A DETECTIVE SEAN DUFF[...]

I HEAR THE
SIRENS
IN THE STREET

BOOK TWO
THE TROUBLES TRILOGY

ADRIAN McKINTY

SEVENTH
STREET
BOOKS™

59 John Glenn Drive
Amherst, New York 14228-2119

Published 2013 by Seventh Street Books™, an imprint of Prometheus Books

First published in 2013 by Serpent's Tail, an imprint of Profile Books Ltd. 3A Exmouth House, Pine Street, London EC1R 0JH; website: www.serpentstail.com

Cover Image © 2013 Media Bakery
Cover design by Grace M. Conti-Zilsberger

Inquiries should be addressed to
Seventh Street Books
59 John Glenn Drive
Amherst, New York 14228–2119
VOICE: 716–691–0133
FAX: 716–691–0137
WWW.PROMETHEUSBOOKS.COM

17   5 4 3 2

Library of Congress Cataloging-in-Publication Data

McKinty, Adrian.
    I hear the sirens in the street : a Detective Sean Duffy novel / by Adrian McKinty.
        p cm. — (The Troubles trilogy ; bk 2)
    ISBN 978-1-61614-787-7 (pbk.)
    ISBN 978-1-61614-787-3 (ebook)
    1. Detectives—Northern Ireland—Fiction. 2. Murder—Investigation—Fiction. I. Title.

PS3563.C38322I22 2013
813'.54—dc23
                                                              2013001497

MARTY MCFLY: Wait a minute, Doc. Are you telling me that you built a time machine ... out of a DeLorean?

DR. EMMETT BROWN: The way I see it, if you're gonna build a time machine into a car, why not do it with some style?

—Robert Zemeckis & Bob Gale,
Back to the Future (1985)

CONTENTS

1: A TOWN CALLED MALICE

The abandoned factory was a movie trailer from an entropic future when all the world would look like this. From a time without the means to repair corrugation or combustion engines or vacuum tubes. From a planet of rust and candle power. Guano coated the walls. Mildewed garbage lay in heaps. Strange machinery littered a floor which, with its layer of leaves, oil and broken glass was reminiscent of the dark understory of a rainforest. The melody in my head was a descending ten-on-one ostinato, a pastiche of the second of Chopin's études; I couldn't place it but I knew that it was famous and that once the shooting stopped it would come to me in an instant.

The shotgun blast had sent the birds into a frenzy and as we ran for cover behind a half disassembled steam turbine we watched the rock doves career off the ceiling, sending a fine shower of white asbestos particles down towards us like the snow of a nuclear winter.

The shotgun reported again and a window smashed twenty feet to our left. The security guard's aim was no better than his common sense.

We made it to safety behind the turbine's thick stainless steel fans and watched the pigeons loop in decreasing circles above our heads. A superstitious man would have divined ill-omened auguries in their melancholy flight but fortunately my partner, Detective Constable McCrabban, was made of sterner stuff.

"Would you stop shooting, you bloody eejit! We are the police!" he yelled before I even had the chance to catch my breath.

There was an impressive dissonance as the last of the shotgun's echo died away, and then an even more impressive silence.

Asbestos was coating my leather jacket and I pulled my black polo neck sweater over my mouth.

The pigeons began to settle.

Wind made the girders creek.

A distant bell was ringing.

It was like being in a symphony by Arvo Pärt. But he wasn't the composer of the melody still playing between my ears. Who was that now? Somebody French.

Another shotgun blast.

The security guard had taken the time to reload and was determined to have more fun.

"Stop shooting!" McCrabban demanded again.

"Get out of here!" a voice replied. "I've had enough of you hoodlums!"

It was a venerable voice, from another Ireland, from the '30s or even earlier, but age gave it no weight or assurance—only a frail, impatient, dangerous doubt.

This, every copper knew, was how it would end, not fighting the good fight but in a random bombing or a police chase gone wrong or shot by a half senile security guard in a derelict factory in north Belfast. It was April 1st. Not a good day to die.

"We're the police!" McCrabban insisted.

"The what?"

"The police!"

"I'll call the police!"

"We *are* the police!"

"You are?"

I lit a cigarette, sat down and leaned against the outer shell of the big turbine.

This room in fact was one enormous turbine hall. A huge space built for the generation of electricity because the engineers who'd constructed the textile factory had decided that autarchy was the best policy when dealing with Northern Ireland's inadequate and dodgy power supplies. I would like to have to seen this place in its heyday, when light was pouring in through the clear windows and the cathedral of turbines was humming at maximum rev. This whole factory must have been some scene with its cooling towers and its chemical presses and its white-coated alchemist employees who knew the secret of turning petroleum into clothes.

But not anymore. No textiles, no workers, no product. And it would never come back. Heavy manufacturing in Ireland had always been tentative at best and had fled the island just as rapidly as it had arrived.

"If you're the police how come you're not in uniform?" the security guard demanded.

"We're detectives! Plain-clothes detectives. And listen, mate, you're in a lot of trouble. You better put down that bloody gun," I yelled.

"Who's going to make me?" the security guard asked.

"We are!" McCrabban shouted.

"Oh, aye?" he yelled back. "You and whose army?"

"The bloody British Army!" McCrabban and I yelled together.

A minute of parley and the security guard agreed that perhaps he had been a bit hasty. Crabbie, who'd recently become a father of twin boys, was seething and I could tell he was for throwing the book at him but the guard was an old geezer with watery eyes in a blue polyester uniform that perhaps presaged our own post-peeler careers. "Let's cut him a break," I said. "It will only mean paperwork."

"If you say so," Crabbie reluctantly agreed.

The security guard introduced himself as Martin Barry and we told him that we had come here to investigate a blood trail that had been discovered by the night watchman.

"Oh, that? I saw that on my walk around. I didn't think too much about it," Mr. Barry said. He looked as if he hadn't thought too much about anything over the last thirty years.

"Where is it?" McCrabban asked him.

"It's out near the bins, I wonder Malcolm didn't leave a wee note for me that he had already called that in," Mr. Barry said.

"If it was blood, why didn't *you* call it in?" Crabbie asked.

"Some rascal breaks in here and cuts himself and I'm supposed to call the peelers about it? I thought you gentlemen had better things to do with your days."

That did not bode well for it being something worth our trouble.

"Can you show us what you're talking about?" I asked.

"Well, it's outside," Mr. Barry said reluctantly.

He was still waving his antique twelve-gauge around and Crabbie took the shotgun out of his hands, broke it open, removed the shells and gave it back again.

"How did you get in here, anyway?" Mr. Barry asked.

"The gate was open," Crabbie said.

"Aye, the hoodlums broke the lock, they're always coming in here to nick stuff."

"What stuff?" McCrabban asked, looking at the mess all around us.

"They're going to ship the rest of that turbine to Korea some day. It's very valuable," Mr. Barry explained.

I finished my cigarette and threw the stub into a puddle. "Shall we go see this alleged blood trail?" I asked.

"All right then, aye."

We went outside.

It was snowing now.

Real snow, not an asbestos simulacrum.

There was a quarter of an inch of the stuff on the ground which meant that the trains would grind to a halt, the motorway would be closed and the rush-hour commute would become chaotic. Crabbie looked at the sky and sniffed. "The old woman is certainly plucking the goose today," he said stentoriously.

"You should put those in a book," I said, grinning at him.

"There's only one book I need," Crabbie replied dourly, tapping the Bible in his breast pocket.

"Aye, me too," Mr. Barry agreed and the two obvious Presbyterians gave each other a knowing glance.

This kind of talk drove me mental. "What about the phone book? What if you need to look up somebody's phone number. You won't find that in your King James," I muttered.

"You'd be surprised," Mr. Barry said, but before he could explain further his method of divining unknown telephone numbers using the kabbalah, I raised a finger and walked to a dozen large, rusting skips filled with rubbish.

"Is this where you're talking about?"

"Aye, over there's where the wee bastards climb over," he said, pointing to a spot where the fence had been pulled down so that it was only a few feet high.

"Not very secure, is it?" McCrabban said, turning up the collar on his raincoat.

"That's why I have this!" Mr. Barry exclaimed, patting his shotgun like a favored reptile.

"Just show us the blood, please," I said.

"Over here, if it is blood. If it is *human* blood," Mr. Barry said, with such an ominous twinge in his voice that it almost cracked me up.

He showed us a dried, thin reddish brown trail that led from the fence to the bins.

"What do you make of that?" I asked Crabbie.

"I'll tell you what I make of it! The kids were rummaging in the skip, one of them wee beggars cuts hisself, heaven be praised, and then they run to the fence, jump over and go home crying to their mamas," Mr. Barry said.

Crabbie and I shook our heads. Neither of us could agree with that interpretation.

"I'll explain what happened to Mr. Barry while you start looking in the skip," I said.

"I'll explain it while *you* start looking in the skip," Crabbie countered.

"Explain what?" Mr. Barry asked.

"The blood trail gets thinner and narrower the further away from the fence you get."

"Which means?" Mr. Barry asked.

"Which means that unless we have a Jackson Pollock fan among our local vandal population then something or someone has been dragged to one of those dumpsters and tossed in."

I looked at McCrabban. "Go on then, get in there, mate," I said.

He shook his head.

I pointed at the imaginary pips on my shoulder which would have signified the rank of inspector if I hadn't been in plain clothes.

It cut no ice with him. "I'm not going in there. No way. These trousers are nearly new. The missus would skin me alive."

"I'll flip you for it. Heads or tails?"

"You pick. It's a little too much like gambling for my taste."

"Heads then."

I flipped.

Of course we all knew what the outcome would be.

I climbed into the skip nearest to where the blood trail appeared to end but naturally that would have been too easy for our criminal masterminds and I found nothing.

I waded through assorted factory debris: wet cardboard, wet cork, slate, broken glass and lead pipes while Mr. Barry and Crabbie waxed philosophic: "Jobs for the boys, isn't it? It's all thieves and coppers these days, isn't it?"

"Somebody has to give out the unemployment checks too, mate," Crabbie replied, which was very true. Thief, copper, prison officer, dole officer: such were the jobs on offer in Northern Ireland—the worst kakistocracy in Europe.

I climbed back out of the skip.

"Well?" Crabbie asked.

"Nothing organic, save for some new life forms unknown to science that will probably mutate into a species-annihilating virus," I said.

"I think I saw that film," Crabbie replied.

I took out the fifty-pence piece. "All right, couple more bins to go, do you want to flip again?" I asked.

"Not necessary, Sean, that first coin toss was the toss for all the skips," Crabbie replied.

"You're telling me that I have to sort through all of them?" I said.

"That's why they pay you the big bucks, boss," he said, making his beady, expressionless eyes even more beady and expressionless.

"I lost fair and square but I'll remember this when you're looking for help on your bloody sergeant's exam," I said.

This had its desired effect. He shook his head and sniffed. "All right. We split them up. I'll take these two. You the other two. And we should probably get a move on before we all freeze to death," he muttered.

McCrabban found the suitcase in the third bin along from the fence.

Blood was oozing through the red plastic.

"Over here!" he yelled.

We put on latex gloves and I helped him carry it out.

It was heavy.

"You best stand back," I said to Mr. Barry.

It had a simple brass zip. We unzipped it and flipped it open.

Inside was a man's headless naked torso cut off at the knees and shoulders. Crabbie and I had some initial observations while behind us Mr. Barry began with the dry heaves.

"His genitals are still there," Crabbie said.

"And no sign of bruising," I added. "Which probably rules out a paramilitary hit."

If he was an informer or a double agent or a kidnapped member of the other side they'd certainly have tortured him first.

"No obvious tattoos."

"So he hasn't done prison time."

I pinched his skin. It was ice cold. Rigid. He was dead at least a day.

He was tanned and he'd kept himself in shape. It was hard to tell his age, but he looked about fifty or maybe even sixty. He had grey and white chest hairs and perhaps, just perhaps, some blonde ones that had been bleached white by the sun.

"His natural skin color is quite pale, isn't it?" Crabbie said, looking at the area where his shorts had been.

"It is," I agreed. "That is certainly some tan on him. Where would he get a tan like that around these parts, do you think?"

"I don't know."

"I'll bet he's a swimmer and that's the tan line for a pair of Speedos. That's probably how he kept himself in shape too. Swimming in an outdoor pool."

Northern Ireland of course had few swimming baths and no outdoor pools, and not much sunshine, which led, of course, to Crabbie's next question:

"You're thinking he's not local, aren't you?" Crabbie said.

"I am," I agreed.

"That won't be good, will it?" Crabbie muttered.

"No, my friend, it will not."

I stamped my feet and rubbed my hands together. The snow was coming down harder now and the grim north Belfast suburbs were turning the color of old lace. A cold wind was blowing up from the lough and that music in my head was still playing on an endless loop. I closed my eyes and tripped on it for a few bars: a violin, a viola, a cello, two pianos, a flute and a glass harmonica. The flute played the melody on top of glissando-like runs from the pianos—the first piano playing that Chopinesque descending ten-on-one ostinato while the second played a more sedate six-on-one.

"Maybe we'll get lucky. Let's see if we can find any papers in the case," Crabbie said, interrupting my reverie.

We looked but found nothing and then went back to the Land Rover to call it in. Matty, our forensics officer, and a couple of Reservists showed up in boiler suits and began photographing the crime scene and taking fingerprints and blood samples.

Army helicopters flew low over the lough, sirens wailed in County Down, a distant thump-thump was the sound of mortars or explosions. The city was under a shroud of chimney smoke and the cinematographer, as always, was shooting it in 8mm black and white. This was Belfast in the fourteenth year of the low-level civil war euphemistically known as The Troubles.

The day wore on. The grey snow clouds turned perse and black. The yellow clay-like sea waited torpidly, dreaming of wreck and carnage. "Can I go?" Crabbie asked. "If I miss the start of *Dallas* I'll never get caught up. The missus gets the Ewings and Barneses confused."

"Go, then."

I watched the forensic boys work and stood around smoking until an ambulance came to take the John Doe to the morgue at Carrick-fergus Hospital.

I drove back to Carrick police station and reported my findings to my boss, Chief Inspector Brennan: a large, shambolic man with a Willy Lomanesque tendency to shout his lines.

"What are your initial thoughts, Duffy?" he asked.

"It was freezing out there, sir. Napoleon's retreat from Moscow, we had to eat the horses, we're lucky to be alive."

"Your thoughts about the victim?"

"I have a feeling it's a foreigner. Possibly a tourist."

"That's bad news."

"Yeah, I don't think he'll be giving the old place an 'A' rating in those customer satisfaction surveys they pass out at the airport."

"Cause of death?"

"We can probably rule out suicide," I said.

"How did he die?"

"I don't know yet—I suppose having your head chopped off doesn't help much though, does it? Rest assured that our crack team is on it, sir."

"Where is DC McCrabban?" Brennan asked.

"*Dallas*, sir."

"And he told me he was afraid to fly, the lying bastard."

Chief Inspector Brennan sighed and tapped the desk with his fore-finger, unconsciously (or perhaps consciously) spelling out "ass" in Morse.

"If it is a foreigner, you appreciate that this is going to be a whole thing, don't you?" he muttered.

"Aye."

"I foresee paperwork and more paperwork and a powwow from the Big Chiefs and you possibly getting superseded by some goon from Belfast."

"Not for some dead tourist, surely, sir?"

"We'll see. You'll not throw a fit if you do get passed over will you? You've grown up now, haven't you, Sean?"

Neither of us could quickly forget the fool I'd made of myself the last time a murder case had been taken away from me . . .

"I'm a changed man, sir. Team player. Kenny Dalglish not Kevin Keegan. If the case gets pushed upstairs I will give them every assistance and obey every order. I'll stick with you right to the bunker, sir."

"Let's hope it doesn't come to that."

"Amen, sir."

He leaned back in the chair and picked up his newspaper.

"All right, Inspector, you're dismissed."

"Yes, sir."

"And remember it's Carol's birthday on Friday and it's your turn on the rota. Cake, hats, you know the drill. You know I like buttercream icing."

"I put the order in at McCaffrey's yesterday. I'll check with Henrietta on the way home."

"Very well. Get thee to a bunnery."

"You've been saving that one up, haven't you, sir?"

"I have," he said with a smile.

I turned on my heel. "Wait!" Brennan demanded.

"Sir?"

"'Naples in Naples', three down, six letters."

"Napoli, sir."

"Huh?"

"In Naples, Naples is Napoli."

"Oh, I get it, all right, bugger off."

On the way back to Coronation Road I stopped in at McCaffrey's, examined the cake, which was a typical Irish birthday cake layered with sponge, cream, rum, jam and sugar. I explained the Chief Inspector's preferences and Annie said that that wouldn't be a problem: she'd make the icing half an inch thick if we wanted. I told her that that would be great and made a mental note to have the defib kit on hand.

I drove on through Carrickfergus's blighted shopping precincts, past boarded-up shops and cafes, vandalized parks and playgrounds. Bored ragamuffin children of the type you often saw in Pulitzer-Prize-winning books of photography were sitting glumly on the wall over the railway lines waiting to drop objects down onto the Belfast train.

I stopped at the heavily armored Mace Supermarket which was covered with sectarian and paramilitary graffiti and a fading and unlikely claim that "Jesus Loves The Bay City Rollers!"

I waded through the car park's usual foliage of chip papers, plastic bags and crisp packets.

Halfway through my shop the piece of music that had been playing in my head began over the speakers. I must have heard it last week when I'd been in here. I got cornflakes, a bottle of tequila and Heinz tomato soup and went to the checkout.

"What is this music? It's been in my head all day," I asked the fifteen-year-old girl operating the till.

"I have no idea, love. It's bloody horrible, isn't it?"

I paid and went to the booth, startling Trevor, the assistant manager who was reading *Outlaw of Gor* with a wistful look on his basset-hound face. He didn't know what the music was either.

"I don't pick the tapes, I just do what I'm told," he said defensively.

I asked him if I could check out his play box. He didn't mind. I rummaged through the tapes and found the cassette currently on the go. *Light Classical Hits IV*. I looked down through the list of tracks and found the one it had to be: "The Aquarium" from *Carnival of the Animals* by Saint Saens.

It was an odd piece, popular among audiences but not among musicians. The melody was carried by a glass harmonica, a really weird instrument that reputedly made its practitioners go mad. I nodded and put the cassette box down.

"I won't play it again, if you don't like it, Inspector, you're not the first to complain," Trevor said.

"No, actually, I'm a fan of Saint Saens," I was going to say, but Trev was already changing the tape to *Contemporary Hits Now!*

When I came out of the Mace, smoke from a large incendiary

bomb was drifting across the lough from Bangor and you could hear fire engines and ambulances on the grey, oddly pitching air.

From the external supermarket speakers Paul Weller's reedy baritone begin singing the first few bars of "A Town Called Malice" and I had to admit that the choice of song was depressingly appropriate.

2: THE DYING EARTH

We stood there looking at north Belfast three miles away over the water. The sky a kind of septic brown, the buildings rain-smudged rectangles on the grim horizon. Belfast was not beautiful. It had been built on mudflats, and without rock foundations nothing soared. Its architecture had been Victorian red-brick utilitarian and sixties brutalism before both of those tropes had crashed headlong into the Troubles. A thousand car bombs later and what was left was surrounded by concrete walls, barbed wire and a steel security fence to keep the bombers out.

Here in the north Belfast suburbs we only got sporadic terrorist attacks, but economic degradation and war had frozen the architecture in outmoded utilitarian schools whose chief purpose seemed to be the disheartening of the human soul. Optimistic colonial officials were always planting trees and sponsoring graffiti clearance schemes, but the trees never lasted long and it was the brave man who dared clean paramilitary graffiti off his own house never mind in communal areas of the town.

I lit a second cigarette. I was thinking about architecture because I was trying not to think about Laura.

I hadn't seen her in nearly a week.

"Should we go in?" Crabbie asked.

"Steady on, mate. I just lit me fag. Let me finish this first."

"Your head. She won't be happy to be kept waiting," Crabbie prophesied.

Drizzle.

A stray dog.

A man called McCawley wearing his dead wife's clothes pushing her empty wheelchair along the pavement. He saw us waiting by the Land Rover. "Bloody peelers, they should crucify the lot of you," he said as he picked up our discarded cigarette butts.

"Sean, come on, this is serious. It's an appointment with the patho," Crabbie insisted.

He didn't know that Laura and I had been avoiding one another.

I didn't know that we had been avoiding one another.

A fortnight ago she'd gone to Edinburgh to do a presentation for a couple of days and after she'd returned she said that she was swamped with catch-up work.

That was the official party line. In fact I knew that something was up. Something that had been in the wind for months.

Maybe something that had been in the wind since we had met.

This was her third trip to Edinburgh this year. Had she met someone else? My instincts said no, but even a detective could be blind-sided. Perhaps detectives in particular could be blind-sided.

For some time now I'd had the feeling that I had trapped her. By putting us in a life and death situation, by getting myself shot. How could she do anything but stay with me through the process of my recovery. She couldn't possibly leave a man who had fallen into a coma and awoken to find that he had been awarded the Queen's Police Medal.

She had protected herself to some extent. She had refused to move in with me on Coronation Road, because, she said, the Protestant women gave her dirty looks.

She had bought herself a house in Straid. There had been no talk of marriage. Neither of us had said "I love you."

Before the recent absences we had seen each other two or three times a week.

What were we? Boyfriend and girlfriend? It hardly seemed so much.

But what then?

I had no idea.

Crabbie looked at me with those half closed, irritated brown eyes, and tapped his watch.

"It's nine fifteen," he said in that voice of moral authority which came less from being a copper and more from his status as a sixth generation elder in the Presbyterian Church of Ireland. "The message, Sean, was to come at nine. We're late."

"All right, all right, keep your wig on. Let's go in," I said.

Cut to the hospital: scrubbed surfaces. Lowered voices. A chemical odor of bleach and carpet cleaner. Django Reinhardt's "Tears" seeping through an ancient Tannoy system.

The new nurse at reception looked at us skeptically. She was a classic specimen of the brisk, Irish, pretty, no nonsense nursey type.

"There's no smoking in here, gentlemen," she said.

I stubbed the fag in the ashtray. "We're here to see Dr. Cathcart," I said.

"And who are you?"

"Detective Inspector Duffy, Carrick RUC, and this is my spiritual coach DC McCrabban."

"You can go through."

We stopped outside the swing doors of the Autopsy Room and knocked on the door.

"Who is it?" she asked.

"DI Duffy, DC McCrabban," I said.

"Come in."

Familiar smells. Bright overhead lights. Stainless steel bowls filled with intestines and internal organs. Glittering precision instruments laid out in neat rows. And the star of the show: our old friend from yesterday lying on a gurney.

Laura's face was behind a mask, which I couldn't help thinking was wonderfully metaphoric.

"Good morning, gentlemen," she said.

"Good morning, Dr. Cathcart," Crabbie uttered automatically.

"Hi," I replied cheerfully.

Our eyes met.

She held my look for a couple of seconds and then smiled under the mask.

It was hard to tell but it didn't seem to be the look of a woman who was leaving you for another man.

"So, what can you tell us about our victim, Dr. Cathcart?" I asked.

She picked up her clipboard. "He was a white male, about sixty, with grey, canescent hair. He was tall, six four or maybe six five. He had a healed scar on his left buttock consistent with a severe trauma, possibly a car accident, or given his age, a shrapnel wound. There was a tattoo on his back—'No Sacrifice Too Grea'—which I take to be some kind of motto or Biblical verse. The 't' was missing from 'Great' where his skin had adhered to the freezer compartment."

"Freezer compartment?"

"The body was frozen for some unspecified period of time. When the body was removed and placed in the suitcase a piece of skin stuck to the freezer, hence the missing 't' in great. I've taken photographs of this and they should be developed later today."

"What did you say the tattoo said?" Crabbie asked, flipping open his notebook.

She shrugged. "A Biblical verse perhaps? 'No Sacrifice Too Great.'"

I looked at Crabbie. He shook his head. He had no idea either.

"Go on, Doctor," I said.

"The victim's head, arms and legs were removed post mortem. He had also been circumcised, but this had been done at birth."

She paused and stared at me again.

"Cause of death?" I asked.

"That, Detective Inspector, is where we get into the really interesting stuff."

"It's been interesting already," Crabbie said.

"Please continue, Dr. Cathcart."

"It was a homicide or perhaps a suicide; either way, it was death by misadventure. The victim was poisoned."

"Poisoned?" Crabbie and I said together.

"Indeed."

"Are you sure?" Crabbie said.

"Quite sure. It was an extremely rare and deadly poison known as Abrin."

"Never heard of it," I said.

"Nevertheless, that's what it was. I found Abrin particles in his larynx and esophagus, and the hemorrhaging of his lungs leaves little doubt," Laura continued.

"Is it a type of rat poison or something?" I asked.

"No, much rarer than that. Abrin is a natural toxin found in the rosary pea. Of course it would need to be refined and milled. The advantage over rat poison would be in its complete lack of taste. Like I say it is very unusual but I'm quite certain of my findings . . . I did the toxicology myself."

"Sorry to be dense, but what's a rosary pea?" I asked.

"The common name for the jequirity plant endemic to Trinidad and Tobago, but I think it's originally from South-east Asia. Extremely rare in these parts, I had to look it up."

"Poisoned . . . Jesus," I said.

"Shall I continue?" she asked.

"Please."

"The Abrin was taken orally. Possibly with water. Possibly mixed into food. There would have been no taste. Within minutes it would have dissolved in the victim's stomach and passed into his blood. It would then have penetrated his cells and very quickly protein synthesis would have been inhibited. Without these proteins, cells cannot survive."

"What would have happened next?"

"Hemorrhaging of the lungs, kidney failure, heart failure, death."

"Grisly."

"Yes, but at least it would have been fairly rapid."

"How rapid? Seconds, minutes?"

"Minutes. This particular strain of Abrin was home cooked. It was crude. It was not manufactured by a government germ warfare lab."

"Crude but effective."

"Indeed."

I nodded. "When was all this?"

"That's another part of the puzzle."

"Yes?"

"It's impossible to say how long the body was frozen."

I nodded.

"Are you sure about that freezing thing? There are plenty of ways a bit of skin can come off somebody's back," McCrabban said.

"I'm certain, Detective. The cell damage caused by freezing is consistent throughout what's left of his body."

"And so you have no idea when all this happened?" I asked.

She shook her head. "It is beyond my capabilities to state how long he was frozen for."

"So you're not able to determine a time of death?"

"I am afraid that I am not able to determine a time or date of death. Although I will continue to work on the problem."

"Poisoned, frozen, chopped up, dumped," McCrabban said sadly, writing it down in his notebook.

"Yes," Laura said, yawning. I gave her a smile. Was she already bored by death? Is that what happened to all pathos in the end?

Or was she just bored by us? By me?

"The rosary pea. That is interesting," McCrabban said, still writing in his book.

"Our killer is not stupid," Laura said. "He's got a little bit of education."

"Which more or less rules out the local paramilitaries," McCrabban muttered.

"They're not that bright?" Laura asked.

"Poison is far too elaborate for them. Too elaborate for everybody really around here. I mean what's the point? You can get guns anywhere in Northern Ireland," I said.

McCrabban nodded. "The last poisoning I remember was in 1977," he said.

"What happened then?" Laura asked.

"Wife poisoned her husband with weed killer in his tea. Open and shut case," McCrabban said.

"So what do you think we're looking at here, then? A loner, someone unaffiliated with the paramilitaries?" I asked him.

"Could be," McCrabban agreed.

"Do us a favor, mate, call up a few garden centers and ask about rosary pea and get cracking on 'No Sacrifice Too Great,' will ya?"

Crabbie wasn't dense. He could read between the lines. He could see that I wanted to talk to Laura in private.

"You'll walk back to the station, will you, Sean?" he asked.

"Aye, I'll walk, I could do with the exercise."

"Fair enough," he said and turned to Laura. "Nice to see you again, Dr. Cathcart."

"You too, Detective McCrabban," Laura said.

When he'd gone I walked to her and took off her mask.

"What?" Laura asked.

"Tell me," I said.

"Tell you what?"

"Tell me what's going on," I said.

She shook her head. "Ugh, Sean, I don't have time for this, today."

"Time for what exactly?"

"The games. The drama," she said.

"There's no drama. I just want to know what's going on."

"What are you talking about?"

"What's going on with us?"

"Nothing's going on," she said.

But her voice quavered.

Outside I could hear Crabbie start up the Land Rover.

I waited for a beat or two.

"All right, let's go to my office," she said.

"Okay."

We walked the corridor and went into her office. It was the same dull beige with the same Irish watercolors on the wall. She sat in her leather chair and let down her reddish hair. She looked pale, fragile, beautiful.

The seconds crawled.

"It's not a big deal," she began.

I closed my eyes and leaned back in the patient chair. *Oh shit*, I thought, *that means it's going to be a really big deal.*

"I've been offered a temporary teaching position at the University of Edinburgh," she said, her voice sounding like it was coming from the bottom of a coal mine.

"Congratulations," I replied automatically.

"Don't be unpleasant, Sean."

"I wasn't."

"It's in the medical school. First year class on basic anatomy with a cadaver. To be honest, I need the break, from, from—"

"Me?"

"From all this . . ."

It didn't have to be about me. Anybody with any brains was getting out. The destination wasn't important. England, Scotland, Canada, America, Australia . . . the great thing was to go.

"Of course."

She explained why it was an exciting challenge and why it didn't necessarily mean the end of us.

I nodded, smiled and was happy for her.

I completely understood. She would leave Northern Ireland and she would never come back. I mean, who tries to get back on board the *Titanic*?

Furthermore her sisters were out of high school and her parents were in the process of moving abroad. The only thing keeping Laura here were her ties to this shitty job and to me and both of those were severable.

"When are thinking of heading?" I asked.

"Monday."

"So soon?"

"I signed a lease on an apartment. I need to get furniture."

"What about your house in Straid?"

"My mum will look after it."

"What about the hospital? Who's covering for you here?"

"The other doctors can pick up the slack in the clinic and I've asked one of my old teachers to do my autopsy work in the interim. Dr. Hagan. He's coming out of retirement to do me this favor. Very experienced. He worked for Scotland Yard for years and he taught at the Royal Free. He says he'll be happy to cover me for a few months. He'll be much better at this kind of work than me."

"I doubt that."

She smiled.

And then there was silence. I could hear a kid crying all the way back at Reception.

"Will you have dinner with me this weekend?"

"I'll be very busy. Packing and all that."

So that's the way it was. Well, I wasn't going to beg. "If you change your mind give me a call."

"I will."

I got up. I blinked and looked at her. Her gaze was steady. Resolved. Even relaxed. "Bye, Laura."

"Bye, Sean. It's only for a term. Ten weeks," she said. She wanted to add something else, but her mouth trembled for a moment and then closed.

I nodded and to avoid a scene left it there. I gave her a little nod as I left the office and half slammed her door. "Heart of Glass" by Blondie was my exit music from the hospital reception.

I went out into the car park and said "Shite! Shite! Shite!" before lighting a fag. I tried to think of a curse but Irish articulacy had clearly declined since the days of Wilde and Yeats, Synge and Shaw. Three "shites" and a ciggie, that was what we could come up with in these diminished times.

I walked over the railway bridge.

A stiff sea breeze was sending foam over the cars on the Belfast Road and there were white caps from here to Scotland. On the Scotch

Quarter, outside the Gospel Hall, a wild-haired American evangelist with a walking stick was entertaining a crowd of pensioners with the promise that the end was nigh and the dying earth was in its final days. I listened for a while and found him pretty convincing. Before I could be "saved," however, a freak wave drenched me and another late arrival and the old folks laughed at this perverse joke of Providence.

The Royal Oak was just opening for the day and was already full of sturdy alcoholics and peelers eager to make good on the police discount.

Alex, the barkeep, was dressed in a tie-dye shirt, furry boots and a full-length velvet cape. Clearly he had discovered a time portal to 1972 or he was off to see Elton John. Neither interested me that much.

I said hello and ordered a stiff Scotch.

"Women or work?" Alex asked.

"Is it always one or the other?" I asked.

"Aye, it is," he said thoughtfully.

"Women then," I said.

"In that case, mate, I'll make it a double on the house," he said compassionately.

3: THE BIG RED ONE

I was tempted to order another double whisky and a Guinness and make this a proper session, but it was a Friday which meant that the lunch special was deep-fried pizza and that stuff reeked of the cardiac ward.

I said hello to Sergeant Burke on the desk, complimented him on his throwback Zapata moustache, and went straight upstairs to the incident room.

"Jesus! Where did you come from?" Matty said, caught throwing darts at the dartboard.

"At the nineteenth level of Zen Buddhism you learn how to teleport—now put them darts away, we've work to do," I said irritably.

Matty threw the final dart and sat at his desk.

He was getting on my nerves, Matty. He had let his hair grow and because of his natural Mick frizz it had gotten *wide*. He had a pinky ring and he'd taken to wearing white jackets over white T-shirts. I'm not sure what this look was supposed to be exactly but I didn't like it, even ironically.

He and McCrabban were staring at me with gormless expressions on their faces.

"Missing persons reports?" I asked.

"None so far, Sean."

"Any luck on that motto?"

"Not yet," McCrabban replied mournfully.

"Keep at it! Remember what Winston Churchill said, 'there'll be plenty of time for wanking when the boats are back from Dunkirk,' right?"

"I don't think Churchill ever said any such—"

"And you, Matty, my lad, get on the blower to garden centers and ask about rosary pea."

We phone-called for an hour.

Not a single garden center in Northern Ireland stocked the rosary pea. I phoned the Northern Ireland Horticultural Society but that too drew a blank. No one they knew had ever shown or grown it. But you'd definitely need a greenhouse they said.

"The killer probably has a greenhouse. Write that on the white-board," I said.

Crabbie added that to our list of boxes and arrows on the incident-room whiteboard.

"Keep the calls going. I'm off to the library," I said.

I walked back along the Scotch Quarter. A tinker was selling a dangerous-looking goat from the back of his Ford Transit. "Goat For Sale. Temper. All Offers Considered," his sign said.

"No thanks, mate," I said and as it began to hail I hustled into Carrickfergus Library and said good afternoon to Mrs. Clemens.

"They say it'll be a lovely day later," I added conversationally.

"Who said this?" she demanded suspiciously.

I liked Mrs. Clemens very much. She was going on seventy-five. She had lost an eye to cancer and wore an eye patch instead of a glass bead. I dug that—it gave her a piratical air. She was dyspeptic and knew the library backwards and hated anybody borrowing anything.

"Plants, horticulture, botany?" I asked.

"581," she said. "There are some good encyclopedias at the beginning of the section."

"Thank you."

I went to 581 and looked up the rosary pea:

abrus precatorius, *known commonly as Jequirity, Crab's Eye, Rosary Pea, John Crow Bead, Precatory Bean, Indian Liquorice, Akar Saga, Giddee Giddee or Jumbie Bead in Trinidad & Tobago, is a slender, perennial climber that twines around trees, shrubs, and hedges. It is a legume with long, pinnate-leafleted leaves. The plant is native to Indonesia and grows in tropical and subtropical areas of the world where it has been introduced. It has a tendency to become weedy and invasive. In India the seeds of the Rosary Pea are often used in percussion instruments.*

"Interesting," I said to myself. I photocopied the page and, with Mrs. Clemens's help, found a book on poisons. The listing I needed was under "Jequirity Seed":

The Jequirity Seed contains the highly toxic poison Abrin, a close relative to the well known poison, Ricin. It is a dimer consisting of two protein sub units, termed A and B. The B chain facilitates Abrin's entry into a cell by bonding to certain transport proteins on cell membranes, which then transport the toxin inside the cell. Once inside the cell membrane, the A chain prevents protein synthesis by inactivating the 26S sub unit of the ribosome. One molecule of Abrin will inactivate up to 1,500 ribosomes per second. Symptoms are identical to those of Ricin, save that Abrin is more toxic by several orders of magnitude. Weaponised high toxicity Abrin will cause liver failure, pulmonary edema and death shortly after ingestion. There is no known antidote for Abrin poisoning.

I photocopied that page too and jogged back to the station through the hail. The place was deserted apart from a tubby, annoying new reservist called McDowell who had come up to me on his first day and asked me point blank if "it was true that I was really a fenian" and it was a lucky break for me that it had been raining just then because I was able to dramatically take off my wool cap and ask him to look for horns. The place had erupted in laughter and Inspector McCallister was gagging so hard he nearly threw a hernia. McDowell had avoided me ever since.

I found everyone in a haze of cigarette smoke up in the second-floor conference room where Chief Inspector Brennan was giving a briefing on the current terrorist situation—a briefing he had just been given at a station chiefs and divisional commanders meeting in Belfast. "Glad you could join us, Inspector Duffy, do have a seat, this concerns you, too!"

"Yes, sir," I said and took a chair at the back of the room next to Sergeants Burke and Quinn.

I listened but I wasn't paying much attention. Brennan told us that we were in what the boys in Special Branch called a "regrouping and reconnaissance period." The IRA's problem was very much an embarrassment of riches. IRA recruitment had soared because of the hunger strikes last year and especially after the martyrdom of Bobby Sands. Volunteers were having to be turned away and money was flowing into the organization through protection rackets, narcotics and pub collection boxes in Irish bars in Boston and New York. The Libyans had supplied the IRA with Semtex explosive, rockets and Armalite rifles. The IRA leadership was currently having difficulty figuring out what to do with all its men and guns but the lull wouldn't last and we were all to be on our guard for what could be an epic struggle ahead.

Brennan's method was only to give us the facts and he didn't bother with a pep talk or encouraging words. We were all too jaded for that and he knew it. He didn't even break out his stash of good whisky which wasn't really on at all.

"Are you paying attention to this, Duffy?" he asked.

"Aye, sir, *ce n'est pas un revolte*, it's a friggin' revolution, isn't it?"

"Aye, it is. And don't talk foreign. All right, everyone, you're dismissed," he said brusquely.

I corralled Matty and McCrabban back into the incident room where our whiteboard gleamed with a big red "1" drawn above the list of known facts about our John Doe.

"What's that for?" I asked Crabbie.

He grinned and got me a sheet of paper from his desk which turned out to be his notes on the First Infantry Division of the United States Army.

"Our boy is a Yank. 'No Mission Too Difficult, No Sacrifice Too Great,' is the motto of the United States Army's First Infantry Division. I did some digging. If our John Doe was World War Two age, his unit was in the worst of it: Sicily, Normandy, the Hurtgen Forest. That's maybe where he got the shrapnel wounds too."

"Excellent work, Crabbie!" I said, really pleased. "This is great! It gives us a lot to go on. An American! Boy oh boy."

"I helped!" Matty protested a little petulantly.

"I'm sure you did, mate," I reassured him.

"An American ex-GI comes to Northern Ireland for his holidays or to visit his old haunts and the poor bugger somehow ends up poisoned," Crabbie said reflectively.

"Aye," I said and rubbed my chin. "Have you been on the phone to Customs and Immigration?"

"We have. They're on it now. We've got them compiling a list of names of all American visitors to Northern Ireland in the last three months," Matty said.

"Why three months?"

"If his body was frozen it could have been any time at all, but any earlier than three months and we surely would have had a missing persons report," Matty said, a little oversensitively.

"Call them up and ask them to go back a full year," I said.

"Jesus, Sean, that could be hundreds of names, maybe thousands," Matty said.

"We'll go back five years if we have to. We're looking for a result here. You heard what the Chief said. We've got the luxury of one case right now. We could be looking at murders a plenty in the next couple of months."

Matty nodded and got on the phone and I shared what I had found about the nature of the poison with McCrabban.

"That's a rare old bird indeed," he said.

"Aye."

"We've got to see who could grow a plant like that, or where you could get the seeds."

"Back on the bloody blower?" he asked.

"Back on the bloody blower, mate."

I went to the crapper and read the *Sun,* a copy of which was always in there. I'll say this for Rupert Murdoch, he made a good paper to read on the bog.

When I came out Matty was looking triumphant.

"What did customs say about the names?" I asked.

"Well, there was a lot of complaining."

"Did you lean on them?"

"Those bastards hate to do any work, but I applied the thumb-screws and they said they'll have them for us by the end of the week."

"Good. Although, in civil service speak that means the end of the year."

"Aye, so what do you want me to work on now?"

"Is that suitcase still around?"

"Of course. It's in the evidence room."

"See if you can find out where it came from, how many were sold in Northern Ireland, that kind of thing."

"What good will that do?" he said with an attitude.

"Matty, in the words of William Shakespeare: just fucking do it, ya wee shite."

"Will do, boss," he replied and went to the evidence room to unwrap the suitcase from its plastic covering.

We called garden centers all over Ireland for the rest of the afternoon. We got nothing. Few had heard of rosary pea and no one had a record of anyone growing it or requesting seeds.

I phoned the General Post Office in Belfast and asked if they had any records of seeds being seized or coming through the mail. They said that they had no idea and would call me back.

McCrabban called UK customs to ask them the same question, and after going through a couple of flunkies, a "police liaison officer" told him that importing such seeds was not illegal or subject to duty so customs would have no interest in them.

The post office phoned back with the same story.

I called Dick Savage in Special Branch. Dick had taken chemistry at Queen's University about the same time as me. He wasn't a high flyer but he'd written several surprisingly acute internal memos on methods of suicide and how to distinguish a true suicide from a murder disguised to look like one.

Dick had heard of Abrin but had never heard of it being used in a poisoning anywhere in the British Isles. He told me he'd look into it.

I went in to see Chief Inspector Brennan and broke the bad news that our John Doe was definitely American but that we had a good chance of finding out who he was through the immigration records.

"When we've got his name we should inform the US Consulate. And we'll probably need the Consulate's help cross referencing our list of names against veterans of the First Infantry Division."

Brennan nodded. "I suppose you want *me* to call them."

"Better coming from you, sir. You're the head of station. More official, all that jazz."

"You just don't want to do it."

"Could be a difficult phone call."

"And?"

"I'm feeling a bit fragile today, sir. I may just have been dumped by my girlfriend."

"That doctor bint you were seeing?"

"Aye."

"I could see that coming. She was out of your league, son."

"Will you make the call, sir?"

"It'll be the start of a shitstorm . . . a dead American—as if we don't have enough problems."

I stood there and let weary resignation overcome his weathered face like melted lard over a cast-iron skillet. He sighed dramatically. "All right. I suppose I'll do it for you, like I do everything around here. You're sure he's a Yank?"

I told him about the tattoo.

"All right, good. Scram. And get Carol's cake, ready. She's in in half an hour."

When Carol came in at three we had her party.

Tea, cake, party hats, both types of lemonade.

Carol had been on planet Earth for sixty years. She ate the cake, drank the tea, smiled and said how wonderful it all was. Brennan gave her a toast and it was Brennan, not Carol, who told us the story of her first week on the job in 1941 when a Luftwaffe Heinkel 111 dropped a stick of 250 kilogram bombs on the station. We'd all heard the tale before but it was a re-teller. The only person who'd been hurt that day was a prisoner in the cells who broke an arm. Course, up in Belfast, where the rest of the Heinkel squadron had gone, people were less fortunate.

The sun came out and the day brightened to such an extent that a few us spilled out onto the fire escape and started slipping rum into the Coke. A pretty female reservist with a tiny waist and a weird Geordieland accent asked me if it was true that "I had killed three men with my bare hands."

She was creeping me out so I made myself scarce, gave Carol a kiss, said goodnight to the lads, locked up the office and headed home.

Coronation Road in Victoria Housing Estate was in one of its rare moments of serenity: stray dogs sleeping in the middle of the street, feral moggies walking on slate roofs, women with rollers in their hair hanging washing on plastic lines, men with flat caps and pipes digging in their gardens. Children from three streets were playing an elaborate game of hide-and-seek called 123 Kick A Tin. Children who were adorable and shoeless and dressed like extras from a '50s movie.

I parked the BMW outside my house, nodded a hello to the neighbors and went inside.

I made a vodka gimlet in a pint glass, stuck on a random tin of soup and with infinitely more care picked out a selection of records that would get me through the evening: "Unknown Pleasures" by Joy Division, "Bryter Layter" by Nick Drake and Neil Young's "After the Goldrush." Yeah, I was in *that* kind of mood.

I lay on the leather sofa and watched the clock. The children's game ended. The lights came on all over Belfast. The army helicopters took to the skies.

The phone rang.

"Hello?"

"Is this Duffy?"

"Who wants to know?"

"I was looking for you at work, Duffy, but apparently you'd left already. Lucky for some, eh?"

It was the weasely Kenny Dalziel from clerical.

"What's the matter, Kenny?"

"The situation is a disaster. A total disaster. I've been pulling my hair out. You don't happen to know who started all this, do you?"

"Gavrilo Princip?"

"What?"

"What's this about, Kenny?"

"It's yet another problem with your department, Inspector Duffy. Specifically Detective Constable Matty McBride's claim for overtime in the last pay period. It's tantamount to fraud."

"Wouldn't surprise me."

"Constable McBride cannot claim for time and a half danger money while also claiming overtime! That would be triple time and believe me, Duffy, nobody, and I mean nobody, is getting triple time on my watch . . ."

I stopped paying attention. When the conversation reached a natural conclusion I told him that I understood his concern and hung up the phone. I switched on the box. A preacher on one side, thought for the day on the other. This country was Bible mad.

Half an hour later Dick Savage called me with info about Abrin. It was an extremely rare poison that he said had never been used in any murder case anywhere in the British Isles. He thought that maybe it had been used in a couple of incidents in America and I might want to look into that.

I thanked him and called Laura, but she didn't pick up the phone.

I made myself another vodka gimlet, drank it, turned off the soup, and put "Bryter Layter" on album repeat and then changed my mind. Nick Drake, like heroin or Marmite, was best in small doses.

As was typical of Ulster's spring weather systems, a hard horizontal rain was lashing the kitchen windows now so I switched the record player to its 78 mode and after some rummaging I found "Into Each Life Some Rain Must Fall" by The Ink Spots with Ella Fitzgerald.

I tolerated the Ink Spot guy singing the first verse but when Ella came on I just about lost it.

The phone startled me.

"Hello?"

"You know the way you're always saying that I'm a lazy bastard and that I don't take this job seriously?"

It was Matty.

"I don't believe that I've ever said any such thing, Matty. In fact I was just defending your honor to that hatchet-faced goblin, Dalziel, in clerical," I said.

"That sounds like a bold-faced lie."

"You're paranoid, mate." I told him.

"Well, while all you lot were copping off with female reservists and buggering away home I've been burning the midnight whale blubber."

"And?"

"I've only gone and made a breakthrough, so I have."

"Go on."

"What's that racket in the background?"

"That 'racket' is Ella Fitzgerald."

"Never heard of him."

"What's going on, mate? Have you really found something out?"

"I've only gone and cracked the bloody case, so I have," he said.

"Our John Doe in the suitcase?"

"What else?"

"Go on then, you're killing me."

"Well, I was on the late shift anyway to cover the station, so I thought instead of breaking out the old stash of *Penthouses* and having a wank I'd do something useful and get back on that suitcase . . ."

"Yes . . ?"

"No forensics at all. No liftable prints. Blood belongs to our boy. But you know the wee plastic window where people write their addresses?"

"McCrabban already checked that window—there was no address card in there. No one would be that much of an eejit."

"That's what I thought too, but I cut it open and I noticed a wee sliver of card scrunched up in the bottom of the window. You couldn't possibly have seen it unless you cut open the plastic and shone a torch down into the gap."

"Shite."

"Shite is right, mate."

"It was an old address card?"

"I got a pair of tweezers, pulled it out, unscrunched it and lo and behold I've only gone and got the name and address of the person who owned the suitcase!"

"Who was it?"

"Somebody local. A bloke called Martin McAlpine, Red Hall Cottage, The Mill Bay Road, Ballyharry, Islandmagee. What do you think about that?"

"So it wasn't the dead American's suitcase, then?"

"Doesn't look like it, does it? It's like you always say, Sean, the concept of the master criminal is a myth. Most crooks are bloody eejits."

"You're a star, Matty, my lad."

"An underappreciated star. What's our next move, boss?"

"I think, Matty, that you and me will be paying Mr. McAlpine a wee visit first thing in the morning."

"Tomorrow? It's a Saturday."

"So?"

He groaned.

"Nothing. Sounds like a plan."

"See you at the barracks. Seven sharp."

"Can't we go later?"

"Can't go later, mate. I'm having me portrait done by Lucian Freud and then I'm off to Anfield, playing center back for Liverpool on account of Alan Hansen's injury."

"Come on, Sean, I like to sleep in on a Saturday."

"Nah, mate, we'll go early, get the drop on him. It'll be fun."

"All right."

"And well done again, pal. You did good."

I hung up the phone. Funny how things turned out. Just like that, very quickly indeed, this potentially tricky investigation was breaking wide open.

4: MACHINE GUN SILHOUETTE

The alarm was set to *Sports Talk* on Downtown Radio which was a nice non-threatening way to start the day. The conversation this morning was about Northern Ireland's chances in the 1982 World Cup. The topic, as usual, had gotten round to George Best and whether the thirty-five-year-old had any game left in him. The last I had heard of Best was his notorious stint playing with Hibernian when he was more famous for out-drinking the entire French rugby team and seducing the reigning Misses World and Universe in the same weekend.

I turned off the radio, made coffee, dressed in a black polo neck sweater, jeans and DM shoes, went outside. I checked under the BMW for any mercury tilt explosives but didn't find any. Right about now seven thousand RUC men and women were all doing the same thing. One or two of them would find a bomb and after shitting their pants, they'd be on the phone to the bomb squad, thanking their lucky stars that they'd kept to their morning routine.

I stuck on the radio and listened to Brian Eno on the short drive to the barracks. Wasn't a big fan of Eno but it was either that or the news and I couldn't listen to the news. Who could, apart from those longing for the end times.

I thought about Laura. I didn't know what to do. Was I in love with her? What did *that* feel like? If she went away it would hurt, it would ache. Was that love? How come I was thirty-two and I didn't know? Was that bloody normal? "Jesus," I said to myself. Thirty-two years old and I had the emotional depth of a teenager.

Maybe it was the situation, maybe Northern Ireland kept you paralyzed, infantilized, backward . . . Aye, blame that.

I nodded to Ray at the guard house and pulled into the police station.

As usual Matty was late and before we could get rolling Sergeant Burke told me that Newtownabbey RUC needed urgent assistance dealing with a riot in Rathcoole. It was completely the wrong direction, I was a detective not a riot cop, and I outranked Burke, but you couldn't really turn down brother officers in need, could you?

With Matty grumbling things like "this isn't what I signed on for," and "I could be fishing right now," we burned up the A2 to that delightful concrete circle of hell known as the Rathcoole Estate.

"Good Friday night?" I asked Matty when his moaning was over.

"Oh, it was a classic, mate. Since I wasn't allowed out, it was a fish supper, a six-pack of Special Brew and a wank to *Sapphire and Steel* on the video."

"David McCallum or Joanna Lumley?"

Matty rolled his eyes.

We arrived at Rathcoole to find that it was only a half-hearted sort of riot that had been running since the night before. About thirty hoods on the ground throwing stones and Molotovs from behind a burnt-out bus, maybe another two dozen comrades offering them assistance by tossing petrol-filled milk bottles from the high-rise tower blocks nearby. The cops under a Chief Superintendent Anderson were keeping well back and letting the ruffians exhaust themselves. I reported to Anderson while Matty stayed in the Rover reading The Cramps' fanzine: *Legion of the Cramped*. Anderson thanked me for coming, but said that we weren't needed.

He asked if I wanted a coffee and poured me one from a flask. We got to talking about the nature of riots, Anderson venturing the opinion that social deprivation was at the root cause of it and I suggested that ennui was the disease of late-twentieth century man. Things were going swimmingly until Anderson began banging on about "it all being part of God's plan" and I decided to make myself scarce.

"If we're not needed, we'll move out, sir, if that's okay with you?" I said and he said that that was fine.

It was when we were safely back in the Rover and heading out of the Estate that we were hit by a jerry-can petrol bomb thrown from a low rise. It exploded with a violent whoosh across the windscreen and it was followed a second or two later by a burst of heavy machine-gun fire that dinged violently off the Land Rover's armored hull.

"Jesus Christ!" Matty screamed while I put my foot on the accelerator to get us away from the trouble. More machine-gun fire tore up the road behind us and rattled off the rear doors.

"They're shooting at us!" Matty yelled.

"I know!"

I hammered down the clutch, switched back into third gear and accelerated round a bend in the road. I got us a hundred yards from the corner and then I hand-break-turned the Land Rover in a dramatic, tire-squealing 180. Fire was melting the Land Rover's window wipers and licking its way down towards the engine block. If it reached the petrol tank . . . I grabbed my service revolver and the fire extinguisher.

"You're not going out there without a bullet-proof vest are you?" Matty said, horrified.

"Call the incident in, ask Anderson to send down help and tell them to be careful," I barked and opened the side door.

"Don't go out there, Sean! That's what they want! It's an ambush."

"Not with half the police force just up the road. They've long gone. Two quick bursts on a machine gun and they'll be heroes in the pub tonight."

"Sean, please!"

"Call it in!"

I got out of the Land Rover, pointed my service revolver at the surrounding low rises but no one was around. Keeping the revolver in one hand and the fire extinguisher in the other I sprayed foam over the windscreen and easily dowsed the flame.

I climbed inside the Rover to wait for back up. We sat there for twenty-five minutes but Anderson's lads never came so I told Matty that we'd write up the incident ourselves later since we had actual work to do this morning.

"Unless—that is—this offends your forensic officer sensibilities and you feel compelled to go back to the scene of the shooting and gather shell cases, pieces of jerry can and other assorted evidence?"

"Bollocks to that!" Matty said and we took the A2 north again. Unfortunately the petrol bomb had burned the rubber off one of the tires and we limped back to Carrickfergus RUC to get a replacement Rover.

This day was destined never to get going. Brennan was in his office now with a nasty look on his once handsome face. I tried to avoid him by sneaking to the incident room while Matty was signing out a new Rover, but the bugger saw and summoned me.

"Hello sir, what are you doing in on a Saturday morning?" I said.

"My duty, Duffy, my duty. What progress have you made on your murder victim?" he muttered, putting his feet up on his desk. He was wearing slippers and some kind of dressing gown and he hadn't shaved. Had he been secretly here all night? Was there trouble on the home front? Should I offer him my big empty house on Coronation Road? Before even the possibility of an Oscar & Felix scenario formed in my brain, I reconsidered: he was a Presbyterian and no doubt he'd take my offer as some kind of insult to his pride.

"A couple of promising leads, sir. We have Customs and Immigration getting us a list of names of Americans who entered Northern Ireland in the last year and we'll cross reference that with any who are the right demographic and have served with the First Infantry Division. I'm optimistic that we should be able to ID our victim pretty soon."

"Good," he said with a yawn. "What else?"

"We found a name in that suitcase our victim was locked up in. Matty found the name, I should say—good police work from him. It was an old address label and we're going to follow up on that this morning."

"Excellent."

"If you don't mind me saying, sir, if you're looking for a place to stay I've got a big empty house on Coronation Road," I blurted out despite myself.

Brennan looked at his slippers, took his feet off the memo pad and hid them under his desk. He was pissed off that I'd accurately deduced his home situation. He had presence, did Brennan, like a fallen actor once famous for his Old Vic Claudius now doing Harp lager commercials on UTV.

"You know what you could do for me, Duffy?"

"What, sir?"

"You could build a fucking time machine, go back forty-five seconds and shut the fuck up after I say the word 'excellent,' okay?"

"Yes, sir."

"And you look bloody terrible. What's the matter with you? The flu?"

"No, sir, Matty and I were out in a Rover and someone threw a petrol bomb. I had to go out and extinguish it."

"Someone threw a petrol bomb at ya? Did you write it up?"

"No, sir, not yet."

"See that you do."

"Yes, sir."

"Have you read the papers this morning, Sean?" he said in a less abrasive voice.

"No."

"Listened to the news?"

"No, sir."

"You have to stay abreast of current events, Inspector!"

"Yes, sir. Anything interesting happening?"

"General Galtieri has decided that his personal manifesto, like all the very best manifestos, needs to be unleashed on the world in a rainy windswept bog, filled with sheep shit."

"General who? What?"

"Argentina has invaded the Falkland Islands."

"The Falkland Islands?"

"The Falkland Islands."

"I'm not really any the wiser, sir."

"They're in the South Atlantic. According to the *Mail* they've got ten thousand troops on there by now."

"Shite."

"You know what that means for us, don't you? Thatcher's going to have to take them back. It's either that or resign. She'll be sending out an invasion fleet. They'll be getting troops from everywhere. I imagine we'll lose half a dozen regiments from here."

"That's going to stretch us thin."

About half of the anti-terrorist and border patrols in Northern Ireland were conducted by the British Army; we, the police, could not easily pick up the slack.

Brennan rubbed his face. "It's bad timing. The IRA's gearing up for a campaign and we're going to be losing soldiers just when they're surging. We could be in for an even trickier few months than we thought."

I nodded.

"And spare a thought for what will happen if it's a debacle. If Thatcher doesn't get the islands back."

"She resigns?"

"She resigns, the government collapses and there's a general election. If Labor wins, and they will, that's it, mate—the ball game is fucking over."

The Labor Party under Michael Foot had a policy of unilateral withdrawal from Ireland, which meant that they would withdraw all British soldiers and civil servants. Ireland would be united at last under Dublin rule which was all fine and dandy except that the Irish Army had only a few battalions and it was a laughable idea that they would be able to keep the peace. What it would mean would be full-scale civil war with a million well-armed, geographically tightly knit Protestants against the rest of the island's four million Catholics. There would be a nice little bloodbath until the US Marines arrived.

"I hadn't thought of that," I said.

"Best not to."

He picked up his copy of the *Daily Mail*.

The headline was one word and screamed "Invasion!"

I noticed that the date on the paper was April 3rd.

"Are you sure this isn't all some kind of belated April Fool's joke?"

"It's no joke, Duffy, the BBC are carrying it, all the papers, everybody."

"Okay."

"We won't get our knickers in a twist. We'll take all this one day at a time."

"Yes, sir."

"Back to work. Get out there and wrap up this murder investigation of yours."

"Yes, sir."

I pushed back the chair and stood.

"One more thing, Duffy. 'A chaperone for a conquistador perhaps?'" he said, tapping his crossword puzzle with his pencil and then thoughtfully chewing the end of it.

It was easy enough. "I think it's an anagram, sir," I said.

"An anagram of what, Duffy?"

"Cortes," I said trying to lead him to the solution but he still didn't get it and he knew that I knew the answer.

"Just tell me, Duffy!" he said.

"Escort, sir."

"What? Oh, yes, of course . . . now piss off."

As I was leaving the office I saw Matty struggling to get a long knitted scarf out of his locker.

"No scarves. Accept it. The Tom Baker era is over, mate," I told him.

Hard rain along the A2.

Matty driving the Land Rover.

Me riding shotgun, literally: a Winchester M12 pump-action across my lap in case we got ambushed on one of the back roads.

I put a New Order cassette in the player. They'd gone all disco but it wasn't as bad as you would have thought.

"Did you hear the news, Matty?"

"What news?"

"You have to stay up with current events, Constable. The Falklands have been invaded."

"The what?"

"Argentina has invaded the Falkland Islands."

"Jesus, when was this?"

"Yesterday."

"First the Germans and now the bloody Argentinians."

"You're thinking of the Channel Islands, mate."

"Where's the Falklands then?"

"Uhm, somewhere sort of south, I think."

"I suppose that's Spurs fucked now, isn't it?"

"How so?"

"Half their team's from bloody Argentina. They'll be well off their game."

"The Chief Inspector wants us to think about the geo-political consequences."

"Aye, geo-politics is one thing, but football's football, isn't it?" Matty said, putting things into a proper perspective.

5: THE WIDOW McALPINE

We drove through the town of Whitehead and hugged the shore of Larne Lough until we were on Islandmagee. Islandmagee was an odd place. A peninsula about six miles north-east of Carrickfergus with Larne Lough on one side and the Irish Sea on the other. It was near the major metropolitan center and ferry port of Larne, yet it was a world away. When you drove onto Islandmagee it was like going back to an Ireland of a hundred or even two hundred years before. The people were country people, suspicious of strangers, and for me their accent and dialect were at times difficult to understand. I got it when they used the occasional word in Irish but often I found them speaking a form of lowland Scots straight out of Robert Burns. They almost sounded like Americans from the high country of Kentucky or Tennessee.

I'd been there several times. Always in my civvies, as I'd heard that they didn't like peelers snooping around. As Matty drove I unfolded the ordnance survey map and found Ballyharry. It was halfway up the lough shore, opposite the old cement works in Magheramorne. On the map it was a small settlement, a dozen houses at the most.

We turned off the Shore Road onto the Ballyharry Road. A bump chewed the New Order tape so I flipped through the radio stations. All the English ones were talking about the Falklands but Irish radio wasn't interested in Britain's colonial wars and instead were interviewing a woman who had seen an apparition of the Virgin Mary who had told her that the sale of contraceptive devices in Dublin would bring a terrible vengeance from God and his host of Angels.

The Ballyharry Road led to the Mill Bay Road: small farms, whitewashed cottages, stone walls, sheep, rain. I looked for Red Hall but didn't see it.

Finally there was a small private single-laned track that led into the hills that had a gate and a sign nailed to an old beech tree which said "Red Hall Manor, Private, No Trespassing," and underneath that another sign which said "No Coursing or Shooting Without Express Permission."

"You think this is the place?" I asked, looking up the road.

Matty examined the map and shrugged. "We might as well give it a go."

We drove past a small wood and into a broad valley.

There were farms dotted about the landscape, some little more than ruins.

A sign by one of them said Red Hall Cottage and Matty slammed on the brakes. It was a small farm surrounded by flooded, boggy fields and a couple of dozen miserable sheep. The building itself was a white-washed single-story house with a few cement and cinder block buildings in the rear. It looked a right mess. Most of the outbuildings had holes in the exterior walls and the farmhouse could have done with a coat of paint. The roof was thatched and covered with rusting wire. The car out front was a Land Rover Defender circa 1957.

"Well, I don't think we're dealing with an international hitman, that's for sure," I said.

"Unless he's got all his money overseas in a Swiss Bank."

"Aye."

"Maybe you should go in first, boss, and I'll stay here by the radio in case there's any shooting."

"Get out."

"All right," he said, with resignation.

We parked the Rover and walked through the muddy farmyard to the house.

"My shoes are getting ruined," Matty said, treading gingerly around the muck and potholes. He was wearing expensive Nike gutties and unflared white jeans. Is that what the kids were sporting these days?

An Alsatian snarled at us, struggling desperately at the edge of a long piece of rope.

"Yon bugger wants to rip our throats out," Matty said.

The chickens pecking all around us seemed unconcerned by the dog but he did look like a nasty brute.

We reached the whitewashed cottage, the postcardy effect somewhat spoiled by a huge rusting oil tank for the central heating plonked right outside. There was no bell or knocker so we rapped on the wooden front door. After a second knock, we heard a radio being turned off and a female voice asked:

"Who is it?"

"It's the police," I said. "Carrickfergus RUC."

"What do you want?" the voice asked.

"We want to talk to Martin McAlpine."

"Hold on a sec!"

We waited a couple of minutes and a young woman answered the door. She had a towel wrapped round her head and she was wearing an ugly green dressing gown. She'd clearly only just stepped out of the bath or the shower. She was about twenty-two, with grey-blue eyes, red eyebrows, freckles. She was pretty in an unnerving, dreamy, "She Moved through the Fair," kind of way.

"Good morning, Ma'am. Detective Inspector Duffy, Detective Constable McBride from Carrickfergus RUC. We're looking for a Martin McAlpine. We believe that this is his address," I said.

She smiled at me and her eyebrows arched in a well-calibrated display of annoyance and contempt.

"This is why this country is going down the drain," she muttered.

"Excuse me?" I replied.

"I said this is why this country is going down the drain. Nobody cares. Nobody is remotely competent at their jobs."

Her voice had a distinct Islandmagee country accent tinge to it, but there was something else there too. She spoke well, with a middle-class diction and without hesitation. She'd had a decent education it seemed, or a year or two at Uni.

The dog kept barking and two fields over a door opened in another thatched farmhouse and a man smoking a pipe came out to gawk at us.

The woman waved to him and he waved back.

I looked at Matty to see if he knew what she was talking about, but he was in the dark too. I took out my warrant card and showed it to her.

"Carrickfergus RUC," I said again.

"Heard you the first time," she said.

"Is this Martin McAlpine's address?" Matty asked.

"What's this about?" she demanded.

"It's a murder investigation," I told her.

"Well, Martin didn't do it, that's for sure," she said, reaching into the dressing-gown pocket and pulling out a packet of cigarettes. She put one in her mouth but she didn't have a lighter. I got my Zippo, flipped it and lit it for her.

"Ta," she muttered.

"So can we speak to Mr. McAlpine?"

"If you're a medium."

"Sorry?"

"My husband's dead. He was shot not fifty feet from here last December."

"Oh, shit," Matty said, sotto voce.

She took a puff on the cigarette and shook her head. "Why don't the pair of youse come in out of the rain. I'll make you a cup of tea before you have to drive back to Carrick."

"Thank you," I said.

The farmhouse was small, with thick stone walls and cubby windows. It smelled of peat from the fire. We sat down on a brown bean-bag sofa. There were spaces on the mantle and empty frames where photographs had once been. Even Matty could have figured out what the frames had once contained.

She came back with three mugs of strong sweet tea and sat opposite us in an uncomfortable-looking rocking chair.

"So what's this all about?"

"I'm very sorry about your husband," I said. "We had no idea. He was shot by terrorists?"

"The IRA killed him because he was in the UDR He was only

a part-timer. He was going up the hills to check on the sheep. They must have been waiting behind the gate out there. They shot him in the chest. He never knew a thing about it, or so they say."

Matty winced.

Yes, we had really ballsed this one up and no mistake.

"I'm very sorry. We should have checked the name before we came out here," I said pathetically.

The Ulster Defence Regiment was a locally recruited regiment of the British Army. They conducted foot patrols and joint patrols with the police and as such they were a vital part of the British government's anti-terrorist strategy. There were about five thousand UDR men and women in Northern Ireland. The IRA assassinated between fifty and a hundred of them every year, most in attacks like the one that had killed Mrs. McAlpine's husband: mercury tilt switch bombs under cars, rural ambushes and the like.

As coppers, though, we looked down on UDR men. We saw ourselves as elite professionals and them as, well . . . fucking wasters for the most part. Sure, they were brave and put their lives on the line, but who didn't in this day and age?

There was also the fact that many of the hated disbanded B Specials had joined the UDR and that occasionally guns from their depots would find their way into the hands of the paramilitaries. I mean, I'm sure ninety-five per cent of the UDR soldiers were decent, hardworking people, but there were definitely more bad apples in the regiment than in the RUC.

Not that any of that mattered now. We should have known about the death of a security forces comrade and we didn't.

"Hold on there, that tea's too wet. I'll get some biscuits," Mrs. McAlpine said.

When she had gone Matty put up his hands defensively.

"Don't blame me, this was your responsibility, boss," he said. "You just asked for an address. You didn't tell me to check the births and deaths . . ."

"I know, I know. It can't be helped."

"We've made right arses of ourselves. In front of a good-looking woman, too," Matty said.

"I'm surprised the name didn't ring a bell."

"December of last year was a bad time, the IRA were killing someone every day, we can't remember all of them," Matty protested.

It was true. Last November/December there'd been a lot of IRA murders including the notorious assassination of a fairly moderate Unionist MP, the Reverend Robert Bradford, which had absorbed most of the headlines; for one reason and another the IRA tended not to target local politicians but when they did it got the ink pots flowing.

The widow McAlpine came back in with a tray of biscuits.

She was still wearing the dressing gown but she'd taken the towel off her head. Her hair was chestnut red, curly, long. Somehow it made her look much older. Late twenties, maybe thirty. And she would age fast out here in the boglands on a scrabble sheep farm with no husband and no help.

"This is lovely, thanks," Matty said, helping himself to a chocolate digestive.

"So what's this all about?" she asked.

I told her about the body in the suitcase and the name tag that we'd found inside the case.

"I gave that suitcase away just before Christmas with all of Martin's stuff. I couldn't bear to have any of his gear around me anymore and I thought that somebody might have the use of it."

"Can you tell us where you left it?" I asked.

"Yes. The Carrickfergus Salvation Army."

"And this was just before Christmas?"

"About a week before."

"Okay, we'll check it out."

We finished our tea and stared at the peat logs crackling in the fireplace. Matty, the cheeky skitter, finished the entire plate of chocolate digestives.

"Well, we should be heading on," I said, stood and pulled Matty up before he scoffed the poor woman out of house and home.

"We're really sorry to have bothered you, Mrs. McAlpine."

"Not at all. It chills the blood thinking that someone used Martin's old suitcase to get rid of a body."

"Aye, it does indeed."

She walked us to the front door.

"Well, thanks again," I said, and offered her my hand.

She shook it and didn't let go when I tried to disengage.

"It was just out there where your Land Rover was parked. They must have been hiding behind the stone wall. Two of them, they said. Gave him both barrels of a shotgun and sped off on a motorbike. Point blank range. Dr. McCreery said that he wouldn't have known a thing about it."

"I'm sure that's the case," I said and tried to let go, but still she held on.

"He only joined for the money. This place doesn't pay anything. We've forty sheep on twelve acres of bog."

"Yes, the—" She pulled me closer.

"Aye, they say he didn't know anything but he was still breathing when I got to him, trying to breathe anyway. His mouth was full of blood, he was drowning in it. Drowning on dry land in his own blood."

Matty was staring at the woman, his eyes wide with horror and I was pretty spooked too. The widow McAlpine had us both, but me literally, in her grip.

"I'll go start the Land Rover," Matty said.

I made a grab at his sleeve as he walked away.

"He was a captain. He wasn't just a grunt. He was a God-fearing man. An intelligent man. He was going places. And he was snuffed out just like that."

She looked me square in the face and her expression was accusatory—as if I was somehow responsible for all of this.

Her rage had turned her cheeks as red as her bap.

"He was going to work?" I muttered, for something to say.

"Aye, he was just heading up to the fields to bring the yearlings in, him and Cora. I doubt we would have had a dozen of them."

"I'm really very sorry," I said.

She blinked twice and suddenly seemed to notice that I was standing there in front of her.

"Oh," she said.

She let go of my hand. "Excuse me," she mumbled.

"It's okay," I said, and took a step backwards. "Have a good morning."

I walked back across the yard towards the Land Rover.

The rain was heavier now.

The Alsatian started snarling and barking at me again.

"That's enough, Cora!" Mrs. McAlpine yelled.

The dog stopped barking but didn't cease straining at its rope leash.

"That is one mean crattur," Matty said as I got into the front seat of the Land Rover.

"The dog or the woman?"

"The dog. Hardly the temperament for a sheep dog."

"What do you mean?"

"Sheep dogs are supposed to like people."

I looked back at the farmhouse and Mrs. McAlpine was still standing there.

"Jesus, she's still bloody staring at us—get this thing going, Matty."

He turned on the Land Rover and maneuvered it in a full circle in the farmyard. The sodden chickens flew and hopped away from us.

We drove out of the gate and began going down the lane.

The man with the pipe across the valley was still there in front of his house looking at us and another man on a tractor one field over on a little hill had stopped his vehicle to get a good gander at us too.

We were the local entertainment for the day.

"Where to now, boss?" Matty asked.

"I don't know. Carrick Salvation Army, to see if they remember who they sold that suitcase to?"

"And then?"

"And then back to the station to see if Customs have that list of names yet."

Matty put the heavy, armored Land Rover in first gear and began driving down the lane keeping it well over on the ridge so that we wouldn't get stuck in the mud.

He stuck on the radio and looked to see if I would mind Adam and the Ants on Radio One.

I didn't mind.

I wasn't really listening.

Something was bothering me.

It was something Matty had said.

The dog.

It *was* a mean animal. An Alsatian, yes, but trained to be a mean. I'd bet a week's pay that it was primarily a guard dog. As Matty pointed out, on a sheep farm you'd want a Border Collie, but Martin McAlpine's herd was so small he didn't need that much help with the round up and so he'd got himself a good watch dog instead.

"Stop the car," I said to Matty.

"What?"

"Stop the bloody car!"

He put in the clutch and brake and we squelched to a halt.

"Turn us around, drive us back to the McAlpines."

"Why?"

"Just do it."

"Okay."

He put the Rover in first gear and drove us back down the lane. When we reached the stone wall, Matty killed the engine and we got out of the Rover and walked across the muddy farmyard again.

I knocked on her door and she opened it promptly.

She had changed into jeans and a mustard-colored jumper. She had tied her hair back into a pony tail.

"Sorry to bother you again, Mrs. McAlpine," I said.

"No bother, Inspector. What else was I going to do today? Wash the windows a second time?"

"I wanted to ask you a question about Cora? Is that the name of your dog?"

"Yes."

"And you say your husband was going up to bring the yearlings in, is that right?"

"Yes."

"And did he normally take Cora with him?"

"Yes."

"So she wasn't tied up?"

"No."

"Hmmm," I said, and rubbed my chin.

"What are you getting at?" she asked.

"Was Cora always this bad-tempered or is this just since your husband was shot?"

"She's never liked strangers."

"And you say the gunmen were waiting just behind the stone wall, right out there beyond the farmyard?"

"They must have been, because Martin didn't see them until it was too late."

"You say they shot him in the chest?"

"Chest and neck."

"Did you hear the shot?"

"Oh, yes. I knew what it was immediately. A shotgun. I've heard plenty of them in my time."

"One shot?" Matty asked.

"Both barrels at the same time."

"And when you came out your husband was down on the ground and the gunmen were riding off on a motorbike?"

"That they were."

"And you couldn't ID them?"

"It was a blue motorbike, that's all I saw. Why all the questions, Detective?"

"Who investigated your husband's murder?"

"Larne RUC."

"And they didn't find anything out of the ordinary?"

"No."

"And the IRA claimed responsibility?"

"That very night. What's in your mind, Inspector Duffy?

"Your husband was armed?" I asked.

"He always carried his sidearm with him, but he didn't even get a chance to get it out of his pocket."

"And you ran out and found him where?"

"In the yard."

"Whereabouts? Can you show me?"

"There, where the rooster is," she said, pointing about half the way across the farmyard, about twenty yards from the house and twenty from the stone wall. Not an impossible shot with a shotgun by any means, but then again, surely you'd want to get a lot closer than twenty yards and if you got closer, wouldn't that have given Captain McAlpine plenty of time to get his own gun out of his pocket?

"Mrs. McAlpine, if you'll bear with me for just another moment . . . Let me get this clear in my mind. Your husband's walking out to the fields, with Cora beside him, and two guys come out from behind the stone wall and shoot him down from twenty yards away. Cora, who was for taking my head off, doesn't run at the men, and he can't get his gun out in time?"

Her eyes were looking at me with a sort of hostility now.

"I'm only telling you what the police told me. I didn't get there until it was all over."

"But Cora was definitely loose?"

"Yes, she was."

"Why didn't the IRA men shoot her? She must have been all over them."

"I don't know . . . Maybe she was frightened."

"She doesn't seem like a dog easily cowed to me."

Mrs. McAlpine shrugged and said nothing.

"And why didn't your husband pull his gun? They come out from behind the wall with shotguns. He must have seen them."

"I don't know, Inspector, I just don't know," Mrs. McAlpine said in a tired monotone.

"Not if his back was turned," Matty added.

"But Cora would have smelt them, no? She would have been going bonkers. They're going to see a slavering Alsatian running at them. Wouldn't that have given him a second or two to go for his gun?"

"Evidently not," she said.

She reached into her jeans, took out a battered packet of Silk Cut and lit one.

She was pale and wan. Not just tired, something else ... *weary*. Aye, that was it.

"They killed him. What difference does it make how they bloody did it?" she said at last.

I nodded. "Yes, of course. I'm sure it's nothing," I said. "Nothing important ... Anyway, I've taken up more than enough of your time."

"Oh, don't worry about that. These days all I've got is time," she said, looking searchingly into my face, but I was the master of the blank expression—training from all those years of interrogation.

She puffed lightly on her fag.

"Maybe we should be heading, boss, before the rain bogs us down," Matty said.

"One final question, if you don't mind, Mrs. McAlpine. I noticed some of the farm buildings back there, but I didn't see a greenhouse. You wouldn't have one at all, would you?"

"A what?"

"A greenhouse. For plants, fruits, you know."

She blew out a line of smoke. "Aye, we have a greenhouse."

"You wouldn't mind if I took a wee look."

"What for?"

"I'm afraid I can't say, but it will only take a minute."

"If it's drugs you're after, you won't find any."

"Can I take a look?"

She shrugged. "Be my guest."

She walked me through the house to the muddy farmyard out the back. A smell of slurry and chicken feed. A few more harassed-looking hens sitting on a rusting Massey Ferguson tractor.

"Over there," she said, pointing to a squalid little greenhouse near a barn.

I squelched through the mud to the greenhouse and went inside. Several panes had fallen in and rain and cold had turned a neat series of plum bushes into a blighted mess. There was mold on the floor and mushrooms were growing in an otherwise empty trough of black soil. There were no exotic plants or indeed any other plants apart from the withered plums.

I rummaged in the trough where the wild mushrooms now thrived, looking for the roots of a plant that might once have been there, but I came up empty—if Martin had been growing anything interesting here all traces of it had been removed.

I nodded and walked back across the farmyard, cleaned my shoes on the mud rack.

"Did you find what you were after?" she asked.

"Did you ever hear of a plant called rosary pea?"

"What?"

"A plant called the rosary pea? Did you ever hear of it?"

She shook her head.

"It's also called crab's eye, Indian liquorice, jumbie bead?"

"Never heard of it in my life."

I nodded. "Sorry to have taken up so much of your time, thank you very much, Mrs. McAlpine. Good morning," I said and walked to the Rover.

"What was that all about?" Matty asked as we climbed back inside. "This thing stinks."

"What stinks? This? It's a dead end, surely?"

I stared out at the boggy farm and through the rearview mirror I watched her go back inside the house.

"Let's get out of here. Let's see if we can't dig a little deeper into the late Mr. McAlpine's murder."

"What the hell for?"

"Just get us going, will ya?"

"Okay."

We got about a hundred yards down the lane but a farmer was blocking the road with his tractor. It had stalled on the edge of the sheugh. He climbed down out of the cab to apologize. He had brown eyes under his flat cap. He was about forty-five. He had a pipe. So far so ordinary, but there was something about him I didn't like. An unblinking quality to those brown eyes that most people didn't have towards cops.

"Sorry lads, won't be a moment," he said. "I was turning this baste of a thing and I misjudged the size of the road."

A road he's driven down and turned his tractor around on a thousand times, I was thinking to myself.

"Oh, that's okay, we're in no hurry," Matty said.

I added nothing.

"Just got to get the front wheel out of the ditch," the man said, climbing back into the cab and turning the thing on.

The wheel came out easily and the man pulled the tractor over to let us pass.

Matty started the Rover and waved.

"What do you think that was all about?" I asked as I looked at the tractor in the side mirror.

"What?"

"The man with the tractor."

"What about it?"

"Him fucking with us like that."

Matty stared at me and when I didn't elaborate he looked back down the road.

"So where to, boss?" he asked.

"Larne RUC," I insisted.

6: SOMEONE ELSE'S PROBLEM

We took the shore road past Magheramorne quarry, where the slag heaps ran next to the road and where the fields were a strange John Deere green.

Radio One decided to torture us by heavily rotating "Making Your Mind Up" to commemorate Bucks Fizz's triumph in the previous year's Eurovision Song Contest. Even Matty couldn't take it and after hunting in vain for another station we rummaged in the Land Rover's cassette stash and found Joan Armatrading's *Walk Under Ladders*.

"You didn't really think she'd be growing rosary pea in that greenhouse, did you?" Matty asked.

"You never know, mate, you have to follow up everything."

"I could have told you it was a waste of time . . . Sort of like this little journey."

"You're quite the lippy wee character aren't you, Matthew?"

"I'm on an emotional rollercoaster, mate, someone fired a machine gun at me this morning, not to mention being harassed by a vicious dog."

"Tell Kenny Dalziel you're putting in for emotional hardship money. That'll make the bastard's head explode."

Larne RUC station was a massive concrete bunker near the harbor. It was known to be one of the safest cop postings in all of Northern Ireland because the town was small with a population that was over ninety per cent Protestant. The IRA would have few, if any, safe houses in the community and an IRA cell from Belfast could not easily make an escape to a nearby haven. In general the worst the Larne peelers had to deal with was drunkenness on Friday and Saturday nights and the occasional fracas between rival gangs of football supporters heading over or back from the ferry to Scotland. As a result of all this, Larne was known as a place where they dumped lazy, old and problem officers who could cause real difficulties elsewhere.

The McAlpine murder had been investigated by an Inspector Dougherty, a red-nosed, white-haired old stager with a tremble in his left hand that to the uneducated eye could be Parkinson's disease or MS or some other malady but which was actually the eleven o'clock shakes. At lunch time he'd slip out to the nearest pub and after a couple of triple vodkas he'd be right as rain again.

We met him in a large book-lined office overlooking the harbor and ferry terminal. The books were mostly thrillers and detective fiction which I found encouraging, but they were all from the '60s and early '70s, which wasn't such a good sign. At some juncture in the last decade he'd lost interest in reading—had lost interest in everything probably. There was no wedding ring on his left hand, but many Presbyterians didn't wear a ring because they considered it a Papist affectation. Even so, the room stank of divorce, failure and alcoholism—the standard troika for many a career RUC officer.

We were both the same rank, detective inspector, but he'd been on the force twenty years longer than me, which made me wonder what the hell he had been doing all that time, and whether I was destined to go the same route.

The rain was still pelting the windows and Scotland was a blue smudge to the east.

"Gentlemen, have a seat," he said. "Cup of tea or coffee?"

"Thanks but no, we're all tea'd out this morning," I replied, with as decent an apologetic smile as I could muster.

Dougherty folded his hands across his ample belly. He was wearing a white shirt and a brown suit that he'd obviously had for quite a few years, which, as he sat down, bunched at the sleeves and gave him an unfortunate comic air. A peeler could be a lot of things: a drunk, a thug, an idiot, a sociopath, but as long as you looked the part it was usually fine. Even in Larne Dougherty would have a hard time currying respect.

"So what brings you gentlemen down from Carrick?" he asked.

"I'd like to ask you a couple of questions about the McAlpine murder," I said, all business.

"The what?"

"Martin McAlpine. He was a part-time UDR captain who was shot at his farm on Islandmagee last December."

"Ah, yes, I remember. What's this pertaining to?"

I explained about the suitcase and the John Doe and how we had traced the suitcase back to Martin McAlpine.

"And what did his wife say happened to his suitcase?" Dougherty asked.

"She says she left it at the Carrickfergus Salvation Army before Christmas," Matty said.

Dougherty looked puzzled.

"She left it at the Salvation Army before Christmas?" he asked.

"Yup," Matty said.

"So, what's his murder got to do with anything? The murderer of your John Doe obviously just bought the suitcase for a pound from the Sally Army and used it to dump a body, right?"

"Almost certainly," I agreed.

"So, why bother dredging up the McAlpine case? Your killer could have grabbed any random suitcase, couldn't he?"

"Yes."

"And the timeline . . . She leaves the suitcase in just before Christmas. McAlpine is murdered back in early December. Your body is discovered this week? In April?"

I shook my head. "The body had been frozen for an indeterminate amount of time, but aye, I'm with you, Dougherty, I agree, it's weak beer; but you see it's not us, it's our Chief; he's going to want us to have pursued every lead out there and as soon as he finds out that the suitcase belonged to a UDR captain who was assassinated by the IRA, he's going to be firing a million questions at me."

Dougherty breathed a sigh of relief. I was not an internal affairs spook come to investigate his work, I was just another working stiff dealing with an arsehole boss.

"I'll get the file," he said.

He opened a metal cabinet and flipped out a thin—very thin—cardboard file.

He spread it on the desk between us and very slowly he sat down again with one hand on the desk and one hand to balance him. Jesus, how far gone was this eejit?

"Okay, let me see . . . Ah yes, Martin McAlpine shot in the chest with a shotgun, at approximately nine twenty in the morning of December first. He died instantly, assailants fled on a blue motorcycle which has not been recovered. IRA claimed responsibility with a recognized code word that evening with a call to the *Belfast Telegraph* . . . We didn't find the murder weapon, or the bike, and we've had no tips."

He put the file down.

That's it? I was thinking. *A man gets blown away and that's bloody it?*

"Can I take a look?"

He passed the file across. His report was one paragraph and they had tossed all the crime-scene photographs except for one which showed Martin McAlpine face up on the ground. The shotgun pellets had ripped apart his chest and throat and a couple had buried themselves in his temple. His dead face seemed to register surprise more than fear or panic but that didn't mean anything. The interesting thing about the picture was the tightness of the grouping on his torso. There was no way this had been done at twenty yards. Twenty feet perhaps, but not twenty yards. The assailants had definitely gotten a lot closer to McAlpine than the wall. How had they done this carrying shotguns without alerting Cora or giving McAlpine a chance to draw his sidearm?

I passed the photograph to Matty.

"Did you take photographs of the bootprints near the body?" I asked.

Dougherty shook his head. "What do you mean?"

"It was December, it must have been muddy, you could have gotten casts of the killers' shoes."

Dougherty raised an eyebrow at me. "No, you're not getting it, Inspector Duffy. They shot him from behind the wall. They didn't come into the farmyard. They were in the field. There were no bootprints."

"It seems to me that they must have been a good bit closer than that."

"They shot him at the wall."

"Is that where you recovered the shotgun shells? The wall?"

"We didn't recover any shells."

"They shot him and then they stopped to take the shotgun shells before running off to their motorbike?"

"Apparently they did," Dougherty said, bristling a little. He was now sitting on his left hand to stop the DTs from becoming obvious.

Matty looked at me and raised his eyebrows a fraction but I didn't mind Dougherty. He was close to retirement and when he'd joined up the RUC must have seemed like an easy life. He couldn't have predicted that come the '70s and '80s it would be the most stressful police job in Europe. Nah, I didn't mind him, but boy he was an indolent fuck, like all them old characters.

"What was the murder weapon? Did your forensic boys get a bead?"

"A shotgun."

"What type?"

Dougherty shrugged.

"Twelve-bore, over/under, single-trigger, double-barrel, what?" I asked.

He shrugged again.

"Pigeon shot, buck shot, deer shot?"

He shrugged a third time.

And this time it made me angry.

They hadn't even spent time doing a basic ballistic inquest?

He could see it in my eyes. He went defensive. "The IRA killed him with a stolen or an unregistered shotgun, what difference does it make what type it was?"

I said nothing.

Silence did my talking for me.

It worked him some more.

"... Look, if you're really interested I'm sure we kept some of the fucking pellets in the evidence room just in case we ever recovered the gun. If you go down there Sergeant Dalway will let you see."

I nodded and wrote "Dalway" in my notebook.

"Were there any other witnesses apart from the wife?" I asked.

"No, and she wasn't really a witness. She heard the shooting but when she ran out McAlpine was dead and the gunmen were already making a break for it on the motorbike."

"And you say you never recovered the gun?"

"No."

"Did you not find that strange at all?"

"Why?"

"Two guys on a motorbike carry a murder weapon with them all the way back to Belfast?"

"Don't be fucking silly! They probably threw it in a sheugh or the Lough. We did look for it but we didn't find it," Dougherty said.

"Why do you think he didn't pull his sidearm on them? He was walking out to the fields and if they were at the wall they were a good twenty yards from him," I asked.

"They had the element of surprise. They jumped up and shot him. Poor devil didn't have a chance."

"And why do you think Cora didn't go for them?" I asked.

"Who's Cora?"

"The dog, a really nasty Alsatian," Matty said. "The dog that didn't bark in the daytime. It's a classic."

"Oh aye, the dog, I don't know. The gunshots probably scared the shite out of it," he muttered.

"Did you find any motorcycle tracks? Were you able to identify the tire or make of the bike?" I asked.

"No."

"No you didn't ID the bike or no you didn't find any tracks?"

"I don't like your tone, Inspector Duffy," he said.

There hadn't been any tone. I'd been careful about that. He was just getting ticked off at the holes I was poking in the case.

"Please, I didn't mean to imply—" I said.

"We didn't find any motorcycle tracks, Inspector, because they drove off on the road. It's tarmac—it's not going to leave any fucking tracks, is it?"

"If they're behind the wall surely they're going to start the bike there, not push it to the road and kick start it there?" Matty said. "There should be tracks."

"Well, we didn't find any."

I frowned. "Look, Inspector, I'm going to ask a question and please don't take it the wrong way . . ."

"Go on," he said, steam practically coming out of his ears.

"Did you look for the tracks or were they just not there?"

His fist clenched and unclenched, but then he closed his eyes for a moment and when he opened them he smiled at us.

"I'm not going to bullshit you, Duffy, I honestly don't remember. Hold on a minute and I'll get my notes."

"Thank you, I appreciate that," I said.

He opened a drawer and flicked through a green jotter. He slid it across to me, but I couldn't decipher the handwriting. I did notice that under "McAlpine" there was less than half a page of text. All in pencil. With a few doodles on the side. When *I* conducted a murder investigation, sometimes I filled two or even three ring-bound reporters' notebooks.

I passed the notebook to Matty, who had been sufficiently pedagogically indoctrinated by me to frown and shake his head. He skimmed the notebook back across the table. Dougherty took it and smiled a little smile of satisfaction as if he was saying, *see, I'm not a fuck up, I even kept my notes.*

"No tracks. But I can't tell if we looked behind the wall or not," he admitted.

I turned to Matty. "Do me a favor, go down to the evidence room and see if you can bag me one of the shotgun pellets. We'll see what they can find out up at the lab in Belfast? If that's okay with you, Inspector Dougherty?"

"I don't see what this has to do with your investigation?"

"Do you object?"

"No. If you want to go around wasting everyone's time, go ahead, be my guest."

Matty got up and left the office.

Dougherty looked at me. "I take it you're not happy with the wife's story then, is that it?" he asked.

So he wasn't a complete fool. At least he saw my angle.

I shook my head. "I don't know about that. She seemed fairly credible to me. I just want to eliminate all the other possible contingencies."

"She came from a good family. Islandmagee locals. Her father was a Justice of Peace and of course she married into the McAlpines."

"What's special about the McAlpines?"

"Harry, the elder brother, is a big wheel. His grandfather did something for the Empire.

They gave him a gong for it."

The clock on the wall reached twelve and with that he breathed an audible sigh of relief and reached in his desk drawer for a bottle of Johnnie Walker.

"A wee one before lunch?" he asked.

"Don't mind if I do," I replied.

He produced two mugs and poured us each a healthy measure.

When he had drunk and topped up his own mug he grinned.

"You like the wife for it?" he asked. "How do you explain the IRA code word? And I still don't see what this's got to do with your suitcase?"

"I'm not saying it was her. But the grouping on that wound is so tight it looks point blank to me. And if a couple of terrorists were marching up to him so close as to do that kind of point blank damage surely the dog would have been on them and he would have had his sidearm out," I said.

"Aye," Dougherty said thoughtfully.

"And besides the IRA don't use shotguns anymore. Not since the early '70s. Not since our Boston friends and Colonel Gaddafi started sending boatloads of proper ordnance. They've got M16 rifles and Uzis and Glock pistols now," I said.

"I suppose," he said, refilling his mug.

"And then there's the lack of witnesses. And no trace of a gun, no shells, no motorbike," I continued.

"But what about the code word?" Dougherty asked.

"Jesus, those things leak like a sieve. Her own husband might have told her the IRA-responsibility code word for late last year."

"Why would she do it? There was no insurance policy. We checked that. And the army pension is pathetic."

"A domestic, maybe? I don't know," I said.

"And your fucking suitcase?"

"Probably unrelated, but you never know, do you?"

He nodded, poured himself a *third* generous measure of Scotch.

"I've heard of you, Duffy. You were the hot shot in Carrickfergus who got himself the Queen's Police Medal. Are you looking to make a big fucking splash in Larne, too?"

He was getting punchy now.

It was time to leave.

"No. I'm not. This isn't my case. I'm done and unless Mrs. McAlpine is involved in my murder somehow you probably won't be hearing from me again."

"Aye, pal, don't forget this is my manor, not yours."

"I won't forget."

I got to my feet and offered him my hand and he reluctantly shook it. I saw myself out.

I waited for Matty by the desk sergeant's desk.

He came back from the evidence room empty-handed.

"What happened, they wouldn't let you in?"

"They let me in all right but the locker's empty boss. Nothing there at all."

"They've moved it?"

"Lost it. A few weeks ago they moved the McAlpine evidence to the Cold Case Storage Room but when I went there the box was empty. The duty sergeant looked through the log and has no idea where the stuff went. He told me shite like this happens all the time."

"Jesus, Mary and Joseph. All right, I better go myself."

We went to the evidence room and searched high and low for half an hour but it was gone. Either lost in a spring cleaning or deliberately thrown out. Incompetence or cover up—both were equally likely. I liked the former better because asking who was covering up for whom raised all sorts of difficult questions.

It was drizzling when we got back outside.

Matty lit me one of his Benson and Hedges and we smoked under the overhang and watched the potholes fill up with water for a couple of minutes.

"I'm not saying that these lads are the worst cops in Ireland . . ." Matty began and then hesitated, unsure if I was going to countenance this level of perfidy.

"Yes?"

"If there's a shittier station than this lot I hope to God I'm never posted there," he concluded.

"Oh, there's worse. I was at a station in Fermanagh where they dressed up as witches for Halloween. Big beefy sergeant called McCrae dolled up as Elizabeth Montgomery was the stuff of nightmares . . . Larne would be okay, you'd be the superstar of the department if you got the bloody days of the week right."

We nailed another couple of smokes and got back in the Land Rover. Matty drove us out of the car park and the Constables at the gate gave us the thumbs up as they raised the barrier to let us out.

Matty drove through Larne past a massive UVF mural of two terrorists riding dragons and carrying AK 47s.

We turned up onto the A2 coast road.

"Where to now, Sean?"

"Carrickfergus Salvation Army," I said. "It's a long shot but maybe they'll remember what happened to that suitcase, if she really did bring it in there."

"Why would she lie about that?"

"Why does anybody lie about anything?"

Matty nodded and accelerated up onto the dual carriageway. The Land Rover was heavily armor plated and bullet-proofed, but the juiced engine still did zero to sixty in about eight seconds.

We put on Irish radio again. It was the same program as before; this time the interviewee, a man called O'Cannagh, from the County Mayo, was talking about the mysterious behavior of his cattle which baffled the local vets but which he felt was something to do with flying saucers. The man was explaining this fascinating hypothesis in Irish, a language Matty didn't speak, so I had to turn it off. Neither of us could stand the constant jabber about the Falklands on news radio so we went for Ms. Armatrading again.

Matty drummed his fingers impatiently on the steering wheel. "I know what you're thinking, Sean, you're thinking we should stick our noses in here, aren't you?"

"Maybe."

"Listen, Sean, what if she's telling the truth about the suitcase but she was, for whatever reason, lying about her husband's murder?"

"What about it?"

"Then it's not our case, mate, is it?" he said.

"And if she killed the poor bastard?"

"If she killed the poor bastard, it becomes, in the coinage of Douglas Adams, an SEP."

"Who's Douglas Adams? And what's an SEP?" I asked.

"If you were down with the kids, Sean, you'd know that Douglas Adams has written this very popular radio series called *The Hitchhiker's Guide to the Galaxy*. I listen to it when I'm fishing."

"I'm not down with the kids, though, am I? And you still haven't answered my question. What's an SEP?"

"Someone else's problem, Sean," Matty said, with a heavy and significant sigh.

I nodded ruefully. Ruefully, for it was the sorry day indeed when my junior colleague felt the need to remind me that in Ireland you swam near the shore and you kept your mouth shut and you never made waves if you knew what was good for you.

"SEP. I like it. I'll bear it in mind," I said.

7: SHE'S GOT A TICKET TO RIDE (AND SHE DON'T CARE)

The Salvation Army was a bust. The lady there, Mrs. Wilson, said that they sold dozens of suitcases every month, especially now that everyone was trying to emigrate. They didn't keep records of who bought what and she did not recall a red plastic suitcase or a Mrs. McAlpine.

"Have a wee think. You might remember her, she was a recent widow. She brought in her husband's entire wardrobe."

"You'd be surprised how many of those we get a month. Always widows. Never widowers. Cancer, heart attack and terrorism—those are the three biggies."

"Well, thank you for your time," I said.

When we got back to the station Crabbie's dour face told me that Customs and Immigration had not yet given us the list of names of all the Americans entering Northern Ireland in the last year.

"What's their excuse?" I asked him.

"They're transferring everything from the card file to the new computer."

"Jesus, I hope to God they haven't lost them. We've had enough of that today."

"Nah, there was no note of panic in their voices, just bored stupidity."

"Par for the course, then," I said under my breath, staring at the other policemen and women in here who seemed to have jobs to do but God alone knew what the hell they were. Crabbie, Matty and myself were detectives, we investigated actual crimes, what these jokers did (especially the reservists and the part-time reservists) was a fucking mystery.

"No luck on the Abrin either. I called the Northern Ireland horticultural society, the Irish Horticultural Society, the British Horticultural Society and no one had any records of anyone growing rosary pea or one of its varieties. It is certainly not a competition or show plant. I phoned UK Customs HQ in London and asked if they had ever impounded any seeds and of course they had no idea what I was talking about. And, you'll like this, I called up Interpol to see—"

"Interpol?"

"Yeah."

"I do like it. Go on."

"I called up Interpol to ask them to fax me any cases of Abrin poisoning that they had on file in any of their databases."

"And?"

"Three homicide cases: all from America: 1974, 1968, 1945. Half a dozen suicides and another two dozen accidentals."

"That's very good work, mate," I said, and told him about our interesting day.

I treated the lads to a pub lunch. Steak and kidney pie and a pint of the black stuff and after lunch I retreated to my office, stuck on the late Benny Britten's "Curlew River" and read the Interpol files on the Abrin murders:

1974: Husband in Bangor, Maine, who was a chemist, poisoned his wife.

1968: Husband who was a banker in San Francisco who grew tropical plants, poisoned his wife.

1945: Young woman, originally from Jamaica, poisoned her parents in New York.

I read the suicides and the accidentals but there was nothing significant or interesting about them. There were no Irish connections or intriguing links to the First Infantry Division.

I called up Belfast Customs and Immigration and politely harangued them about their abilities and their propensity for sticking their heads up their own arses.

They said that they were working on it but the new computer system was a nightmare and did I know that it was a Saturday and there were only two people in the office, one of whom was Mrs. McCameron?

I said that I knew the former but not the latter and asked them to do their best. I avoided the obvious Mrs. McCameron lure, which sounded like a standard civil service crimson clupea. There probably was no Mrs. McCameron.

At around three o'clock someone put on the football but I grew bored and found myself at another table listening to a reserve constable called Wilkes who was also in the Royal Navy Reserve and who'd just gotten a phone call telling him that he was on his way to the South Atlantic as a fire control officer on *HMS Illustrious*.

"That's going to be the fucking Admiral's ship!" he said, with obvious excitement.

"Aye and the best target in the fleet for the Argie submarines. Classic frying pan/fire situation for you, my lad. This time next month you'll be some penguin's breakfast," Sergeant Burke muttered. I gave him a cynical grin and went to get a coffee.

The lads plied Wilkes with questions and when the clock finally got its bum round to five we hit the bricks.

Since it was indeed a Saturday I got a Chinese takeaway and ate it with a bottle of Guinness back in Coronation Road. It was the dinner of sad single men across Ireland. To really trip on the mood I scrounged up some fuzzy Moroccan black and dug out the copy of the ancient *Times Literary Supplement* I'd lifted from the doc's. I flipped through the pages until I found what I was after, which was a poem by Philip Larkin called "Aubade." I read it twice and decided that it was the greatest poem of the decade. I wanted to share this information with someone, but here at 113 Coronation Road, Carrickfergus there was no one to share it with. My parents wouldn't be interested and Laura had no time for poetry. And my friends, such as they were, would think I was taking the piss.

I finished my spliff and called my parents anyway, but they weren't home.

I looked at the phone and the rain leaking in the hall window.

I made myself a vodka gimlet in a pint glass and called Laura. Her mother answered.

"Oh, hello, Sean," she said cheerfully.

"Hi, Irene, is Laura there at all?" I asked.

"No. No, I'm afraid not. Her father drove her to the airport."

This took several seconds to sink in.

"She's leaving *tonight*?"

"Yes. Didn't she tell you?"

"She said it was next week."

"We had to change the plans. She's been trying to call you all day. We're going to take the ferry over with her car on Tuesday and she's going by plane tonight to get everything sorted."

"She tried to call me?"

"Yes—where were you this afternoon?"

"Working."

"On a Saturday?"

"Aye, on a Saturday. The crooks don't take the weekends off."

"I'm sure she'll try you again at the airport. The plane doesn't leave until seven."

"Okay, I better get off the line then," I said.

I hung up and childishly punched the wall.

"Fucking lying bitch!" I yelled, which wouldn't be the last time such edifying dialogue would be heard in Victoria Estate on a wet Saturday night.

I made myself another pint of vodka and lime juice, walked out the back to the garden shed, opened an old can marked "Screws" and found the stash of high-grade Turkish hashish I'd liberated from the evidence locker before they'd torched it and a couple of bags of brown tar heroin in a ceremony for the *Carrickfergus Advertiser*.

I got a Rizla King Size, made myself a joint and smoked it as I walked back to the house.

The phone was ringing and I almost slipped and broke my neck as I sprinted for the bastard.

"Sean! At last!" she said.

Laura. She was calling from Aldergrove Airport. Her plane left in five minutes.

I don't remember any of the rest of it.

It was a story. A fairy story.

And promises neither of us would keep.

Five minutes?

It didn't last two.

Her words were frozen birds fallen from the telegraph wires.

I responded with a vacuum of lies and banality, sick of my own material.

She finally took mercy on us and said goodbye and hung up the phone.

I sat in the living room and relit my joint. The Turkish was the shit and it wasn't ten minutes before I was as high as a fucking weather balloon floating over Roswell, New Mexico.

I expectorated in the back yard and watched The Great Bear's snout bend down and touch the lough. Spacing, I was. "Bear mother, watch over us," I said. "Like you watched the old ones . . ."

There was a good quarter inch left but I tossed the joint, went back inside, put on *Hunky Dory*. *Hunky Dory* became Joan Armatrading became *Dusty in Memphis*.

At eleven o'clock there was a knock at the door.

I got my revolver from the hall table and said "Who is it?"

"Deirdre," I think she said.

"Deirdre who?"

"From next door."

I opened the door. It was Mrs. Bridewell. She was holding a pie. It had got wet in the rain. *She* was wet. Mrs. Bridewell with her cheekbones and bobbed black hair and husband over the water looking for work . . .

"Oh, hello," I said. "Come in."

"No. I won't stop over. I've left Thomas with the weans and a bigger eejit never stuck his arm through a coat."

"Come in out of the rain, woman."

She took a cautious step into the house. She looked at my picture of Our Lady of Knock and suppressed a skewer of polemic against the Papists.

"I only wanted to leave this off. I made it for the church bake sale tomorrow but it's been canceled because of the war."

"What war?"

"Argentina's invaded the Falkland Islands!"

"Oh, that war."

"None of my lot can eat a rhubarb tart. But I know you like it."

I turned on the hall light. She'd put on lipstick for this little sally next door and she was beautiful standing there with her wet fringe and puzzled green eyes, tubercular pallor, dark eyelids and thin, anxious red lips.

"Mr. Duffy?" she said.

There was no one in the street. Her kids would be abed. The air was electric. Dangerous. It was fifty-fifty whether we'd roo like rabbits right here on the welcome mat. She could feel it too.

"Sean?" she whispered.

Christ almighty. I took a literal step back and breathed out.

"Yes . . . Yes, a rhubarb tart. Love them."

She swallowed hard.

"M-make sure you eat it with cream," she said, left it on the hall table and scurried back to her house.

I left the pie where it was and broke out the bottle of Jura instead. At midnight I put on the news to see if there had been any plane crashes but all the telly wanted to talk about was Argentina and I had to sit through several angles on that story before it became obvious that there hadn't been any airline disasters and that Laura was completely safe.

8: VETERANS OF FOREIGN WARS

On Sunday an Atlantic storm parked itself over Ireland and it was raining so hard it could have been the Twelfth of July or one of those other holidays when God poured out his wrath on the Orangemen marching through the streets in bowler hats and sashes. I didn't leave the house the whole day. I was so bored I almost went to the Gospel Hall on Victoria Road where, allegedly, they spoke in tongues, danced with snakes and afterwards you got a free slice of Dundee cake. Instead I listened to music and read *One Hundred Years of Solitude* which had come from the book club. It was a good novel but, as the man said, maybe seventy-five years of solitude would have been enough.

Dozens of different birds had stopped in my back garden to take shelter from the weather. I was no expert but I was my father's son and with half a brain noted starlings, sparrows, blackbirds, thrushes, swifts, magpies, rock doves, robins, gulls of every kind.

On Monday the birds were still there and Mrs. Campbell from the other side of the terrace was in her back garden in a plastic mac throwing bread to them. You could see her jabbers through the mac, which me and Mr. Connor in the house opposite were both appreciating through our kitchen windows. The Campbells were a mysterious people and although I shared an entire wall with them I never really knew what was going over there, if her husband was working or at home, or how many kids and relatives' kids she was looking after. She was an attractive woman, no doubt, but the stress and the smokes would get to her like they got to everyone else.

And speaking of ciggies, I lit myself a Marlboro, put The Undertones on the record player, showered, ate a bowl of cornflakes and hot milk, dressed in a shirt and jeans and headed out for the day. I checked under the BMW for mercury tilt bombs and drove to the station.

When the list of American citizens who had entered Northern Ireland in the previous year finally came in at eleven on Monday morning it was longer than we'd been expecting. Six hundred names. Five hundred of whom were men. Northern Ireland during the Troubles was not a popular tourist destination but the hunger strikes had sucked in scores of American journos, protesters, politicians and rubberneckers.

"How are we going to tackle this?" McCrabban asked dourly. His default method of asking anything.

"We'll break the list into three and we'll start making phone calls. We'll begin with the over-forties first," I said.

Fortunately each visitor to Northern Ireland had to fill out a full information card giving his or her home address, phone number, emergency contact, etc.

There were three hundred and twenty American men over forty who had entered the Province in the previous twelve months.

"All these calls to America are going to cost us a fortune," Matty said. "The Chief won't like it."

"He's going to have to lump it," I told him. "And let's hope that our boy hasn't been frozen for years."

"Wait," McCrabban said. "I've thought of another problem."

"What?" I said, somewhat irritated because I was keen to get started.

"We can't make any phone calls before one o'clock. They're five hours behind, remember?"

"Shite," I said, slapping my forehead. He was right. It wasn't decent to call people up first thing in the morning.

"So what are we going to do in the meantime?" Matty asked.

"Do what everyone else does around here. Pretend to work," I said.

Matty opened up some files and spread them on his desk, but read the *Daily Mail*. The *Mail* and every other paper was all Falklands all the time. The country was mad for the war. Thirty years since the last good one, not counting what had been going on in our little land.

McCrabban took out his notebooks and started studying for his sergeant's exam.

I looked through a couple of theft cases to see if anything would leap out at me. Nothing did. Theft cases rarely got solved.

On a hunch I called up every life insurance company in the book to see if there had been any payouts on anyone called McAlpine in the last four months.

Nope.

At eleven the phone rang.

"Hello?" I said.

"Hello, is this Inspector Duffy?" a voice asked.

"Yes."

The voice was Scottish, older. I immediately thought that something had happened to Laura in Edinburgh and she'd put me down as her emergency contact.

"Is this about Laura?" I asked breathlessly.

"Well, yes and no," the voice said.

"Go on."

"I'm Dr. Hagan, Laura, er, Dr. Cathcart's replacement at Carrickfergus Clinic. I was reading over Dr. Cathcart's report on the torso in morgue number 2."

"Yes?"

"The John Doe torso."

How many torsos did he think we got in a week?

"Yes?"

"Well, something occurred to me that I thought I should share with you."

"Go on, Dr. Hagan."

"Well, Laura has written down in her notes 'victim frozen, time and date of death unknown.'"

"That's right."

"But, she's also written down that the victim's last meal was a Chicken Tikka Pot Noodle."

"So I read."

"In case you don't know, Sergeant Duffy, that was a really quite extraordinary bit of forensic medicine. She must have analyzed the stomach contents and then compared them with a list of ingredients for every Pot Noodle that Golden Wonder makes."

I wasn't really in the mood to hear Laura praised to the skies.

"Okay, so she was extremely diligent at her job—how does this help me, Dr. Hagan?"

"It helps you because it considerably narrows down the window in which the victim died. Since I retired from full-time practice I've been fishing a lot more and on occasion I've taken a Pot Noodle and a thermos of hot water with me . . ."

I was getting excited now. The old git was on to something.

"I know for a fact that the Chicken Tikka Pot Noodle was only introduced in November of 1981. I'd seen the advertisements for it and I made a point to try it when it came out as I spent quite a few years in Malaya and thought it might be a nice blend of Indian and Chinese cuisines. Unfortunately it wasn't that tasty . . . but this is me running off on a tangent—do you get my drift, Sergeant Duffy?"

"The victim couldn't possibly have been killed before November of last year," I said.

"Yes."

I thanked Dr. Hagan and shared the news with the boys.

We called Golden Wonder to confirm the release date of the Chicken Tikka Pot Noodle and they told us that it had been shipped to shops and supermarkets on November 12. It helped a little. Yes, the victim had been alive in November, but he still could have entered Northern Ireland anytime in the last year. Tourists overstayed their ninety-day visas all the time, as did journalists and businessmen. But still, assuming he was a law-abiding citizen, we could cut off the list of names at, say, 30th June 1981 for our initial series of phone calls.

That winnowed the list down to a measly two hundred and fifty over-forty American males who had entered Northern Ireland between 30th June 1981 and 30th March 1982. I drafted in a reserve constable with the unlikely name of John Smith so that we could divide the effort in four. Sixty names each didn't seem that onerous.

Matty wondered if any Canadians or Brits abroad had joined or been seconded into the First Infantry Division and it was a damn fine point but we couldn't afford to get sidetracked this early. We took it as a useful fiction that they had not.

We started making phone calls at 1 p.m., which was 8 a.m. on the East Coast.

For once we caught a break and by just three forty-five we had a first-class lead on our hands.

Matty did the call. A man called Bill O'Rourke had put the number of his Veterans of Foreign Wars Lodge as his emergency contact. VFW Post 7608 in a place called Newburyport, Massachusetts, which we discovered was a hop, a skip and jump north of Boston.

A guy called Mike Lipstein was happy to fill Matty in on his buddy Bill who no one had heard from since before Christmas 1981.

Bill was a former IRS inspector who had indeed served in The Big Red One, in North Africa, Sicily, France and Germany. He was an enlisted man who had risen to the rank of First Sergeant by the end of hostilities.

He was also a widower who had retired from the IRS in Boston to take care of his wife Heather who was dying of terminal breast cancer. She had died in September of 1980. It had hit him hard and everyone had told him that he had to get away somewhere. He had taken a trip to Ireland just before Halloween to visit the old country and retrace his roots. He'd gone for a few weeks, loved it and said he was going back to do some more exploring. This second trip was just before Thanksgiving and no one had heard from him since.

"Did he say why he was going to *Northern* Ireland?" Matty had asked.

His paternal grandparents had come from County Tyrone, Matty had been told.

"Did he keep himself fit by swimming at all?" Matty had wondered, and had been informed that Bill was a keen swimmer and further that he had a condo in Fort Lauderdale, Florida where he usually spent the winters...

"I think I have the bastard!" Matty yelled.

Crabbie and I put down our phones.

"Matty my lad, you have the moves, son," Crabbie said.

He laughed. "I am sweet to the beat, boys!" and told us all about Mr. O'Rourke.

To be on the safe side we worked our way through the other names on our list but not a single one of them had served in the First Infantry Division.

Now it was action stations. We called the Newburyport Police Department and talked to a Sergeant Peter Finnegan. We explained the situation and Sergeant Finnegan gave us Bill's dates and social security number and promised to fax us a copy of his driver's license from the DMV. Sergeant Finnegan didn't know about kids or next of kin but said that he would look into it for us.

I also put in a call to the FBI and after half a dozen suspicious flunkies I got someone who said that he would let me know if Bill had a criminal record. This information had only been forthcoming after a threat to go through the State Department "or the President himself," which had Matty and Crabbie cracking up in the aisles.

I went in to tell the Chief.

"We may have our John Doe, sir."

"Who is it?"

"A retired IRS inspector called Bill O'Rourke from Massachusetts."

"What's the IRS?"

"Internal Revenue Service. He was a taxman."

"A taxman. Jesus. There's your motive."

"A retired taxman. Born 1919. Apparently he had come here to trace his roots. He's the right age, he's a veteran of the right regiment and no one's heard from the bugger in months."

"1919, eh? Lucky baby to have survived the influenza."

"Not so lucky now, of course."

Brennan nodded. "Who are you following up with?"

"I've asked the Yank cops to fax me a copy of his driver's license and after a lot of pushing and shoving I even got the FBI to come on board and send me any files they have on him."

"Why bother the FBI?"

"It's an unusual case. I just want to be sure that he wasn't mixed up in anything he shouldn't have been mixed up in."

Brennan grinned and slapped his hand into his fist. "You're dotting the i's, crossing the t's. It's an American after all. I'll confirm the bad news with the Consulate. They'll want to know one of their own has definitely met with a sticky end. And the press too, they'll want a piece of this. The Irish press, the English press, the American press," Brennan said, starting to see other angles in this case. PR angles. Promotion angles.

"Hold your horses, Chief. If we go to the media everybody's going to be looking over our shoulder and we're not *completely* sure that he's our stiff," I complained.

"The newspapers will want this, Duffy. A dead American's worth a hundred dead Paddies any day of the week," Brennan said.

Brennan opened his desk drawer and took out the Tallisker single malt. I sat down and was persuaded into a glass.

"Speak now or forever hold your peace," he said.

"Maybe we should wait a day or two before turning on the spotlights," I said, trying to erase his overconfident grin.

"O'Rourke's our lad! I can smell it."

"What does this magic nose of yours tell you about who killed him?"

"Don't mock your elders! My intuition comes from years of experience. I had a premonition about Elvis's death two weeks before he passed on, God rest his soul. I told Peggy and she said I should call Graceland. I didn't of course. Shame . . . Lost my train of . . . What were we . . . Oh, yes—if it makes you happy, we'll say that he's a 'possible victim' in a 'possible homicide,' will that satisfy you?" he asked.

"I suppose so, sir."

I drank another round of Tallisker and Brennan opened a packet of Rothmans, fired one across to me and lit one for himself. I noticed a sleeping bag bundled up in the corner of the office. I decided not to comment on it.

"Any leads on the poison angle?" Brennan asked.

"None at all, sir, I am sorry to say. Abrin is an extremely rare substance. I don't know who the hell would have taken the trouble to refine and process it or why they would have used it as a murder weapon on an island filled to the brim with guns."

He nodded and blew smoke at the brown stain on the ceiling that uncannily resembled Margaret Thatcher's hairdo. "I'm sure it's going to take you into some interesting areas, but do me a favor, don't let it get too complicated, will you, Sean?" Brennan muttered. He shifted his weight from his left to his right side. He grunted and rubbed his eyelids. "Do you hear me, son?"

"Yes, sir," I replied. "I'll keep it simple, you know me."

"I do know you, pal, that's the bloody trouble."

I nodded, drank the rest of the whisky and got to my feet.

"And Duffy?"

"Yes, sir?"

"That Elvis story is just between us," Brennan said.

"Of course, sir," I replied and exited the office.

9: BLOOD ON THE TRACKS

Someone passed me a brandy to help "batten down the hatches on our breakfasts." I'd only had a coffee but I took a swig of the flask anyway and passed it back.

I walked to the top of the hill and waved away the oncoming traffic. I wasn't properly in uniform. No shirt, no tie, just black trousers and a black sweatshirt under my flak jacket which said "Police" on it in yellow letters. I was wearing my green uniform hat and fidgeting with a Sterling submachine gun loaded with a 25-round clip. The same gun I'd used to repel the attack on Coronation Road and win me my police medal and my invitation to Buckingham Palace.

I was fiddling with the gun rather than looking downhill at the carnage. Everyone was compensating in their own way. One guy was whistling, two other cops were talking about the football. That was their way of not being in the present. "We have better things to do with our time than direct traffic," Matty was grumbling to Crabbie because he knew better than to grumble to me.

"You do what you're told to do and that's an end to it," Crabbie told him and like a good Free Presbyterian refused the brandy and passed it back to me. I shook my head and walked along the lane to where a dead cow was lying in the sheugh. Killed by the concussion shock wave or a random piece of debris. I looked down into the valley. The helicopter's spotlights were still scouring the scene in the predawn light, even though everyone was now accounted for: the dead, the dying, the miraculously survived. I lit a Marlboro and drew in the good, safe, dependable American tobacco. It comforted me. I sat on a tree stump and watched the helicopter's powerful incandescent spotlight beams meditating on the pulverized brick and stone, on the smashed cinder block walls, on the cars ripped inside out. I watched as the rotors sucked embers, paper fragments and debris into the sky in huge anticlockwise spirals.

That comforted me too, making me feel that something, *anything*, was being done. Half an hour passed this way, then dawn made its presence felt across the landscape and the chopper banked to the left and flew back to RAF Aldergrove.

I could see the full havoc wrought on Ballycoley RUC station, now.

It was a country police barracks and with only a thin brick wall around the perimeter, which was why it had been chosen for the terrorist attack. The main building itself had been flattened and a portacabin structure in the rear had been tossed halfway up the nearest hill. Many of the surrounding houses had been wrecked, part of a railway line had been ripped up and an electricity substation destroyed. It was lucky that the number of civilian casualties wasn't higher.

With the Wessex gone the valley was relatively quiet.

Cops talked to one another, radios crackled, generators hummed and a massive yellow digger pawed at the rubble like a brachiosaurus over its dead young.

I went back to the other officers and we shared smokes and turned away a milk delivery lorry and explained what had happened to the bemused driver. "There's been an incident, the road's closed for the time being, mate, you'll have to find an alternative route . . ."

"What happened?"

"A bomb blast in the wee hours down at the police station there."

"Anybody dead?"

"Aye. Four."

The driver nodded and turned his car around. Ballycoley RUC was only six miles from Carrickfergus but I didn't know any of the deceased. Two of them were peelers, one was the driver of the bomb vehicle and one was a civilian woman, a widow who lived across the road and who apparently had been eviscerated by her own disintegrating bedroom windows.

Matty yawned. "How much longer are we going to have to stand here like eejits, Sean?" he asked me.

I shook my head. "I'll go down there and find out."

I walked down the slurry slope into the former police station compound.

The air smelled sweetly of cordite, sawdust, blood and diesel leaking from the portable generator. Now that the rescue portion of the job was over the scene was filled with white boiler-suited forensic officers gathering material and taking photographs.

I found the chief investigating officer and introduced myself.

"Detective Inspector Duffy, Carrick RUC," I said.

"Detective Chief Superintendent McClure, Special Branch," he said and offered his hand. I shook it. His handshake was even limper than mine. We were both exhausted. He was a grizzled man with a grey moustache and black eyebrows. About fifty. He favored his left hand side and was smoking a little cigar.

"You were up there on traffic duty?" he asked in a faint Scottish accent.

"Aye."

"They've got a detective inspector on bloody traffic duty? What's the bloody world coming to?"

"I suppose they're a bit short-handed. Apparently the army units they were going to deploy in East Antrim are off to the Falklands," I said.

He spat. "Fucking Falklands. Fucking sheep. That's all that's there. I know, I've been. Military Police. You're not the Duffy that Tony McIlroy's always going on about, are you?" McClure asked.

"Tony talks about me?"

"He said we should recruit you for Special Branch, he says that you're good."

"That's nice of him."

"Can't stand the man myself. Very showy."

"When we arrived last night somebody told us that this is some new IRA technique?" I asked, to change the subject.

"Oh, yes. Come and see."

He lifted the "RUC: Do Not Cross" tape and I followed him across the site of the former police station. He showed me where the lorry had driven through the police station's barrier and then exploded. "It's a very impressive new technique," he said. "We'll have to re-evaluate security at every barracks in Ulster. Apparently the man who drove the lorry was forced to do it. His family had been taken hostage by the IRA and he was told that if he didn't drive the vehicle right into the station they'd all be shot. As soon as he breached the barrier another IRA team blew up the lorry by remote control. As you can see it was a big bomb. A thousand pounds, maybe."

"You've seen this sort of thing before?"

"Once before. Two makes it a pattern. It's a pretty devastating new ploy. Between us, Inspector, the higher ups are keeking their whips."

"I'll bet they are. Every police station in Ulster will be vulnerable."

"Aye."

"What about the guy who drove the lorry? Was he a copper too?"

"No. Catholic bread-van driver. He delivered to the peelers so they're calling him a 'collaborator.' He delivers bread for a living and he's a collaborator. That's the world we're living in, Inspector."

We walked among the smoking debris and the Chief Superintendent picked up the twisted remains of a steering wheel. "Look at this," he said, showing me the plastic wheel which had been warped and melted into an amazing spaghetti sculpture. I noticed a bent ring of metal around the wheel. "They didn't trust him completely, did they?" I said, pointing at the metal ring.

"Why do you say that?"

"They handcuffed the poor bastard to the steering wheel."

Davey looked at the wheel and nodded. The sun was burning through the low clouds now. I yawned. It had been a long night. "Listen, sir, I was wondering if my team could be released from traffic duty, I've got an interview at the US Consulate later this morning and—"

"Aye, aye, spare me the details. You and your lads can go. How many CID are up there with you?"

"Just two."

"Good. Leave the others. I can't afford to lose a man down here."

"Thank you, sir."

I walked back up the hill and grinned at Matty and Crabbie.

I pointed at Matty. "You can go to bed."

"Ta, mate."

I pointed at Crabbie. "You can come with me."

Some of the other peelers from Carrickfergus looked at me expectantly.

I shook my head. "Sorry lads, they need the rest of you here for the foreseeable. I'm really sorry."

Before there was a police mutiny I got Matty and McCrabban into the nearest Land Rover and we drove off. Up on the hills debris from the explosion had set the gorse on fire. A line of flame was snaking its way over the mountain top. We called it in to the fire brigade and drove through: Ballyclare, Ballyeaston, Ballynure, Ballylagan and finally Carrickfergus. We dropped Matty at his house up the Woodburn Road. His mother invited us in for a cup of a tea, but we had to say no.

McCrabban and I hit the station, shaved, splashed water on our faces, grabbed an instant coffee, put on shirts and ties.

The Chief saw us on the way out. "Oi, lads, what are you doing here? Get your arse in gear, you've got a meeting at the US Consulate in Belfast at nine. Chop fucking chop, Duffy. Don't embarrass us."

"We were just on our way out, sir, they had us on emergency traffic duty at Ballycoley."

"That's the service. All hands on deck. Tragedy up there. Two brother officers killed. You're not complaining, are you, Duffy?"

"No sir."

"Good, now don't stand there with your bake open, off ya go!"

We hit top gear on the M5 even sticking the siren on so we'd make our appointment on time and not "embarrass the station." As it was we were ten minutes late.

A lackey showed us into a formal meeting room with a chandelier, William Morris wallpaper and large photographs of President Reagan,

Vice President Bush and the Secretary of State, Alexander Haig. There was a polished oak oval table and a dozen straight-backed uncomfortable-looking oak chairs on a plush red carpet.

A secretary came in to take minutes, a nice wee lass with pale skin and green eyes, followed by a skinny character who was obviously a diplomat. He was about thirty, cadaverous, reedy, brown-eyed, a slightly misshapen head. He was wearing a tweed jacket, a pink shirt and a black tie. He was carrying a briefcase which he placed on the desk in front of him.

I gave Crabbie a look which told him that I wanted him to run the meeting and he nodded. "Detective Inspector Duffy, Detective Constable McCrabban," he said.

"James Fallows, US Department of State. Would either of you gentlemen like tea or coffee?" Fallows asked in a pleasant baritone.

"Coffee would be lovely," I said. "Milk, two sugars."

"Mine's a tea, no milk, no sugar," McCrabban said.

The secretary put down her yellow legal pad and without a word exited the room.

"I heard about the bombing this morning. I'm very sorry," Fallows said.

"Thank you," Crabbie replied for both of us.

"They're saying on the news that there were three deaths?" Fallows continued.

"Four. Four confirmed dead at the scene. Two policemen dead, two seriously injured. The driver of the lorry died in the explosion and a civilian was killed in a nearby home," I said.

"Ah, yes, but the driver of the lorry was surely a terrorist," Fallows said with a thin smile that I didn't really like.

"We don't know that at this stage," McCrabban said.

The secretary came back with the hot drinks and a plate of American cookies.

I took a sip of my surprisingly good coffee and took a bite of cookie.

Aaron Copland began piping through the air from somewhere.

"So, down to business. Apparently one of our countrymen called William O'Rourke has been murdered?"

"Yes."

"Are you quite sure it's a murder?"

"We're sure," Crabbie said.

"Poisoned?"

"Poisoned, yes."

He opened his briefcase and looked at the notes in front of him. "I've never heard of this 'Abrin'—it's rare, is it?"

"Very rare. In fact, one of the things we wanted to ask you about was whether you can provide any information for us about Mr. O'Rourke's horticultural connections. Did he have a greenhouse, was he a grower of exotic plants, were any of his relatives engaged in that kind of activity?" Crabbie asked.

"I wasn't aware that you were here to solicit help with your investigation," Fallows said.

"Why did you think we were here?" I asked.

"I had been led to believe that this was merely a formal briefing."

"You're not refusing to help us with our inquiries, are you?" I asked incredulously.

Crabbie and I exchanged a look.

"Of course not," Fallows ululated. "You will be given the full and complete cooperation of the United States Embassy to the Court of St James."

"That's what we were hoping for," I said. "For a start, the local police force in Newburyport is having some trouble faxing Mr. O'Rourke's driving license to us. Apparently that requires another level of authorization or something. I'm not sure what the holdup is but I was wondering if you could—"

Mr. Fallows slid a cardboard file across the desk.

"You can keep this," he said.

It contained a photostat of Bill O'Rourke's driver's license and passport. He was a handsome man, was Bill. Lean, tanned, with dark black hair greying only slightly on the left hand side. He had an intelligent, unyielding face and there was that certain something about him that commanded respect. Maybe it was all that horror he'd experienced in World War Two.

"We've never had an American murdered in Northern Ireland in all my time here," Fallows said. "Surprising, given the level of violence."

"There's got to be a first time for everything," Crabbie said.

"We'll also need his work records from his employer and any possible criminal records from the FBI," I added.

"You ask for a lot."

"And I'll need a local police officer to investigate his house and report back to me about what he finds."

"Oh, they won't like that," Fallows sniffed. "That's vague. Report back about what?"

"I'll need a full report on his home—homes, I should say—his recent activity at the bank, that kind of thing. The cops will know what to do."

"And whether he has a greenhouse. And we'll need to know if he has a plant in that greenhouse called rosary pea," McCrabban added.

"Rosary pea?" Fallows said, and couldn't quite meet our gaze.

I shot another quick glance at McCrabban. Yup, he'd seen it too. This fucker was hiding something.

"*Rosary pea* rings a bell, does it?" I asked.

Fallows shook his head. "Never heard of it in my life."

"Are you sure?"

"Quite sure. Never heard of it before you mentioned it."

"Your last diplomatic posting wasn't Trinidad, was it?" McCrabban asked.

"No. Six years in Canada and then here. Why?"

I smiled and shook my head. "No reason."

We fired a few more questions at him but he gave us back nothing that we wanted. We made sure that he got the message about the cooperation of the Massachusetts police and the FBI and he said that he would see what he could do.

When we got outside we rubber-banded the file and headed for the Rover. Queen's Street was one of the places where you could get into the center of Belfast through the steel security barriers erected across the road. Every single pedestrian going into Belfast had to be patted down and their bags searched in an effort to stamp out bomb attacks. Of course we peelers just flashed our warrant cards and jumped straight to the head of the line.

"Fucking cops," someone muttered behind us in the queue.

"Aye," someone else agreed. "They think they run the fucking world."

When we were through the barrier I patted McCrabban on the back, something which the big phobic Proddy ganch always hated. "That was a good question, mate, *rosary pea* seemed to take that skinny wee shite aback a bit, didn't it?"

"Maybe the local American cops have already found something in O'Rourke's greenhouse?" Crabbie said, shrinking from the touch of a fellow human being.

"Maybe, Crabbie, maybe. But, as Bobby D. says, there's something funny going on, I can just feel it in the air."

"A complication?"

"Brennan's not going to like it, but yeah, it's beginning to sound that way, isn't it?"

10: GOOD PROGRESS

The case was flying now. We had made a shit load of progress and as I looked at myself in the mirror and shaved with an electric I saw a man who was at least professionally content, if not exactly happy in any other aspect of his life. I certainly wasn't worried about meeting the Chief this morning. He'd kept off my back for a few days and I was determined to show him that his faith in the long leash was justified.

I finished shaving, put the kettle on and went outside. The starlings had been at the milk: clever wee shites, they had figured out that gold-top bottles contained the full cream stuff and silver top the ordinary milk. Their intelligence was a rare commodity round these parts. I grabbed a gold-top, made coffee and toast and I was about to head out to the car when the phone rang. It was Carol, who told me that the Chief Inspector wanted to meet me at the police club in Kilroot, not at the station.

"Fine by me," I lied.

I checked under the BMW for bombs, didn't find any and drove down Coronation Road.

I was stopped at an army checkpoint outside of Eden Village. Two Land Rovers and half a dozen jittery squaddies from the Parachute Regiment. Everyone knew that the Paras were being shipped out of Northern Ireland to be the tip of the spear in the Falklands invasion. It was good riddance. Most Catholics I knew still hated the Parachute Regiment for the Bloody Sunday massacre in Derry. I still hated them for that too, as irrational and conflicted as that sounded.

The weekend after Bloody Sunday was one of the hinge points of my life, when I very nearly joined the PIRA, only to be turned down by an old school friend of mine, Dermot McCann, the IRA quartermaster in the city who told me that I should stay at university because "the movement needed thinkers."

Of course, by joining the police I had betrayed Dermot and the movement.

I don't know how honor is to be properly measured, but when you saw the Parachute Regiment march the streets of Ulster and you knew that they were your brothers in arms, it certainly didn't sit well . . .

I showed the soldiers my warrant card and a big sergeant within an even bigger moustache waved me through the checkpoint.

Another checkpoint took me into the police club.

I parked the Beemer and went downstairs.

I found Brennan at the bar and he suggested a game of snooker, a fiver the winner, while I debriefed him.

Brennan broke and potted the pink with a completely flukey shot off two cushions and a red. Just then the strip lights flickered and the barman flinched as if he was expecting some kind of trouble. He was a civilian. None of the cops moved a muscle.

The cue ball rolled across the baize and came to stop perfectly aligned at another red.

"A-ha!" Brennan said triumphantly, reached into his pocket and put another fiver on the table.

"You want to increase your wager?" he asked, with a malevolent grin.

"You have a ways to go before you make it as a snooker hustler, sir. Displaying your prowess first isn't usually a good idea."

He laughed again. "You haven't seen the half of my prowess, matey boy."

His mirth seemed hollow in here where the mood was pretty grim. Not grim because of the recent attacks on police stations or because confirmation had come through that several battalions of British Army soldiers were being transferred from Ulster to the Falklands Islands Task Force, no, the mood in here was grim because it was always bloody grim. The Police Club was nothing more than a windowless bunker with thick, bombproof concrete walls, concrete floors, a utilitarian bar, a couple of snooker tables and a dartboard. TV reception was difficult through all that bomb-proofing so the only reason at all why you'd come here was to drink the heavily subsidized booze with brother officers.

As far as I could see I was the sole copper in here who wasn't a middle-aged, chronically depressed alcoholic. But fast forward to five years from now ... if I was still alive ...

Cut to the boss: unkempt, unshaven, and he'd been wearing the same shambolic suit for a week. Definitely trouble chez Brennan and although I would certainly put him up if he wanted, if I suggested it again he'd have me guts. Presumably this place had become a sort of home from home and I wondered if this was where he was kipping too.

He potted another red and lined up the blue.

"So what have you found out, Duffy?" he asked.

"About the case?"

"No, about the bloody meaning of life."

"Like I say, sir, we've been making excellent progress."

"Do tell."

"Well, sir, we've learned about Bill O'Rourke's war service. Operation Torch in North Africa—easy sailing against the Vichy French but then a rough time of it with Rommel's Panzers. Then Normandy, where he was wounded taking a pill box. Silver Star and a Purple Heart for that one. A second Purple Heart at Hurtgen Forest."

"Good for him."

"He rose from Private First Class to First Sergeant of his company in just two years. An impressive guy."

"Sounds it," Brennan said, potting the black and lining up another red. "Go on."

"After the war he takes chemical engineering at the University of Massachusetts and then switches to accountancy. Joins the IRS in '49 where he works for the rest of his life, it seems."

"Criminal record?"

"The FBI faxed us a very thin dossier on him. O'Rourke apparently had no criminal record of any kind and had never been investigated by any government agency. An FBI team visited his house in Newburyport and found nothing of a criminal nature."

"You sent the FBI to look at this guy's house?"

"No, I asked the Consul if the local police could do that, but somehow the FBI got involved. It actually got DC McCrabban and myself a little excited, but it was all moot because the Feds didn't find anything."

Brennan glowered at me. "You're not trying to make things complicated, are you, Duffy?"

"No, sir, and in any case, like I say, it was a bust. The FBI found nothing suspicious among Mr. O'Rourke's personal effects and nothing in the background check. One speeding ticket from the '60s."

"A model citizen."

"Indeed, although I suppose there could be misdemeanors that didn't make it into the files."

"What else?" Brennan said, potting the red and crashing into the yellow with a very lucky lie.

"The boys and myself have done some leg work and we've begun piecing together our victim's last movements. It seems that he took two trips to Ireland. The first was uneventful. He arrived in Belfast on the train from Dublin on October twenty-sixth of last year, stayed for a week and left again. He stayed in the Europa Hotel in Belfast for all seven nights and then checked out. His family on his father's side was from Omagh and presumably he went to Tyrone to investigate his roots, but if so, no one remembers him. I called librarians, local history organizations, that kind of thing. They do get a lot of Americans and they don't keep records. Anyway, he didn't make an impression."

"What about this second trip?"

"That's where the story gets interesting, sir. Okay, so he goes back to America. Tells some of his pals that Northern Ireland is a wonderful place and he's going back for more. This is last year, sir, right after the hunger strikes . . ."

I looked at Brennan, who stopped lining up the cue ball and

nodded. We both knew what Northern Ireland had been like last year. Worse than now and now was bad.

"So obviously O'Rourke's either a deluded old fool or a bit of a liar," Brennan said.

"Americans can get sentimental about the Old Country, sir."

"Indeed. Carry on, Duffy."

"Second time around he arrives in Belfast on November eighteenth, stays at the Europa again for five days. Apparently he ate in the hotel restaurants most nights and he tipped fifteen per cent. He made no fuss, seemed to be enjoying life as a tourist, asked the bell hops no questions about hoors or product. He paid his bill with an American Express Card. Apparently there was no problem with the transaction."

"That'll do nicely," Brennan said, and potted the blue.

"Quite a few people in the Europa actually remember him because he was so courteous and pleasant. One of the maids said that he was, quote, a real charmer and a bit of a smoothie, unquote, but again, there was no hint of any impropriety."

"That's when he disappeared?"

"No. Not quite. He next surfaced in the Londonderry Arms hotel in Carnlough on November twenty-fourth. We drove up there too and interviewed the staff, and again Bill had been a model citizen, attracting no adverse attention and tipping well."

"This is good stuff, Duffy, go on."

"Well, this is where it gets tricky, sir. He disappeared for two days after that until he paid a very large credit card bill at a bed and breakfast in Dunmurry called the Dunmurry Country Inn."

"How much is very large?"

"Seven hundred quid."

"Jesus!"

"Yesterday Detective McCrabban went to see the proprietor of the Dunmurry Country Inn and was refused entry. The place is owned by a Richard Coulter, and either he or one of his employees demanded to see DC McCrabban's search warrant, which is why I've come to see you, sir."

Brennan potted a red and a black. He was leading by seventy points now and it was mathematically impossible for me to win the frame.

"So you want me to call up a friendly judge and get you a universal search warrant for the Dunmurry Country Inn?"

"I've already taken care of that, sir. There are some other difficulties. We'll be stamping all over Dunmurry RUC's patch and I don't want to make any waves."

Brennan stopped mid-shot and straightened his back.

He got the message.

"Coulter's protected, is he?"

"In a way, sir."

"How so?"

"He comes from a prominent family in Ballymena. He has money, sir. He runs several small hotels and bed and breakfasts. He's also well known for his charity work. He set up a shelter for abused women and runaway kids."

"Classic cover."

"Exactly, sir."

"Is he untouchable?"

"I'm sure he pays off to the right people. He's not small fry and I doubt very much that Coulter filed the clearly fraudulent American Express claim but someone who works for him did and Coulter doesn't want us to push too deeply into it. Fraud's a serious business, sir. Murder's murder but defrauding a CC company might even get the attention of Scotland Yard."

"This Coulter, what is he, a terrorist? A paramilitary?"

"No, sir, not in the least. But he's a known associate of Cyril Lundy who I'm sure you're aware is the commander of the Rathcoole Brigade of the UDA. Coulter's more of a shady businessman than either a gangster or someone actively involved in sectarian conflict."

"But not someone you want to fuck with. Not with your track record, eh, Duffy?"

"No, sir."

Brennan sighed, lurched towards me and let a big paw rest on my shoulder.

"I'm glad we had this little chat. When's your warrant for?"

"This morning."

"This morning, eh?"

"Yes, sir."

"Okay, I can square things with the cops in Dunmurry."

"I was hoping that you'd say that."

"But there's a price for my assistance."

"A price?"

"I want to come with you. I want to come, and I'll do lead if that's okay with you? Funny how bored a man can get even in the middle of a so-called civil war."

"I'm not sure that's a good idea. I think I can handle this one on my own."

"I said I'll come with you, Duffy, and I'll do lead if that's okay with you?" he reiterated in a growling undertone.

"It's absolutely fine with me, sir."

11: NO PROGRESS

Awet April morning in a small provincial city on the fringe of Europe. A bunch of cops carrying out one of the most basic of all cop activities: executing a search warrant. And although everywhere the serving of search warrants is a protocol driven, largely crepuscular activity, nowhere in the "civilized" world does the task come with so much palaver as in Northern Ireland.

Three grey armored Land Rovers driving up a dreary motorway towards Dunmurry, a drab, soulless sink estate in North Belfast, recently saved from perfect entropy by the DeLorean Motor Company which had been established here precisely for the purpose of resurrection.

Elsewhere on Eurasia in this spring of 1982 men are working in factories, making consumer goods and cars, harvesting winter wheat and barley, toiling in terraced rice paddies; from Shanghai to Swansea there is order, work and discipline and only here, at the edge of the continent, is there war. Funny that.

Getting the warrant has been easy and the Chief has wielded his magic with the local brass. He gathers Crabbie, Matty and myself in his pungent office to share the news. "We have our warrant and we have an okay from the RUC and Army chiefs. This is how the system works, lads. You just gotta be nice and humble to the higher ups," he says, presenting the wisdom of the ages as some kind of hard-won insider scoop.

Chief Inspector Brennan, Sergeant Burke and Inspector McCallister are in one Land Rover. In a second there are half a dozen police reservists dressed up in riot gear. In a third Matty, Crabbie and myself.

As we drive through the seething estates, the locals make us welcome by throwing milk bottles filled with urine from tower blocks and the flat roofs of houses. Of course, if it was night time or an occasion of particular tension, burning vodka bottles filled with petrol would be arcing in our direction.

The convoy pulls up outside a bed and breakfast which lies at the end of a terrace. Reserve constables fan out of the second Land Rover to guard the perimeter. We get out of ours. I am not wearing full riot gear but a simple blue suit and a black raincoat.

Matty is unimpressed by the Dunmurry Country Inn, which looks like a bit of a shitehole. "What was O'Rourke staying here for?" he asks.

An excellent question, that will, no doubt, be asked many times before this investigation is over.

"This way, lads," Chief Inspector Brennan announces, and we follow him down the path. Sergeant Burke is with him for protection. Sergeant McCallister is waiting back in the Rover with his machine gun at the ready.

We knock on the door.

We are expected.

The door opens. A man called Willy McFarlane opens it and stands there large as life and twice as ugly. He's five eight, lean, with a handlebar moustache, a black comb-over, aviator sunglasses. He's wearing a loud blue polyester sports jacket over a yellow *Six Million Dollar Man* T-shirt. Knife scars. Jail house ink. I dig the T-shirt.

"Are you gentlemen looking for a place to stay?" he says, with a chuckle.

"We're looking for Richard Coulter," I tell him.

"Mr. Coulter is at a charity lunch in London. Princess Diana is going to be there," Willy McFarlane says.

"Is this his place of business?" I ask.

"One of many."

"Who are you?"

He tells us who he is.

"We have a warrant to search these premises, Mr. McFarlane," Brennan announces.

"Be my guest," McFarlane says with another wee laugh.

"Work your way through from top to bottom and back again. I'll question Mr. McFarlane here."

The bed and breakfast is small. Two terraced houses knocked into one. Four guest rooms. O'Rourke had been staying in room #4 and I know McCrabban will pay special attention there but I ask him to check all the bedrooms to look for *any* possible evidence. I'm letting Crabbie lead the search while I run the wheel on McFarlane.

"Upstairs, downstairs. Meet me in the back kitchen," I tell him.

The back kitchen.

The smell of lard and Ajax. Flypaper hanging against the wall. Clothes drying on an internal clothes line. A checkered linoleum floor: the kind that blood cleans up easily from. Mrs. McFarlane, a small bird-like woman, is making tea, humming to herself contentedly.

She's not a stranger to unusual guests or peelers with machine guns.

McFarlane's smoking Bensons. Relaxed.

Let's unrelax the fucker.

"You know why we're here?"

"No," McFarlane says, unconcerned.

"Mr. Coulter's account charged seven hundred pounds on one of your guest's American Express Cards last November. A Mr. Bill O'Rourke from Boston, Massachusetts," I say.

"What about it?"

"Your room rates are twenty pounds a night and he checked out after two nights. It doesn't compute, does it?"

William McFarlane is not fazed. He rubs a greasy fist under his chin. "I charged that bill. Mr. Coulter has nothing to do with it and I'll thank you not to mention his name again."

"You charged the bill? So you admit it?"

"Aye. I remember yon boy. He wanted Irish Punts. He wanted six hundred quid's worth of Irish Punts. I got them for him, legally I might add, from the Ulster Bank in Belfast. In fact I think I might have the receipt right here."

He produces a piece of paper from his trouser pocket.

What a joke. What a frigging laugh riot. He knew we were coming and why we were coming. Someone tipped off his boss and his boss tipped him.

I take the receipt and read it.

It's exactly what he says it is. A receipt for six hundred and fifty Irish pounds from the Ulster Bank on Donegall Square, Belfast. Transaction dated 25 November 1981.

I bag it and put it in my jacket pocket.

"What did he want the money for?" I ask.

"He didn't say."

"He just stayed here two days and left?"

"That's right."

"Did he say where he was going?"

"No."

"He paid his bill in full?"

"Aye. No problems."

"How many other guests did you have?"

"At that time?"

"Yes."

"None."

"You're a bit out of the way here, aren't you? A bit off the tourist trail."

"Aye, I suppose so."

"How many guests do you get a month, would you say?"

"Well, it depends."

"On average?"

"I don't know. A dozen. Maybe more, maybe less."

Hmmmm.

Mrs. McFarlane brings me a mug of tea, a Kit Kat and a publication called *Teetotal Monthly* whose headline for April is "Hibernia Despoiled By Demon Gin." I thank her.

"Eat that up, love, you're skin and bones and you look hungry enough to eat the beard of Moses," she says.

I drink the tea and light a cigarette. McFarlane and I look at one another and say nothing. I read Mrs. McFarlane's pamphlet. There's a nice exegesis of the wedding feast at Cana which explains that Jesus Christ turned the water not into wine but into a form of non-alcoholic grape juice.

McCrabban comes back downstairs.

He shakes his head.

Brennan and Sergeant Burke appear from wherever they've been. Mrs. McFarlane offers to make them tea. Brennan accepts. Sergeant Burke goes outside to have a smoke.

I let McCrabban ask McFarlane all the questions I have already attempted in order to ascertain if there are any inconsistencies.

There are none.

We drink our teas and assume that Edwardian Belfast fake politeness that coats this city like poison gas. Matty finally comes down with his fingerprint books and forensic samples.

"Are you all done, mate?"

"Aye," he says. He's got something in his hand. He shows it to me. It's from the pantry. A Chicken Tikka Pot Noodle.

"Well done," I tell him.

Perhaps a flash of concern flits across McFarlane's eyes.

I go up to bedroom #4 and ask Crabbie to follow.

Chintz wallpaper on the staircase, thin orange carpet, pictures of Belfast that look as if they are framed postcards. There's a smell too: vinegary and sour.

I pause on the top step.

"What was O'Rourke staying in a place like this for?"

Crabbie shrugs. "He was only here for two nights."

"Why here? Why Dunmurry? No one visits Dunmurry."

"Some people must do so otherwise there wouldn't be a bed and breakfast," Crabbie says.

"Wise up, mate, this place is clearly a money-laundering scheme."

We go along the landing to room #4.

Typical Belfast terraced bedroom: small, damp, depressing, with an old fashioned bed covered in many layers of itchy woolen blankets. Also: a grainy window that does not open; a huge Duchess chest of drawers with a large fixed mirror; an elm desk and a plastic chair next to the window; fleur-de-lis wallpaper from a bygone age; sepia prints on the wall of 1920s Ireland. And that smell: mildew, vinegar, cheap cleaning products. I look under the bed and examine the Duchess chest of drawers which is a monstrosity of a thing, the wood dyed to look like mahogany, but really pine. The drawers are empty and the mirror could do with a good wipe down.

I examine the desk but there's nothing there and again we look at the chest of drawers. There are strange wear marks on the carpet, an ugly case of rising damp on two of the walls.

"We found nothing, either," Crabbie says.

"McFarlane says he wanted Irish currency. That's why there was such a big bill," I tell Crabbie.

"So he went down to the Republic?"

"Could be."

"Maybe he was murdered down there?"

"How did the body end up here?"

"A million ways. They dump the suitcase in a truck or a bin lorry going north?"

I shake my head. "We're not getting off that easy. The suitcase came from here and the body was found here. This is *our* problem."

We take a last look around.

"What do you think those marks are on the carpet?" I ask Crabbie.

He shrugs. "Is that where people kick the chair over when they hang themselves from the light fitting?"

We go back downstairs.

Brennan looks at me. "Well?"

"Well what?"

"When do we depart this royal throne of shit, this cursèd plot?"

"We'll go when I think we're done," I say.

"Some of these men are on overtime, Duffy."

"I didn't ask you to bring them, sir."

"It's a tough manor."

"Everywhere's a tough manor."

Brennan pulls a pipe out of his raincoat pocket and begins to fill it.

"How long, Duffy?" he insists.

"Give me five more minutes. Let's see if the bugger's got a greenhouse at least . . . Matty, come with me!"

We push through the kitchen into the wash-house where more clothes are hanging out to dry and coal is piled high in coal buckets and an old bath.

Sergeant Burke is leaning against a wall, vomiting.

"Are you okay, mate?" I ask him.

"Have you got any hair of the dog, Duffy?" he asks.

I look at Matty, who shakes his head.

"Go get the hip flask from Inspector McCallister," I tell Matty. "Tell him it's for me."

He nods and goes back inside.

"Are you okay?" I ask Burke.

"I'm all right. I'm all right. Collar's too tight or something."

"Shall I get a medic?"

"I'm fine!" he says.

Matty comes back with McCallister's brandy. Burke grabs it and swallows half of it. He wipes his mouth and nods.

"Knew that would sort me," he says, with an unpleasant smile.

He goes back inside on unsteady legs.

When he's gone I whisper to Matty: "You and me a few years from now, if we don't watch out."

"I've got fishing, what have you got, mate?" Matty asks.

"Uh . . ."

"You should get a pet. A tortoise is good. They're lots of fun. You can paint stuff on their shells. My sister's looking to get rid of hers. Twenty quid. It's got a great personality."

"A tortoise isn't my idea of—"

"Hey, boy! Does your warrant cover the back garden?" McFarlane yells at Matty from the kitchen window.

"Show him the warrant, will you, DC McBride? And tell him that if he calls you boy again you'll lift him and bring the fucker in for a comprehensive cavity search."

Matty shows McFarlane the legalese and yells back to me: "Inspector Duffy, it sounds like somebody's not keen for us to investigate his back yard."

"Aye, I wonder what we'll find," I say.

What we find is a back garden which is a dumping ground for assorted garbage: old beds, old tires, mattresses. In many places thin reed trees and ferns are growing through a thicket of grass. Along the wall there seems to be an ancient motorbike; but more importantly, there in the north-west corner, there's a greenhouse.

We open the door and go inside. It's clean, humid, well-maintained and all the windows are intact. There are a dozen boxes of healthy tomato plants growing in pots along the south-facing glass.

"Tomatoes," Matty says.

Matty puts on his latex gloves and begins digging through them to see if there's anything else growing in there, but in pot after pot he comes up only with soil.

"Nowt," Matty says.

"Look through those bags of fertilizer."

Nothing in there either. We stand there looking at the rain running down the thirty-degree angled roof in complicated rivulets.

He looks at me.

"You're feeling it, too?" I ask him.

"What?"

"A feeling that we're missing something?"

"No."

"What were you looking at me like that for?"

"I just noticed all those grey hairs above your ears."

"You're an eejit." I examine the plants, but Matty's right: these really are genuine tomato plants and there is nothing secreted in the pots.

McFarlane gurns at us through the glass before going back towards the house.

"He's lying about something, Matty, but what?"

"I don't know. Maybe he's Lord Lucan. Maybe he shot someone once from a grassy knoll. Do we head now? The Chief's getting shirty," Matty asks.

I walk outside the greenhouse and do a thorough three-sixty perimeter scan—and low and behold, between the greenhouse and the wall I spot a plant pot sitting on a compost heap: red plastic, hastily thrown away. There's no plant in it now but clearly there once was and perhaps residue remains.

"What do we have here?"

"What is it?"

"Gimme a bag, quick," I tell him.

We put the plant pot in a large Ziploc to protect it from the rain.

We march back into the house.

"What have you got?" the Chief asks.

"Evidence, boss!" Matty says with an unconcealed note of triumph.

I look at McFarlane.

His face is blank.

The complaining, however, has dried up, which can only be a good sign.

I thank Mrs. McFarlane for the tea and her hospitality.

We file outside.

A crowd.

A rent-a-mob. Three dozen youths in denim jackets.

The reserve constables looking nervous.

"SS RUC!" a kid yells and the chant is half-heartedly taken up by the others. Someone from the back throws a stone.

"Time to head, gentlemen, these fenian scum will make it hairy in a minute or two," Brennan says.

These fenian scum.

The word throws me. Gives me a strange out-of-body dissonance for the second time today. How did it happen that I'm on the side of the Castle, on the side of the Brits? One of the oppressors, not the oppressed...

"Come on lads, let's go!" Chief Inspector Brennan says.

We get back into the vehicles as a hail of bricks, bottles and stones came raining down on the Land Rover's steel roof.

We make straight for the M2 motorway, the shore road, Carrickfergus Police Station.

"What now, boss?" Matty asks.

"Take a Land Rover and a driver and get this plant pot up to the lab. I want it examined by the best forensic boys on the force and I want you to stay with those fuckers until the job is done. If they find any rosary pea material in here at all it'll be enough to hang McFarlane."

Matty takes the plant pot and streaks off like Billy Whizz.

The rest of us head home.

#113 Coronation Road.

I put on "For Your Pleasure" by Roxy Music.

I fry some bacon and onions.

I eat my dinner and listen to both sides of the LP which I haven't played in seven or eight years.

When it's over I put on my raincoat walk back down to the station to wait for Matty. He shows up at nine.

"Good news?"

He shakes his head. "The only organic material in that pot was a withered tomato plant."

"Are you sure?"

"The lads were 100 per cent sure. A dead tomato plant. Nothing else."

"No rosary pea or indeed anything weird?"

"No."

"Shit."

"Sorry, boss."

"Thanks, Matty."

No rosary pea. No Abrin.

"Do you want to go next door to the pub?" I ask him.

"Is that an order?"

"No."

"Well, in that case I'd rather not, if you don't mind."

"All right, I'll catch you another time. I'll go myself."

I juke next door and order a pint of Guinness and a double Scotch. A redhead called Kerry asks me if I will buy her a drink. She drinks a blackcurrant snakebite, which apparently is equal parts lager and cider with a dash of blackcurrant in a pint glass. After two she's toast. I tell her the joke about the monkey and the pianist in the bar. She thinks it's hilarious. She asks what I do for a living and I let slip that I'm a copper ... And that, my friend, is it. She's either Catholic or has your bog standard hatred of the police. When I come back from the toilet she's gone. She's been through my wallet, but she's only taken a twenty-pound note to get a taxi, which, when you think about it, isn't so bad.

I order a double Bush for the road, hit it and walk back through the rain.

My head's splitting. I stop to urinate outside the Presbyterian Church and an old lady walking her mutt tells me that I'm a sorry excuse for a human being. "I agree with you, love," I say but when I turn round to make the argument there's no one there at all.

12: A MESSAGE

A week went by without any developments.
Like the majority of murder cases in Northern
Ireland this one was starting to die. No new
information from America. No eyewitness testimony. No calls on the Confidential Telephone.
Mr. O'Rourke had last been seen in Dunmurry.
He'd got some Irish money, checked out of his
crummy B&B and then he'd turned up dead.
In another week or so the Chief would tell me
to put the O'Rourke case on the back burner. A
week after that, we'd move it to the yellow fold-
ers: open but not actively pursuing . . .

It was a Wednesday. The rain was hard and cold and coming at a forty-five-degree angle from the mountains. The sound of shotguns some-where up country woke me at seven. I listened for a moment or two but there was no return fire and it was probably just a farmer going after foxes.

I put on the radio.

The local news was bad. An army base in Lurgan had been attacked with mortars, a firebomb had destroyed a bus depot in Armagh and an off-duty police reservist had been shot dead at the wheel of his tractor in Fermanagh.

The national news was about the Falklands War. Ships were still sailing south, the Pope wanted a peaceful resolution, the Americans were doing something, the EEC was calling for sanctions against Argentina.

I lay under the sheets for a while and finally wrapped myself in the duvet and dragged my ass downstairs.

I called my mother. She said she was just going off to play bridge. Dad was also on his way out, going birding up the Giant's Causeway.

"What do you see up there?" I asked, faking interest.

"Buzzards, kestrels, peregrines, sparrowhawks, gannets, occasional black and common guillemots, razorbills, eider ducks, purple sandpipers, colonies of fulmar, kittiwakes, Manx shearwaters, puffins, twites."

"You're making half those up."

"I am not."

"There's no such bird as a fulmar or a twite. I wasn't born yesterday."

"Fulmar from the Norse 'full,' meaning foul, 'mar' meaning gull, 'fulmar,' because of their oily bills. They're a type of seagull. Highly pelagic birds . . ."

"Which means?"

"They spend most of their life out at sea, like albatrosses."

"And a twite?"

"A small passerine bird in the finch family."

We both knew that I didn't know what a passerine bird was, but an explanation would weary me. "I have to go, Dad."

"Okay, son, see you, take care of yourself."

"I will."

I hung up and put on Radio Albania to get a Maoist version of the world news. I put Veda bread in the toaster and made a Nescafé. I ate the toast at the kitchen table and thought about my folks. They'd never spoken about why they'd only ever had one kid. I hadn't been deprived of love, but I'd just never really connected with either of them. Dad was into fishing, bird watching, hare coursing, fell walking, hiking, that kind of thing, and as a wean I'd thought that I was interested in it too, but I was only fooling myself. When I told them I was going to be a cop they neither approved or disapproved. If I'd told them I was going to be a terrorist I probably would have gotten the same reaction.

I carried the coffee into the living room.

I put on all three bars of the electric heater and stared out stupidly at the front garden. Radio Albania's spin on the Falklands War was that it was a struggle between two fascist regimes in an attempt to repress revolt among their own working classes.

I trudged back into the kitchen, changed the channel to Radio Four to get confirmation that this really was a Wednesday. I had accumulated a lot of leave and in a deal with Dalziel in clerical I was taking two Wednesdays a month off until my leave was back down to manageable levels.

I made another cup of coffee and when I discovered that it was indeed a Wednesday I retired to the living room with a Toffee Crisp and my novel.

I was reading a book called *Shoeless Joe* which had gotten a good review in the *Irish Times* and was about a man obsessed by baseball and J.D. Salinger—but not in a creepy Mark David Chapman way.

The phone rang.

I trudged into the hall and picked it up.

"Hello?"

"Is this Duffy?"

"It is."

"Can you be at the shelter in Victoria Cemetery in ten minutes?" a woman asked. A young woman, with an odd voice. English. Old fashioned. So old fashioned it sounded like she was doing an accent or something.

"Sorry?"

"Can you be at the Victoria Cemetery shelter in ten minutes?" she repeated.

"I can, but I'm not going to be."

"I've got information about one of your cases."

"Come down my office, love, anytime," I said.

"I'd like to meet with you in person."

"I don't do graveyards. It'll have to have to be at the office."

"This will be worth your while, Duffy. It's information about a case."

"Listen, honey, they pay me the same wages whether I solve the cases or not."

The lass, whoever she was, thought about that for a second or two and then hung up.

She didn't call back.

I looked out the window at the starlings for ten seconds. One of the little bastards shat on my morning paper.

"Fuck it," I muttered, ran upstairs, pulled on a pair of jeans and gutties. I threw a raincoat over my Thin Lizzy T-shirt and shoved my Smith and Wesson .38 service piece in the right hand coat pocket.

"I don't like it," I said to myself and sprinted out the front door.

The graveyard was on the other side of Coronation Road, over a little burn and across a slash of waste ground known as the Cricket Field—the de facto play area for every unsupervised wean in the estate.

The sky was black.

The wind and rain had picked up a little.

I jumped the stream and scrambled up the bank into the Cricket Field: burnt-out cars and a gang of feral boys throwing cans and bottles into a bonfire.

"Hey, mister, have ye got any fags?" one of the wee muckers asked.

"No!" I replied and hopped the graveyard wall.

I circled to where I could see the concrete shelter that had been built to give protection to the council gravediggers while they waited for funeral services to be concluded. This part of Carrick was on a high flat escarpment exposed to polar winds, Atlantic storms and Irish Sea gales. I'd been to half a dozen funerals here and it had been pissing down at every one of them.

I had envied the men in the shelter, although I had never actually been in it myself. It was large and could easily accommodate a dozen people. If I remembered correctly there were several wooden benches that ran along the wall. There were no doors to get into it as it was open to the elements on the south side like a bus shelter.

If I could circle due south through the petrified forest of graves I could easily see if someone was waiting in there or not.

I ran at a crouch through the Celtic crosses and granite headstones and the various family plots and monuments.

I made it to the perimeter wall on Victoria Road due south of the building. I looked across the cemetery and squinted to see into the shelter and moved a little closer and looked again.

No one was there.

I walked a few paces forward until I was behind a large monument to a family called Beggs who had all been killed in a house fire in the '30s.

I watched the cemetery gates and the shelter.

No one came in, nobody left.

There appeared to be no one else here but me.

Rain was pouring down the back of my neck.

It was cold.

And yet I knew that the place was not deserted.

She was here, whoever she was.

She had called me from the phone box on Victoria Road and now she was here, waiting for me.

Why?

I put my hand in my pocket and clicked back the hammer on the revolver and stepped out from behind the Beggs family headstone.

I walked slowly to the graveyard shelter, scanning to the left and right and whirling one-eighty behind me. I raised my weapon and carried it two-handed in front of me.

She was here. She was watching. I could feel it.

I entered the shelter and turned round to look back at the graveyard.

Nothing moved but there were many hiding places behind the trees, the tombstones and the stone walls.

There was no glint from a pair of binoculars or a rifle scope.

"I came. Isn't that what you wanted?" I said aloud.

A crow cawed.

A car drove past on Victoria Road.

I sat on a long bench that had been vandalized down to a couple of wooden slats.

I stared out at the dreary rows of headstones, Celtic crosses and monuments.

Nope. There was nothing and nobody.

She was more patient than me and that was not a good thing. Impatient coppers got themselves killed in this country.

Thunder rumbled over the lough.

The rain grew heavier. Rivers of water were gushing down the Antrim Plateau and forming little pools in the cemetery. I pulled out me Marlboros and lit a cigarette.

I walked to the edge of the shelter and looked out. Worms by the hundred were disgorging themselves from their human feast and writhing on the emerald grass.

Grass so green here that it hurt to look at it.

Why? Why had she called me? What was this about? Had I disrupted her plans by coming over the wall and not through the gates? Had she got cold feet? Was it just a regular crank call?

I sat there, waited, watched.

She waited too.

The sky darkened.

Magpies descended to feast on the snails and earthworms.

"Hello!" I yelled out into the weather. "Hello!"

Silence.

I turned and walked back and it was only then that I noticed the envelope duct-taped to the back of the bench.

I immediately looked away and lit another cigarette.

When the cigarette was done, I turned round with my back to the exposed south entrance. If she was watching she wouldn't know what I was doing. Perhaps she would think that I was pissing against the wall.

I took out a pair of latex gloves from inside my raincoat pocket and put them on.

I checked for wires or booby traps and finding none ripped the envelope off. I examined it. It was a green greeting card envelope. Keeping my back facing south, I opened it. Inside there was a Hallmark greeting card with a shamrock on the cover.

I opened it. "Happy Saint Patrick's Day" was the message printed inside.

At first I thought there was no message at all but then I saw it opposite the greeting.

"1CR1312," she had written in capital letters in black pen on the top of the page.

You could, perhaps, have mistaken it for a serial number.

I noticed that actually there was a space between the 3 and the 1 so that really it read: "1CR 13 12."

Even a non-Bible-reading Papist like me knew what it was.

It was a verse from the New Testament.

Paul's first epistle to the Corinthians, chapter 13, verse 12.

And not only that—it was something familiar. Something I should know.

The answers would be in my King James Bible back home. My house was only two minutes away, but there was something I had to do here first.

I put the card back in the envelope and re-taped it to the seat back.

I pretended to zip up my fly, then I turned round and lit another cigarette.

I did up the collar on my coat and walked out of the shelter towards the cemetery exit. I didn't look to the left or right, instead I hurried on down Coronation Road and only when I was at Mrs. Bridewell's house did I stop and turn and look: two kids playing kerby, a woman pushing a pram, a stray dog sleeping in the middle of the street; no one else, no strangers, no unknown cars.

I ran up the path and knocked on Mrs. Bridewell's door.

She opened it almost immediately. She had curlers in and she was smoking a cigarette. She was wearing a pink bathrobe, pink fuzzy slippers and no makeup. She seemed about twenty. She was really very good-looking.

"Oh, Mr. Duffy, I thought it was the milk man come back to replace those bottles that the—"

"I'm sorry to bother you, Mrs. Bridewell, but your front bedroom must have an unobstructed view of the graveyard—from mine the big chestnut tree at the cricket field is in the way."

"We can see into the graveyard—what's this all about?"

"Do you mind if I run up there? We've been getting reports about vandals spray-painting the shelter and stealing flowers from the graves and I think I just saw one of the little buggers go in there."

"Of course. Of course. That's shocking, so it is. I've complained about them weans to the police but nobody ever pays any mind."

I ran upstairs to her bedroom. Her husband wasn't here as he was still over in England looking for work. The bedroom smelled of lavender, there was a white chest of drawers, the bed sheets were peach, the wallpaper had flowers on it. A black lacy bra was sitting at the top of a laundry basket. It distracted me for a second, before the bra's owner followed me into the room.

"Why didn't you just wait for him in the cemetery?" she asked.

"It's a she. And if she sees me in the graveyard she won't do anything, will she? But if I can catch her in the act from up here, then Bob's your uncle, I'll have physical evidence and we can haul her up before the magistrate."

"Won't it just be your word against hers? You should have brought a camera," Mrs. Bridewell said, which was her way of letting me know that she was not going to be dragged into this. Like everyone else on Coronation Road, testifying against criminals—be they paramilitary mafia or mere teenage vandal—was not an option.

"Aye, but the beak will always take the word of a peeler over a wee mucker any day of the week."

I took up a position at the window.

I could spy out the whole graveyard from up here and could easily see if someone approached the shelter even through the heavy rain. It was possible that she'd already gone to check if I'd taken her envelope in that brief window between me leaving the cemetery and reaching here, but I doubted it. She was the careful type. She'd wait until she knew I was long gone.

If she was still there at all. The really smart play on her part would be to leave the envelope and never come back. But most people weren't like that. That took real dedication. Or years of training. If she didn't come back at all it might be reasonable to infer that she was a spook.

"Would you like a cup of tea?" Mrs. Bridewell asked.

"Love a cup."

"I'll just go downstairs," she said.

"Where are the kids?" I was going to ask, but of course they were at school.

It was just me and her.

Steady lad, I told myself.

I opened the window and stared across Coronation Road towards the graveyard.

Mrs. Bridewell came back in with a stool and a pair of binoculars.

"They're me Dad's ten-by-fifties, they're good," she said.

"Thank you."

"I'll get you that tea," she added, with a Mona Lisa half-smile.

"Ta."

Our eyes locked. I noticed that she had fixed her hair.

I am weak, I thought.

I am a weak man.

A stupid man.

She nodded, turned and went downstairs.

If my mystery caller didn't show up it would mean big trouble here in the Bridewell household.

I focused the binocs and gazed through them towards the shelter.

A pigeon, a friggin' seagull. Nothing else.

I scanned along the graves and the stone wall. Nada.

Mrs. Bridewell came back with the tea and chocolate digestives. The tea was in a Manchester United mug, the biscuits were on a Manchester United plate.

"Thank you," I said.

"You're welcome. So this is what they call a stakeout then, is it?"

I grinned. "I suppose, although its hardly *The French Connection*, is it? Catching a teen graffiti artist won't get me a promotion."

"You've done more than enough, Mr. Duffy. There's many round here that were dead proud of you last year but they wouldn't say it to your face, 'cause, you know . . ."

I'm Catholic? I'm a cop? Both?

"Yeah, I know," I said.

She put her hand on my shoulder.

Oh, Jesus.

"Listen, uh, Mrs. Bridewell, you wouldn't have a copy of the King James Bible handy, would you?"

"Pardon?"

"The King James Bible—I need to look something up."

The hand fled from my shoulder and tapped the back of her hair.

"Of course!" she said, a touch indignantly. "Of course we have a Bible, just hold on a minute there and I'll get it."

I took a sip of tea and resumed scanning the graveyard.

I ate a chocolate biscuit.

And there she was!

She was wearing a black knit cap, a black leather jacket, blue jeans, white Adidas gutties. Her back was to me, but I could tell that she was of medium height, and limber.

I put down the binoculars and ran out of the bedroom.

I almost collided with Mrs. Bridewell coming up the stairs.

"She's there, if I leg it I'll get her!" I called out.

"Oh! Go on!" Mrs. Bridewell said, excited by the hunt.

I opened the front door and sprinted up Coronation Road, turned left on Victoria Road and was through the cemetery gates in under forty-five seconds.

My girl had arrived at the shelter.

I took out the Smith and Wesson and marched towards her.

Rain was bouncing off the polished marble headstones and thunder rumbled to the west. It was quite the scene. If Mrs. Bridewell were watching through the binocs she'd be well impressed.

"Hey you! Police!" I called out. "Put your hands up!"

She didn't even turn to look at me. She ran out of the shelter and kept running towards the graveyard wall.

"Halt or I'll shoot!" I yelled, but she didn't believe me.

She kept on running.

My mind raced. There was no clear shot and if I did shoot her it would be an inquiry at the very least, and if she was just some harmless lunatic I'd be dismissed from the force or (if the Sinn Feiners made an issue of it) charged with involuntary manslaughter.

"Halt!" I screamed again.

Not for a second did she stop.

Fucker!

I let the hammer drop on the Smith and Wesson and ran after her.

Christ, she was fast. She ran between the headstones and down the row of sycamore trees that led to the back gate. She stumbled on a tree root that curved above the surface. She lost her balance, regained it, lost it again, spilled.

"Okay love, that's enough fun and games!" I shouted at her.

I pulled out the trusty .38 again.

I thought I heard a crack.

It may have been a gunshot, it may have been a car backfiring.

I dived to the ground and scrambled behind a headstone.

"The bitch is shooting!" I exclaimed, caught my breath and carefully stood up behind the grave.

In the ten seconds I had taken to do all that, she had gotten to her feet and sprinted towards the cemetery wall.

"Jesus!"

I ran after her but before I'd covered half the distance she hopped the wall and vanished into the Barley Field.

I heard a motorcycle kick and then saw a green Kawasaki 125 trail bike zoom across the field. It jumped a stream and cut down the lane to Victoria Road. It drove straight across the road heading into Down-shire Estate. By the time I made it to the wall I couldn't even hear it any more.

I jogged home and called it in.

"Female motorcyclist in black leather jacket heading through Downshire Estate, Carrickfergus on green Kawasaki trail bike. Indeterminate age, possibly dangerous."

It was unlikely that they'd catch her but you never knew.

The doorbell rang.

I opened it.

Mrs. Bridewell looked concerned. She had evidently watched the whole thing through the binoculars.

"Are you all right, Mr. Duffy?"

"I'm fine."

"Are you hurt?"

"No, I took a spill is all."

"Them vandals are getting more brazen every day. They have no respect for the law. I have half a mind to tell Bobby Cameron."

Bobby Cameron was the local UDA commander. His method would be to kneecap the next kid who was found with a spray can.

"No, no, there's no need for that! I'm sure we'll find the culprit. I've called it in."

"They're putting out an APB? Like on *Kojak*?"

"Exactly like *Kojak*."

She quivered for a moment in the rain.

"Oh, Mr. Duffy," she said, and folded into my arms. "I was so worried."

I held her for a moment.

She cleared her throat.

"Well," she said. "I suppose I better go get the weans."

"Yes. Of course."

She walked back down the path.

As I watched her arse jiggle away in that yellow dress I saw a black woman walking down the street from the other direction. She was tall and elegant, wearing jeans and a green sweater.

I had never seen a black person before in Carrickfergus and contextually it was pretty surprising. Because of the Troubles Northern

Ireland had had virtually no immigration. I mean, why would anyone emigrate to a war zone that had bad weather, bad people, bad food and sky-high unemployment? Carrickfergus was as ethnically complex and diverse as a joint Ku Klux Klan-Nazi Party rally.

I stared at the woman for a second.

It wasn't nice but I couldn't help myself.

She must have felt my gaze because she turned to look at me and smiled.

"Hello," I said.

"Hello," she replied, in an African accent.

I went back inside #113 and closed the front door.

I checked with the emergency dispatcher at Carrick Station.

No motorcycle.

I asked them to patch it up to central command.

They said they would.

Every RUC and British Army patrol that came across a green motorcycle for the next twenty hours would stop the bike and question the rider.

In theory it sounded good. But presumably the bike would be burnt out at the first opportunity and never ridden again.

The whole thing was baffling. Was it just a crank? Some kid fucking with me? I went back to the graveyard to see if the envelope was still there but she'd lifted it. Didn't matter. I remembered the verse. I ran the bath, poured myself a vodka and lime and dug out the King James Bible. I looked up Paul's first letter to the Corinthians, chapter 13, verse 12.

Of course I recognized the passage: "For now we see through a glass darkly; but then face to face: now I know in part; but then shall I know even as also I am known."

What's that all about? I asked myself repeatedly for the next two hours and got no answers at all.

13: THE GIRL ON THE BIKE

I was in Ownies getting a pub dinner when the beeper went. I asked Arthur if I could borrow his phone and when I tracked it down it turned out to be a message from central dispatch in Ballymena. They had got my girl! An army patrol had nabbed her on her motorbike heading north out of Carrick and they'd handed her over to the police. She was now at Whitehead Police Station.

"Well, well, well," I said, and grinned at Arthur.

"Good news?"

"Aye, could be, mate. Could be."

I ran back to the barracks, jumped in the Beemer, hit a ton on the Bla Hole road and was at Whitehead Cop Shop in eight minutes. It was a small police station, unmanned at the weekends. Four police reservists and an inspector ran the show.

I found the duty officer, a freckly kid called Raglan with a David Soul haircut and a feeble ginger tache.

"I need to interview your prisoner," I said.

"The prisoner?"

"Aye, presumably you've only the one."

"She's left already," Raglan said.

"What?"

"She left."

"Who the fuck with?"

"A couple of superintendents from Special Branch."

"You get their names?"

"McClue was one of them, I forget the other. Is there a problem?"

"I don't know. I suppose I'll follow up with bloody Special Branch and see."

"You just missed them by about half an hour."

"Tell me about her—what did she look like? Was she English?"

"She didn't talk a lot. She was good-looking. She looked Scottish. Sort of blondy-reddy hair. About thirty, maybe younger, maybe older. Sort of not very interesting. A bit old to be joyriding a stolen motorbike, I thought."

"Did you take her photograph, her prints?"

"Special Branch called us and told us to hold off on that."

"Special Branch phoned you up and told you not to fingerprint her?"

"Yes."

"That's a bit strange, no?"

"Well, them boys in Special Branch are always a bit strange, aren't they?"

"You must have searched her."

"Of course."

"And?"

"I wrote it down here."

He looked up a notepad and read: "On her person there were: a set of keys, a pair of gloves, a notepad and a paperback book called *Doctor Faustus*."

"And where is all that stuff now?"

"Special Branch took it with them."

I nodded.

"When was she brought in?" I asked.

"The Army dropped her off around four."

"You didn't process her then?"

"No. Not at that time. We took her right to the cells and give her a pillow and a blanket."

"And she said nothing?"

"Not then."

"Did you ask her name at least?"

"Aye. Of course!"

"And?"

"Alice Smith."

"Alice Smith?"

"Alice Smith."

"Hmmm. And how did Special Branch get involved?"

"About six I brought her a cup of tea and she thanked me and asked if she could make her phone call."

"And you let her?"

"It's her right, isn't it?"

"And then what happened?"

"Well, she made her call and ate a biscuit and I escorted her back to her cell and about five minutes later I get a call saying Special Branch is on their way and not to process her."

"You didn't think that was odd? The timing, I mean."

"No."

"And they show up when?"

"About half an hour ago, like I said."

"Were they in uniform?"

"No."

"They have ID?"

"I didn't think it was necessary to check. I mean, they said they were on their way and then they showed up."

"Describe them."

"Just a couple of blokes. Suits, ties . . . I wasn't really paying attention."

"Did they sign for her? Anything like that?"

"Are they supposed to?"

"You let two strangers come in here and take a suspect out of the cells and you didn't check their IDs or ask them to sign for her?"

"She was only in for bike theft, wasn't she?"

I walked down to the cells to see if she'd left anything there.

She hadn't.

I spent the next hour calling Special Branch.

Of course there was no Superintendent McClue and no officers had been sent to Whitehead Police Station to pick up a suspect. This was as I had expected. I ran the name Alice Smith through the database but nothing of interest came up.

I walked to the nearest Eason's in Carrick and bought myself a copy of *Doctor Faustus*. Baroque wasn't the word. Made Henry James seem like Jackie Collins. Not the kind of book I'd bring on a stakeout, but none of this play was the way I would have done things. It was very much amateur hour which could mean anything from civilians on a jape to the goons on Gower Street who still prided themselves on their "amateur" status.

Bath. Vodka gimlet. King James Bible. No luck on seeing through the glass darkly. Ask Presbyterian church elder McCrabban in the morning and get his take. Probably bollocks. Cryptic messages were for spy films and crazy people. In my experience when people wanted to tell you something they bloody told you. That was the Ulster way. Best to say nothing but when you do speak make sure that you are understood.

I went to bed with *Doctor Faustus* and its powerful soporific qualities became readily apparent.

14: A VERY ORDINARY ASSASSINATION

The clock radio woke me at 7:06. I'd been fiddling with the alarm for several days now and I had precisely timed it for when the news bulletin ended and BBC Radio One would only be playing music. These days only a madman would want to wake to the actual news. The Beeb could be relied upon to do things on schedule. The talk and the bulletin were indeed over and the song was "Hanging on the Telephone" by Blondie.

I listened to the song, had a quick Debbie Harry fantasy, and got out of bed.

Stairs. Kitchen.

Doorbell. It was a tinker disguised in drink, offering to pave my driveway for twenty quid. When I told him I didn't have a driveway he said he'd fix my broken electrical appliances or recite a verse from the *Tain* for a shilling. I let him recite me some poetry and gave him fifty pence if promised not to tell his mates I was a soft touch.

After toast and two cups of coffee I finally put on the eight o'clock Radio Ulster News. The policeman's murder was not the headline. It was only the fourth lead after three separate stories about the Task Force's adventures in the Falkland Islands. Some wars, it seemed, were more important than others.

"In Ballygalley, north of Larne, a full-time RUC officer was shot dead outside his home late last night. Inspector David Dougherty, fifty-nine, was divorced with one child. The Provisional IRA claimed responsibility for the attack in a phone call to the BBC using a recognized code word. Ian Paisley, the MP for the constituency, called Inspector Dougherty's murder "a reprehensible act of murder in the continuing IRA campaign of genocide against the Protestant people." The Inspector's widow could not last night be reached for comment. In other news Harland and Wolff shipyard have laid off a further five hundred welders under a restructuring—"

There could only be one Inspector David Dougherty at Larne RUC.

I switched off the radio, went back upstairs, got dressed in my black polo neck sweater, black jeans, DM shoes, black raincoat. I put my leather shoulder holster under the raincoat, picked up my Smith and Wesson and checked that there were six rounds in the barrel.

"Right," I said, and slipped outside.

I looked under the car for a mercury tilt bomb, found nothing, opened the door, wound down the windows, put the key in the ignition.

There was a whoosh through the vents which, for a brief unhappy moment, I thought was the percussion wave of an explosion, but it was just a whoosh of cold air.

At that moment the black woman I had seen before came out of the vacant house at the end of Coronation Road. She was wearing a purple dress with a red trim. Carrickfergus women didn't wear purple dresses. And again, for another half a beat, I wondered if I hadn't in fact just been killed in an explosion.

The engine turned over and the BMW roared into life.

I let out the hand brake, engaged the clutch and drove past her. She looked at me through the windscreen. I nodded a good morning. She smiled. She was very thin and very good-looking—the women on Coronation Road would no doubt begin spreading rumors about her immediately. Was she a student? A refugee? If so, God help her that she had ended up in Northern Ireland.

I was in the mood for no more news so I put on Radio Three and endured Brahms for ten minutes before switching off the radio and listening to nothing but the German-engineered pistons going about their efficient business.

Ballygalley was fifteen miles up the coast, just beyond Larne.

Nice little place with a castle, a beach, a caravan park and a couple of shops. Dougherty's house wasn't hard to find. The one with all the police Land Rovers and the van from the BBC outside.

It was a bungalow on a little rise at the end of a cul-de-sac.

I parked down the street, flashed my warrant card to the reserve constables protecting the crime scene and found the detective in charge, Chief Inspector Tony McIlroy, who was an old mate from my days in Bandit Country on the South Armagh border.

Tony was one of the lead detectives in the RUC Assassination Unit which investigated all police murders in Northern Ireland. The RUCAU looked for similarities, common weapons, common strategies etc. in crimes against coppers. We took it personally when the terrorists killed one of our own and it wasn't unfair to say that the murder of a peeler attracted more money and resources than other murders in the Province. The miserable clearance rate, of course, was about the same: less than ten per cent. Unless the terrorists made a mistake or someone grassed, very few of these murders ever resulted in a prosecution (although quite often we would find out who the trigger man on a particular hit had been).

Tony had a degree in criminology from Birmingham University, a wife who was the daughter of a Conservative English MP, a father who was a prominent Belfast barrister, and he had spent a year on secondment to the Met. He was a high-flyer even back then in South Armagh when he'd been a lowly detective sergeant and I a freshly minted DC. Tony would be a chief superintendent by the age of forty and probably chief constable by fifty (chief constable of a force over the water that is, for Northern Ireland was too small a place to contain his ambitions forever).

He shook my hand. "What's the good word, Sean, me old mucker?"

"Tony, everybody knows that the bird is the word."

"They do indeed. What have you been up to, Sean?"

"The usual. I've got a play opening in the West End, oh, and fingers crossed, I think I've just discovered a tenth planet. Gonna name it after me mum. You look good, Tony, wee bit tubby, but who isn't," I said.

"You look as if you're on the heroin diet. And grey hairs? Must be your guilty conscience, Sean, my lad."

"Grey hairs from hard work, mate."

He leaned in. "Hey, seriously, congratulations on the medal and the promotion," he said, with genuine affection.

"Cheers, mate," I replied with equal amounts of fondness.

He was pale-skinned, and some of that famous shock of red hair was also greying at the temple, but he looked fit, focused, professional. He had acquired rectangular glasses that gave him a professorial air.

"What brings you out here, Sean?"

"I knew Dougherty a little bit. What can you tell me about this business?"

Tony shook his head and took a cigarette from my packet of Marlboros.

"Standard stuff, Sean."

"Nothing special about it?"

"Nah. Your common or garden IRA hit. Two shooters probably. Or one shooter, one driver. Parked outside his house, a little ways down the street, waited until our boy got home. Popped him as soon as he exited his car. Pretty soft target living here at the end of the cul-de-sac."

"A bead on the shooters?"

"If I had to guess I'd say it was the West Belfast Brigade, probably a team under Jimmy Doogan Reilly."

"Pretty adventurous for them to come way up here, no?"

"Nah, they're always looking to expanding their op zones and if you hoofed it you could be back in Belfast in half an hour."

"Definitely IRA then?"

"Well, not definitely, but almost certainly."

Almost every peeler who was murdered in Northern Ireland was murdered by the IRA, usually in one of three methods: a mercury tilt bomb under their car, an ambush by an IRA assassination cell, or in a mass bomb attack on a police station.

"If you've got the time, you couldn't lead me through the physical evidence?"

Tony looked at me askance. "Was this a really good mate of yours or something?"

"Not really, I only knew him through a case of my own."

Tony opened his mouth, closed it again, perhaps thinking that when the time was right, I'd tell him.

"Okay," he said, "Over here."

We walked to the top of the driveway where Dougherty's Ford Granada was still parked. There was dried blood on the gravel but the body of course was long since gone to the morgue in Larne.

"They shot him at point blank range. Poor bastard managed to get his sidearm out but it was too late. He was done for. Didn't even get a round off."

The Ford Granada's door was closed, which meant they'd waited until he was fully out of the car and was walking towards the house.

"He got his sidearm out?" I asked, surprised.

"Aye."

"He was shot in the front or the back?"

"The front, why?" he asked, his eyes, narrow, sensing an angle like a stoat on a rat.

"Why didn't they just shoot him in the back? Bang, bang, bang, you're dead, John Lennon style."

"Nah, nah, there's nothing untoward, mate. They did try and shoot him from behind but the fuckers missed. Our pal Dougherty turns to confront them, half draws his piece and they plug the poor unfortunate sod in the ticker."

"How do you know they missed?"

"Three bullets in the garage door, look."

Sure enough three bullets in the garage door.

But didn't that make things even stranger?

"Okay, so they missed him and he turns to face them and he almost draws his piece and then they plug him. Right?"

"Right."

"But that raises an additional question."

"Which is?"

"The question of why they missed?"

"What? Why they missed?"

"Aye. This is a professional hit team, isn't it?"

"It's a bloody gun battle, Sean, a couple of bullets are bound to go a bit wild, aren't they? Even Lee Harvey Oswald missed with his first shot, didn't he?"

"Did they find the murder weapon?"

"No. And we won't. It'll be at the bottom of the Irish Sea by now."

"The IRA called it in?"

"They did. Admitted responsibility with a recognized code word."

"What were their exact words?"

Tony took a notebook out of his sports jacket pocket and flipped it open. He read the IRA statement. "They said, they regretted that this killing was necessary but that the cause of it was the British occupation of Ireland."

"What was the IRA code word?"

"Wolfhound."

"Which has been current since?"

"January."

"January of this year?"

"Yes."

"So it's authentic?"

"Oh, aye."

I nodded.

Tony squeezed my arm. "What's this all about?" he asked. "Tell me." Tony was slightly taller than me and he was certainly bigger framed. When he squeezed you it hurt.

I sighed and shook my head. "It's probably nothing."

"Go on. Spill," he said.

"I was talking to Dougherty about one of his old cases. It was a loose end. Nothing really to do with me at all. I'm working on something else."

"What?"

I filled him in on the body in the suitcase and Mr. O'Rourke from Massachusetts.

"And how does it tie to Dougherty?"

"It doesn't. Not really."

He squeezed me again. "No secrets, Sean."

"It's not a secret. It's just a bit of a wild goose chase that I'm slightly embarrassed to bring up in front of such an august detective as yourself."

He laughed at that but he kept staring at me in a way which made me see that I wasn't going to get away with anything less than the whole story.

"The suitcase O'Rourke was buried in had an old address card squeezed into that plastic pocket near the handle. The killer or the person dumping the body hadn't noticed it. We were able to decipher it as belonging to a Martin McAlpine who was a captain in the UDR until he was murdered last December. December first, I think. So I went to interview the widow McAlpine and she told me about her husband's murder and the fact that she had left her husband's old things including that suitcase at the Salvation Army in Carrickfergus just before Christmas."

"What's any of that got to do with Dougherty?"

"He was the investigating officer on the husband's murder."

"And?"

"Well . . . I think he botched it."

"How?"

"I think there's at least a chance that she killed him. In Dougherty's theory the gunmen shot at him from behind a wall twenty yards away but he was clearly shot at point blank by someone who knew him."

"Why someone who knew him?"

"He let the killer walk right up to him, he didn't draw his gun, his vicious guard dog didn't get involved."

"And you went and told Dougherty about these doubts?"

"Yes."

"And left it at that?"

"And left it at that. It was a tangent. As my youthful sidekick explained to me, it was an SEP: someone else's problem."

Tony nodded and rubbed his sideburns. "So, what? You think you might have shaken Dougherty out of his hammock and the old geezer went to stir some shit?"

"I don't know. Maybe. Mind if I look around?"

"Be my guest."

I walked the length of the driveway and stopped in front of the garage. I peered at the bullet holes. They were wildly far apart. Feet, instead of inches.

"He was shot three times in the chest?"

"That's what they tell me. Three in the chest, three in the garage."

"What's normally the next step in a case like this?"

"Our next step, Sean, will be to attempt to trace the gun by analyzing the slugs. Canvass for witnesses, of which there won't be any, none that will testify certainly. Put the word out for tips, offer a reward . . ."

We had finished our smokes now and Tony fished into his pocket and took out his packet of Player's.

He lit me one. "Smoking can cause cancer," it said on the packet. It was a fine time to bring that up.

The day had turned cold and fog was rolling down the hill and where it met the electricity pylons little halos of Saint Elmo's fire were forming, vanishing and reforming again.

I took a puff of the Player. It was pretty rough.

"In other words, Chief Inspector, after the condemnation by the politicians and after the church service ends and the TV cameras leave, this case will go nowhere."

He was a little ticked at that. "I don't know how things are done in your manor, mate, but we take every case seriously. It's not my fucking fault that it's nearly fucking impossible to break up an IRA cell, is it?"

I nodded and threw the ciggie away. I walked over to the garage again.

"Three rounds in the garage."

"So."

"When does an IRA hit team miss not once, not twice, but three times?"

"I'd stake my pension that this is an ordinary assassination by an ordinary IRA cell."

"Stake something worth a damn. None of us are making old bones, are we? But let's give it your best-case argument. Let's say they've brought along a newcomer who's on his first job. They have to blood the newcomers somehow, don't they? Every killer has a first time."

"Aye."

"So after the new boy misses and sticks three in the garage door and Dougherty gets his gun out, then his partner can't take any more of it and shoots him in the chest."

"Sounds reasonable," Tony admitted.

"Two things, Tony. Two things. First, Dougherty is old and fat and drunk and fucking *slow*! For him to get that gun out of that leather holster, this team must really be shite."

Tony nodded. "What's the second thing?"

"The second thing is that in this scenario the slugs can't all have come from the same gun. The ones in the garage will be from a different weapon from the ones in Dougherty . . . But they're not, are they?"

"Aaahh," Tony said and shook his head. "Missed that. No, you're right. Preliminary ballistics suggests that—"

"Let's say the widow McAlpine comes up here. She's never fired a hand gun before in her life, she squeezes one off, she misses, he turns, she misses again, he starts fumbling for his gun, she misses again, he's nearly got the .38 out and she finally hits the fucker and hits him again and again."

"Why?"

"Let's say you wanted to kill a copper. For whatever reason. Maybe he fucked your wife or embezzled you or something. Say anything. Now, if you or someone close to you was in the security forces, it would be pretty easy, wouldn't it? You get yourself a gun—anywhere—you put on a balaclava, shoot the bugger and then call the *Belfast Telegraph* with a recognized terrorist code word. Peelers like you and me show up at the crime scene and because the IRA has claimed responsibility we don't look too hard at it 'cause we more or less know who did it and we know that we'll never catch them in a million years."

He finished his fag and nodded thoughtfully.

"Your case hangs on the fact that Dougherty went digging after his wee talk with you."

"Maybe he did, maybe he didn't. Easy to check."

"He goes back to the widow, starts throwing accusations around.

She goes all panic stations, gets herself a piece, comes here and shoots him? You think that's more likely than an IRA hit?"

I laughed and looked at my DMs. "I suppose it's a bit thin, Tony, but I can't help thinking that these three holes in the garage mean *something.*"

He looked at me, squinted into the sun juking between the clouds over the Antrim Plateau and grinned. "You know what I liked about you when we worked together in the County Armagh?"

"What?"

"Even when you were completely wrong about something, the journey into your wrongness was always fucking interesting. Come with me."

We walked over to a tall, lean guy with a big Dick Spring moustache.

"Gerry, take over here, I'm going down to Larne RUC to have a wee look at Dougherty's current case load. Could be personal, not random, you never know, do you?"

"Aye," Gerry agreed.

Tony had come in a cop Land Rover so we took my car.

It was a ten-minute run from rural Ballygalley to the grey misery that was Larne. We chatted a little and Radio One played "Ebony and Ivory," a new song by Paul McCartney and Stevie Wonder. The breakfast DJ Mike Read played it two times in a row which was pretty hardcore of him as it was clearly the worst song of the decade so far, perhaps of the entire century.

Larne RUC.

With one of their own gunned down, the atmosphere was apocalyptic and doom laden. We paid our respects to the duty sergeant and ostentatiously put a few coppers in the widows and orphans box.

We met with the Superintendent, expressed our condolences, told him that we wanted to look into Dougherty's old cases and Tony explained that this was nothing more than Standard Operating Procedure.

The Super couldn't have cared less. He was new on the job, had barely interacted with Dougherty and now he had a funeral to suss and with the Chief Constable and half a dozen VIPs coming it was going to be a friggin' nightmare.

We left him to his drama and found Dougherty's office.

A shining twenty-three-year-old detective constable called Conlon showed us in. I asked him to hang around to answer questions while Tony looked through Dougherty's files.

"Was Inspector Dougherty a family man?" I asked conversationally.

"Wife and a grown daughter. Ex-wife. He was divorced."

"Where's she? The wife, I mean."

"Wife and daughter are both over the water, I gathered."

"Whereabouts?"

"I don't know. London somewhere?"

"Was he a social man—did you all go out for drinks come a Friday night?"

Conlon hesitated, torn between loyalty to the dead man and a desire to tell me how it was.

"Inspector Dougherty wasn't exactly a social drinker. When he drank, he drank, if you catch my meaning."

"I catch your meaning. Was he the senior detective here?"

"Detective Chief Inspector Canning is the senior detective here. He's in court today, I could try and page him?"

"No, no, you'll be fine. Tell me more about Inspector Dougherty; what sort of a man was he?"

"What do you mean?"

"Friendly, dour, a practical joker, what?"

"Well, he was, uh, sort of semi-retired, so he was. Nobody really... I didn't have much to do with him."

"Was he working on anything in particular in the last couple of days?" I asked.

"I thought this was all a random IRA hit?" Conlon asked suspiciously.

"It *was* a random IRA hit," Tony said, looking up from the filing cabinet.

"Did Dougherty mention any threats or anything that was troubling him?"

"Not to me."

"To anybody else?"

"Not that I'm aware of."

"What was he working on the last few days?"

"I didn't know him very well," he said, hesitated, and looked out the window.

"You don't want to speak ill of the dead . . . is that the vibe I'm catching here?" I asked him.

DC Conlon reddened, gave a little half nod and said nothing.

"The Inspector didn't do much but come in late, sit in his office, drink, leave early, drive home half drunk, is that it?" I wondered.

DC Conlon nodded again.

"But what about the last couple of days? Did he seem different? More fired up? Onto anything?"

"Not so I'd noticed," Conlon said.

"Nothing out of the ordinary at all?"

Conlon shook his head. His hair seemed to move independently of his head when he did that and it made him look particularly stupid.

"How did he get assigned to the McAlpine murder if he was such a bloody lightweight?" I asked.

"Chief Inspector Canning was in for his appendix," Conlon said.

"And after he came back from his appendix?"

"Well, that was an open and shut case, wasn't it?"

"It's hardly shut, son, is it? No prosecutions, no convictions?"

Conlon coughed. "What I mean is, I mean, we know who done it, don't we?"

"Do we? Who done it? Gimme their names and I'll have them fuckers in the cells within the hour," I said.

"I mean, we know who done it in the corporate sense. The IRA killed him."

"The corporate sense is it now? The IRA did it. Just like they killed Dougherty himself."

"Well, didn't they?" Conlon asked.

"Yes, they did," Tony said. He waved a file at me.

I looked at Conlon. "That'll be all. And do us a favor, mate, keep your mouth shut."

"About what?"

"Exactly. Now fuck off."

He exited the office and I closed the door.

"What did you find, mate?" I asked Tony.

"Nothing of interest in any of them. Dougherty has nothing in his 'active' file and there's a layer of dust on everything else."

"I take it that's the McAlpine file?"

He slid it across the table to me.

The last notes on it had been made in December. He'd added nothing since my visit.

I shook my head. Tony squeezed my arm again. "Everybody can't be as impressed by you as I am, mate. I'm afraid you didn't wow Dougherty as much as you would have liked."

"I suppose not."

Tony was almost laughing now. "Maybe you should have worn your medal or told him about that time you met Joey Ramone."

"All right, all right. No point in raking me. Let's skedaddle."

We straightened the desk, closed the filing cabinets.

"And look, if you find a case notebook in the house or the car or anything, I'd be keen to take a look at it," I said to Tony.

"You got it, mate," Tony assured me.

"And I did see Joey Ramone, he was right across from me in the subway."

"Big stars don't ride the fucking subway."

We had almost made it out of the incident room when young Conlon approached us diffidently. "Yes?" Tony wondered.

"Well, it's probably nothing."

"Go on," I said encouragingly.

"There was one thing that was a wee bit of the ordinary," Conlon began.

"What was it?" I asked, my heart rate quickening.

"Well, Dougherty knows that I'm from Islandmagee, doesn't he?

And he knows that I take the ferry over here every morning, instead of driving round through Whitehead. It saves you twenty minutes."

"Go on."

"Well, I suppose that's why he asked me how much it cost."

"He asked you how much the ferry cost from Larne to Islandmagee?"

"Aye."

"And that was strange, was it?" Tony asked.

"A wee bit. Because he hadn't spoken to me at all this year. You know?"

I looked at Tony. "He was going to take the ferry over to Islandmagee and he wanted to check the price."

Tony nodded.

"Did he say anything else?" I asked.

"Nope. I told him it was twenty pence for pedestrians and a quid for cars. And he thanked me and that was that."

I looked at Tony. He gave me a half nod.

"You done good, son," I told DC Conlon.

Tony and I did the rounds, said hello to a couple of sergeants and left the station. We got in the Beemer and headed out into the street.

"When he investigated McAlpine's murder he would have had a driver. He would have gone over there in a police Land Rover the long way round through Whitehead. But he was going over himself in his own car," Tony said.

"Going to question Mrs. McAlpine," I said.

"Possibly. What time is it?"

I looked at my watch. "Nine thirty."

"I feel like that ad for the army: 'We do more things before breakfast than you'll do all day.'"

"Aye, more stupid things."

"Yeah."

"Shall we go do one more stupid thing?"

"Aye."

I drove the BMW down into Larne and easily found the ferry over the Lough to Islandmagee. We paid the money and drove on. It left on the half hour and five minutes later we docked in Ballylumford, Island-magee. "Let's go see what alibi this bint of yours has cooked up for her whereabouts last night," Tony said.

15: SIR HARRY

I drove the car over the cattle grid and up the lane marked "Private Road No Entry." "What's all this?" Tony asked, pointing out the window.

"It's a private road on private land."

"The IRA drove all the way up here on private land just to murder this woman's husband?" Tony asked.

"That's what we're supposed to believe."

"Well, I've seen stranger things."

"Me too."

The trail wound on, over a hill and down into the boggy valley.

Tony sighed. "So, what about you, Sean? I haven't really seen you since the hospital."

"I'm okay. What about you? How's the missus? Any kids on the way?"

"Nah, not yet. She's keen as mustard but I'd rather wait until, uh, we're more settled. You can't bring kids up in a place like this . . . What about you and yon nurse lady?"

"Doctor lady. She's gone. Over the water."

"Over the water? Well, you can't blame her, can you?"

"No. You can't."

"Hopefully that'll be me in about a year. Then we can do kids, mortgage, the whole shebang."

"You've actually put in for a transfer?"

"The Met. Keep it between us for now. There's no future here, Sean. Bright young lad like yourself should consider it too. How tall are you?"

"Five ten."

"You'd be fine. I think."

"What if I stood on tip toes."

"What's keeping you here, Sean?" he asked, ignoring my facetiousness.

"I wanna stay and be part of the solution."

"Jesus. They must be putting something in the water or planting subliminal messages in those health and safety films."

I laughed and we were about to turn into the McAlpines' farm when a man with a shotgun came hurrying towards us.

I put the Beemer in neutral and wound the window down.

Tony put his hand on his service revolver.

"Oi, youse! This is a private road," the man yelled.

"Put the gun down!" I yelled at him.

"I will not!" he yelled back.

"We're police! Break open that gun this instant!" I howled at the fucker.

He hesitated for a moment, but didn't break open the shotgun and kept coming towards us at a jog. He was in green Wellington boots, khaki trousers, a white shirt, tweed shooting jacket and a flat cap. He was dressed in a previous generation's get up but he was only about forty if he was a day.

We got out of the Beemer, drew our weapons and put the car between him and us.

"First time I've drawn my gun in two years," Tony said.

"A man shot at me with a shotgun just the other week," I said.

"I've been on the job eight years and I've never had anyone shoot at me."

"I've been shot at half a dozen times."

"What does that tell you about yourself?"

"What does it tell you?"

"It tells me that people don't like you. You rub them the wrong way."

"Thanks, mate."

The man jogged along the track towards us. He had a couple of beagles with him. Beagles I noted, not border collies, so he wasn't a farmer, or at least he wasn't farming today. He arrived at the Beemer slightly out of breath but not in too bad nick considering his little run down the hill. He had a grey thatch, a long angular face and ruddy cheeks. His eyes were blue and squinty as if he spent all his down-time reading and rereading *Country Life*.

"This is private property and you are trespassing," he said.

"We're the police," I said again.

"So you claim," he said, and then after a brief pause he added, "and even if you are, you'll still need a warrant to come onto my land."

His accent was a little peculiar. Not Islandmagee, not local. It sounded 1930s Anglo-Irish. He'd clearly been educated at an expensive private school, one where they learned you to say "leand" instead of "land."

"We're here to see the widow McAlpine," I said.

"She's a tenant on my property and this is a private residence. I would prefer it if you would come back stating the precise nature of your business on a warrant."

I ignored him and turned to Tony. "This is the influence of American TV. Second time this week I've been told to get a warrant by some joker. Not like this in the old days."

Tony cleared his throat. "Listen, mate, you don't want to mess with us. We're conducting inquiries into a murder investigation. We can go wherever the hell we like."

The geezer shook his head. "No, you cannot. It was my younger brother who was murdered and I have seen the efficacy or lack thereof in your procedures. The RUC have not impressed me with their competence these last months."

"You're Dougherty's brother?" I asked.

"Who's Dougherty? I am speaking of Martin McAlpine, Captain Martin McAlpine. My brother."

"No, sir, we're not investigating that murder. Not as such. We're looking into the death of Detective Inspector Dougherty who was murdered last night in Larne. We wanted to ask Mrs. McAlpine a few questions."

"What on earth for?" the man asked.

"We'd like to speak to her about it, sir," I insisted.

"I'll not have Emma disturbed. She's already had several visits from so-called detectives coming out to see her this week on various wild goose chases. I suppose her name popped up on one of your computers—well, let me tell you something, young man, I am not going to stand for it. She's been very upset by all this. She's a strong woman but this nonsense has taken a toll. You fellows are messing with people's lives."

"Sir, it's our duty to investigate Inspector Dougherty's murder and we know for a fact that he came here recently to see Mrs. McAlpine. We need to find out what they were talking about and so we will be questioning Mrs. McAlpine and there is nothing, sir, that you can do about it," I said with authority.

His cheeks reddened and he made a little grunting sound like a sow rooting for truffles. He rummaged in one of the pockets of his shooting jacket and removed a notebook and pencil.

"And what is your name, officer?" he asked me.

"Detective Inspector Sean Duffy, Carrickfergus RUC."

"And yours?" he asked Tony.

"Detective Chief Inspector Antony McIlroy, Special Branch."

"Good," he said, writing the names in his book. "You will both be hearing from my solicitors."

"I'll look forward to that," Tony said, and then went on: "May we inquire as to your name, sir?"

"I am Sir Harry McAlpine," he announced, as if that was supposed to make us fall to our knees or genuflect or something.

"Fine, now if you'll kindly move to one side, we'll be about our business," Tony said.

He moved. We got back in the BMW.

"Watch your dogs," I said, and turned the key in the ignition.

"Funny old git," Tony said.

"I'll tell you something funny," I began.

"What?"

"He lets two armed men go to his sister-in-law's house only a couple of months after her husband, his brother, has been shot by a couple of armed men on a motorbike."

"We told him we were police," Tony protested.

"Aye, we *told* him, but he didn't actually ask to see our warrant cards and he wasn't surprised to see us, was he?"

"Which means?"

"He knew we were the police and he knew we were coming."

"Because of Dougherty?"

"Because of Dougherty."

"Why fuck with us, then?"

"He wanted to introduce himself, he wanted us to know that Emma McAlpine was the sister-in-law of Sir Harry McAlpine."

"What good does that do?"

"He wanted to put the fear of God up us."

"It didn't work because neither of us have bloody heard of him."

"I have an ominous feeling that we're going to though, eh?"

Tony nodded and we drove into the familiar McAlpine farmyard. Cora was chained up under an overhang, but soon began barking and snapping at us.

"Friendly dog," Tony said.

"She does that, when she's not tearing your throat out or watching calmly while two terrorists shoot her master."

We got out of the car and walked across the muddy farmyard. The hens were out, pecking at crumbs, and a proprietary rooster gave us the evil eye from a fence post.

There was a note on the front door:

"Gone to get salt. Back soon."

I took it off and showed it to Tony, who was a little nearsighted.

"You think she means that literally?" Tony asked.

"What else could she mean?"

"I don't know. Could be a country euphemism for something."

Tony looked at his watch. This had been fun and all. But he was a man in a hurry and he had things to do. It didn't matter about my time but his was valuable.

"I suppose we'll wait for her," I said.

"Aye," Tony answered dubiously.

"Speaking of notes . . . Uhm, in your long and storied career has anyone ever sent you an anonymous note about a case?"

"All the time, mate. Happens all the time. In fact, I'd say that I get more anonymous tips than ones from people who actually come forward to be identified. Why, what did you get? You look worried."

"Some character left me a note that was a verse from the Bible."

Tony laughed. "Ach, shite, is that all? You should see the bollocks we get in Special Branch. Bible verses, tips about who may or not be a Soviet agent or the Antichrist . . . you name it, Sean. Last week we had a boy who got passed up to us from Cliftonville RUC, who had convinced them that he was 'the real Yorkshire Ripper.' The cops in Cliftonville actually thought we might want to interview him."

"'Now I see through a glass darkly' was the verse."

"I remember that one. That's popular with the nuts. Is that from the Book of Revelation?"

"Corinthians. It was a woman who left me the note. English accent maybe. She left me a note at Victoria Cemetery and then she went off on a motorbike."

Tony pulled out his smokes and offered me one. We went over to the stone wall and sat down on it. Two fields over a horse was tied up against a tumbledown shed. Three fields the other way there was chimney smoke coming from the big house at the top of a hill—almost certainly the home of the lord of the manor. The rain, thank God, had taken a momentary breather in its relentless guerrilla war against Ireland.

"Go on," Tony said.

"I called it in and they found the girl and arrested her and took her to Whitehead RUC. She spent a few hours in the cells and then she was supposedly taken away by a couple of goons from Special Branch. One of them was a guy called McClue—a fake name if ever I heard it—and of course when I called up Special Branch there was no McClue and no one had been sent to get her in Whitehead."

Tony frowned. "Several things occur to me. First, if you had found her, what would you have charged her with? Leaving you a strange message and riding away on her motorbike? What crime is that? You'd be looking at a bloody lawsuit, mate. Secondly, who is she? Certainly not a lone nut if she had a couple of friends who were willing to pose as Special Branch agents to come get her."

"So, not a nutter."

"Or maybe she could be a very persuasive nutter. It's the sort of thing a student would do, or a bored paramilitary or . . ."

"Or what?"

"You know what. A ghost. A fucking spook. Northern Ireland is thick with them."

"MI5?"

"MI5, Army Intel, MI6. Or, like I say, a nutter, a student, one of your no doubt many dissatisfied lovers, a bored paramilitary playing you for a sap or a very bored spook also playing you for a sap."

Tony's pager went. He picked it up and examined the red flashing light.

"They're looking for me. You think I could break into the widow McAlpine's house and use her phone?"

"What would Sir Harry think? He's probably watching us through a set of field glasses."

"I doubt that. I'll bet he's furiously writing a letter to the Secretary of State for Northern Ireland who, no doubt, is a second cousin twice removed."

I nodded and blew a double smoke ring. Tony's pager went again.

"Fucksake!" Tony said. "I should never have left the bloody crime scene. The fuck was I thinking?"

"Tony mate, go back in the BMW, tell them you were following a lead and send some reservist back here with the car. I'll wait until the widow McAlpine shows up."

"I can take your wheels?" Tony asked.

"Sure."

"I wouldn't normally, but I am lead and maybe we shouldn't

be buggering off round the countryside like Bob Hope and Bing Crosby."

"Hope and Crosby? Christ, Tony, you need new material, mate. Have you heard about this rock and roll phenomenon that's sweeping the land?"

"You're sure I can take the car?"

"Aye!"

"You're a star. And you'll be okay?"

"I'll be fine."

The deal was done. Tony pumped my hand and got in the Beemer. He wound the window down. "Stay away from trouble," he said.

"You should warn trouble to stay away from me."

"Young widows in lonely farmhouses . . ." he said with a sigh, revved the Beemer and forced the clutch into an ugly second gear start.

16: SALT

I was glad that he was gone. I wanted to talk to Mrs. McAlpine alone and to follow up with Sir Harry alone. Tony was too much of an equal. It required weight to deal with him and I needed the emotional space to think.

I walked to the farmhouse again and tried the door.

She'd locked it.

What country person locks their door?

"Maybe one who's just had her husband gunned down by strangers," I said to myself.

Cora barked at me.

The rooster gave me the eye.

I looked at the horse tied up across the fields and I looked at the track up to the manor.

The latter was less muddy than the former.

"The big house first, I think," I said.

The slope was on a one in seven gradient that was a little taxing and I had to catch my breath at the top of it when I reached the stone wall around the house and the estate. There was an old lodge that had been boarded up but no actual gate itself.

There were assorted farm buildings along the wall and a short drive to the house lined with palm trees. Coconut palms, by the look of them, always an odd sight in Ireland but not uncommon: sailors had been bringing them back in pots for centuries.

A brisk walk underneath them brought me to the house.

There were two cars parked outside: an Irish racing green Bentley S2 Continental and a black Rolls-Royce Silver Cloud. Both vehicles were about twenty years old and had certainly not been designed for country living. They were the worse for wear, particularly the Bentley, which was rusted almost to scrap. I wondered if the engine still turned over, but if it did the best you could have done with it was drive it to the junk yard. The Roller was in better nick but not much: the rear suspension was gone, the fenders were dinged and the original paint job had been touched up with what looked like house paint. Both vehicles were caked with mud and bird shit. I loved cars and this was a crying shame.

I gave the house a butcher's: mid-century Georgian, red sandstone, three floors, a steep slate roof and a large wooden door that once had been painted a garish bright blue but which now had faded into a pleasing mottled indigo. The original, elegantly high, curved windows had been replaced by squat square jobs in brown frames. A black, sinister ivy was growing over two thirds of the house and all the third-floor windows were a suffocated tenebrous jungle. At least the ivy helped conceal the house's shambolic condition, but if you looked closely you could see the unrepaired cracks in the walls, the missing tiles in the roof and the strange lean of the entire structure a good ten degrees off the vertical.

I was vibing a classic case of the aristo fallen on hard times: big empty rooms, mad woman in the attic, eldest daughter marrying some garish Yank with money.

I crunched on the gravel and walked up moss-covered granite steps to the porch.

I rang an ancient-looking push bell and contemplated a sour-looking cat who was sleeping on a heap of old newspapers. At least, I assumed he was sleeping, as he didn't seem to breathe once.

A middle-aged woman came to the door. She was wearing an apron and looked annoyed. "He's not in, so he's not," she said in a pissed-off West Belfast accent.

"Where is he?"

"Out with the dogs, so he is."

I showed her my warrant card.

"Poliss, is it? Is there anything wrong? Will I get Betty?"

"Who's Betty?"

"The housekeeper, Mrs. Patton."

"And who are you?"

"Cook. Aileen."

"Who is else is in the house?"

"No one else. Ned will be with the horses."

"Is that everyone?"

"Yes."

I wrote the names in my notebook.

"Is there a wife, girlfriend?"

"No."

"Can I come in?" I asked.

"I suppose so," Aileen said.

I followed into her a rather gloomy looking hall with dark wood paneling and a staircase curving to the upper floors. There were hunting trophies on the wall, something I had not seen before anywhere in Ireland. Huge stags but also lions, leopards, a cheetah—all from another age.

The place was dusty and it smelled of mildew. The smell was so bad, in fact, that I gagged, and to cover my embarrassment I pointed at the beheaded animals.

"Do they not give you the willies, love? All them eyes looking down at you," I said in the demotic.

She laughed. "Aye, they're desperate so they are."

"Is it from himself?" I asked.

I could tell now that Aileen was a Catholic. It was hard to say how I could tell but I could. Accent, body language, who knew? Sir Harry wasn't a raging bigot then.

"No, no. From his da or his grand da more than likely," she said.

"What does *he* do for fun?"

"When he's not in his office in Belfast he just likes the quiet time. Potters around the garden, reads in his library."

"Terrible about his brother, the captain in the army."

"Shocking, so it was. Shocking."

"I suppose you didn't hear the killing from here?"

"Oh, no. It's too far away. We didn't hear anything."

"And there were no witnesses?"

"From up here? No."

"Was Sir Harry at home that day?"

"He was out in the garden, I think. He went over straight away. Of course there was nothing he could do."

"No. Martin was his younger brother?"

"Yes. Eight or nine years between them, I think."

I shook my head. "Must have been awful that morning."

"Oh yes, I'll never forget that day. Shocking, so it was. Such a cowardly act. They're vermin. Vermin shooting a man in the back."

"He was shot in chest,"

Her eyes scolded me. "What does it matter! What does that matter? What are you here for, anyway? I told you Sir Harry was out. Wait here."

Before I could call her back she vanished through a door and a rather different woman appeared in blue suit, white pearls and a black bouffant. She was about forty, thin, thin-lipped, and there was a touch of old Hollywood in her heavy lidded eyes and defiant unfeminine chin.

She walked towards me, all systems bristling. "May I see your identification?" she asked.

I showed her the warrant card.

"I take it that you're Mrs. Patton?" I asked.

She nodded. She was from Derry, by the sound of it. Brisk and business-like. I dug the whole *Rebecca* scene, but if she was Mrs. Danvers and Sir Harry was Max de Winter, what did that make me—Joan fucking Fontaine?

I took out my fags.

"Oh, there's no smoking in here," Mrs. Patton said.

I put the cigarettes back in my pocket with a mumbled "Excuse me."

A little victory for the home team, there.

"And how can we be of service today?" she asked.

"I need to see Sir Harry. I was wondering if I could, uh, if I could wait for him in your lovely garden," I said, putting on a bit of my Glens accent.

"The garden? Why?" she said, both disarmed and suspicious.

"I'm a bit of flower nut and I thought I could spend some time there until Sir Harry comes back. I've heard wonders about his garden."

"You wish to wait for Sir Harry in his garden?"

"If it doesn't put anyone out."

"No . . . I, uh, I don't expect that it would."

She looked at me and nodded curtly. "Follow me," she said.

We went through a spotless kitchen, all gleaming surfaces and pots on hooks. The appliances had all been brand new in about 1975. Sir Harry didn't seem like the sort of man who would let his cars rot but get expensive kitchen gear. It must be a feminine influence. His wife had bought that kit, a wife who was, now, where exactly?

I walked through the back door and out into the kitchen garden.

"Here you go," she said.

I pretended to be fascinated by an ugly yellow smudge of daffodils—the only thing at all growing back here.

Of course I had already seen the greenhouse through the kitchen window.

Mrs. Patton said "I'll leave you to it," and disappeared back inside. I lit a cigarette.

I knew that she'd be spying on me but there was a hedge blocking the rear entrance to the greenhouse from the back windows of the residence. I finished my smoke, inspected more of the flowers and walked behind the hedge. I waited a moment for a cry or footsteps hurrying towards me but I heard nothing. I turned a rusted iron handle and went inside the greenhouse. I didn't know what I was expecting to find but I was not counting on a completely empty space. No plants, no pots, nothing. I wrote "a clean concrete floor, a few gardening tools," in my notebook. The gardening tools were one rake and one hoe.

I had got what I came for on this trip.

I wrote "Down at heel scion. Hiding something or just an arse? No rosary pea or anything else in the greenhouse" in my notebook and walked into the house again.

Mrs. Patton intercepted me in the gloomy hall.

"Inspector Duffy, is anything amiss?" she asked.

"No, nothing's amiss, Mrs. Patton. However, I've just remembered that I have to be somewhere else. I was so taken with your daffodils that I completely forgot. You'll have to excuse me, ma'am. Thank you for your hospitality."

"Oh . . . oh, what shall I tell Sir Harry?"

"No message, thank you," I said.

I walked briskly out of the hall and onto the crunchy gravel drive. I gave the Bentley and the Roller a sympathetic look and I juked under the palm trees.

Thunder rumbled in a grey skin and it began to rain with big heavy, sporadic drops. At the hill's summit I surveyed the broad wet valley filled with cows and sheep and fields too boggy to accommodate man or beast.

The prospect to the north was of Larne Lough and Magheramorne on the far shore.

The widow McAlpine's farm was a good mile off on the far side of a hill. You wouldn't be able to see it even from the third floor of this house. No one inside could possibly have witnessed Martin's murder. There would be no teenage maids too frightened to testify but who could be broken by the age-old tactics of question after question after question.

I dandered down the hill and in twenty minutes I was back at the farm.

I went round the back of the house and tried the rear door.

It too was locked. Cora was barking herself hoarse now. A side window was open, but it was too small for me to squeeze through. I lit my last ciggy, climbed a style over the stone wall and strode out across the fields in the direction of the tied-up horse.

The pasture was little better than a bog with some tuft grass and sodden heather, and in a few moments my DMs were soaked through. Sheep pellets were everywhere and in a slurry pond there was the carcass of an old ewe, suspended just beneath the surface.

The horse was an old white mare who barely registered my presence as I approached. I stroked her head, but I had no sugar to offer her. I grabbed some moist dandelion leaves and held them under her nose but she turned her head away disdainfully. "Spoiled rotten, so you are," I said, and gave her a pat on the neck.

I was curious about the shed so I knocked on the door, but there was no answer. I opened it and saw a lantern hanging from the ceiling and a ladder leading underground.

"What's all this?" I muttered, but the mare kept her thoughts to herself.

I looked down into the hole. It was a vertical tunnel lit by a series of incandescent bulbs. The walls were white, chalky and crumbly and I wasn't encouraged that the rickety metal ladder was bolted to them. There was a slightly unpleasant, sulfurous smell which also boded ill.

I hesitated at the top of the ladder for a moment and then decided to climb down. Twenty rungs to the bottom. A narrow passage lead to a door which said: No Entry Except By Authorized Personnel.

I pushed on the door and entered the chamber. It was like a cave really and everything a cave should be: big, cathedral-like, sonorous, intimidating and impressive.

Two bright arc lamps lit the white, chalky and oddly beautiful walls and cast shadows deep into the back recess of the cavern. To one side there were several metal cupboards and in the middle of the room Emma McAlpine was sitting on a sofa next to a generator which didn't appear to be running. (How the lights were working was the first of the several mysteries.)

She must have heard me coming down the ladder but she did not look up.

"What are you reading?" I asked. "It's not the Bible, is it?"

"Inspector Duffy," she said, and set the book on her lap. It had yellow binding; not many Bibles had yellow covers, not even The Good News.

She was dressed in jeans, an Aran sweater and a wax jacket. Riding boots, of course, but she had kicked those off. Her hair was tied back in a ponytail. Under the fluorescent lights she looked wan, sickly, not a million miles removed from Elizabeth Siddal in *Ophelia*.

I walked towards her. "I get the feeling that you were expecting me," I said.

"Why would I be?"

"Because you heard the news."

She nodded. "Inspector Dougherty. I'm sorry," she said.

"Sorry for what?"

"Dougherty was a brother officer, wasn't he?"

"Yes."

"Would you like some tea? I brought a flask. It's already made up with milk and sugar. Scandalous, I know."

"Sure."

"Have a seat."

I sat next to her on the leather sofa. She smelled of horse and sweat and leather. The sofa was covered in a layer of powdery white shit from the crumbling ceiling; I brushed myself a space with the back of my hand and sat down. She produced a flask with a paisley design on the side, unscrewed the plastic lid and poured a cup of tea into a white plastic mug.

"I also brought a flask of gin, if you want to slip that in there," she said, as if that would be the most natural thing in the world.

"No, you're all right, thanks."

I took the tea, which was weak and very sweet. The way I liked it. The type of tea you were supposed to give to people to stop them going into shock.

"Dougherty came to see you, didn't he?" I asked.

"Yes."

"What about?"

"I think he may have been drunk. He had certainly been drinking."

"What did he talk to you about?"

"In an extremely vulgar manner he demanded to know exactly where I had been when Martin got shot."

"And what did you tell him?"

"I told him that I was in the kitchen."

"And what did he say to that?"

"He said that he didn't believe me. He said that I wasn't telling him everything."

"And what did you say to that?"

"I told him that no one could call me a liar in my own home and I asked him to leave."

"And did he leave?"

"No. He did not. He abused me in the most disgraceful language. At one point I felt that he was going to strike me."

"And then?"

"Well, then he did leave, but not before melodramatically promising that he would return."

I rubbed my chin and leaned back into the sofa cushions.

"But he didn't return, did he?"

"No."

"Did he call you or have any other communication with you?"

"No."

"And you didn't go see him?"

"Of course not."

She looked at me. Her blue eyes were not entirely pleasant. They radiated an icy quality. Not quite contempt but not far off it. Distance, a lack of concern.

"What are you reading?" I asked in a lower register.

"It isn't the Bible, since you ask."

"The Bible was on my mind. Someone called me up and asked me to meet them and when I went there they had left a note," I explained, leaving out the chase scene.

"That sounds like fun," she said. "What did the note say?"

"It was a Bible verse."

"And?"

"'Now I see through a glass darkly.'"

"What does that mean?"

"I have no idea."

She grinned and slapped her thigh. "Oh, I get it. You thought I was reading the Bible and that maybe I was the person who left you the note, is that it?"

"It *was* a woman on the phone. But it was an English woman."

"Maybe I was disguising my voice."

"Maybe you were."

"I didn't call you and I didn't leave you a note. How would I get your number anyway?"

"I'm in the book."

"Oh."

"And I went to see your brother-in-law."

"Why?"

"Just to be nosey."

"And what did you find out?"

"His cars are in a bad way."

"His cars?"

"The Bentley and the Roller. Beautiful machines sadly gone to pot. He should at least keep them in a garage."

"Are you aware of the Japanese concept of *mono no aware*, the bitter sweetness of things?"

"I'm afraid not."

"The Japanese sages say the best way to appreciate beauty is to focus on its transient, fragile and fleeting nature."

I nodded. "Is that what your brother-in-law's doing? I thought he was just a careless fucker."

"And what else did you learn from your visit to Red Hall?" she asked.

"He's a knight. It's *Sir* Harry McAlpine. He's been to see the Queen. Somebody gave him a knighthood."

She shook her head. "Nobody gave him a knighthood. He's a baronet."

"What's a baronet when it's at home?"

"It's the lowest order of peerage."

I must have looked blank because she elaborated. "It goes Prince, Duke, Marquis, Earl, Viscount, Baron, Baronet. It's hereditary. It goes to the eldest son. Harry is the third Baronet. It means very little."

"I wouldn't say that. He's got a title and he's got money."

"Money!" she laughed. "He's as poor as a church mouse."

"He's got that big house, all this land . . ."

"Heavens, Inspector. This land? Well, yes, he owns everything from here to the sea and I'm a tenant and there are half a dozen farms on the other side of the hill, but none of that matters: it's all bogland, it's practically worthless and that big house is a shambles. The top floor is shut up, the walls are crumbling . . ."

"The house isn't in great nick, but with all this property he's hardly a candidate for the poor house, is he?"

"That's where you're wrong again. Red Hall is entailed. He can't touch the freehold or sell it or lease it out. It's all going to his eldest son."

"He has kids?"

"Two."

"One of each?"

"Two boys. They live with their mother. Actually they're both at Harrow."

"Harrow over the water?" I asked stupidly.

"Do you know any other Harrow?"

"He's divorced, then."

"You really are a detective. A regular Poirot," she said, with a sweet teasing smile that got her back into my good books. She snugged her legs up underneath her body. Riding horses had given her powerful thighs and done wonders for her complexion.

"I'll take that," she said, holding my wrist and removing the empty tea cup. I've known judo instructors with a less impressive grip. And that assurance, too. This was no blushing, weeping widow. Not now.

"What about you? How are you doing for money?" I asked.

"Since my husband's murder, you mean? Is this also part of your investigation? Could I be compelled to answer?"

"Perhaps."

"Don't you find question and answer a rather tedious form of discourse? Wouldn't you rather have a conversation?"

"When time is a factor there's really no other way, I'm afraid."

"Is time a factor here? My husband was killed in December. It's April."

"Time is always a factor in police work, Mrs. McAlpine."

She sighed. "I live on Martin's army pension of seventy-five pounds a week. I pay twenty-five pounds of that to Harry. For rent."

I nodded. "And how much does the land bring in?"

She laughed. "Are you serious?"

"Aye."

"I have forty sheep. Shorn, I'll get perhaps three pounds a fleece; come lambing season, perhaps another five pounds a lamb. This year I may make two hundred pounds from the entire acreage."

"Can't you grow something? I'm always hearing things about the high cost of wheat."

"No arable crops will grow here. It's a marsh. This whole part of Islandmagee is one enormous swamp."

"Where were you last night, Mrs. McAlpine?" I asked, abruptly changing tack.

"When Dougherty was killed, you mean?"

"Yes."

"I was at home. Reading. In other words, I have no alibi."

"What were you reading?"

"*Middlemarch.*"

"I see."

"George Eliot."

"I know . . . Is that what you're reading now?"

"Yes."

She passed me the book. I flipped through it and gave it back.

"Why would I kill poor Inspector Dougherty?" she asked while I was thinking of my next question.

"Why indeed?"

"No, let's not play that game. Why do *you* think I may have done it? What possible motive could I have had?"

I was looking for a little more outrage from her: *How dare you accuse me of such a terrible thing!* Not that that would have had much probative value one way or the other. Maybe she just wasn't the demonstrative type.

"Because I got him all riled up about your husband's murder. Because I put a seed of doubt in his head that maybe you weren't telling everything you knew and because he came barging down there to ask you a whole bunch of questions," I said.

She smiled. "Then I got a gun from heaven knows where, found out where he lived and shot him?"

And then dumped the weapon, drove to a phone box and claimed the hit on behalf of the IRA using a recognized IRA code word.

"The assumption, naturally, is that I killed my husband for whatever reason and I was worried that Dougherty was getting close to discovering that I had done it and so he had to go too. Is that it?"

"I suppose so," I agreed.

"Let me dissect this theory of yours a little . . . if I may."

"Be my guest."

"First of all, I didn't kill Martin. Everything I've told you about his murder is completely true. I loved him. He loved me. We rarely argued. And what possible motive could I have had to do it? Fiduciary? For the pathetic lump sum I'll get years from now from the compensation board? For the army pension? We had no life insurance—"

"Why didn't he take out life insurance?"

"The weekly rates for a serving army officer are astronomical."

"Of course."

"Let me continue . . . So, no life insurance, a pathetic pension and then there's the farm. What's to stop Harry from kicking me out once Martin's dead? I lose my husband, his income and my house? For what?"

"There are other motives."

"Like what?"

"Like the oldest motive in the world."

"Martin wasn't having an affair."

"Are you sure about that?"

"Quite sure, he wasn't the type."

"All women think that about their husbands right up to the moment when they receive undeniable proof and quite often after they receive undeniable proof."

"Even if he had been having an affair I wouldn't have shot him."

"Why not?"

"*I'm* not the type, Inspector."

I felt a crick in my neck and I was getting a stress headache in this uncomfortable sofa. I got to my feet and stretched. "What is this place, anyway? Some kind of salt mine?" I asked.

"That's exactly what it is."

"Do you come down here often?"

"I do. I read down here. It's so quiet. No planes, no cars, nothing. Not even wind. They could have a nuclear war out there and I wouldn't know about it."

"I was wondering how you power the lights."

"We steal electricity from the grid. Harry rigged it up." She patted the generator. "This thing is only to pump out water."

"I suppose if I'm to buy into this theory of family poverty then I can only assume that the seams are worked out."

"They are. For all commercial purposes anyway. The mines incidentally are what got Sir Harry his 'Sir.' His grandfather supplied salt for the Empire. It's also why Harry couldn't sell this land even if he wanted to. You can't build on it."

I smiled and she looked at me strangely.

"What are you thinking right now, Inspector?"

"Right now?"

"Right now."

"I'm thinking, Mrs. McAlpine, that most people would be keeking their whips if they were being questioned about a murder for which they had no alibi and a possible motive. But not you. You're as cool as a cucumber."

"Because I didn't do it. I've nothing to be worried about. Why do you think I did it? Is it one of those policemen's hunches I'm always hearing about?"

"Hunches are overrated."

"How does one solve crimes, Inspector?"

"Most criminals aren't that bright. They screw up and we find the screw up pretty quickly and we can usually go to trial, except if the screw up involves eyewitness testimony."

"What happens if it's eyewitness testimony?"

"The eyewitnesses are intimidated into not testifying. Those cases usually collapse."

"And what about the hard cases? Like your body in the suitcase? That's still your case, isn't it? Or have you turned your attention to me and Inspector Dougherty now?"

"No, that's still my case. My only case. A colleague of mine is looking into the death of Inspector Dougherty, and your husband's murder, I'm sorry to say, is probably never going to be solved."

"I see," she said and pursed her lips.

"Have you ever fired a pistol before, Mrs. McAlpine?"

"A pistol, no. A shotgun many times."

I looked at my watch. I had been at this for twenty minutes and I wasn't really getting anywhere. If this was my case, maybe Crabbie and me would make more progress down the station in a windowless interview room. But it wasn't my concern, was it? I looked at her for a beat or two. "Well, I suppose I must be going. Thank you for the tea," I said.

"That's it, you're not going to cuff me and drag me off?"

"No."

"Why not? Do you believe me?"

"I don't know. But you're tangential to my investigation. Chief

Inspector McIlroy may want to interview you about Dougherty, but I'm done here."

"I'll walk you out, if you like," she said.

I'd been hoping for some sign of relief from her—a blush or a sigh or anything, but grief had washed everything out of Mrs. McAlpine already.

I climbed the ladder and she followed me up. Out into sunlight. Or more exactly into the ambient light and rain. The horse whinnied excitedly when he saw Emma and she gave him a sugar lump.

There were several dirty-looking gulls in the fields taking shelter from the wind.

"Do you think those are fulmars?" I said absently.

"Fulmars?"

"Ful from the Norse meaning foul, mar meaning gull."

She grinned at me. "A man of many interests."

"Not really."

We walked the horse back across the bog to the farm. We didn't speak because half a dozen Army Gazelle helicopters were flying south east, at a low ceiling, in a tight menacing formation.

When the choppers had gone she asked me if I'd always wanted to be a policeman. I told her no. I'd been studying psychology at Queens.

She told me that she had done a degree in history.

We talked a little about the university. We'd had no mutual friends and our paths hadn't crossed in the Students' Union. It wasn't surprising. She was seven or eight years younger than me.

"Is Queen's where you met Martin?"

"Well, I'm a local Islandmagee girl so I already knew Martin, but that's where we started going out. He was doing law but he dropped out when he joined the UDR. I stayed on for a bit, and then, well . . . we got married."

She was blushing. There was a story there, too. A pregnancy? A miscarriage? We reached the farmhouse. My car was there and next to it a shining female constable in a dark green uniform and a dark green Kepi.

"Your chauffeur?" Emma asked.

"Indeed."

She offered me her hand. "I assume this is where we take our leave?" she said.

"I expect so," I said, shaking her hand.

She looked into my eyes. "You're disappointed, aren't you? You think I've gotten away with something."

I said nothing.

"I promise you, Inspector Duffy, I did not kill my husband, and I had nothing to do with the killing of Inspector Dougherty."

"Okay," I said, "how about we just leave it there."

17: THE TREASURY MAN

I dropped Reserve Constable Sandra Pollock back at Larne RUC and drove on to Carrickfergus in the Beemer. Somewhere in County Antrim an Army Puma helicopter had been shot at with either an RPG or a surface to air missile and as a result the highways and byways were flooded with angry soldiers in green fatigues idiotically stopping every third car. Of course, I was one of the lucky stopees. I showed the squaddies my warrant card but they ignored it. Two of them pointed FN FAL rifles at me while their mates went through my boot.

"What's this?" an acerbic Welshman asked me, holding up a flare gun.

"A flare gun."

"What's it for?"

"For firing flares."

This could have gone for a while or until one of Taffy's mates shot me, but they decided to let me go instead.

Back in Carrick the peelers were yukking it up over a fake version of the *Belfast Telegraph* that a Republican group must have printed up samizdat fashion. One of the headlines was "Polar Bears Capture Falklands Task Force," which wasn't even geographically astute.

"Take a look at this, Duffy," Sergeant Quinn said.

"Uh, no thanks, some of us have work to do," I said pointedly.

In the CID incident room McCrabban had news. After a bit of prodding the Consul General in Belfast had sent us a second, slightly lengthier FBI file on Bill O'Rourke. We knew most of it already. O'Rourke had worked for the IRS his entire life. He was not involved in any fraudulent or other criminal activities and as far as the FBI could see his only offense was that speeding ticket the local cops had told us about. The report was really rather curt. Three paragraphs. A couple of spelling mistakes. It was signed by a Special Agent Anthony Grimm. Something about it still didn't feel quite right.

"Maybe we should talk to him," I said.

"Who?"

"Grimm. Sounds like another fake name to me."

"You and your fake names. You're still not happy?" Crabbie asked.

"Clearly they did the bare minimum here. I want you to lean on the Consul again and see if anything else squeaks out," I said.

"The consulate is fed up with us already," McCrabban complained.

"You'll do your best, I'm sure," I insisted.

I filled him and Matty in about my day's adventures in Larne and Islandmagee. While they were digesting that, I told them about the anonymous note and the verse from the Bible, the mysterious woman and her arrest.

"Yeah. So what do you think, lads? Is it something or is it nothing?"

Matty was unimpressed. In his experience women were capable of any kind of madness just to get in your head, but McCrabban lapped it up, liking anything which involved Biblical exegesis.

"Have a wee think, boys, will ya?" I said, and went to the kitchen, made three mugs of tea, got some chocolate biscuits and brought them back to the lads.

"Well? Any brainwaves?" I asked.

"The McAlpine angle seems more and more like a distraction. The note is slightly more interesting, but not much. The woman? Someone you met in a pub stalking you? It's probably not relevant for us, in this particular case, is it?" Matty said.

"Your take, Crabbie?"

"I agree with young Matty. The McAlpine angle might be something but it's Larne RUC's something. Or Special Branch's something. The note? Well, I'll have to have a think about that. There's some really good stuff in Corinthians."

"Should we drop the McAlpine angle?"

"I don't think that's the best use of our resources, Sean. The fact that O'Rourke's killer used Martin McAlpine's old suitcase that he picked up in the Salvation Army is neither here nor there. If he'd used Princess Diana's old suitcase we wouldn't spend all this time investigating her." Crabbie said soberly.

"Knowing Sean, I'd say that he definitely would, the old horn dog," Matty chipped in.

They were both content to close the book on Emma McAlpine, at least for now. I took a chocolate digestive and we had a collective think about the note, but it was impossible to say if someone was messing with us or not. I wrote it all up in the case file anyway, in case it became significant.

No one could think of anything else. I went to my office and pretended to work, but really spent time drawing glasses and moustaches on every wanker in the *Daily Mail*, and that is a lot of wankers.

A knock at the door. It was McCrabban, jacket off, revealing a yellow shirt and green paisley tie underneath.

"Come in."

"Fallows from the Consul's office called." McCrabban said. "They want the body released from the morgue. They'd like to bury O'Rourke in the Arlington National Cemetery. It's a big deal apparently. A real honor."

"I don't trust that Fallows guy. I wasn't entirely happy with some of his answers," I said.

"Aye, he looked shifty," McCrabban agreed.

"You think everybody not raised in the Free Presbyterian Church religion is shifty. Still, maybe the Consulate are trying to sweep this under the rug? What say you?"

Normally Crabbie would leap at any hint of conspiracy, but I could see the skepticism in his eyes. He knew and I knew that the avenues were beginning to close one by one. The whole McAlpine diversion had been an attempt to hide the fact that this entire case was slowly grinding to a halt.

"I don't know, mate," he muttered.

"Tell them they can have the body," I said.

"Okay."

I ate a biscuit, looked at the sea, continued my work on the *Mail*. Time passed.

Maybe somebody somewhere would come up with something.

Another knock at the door and Crabbie came in.

"Well?"

"I talked to your man, Fallows. I don't think he knows anything. He's just a functionary. I told him he could ship the body home. He seemed happy with that," Crabbie said.

I yawned. "All right, I'll write this all up tomorrow. Tell Matty we can head on home," I said.

"I'll stay and write it up. I want to study for my sergeant's exam anyway," McCrabban muttered.

"Suit yourself, mate," I said, but later I thought that I should have said "Thank you very much, Crabbie."

I went outside, turned the collar up on my raincoat.

I got inside the BMW and had a reasonably straight run home. Only one patrol stopped me this time. A bunch of Gurkha rifles who were a long way from Nepal. None of them could speak English, which made explaining my cop I.D. a barrel of laughs.

When I finally got back to Coronation Road the street was full of kids playing football. I didn't have the heart to break up their game so I parked on Victoria Road and walked the rest of the way.

I was turning into the house when Bobby Cameron saw me at the door.

"Oi, Duffy, need your help," he said.

Bobby was not only the local paramilitary commander but also a man that I owed my life to when he had shot a man shooting at me a year ago. He knew that I was obliged to him and he loved that.

"Yes?" I said.

"Follow me," he muttered.

"Where?"

"Just follow me. We have a wee problem."

"Tell me what this is about."

"Just come!"

"Not until you tell me."

He glared at me. The rain was light but we were both getting soaked. "Fine! When the trouble comes just remember that I fucking tried to prevent it and you couldn't fucking be arsed," he said.

"What trouble?"

"Too late! You had your fucking chance, peeler. You had your fucking chance!" he said huffily.

I went inside and closed the door. I took off my raincoat and let it fall on the floor. It had been a psychically draining day and I was shattered. I made myself a vodka gimlet and plonked myself down in front of the TV. I watched *The Rockford Files*. You had to like the fact that Rockford got shat on all the time and was living in penury with his old man in a caravan. Seemed about right for a detective.

The phone rang. "Tell me about the bint and her alibi," Tony asked.

"No alibi. She said she was reading George Eliot."

"*Animal Farm* and all that?"

"You're thinking of George Orwell."

"Did Dougherty come to see her?"

"He did. She said that he was drunk and raving, not making a lot of sense."

"Does that sound like him?"

"Yeah, it does. I asked her if she'd ever shot a pistol," I said.

"And what did she say?"

"She said she hadn't, but she'd fired a shotgun many times."

"Who hasn't? So what do you think? Did she kill him?"

"Which 'him'?"

"Dougherty."

"I don't know."

"You gave her the third degree?"

"Yes. Well, maybe the second degree."

"And?"

"I have no idea."

"Jesus. You're no help, are you?"

"No."

"I suppose I'll have to see her too, then."

"I suppose you will."

Tony decided to let it go at that. He detected some note in my voice that he didn't quite like. "Are you all right, mate? I mean, are you doing all right?" he asked in a big brother tone.

"Yeah, I'm fine."

A long pause.

"When I'm over the water I can look for a place for you, too, you know," he said.

"Thanks. . .but you know how I feel."

"Have a wee think. I mean, really, this place is finished, there's no future here. Especially not for bright boys like you and me."

"Sure, Tony. I'll think about it."

"I know you won't, but you should. That doctor friend of yours. She's doing the right thing."

"I know."

"Any more mysterious women leaving you Valentines?"

"Not today."

"If it was anything serious she would have just told you, she wouldn't have left you a cryptic note. That stuff's strictly for the flicks."

"I was thinking the same thing myself."

Dead air for a second or two. "Don't let the job get to you. Okay?"

"Okay."

"Take care now."

"I will."

He hung up. I made another vodka gimlet, dimmed the lights and put on Pink Floyd's *Wish You Were Here*. I moved the stylus to "Shine On You Crazy Diamond"—the song about Syd Barrett's mental breakdown—and put the record player on repeat. I called up Carrick RUC and asked for DC McCrabban.

"McCrabban," he said.

"Christ, are you still there?"

"You shouldn't take the Lord's name. And yeah, I am still here."

"What are you doing, Crabbie, studying?"

"Aye. Got the old law books out. It's quiet here, although intelligence has been coming through about prep for trouble in Belfast."

"You better get out of there before you get dragooned into riot duty."

"I wouldn't mind riot duty. Double time and danger money. We could do with the cash."

"Just don't put in for triple-time, that wee shite Dalziel will be all over you."

"I've been working on the case, too," he said, without much enthusiasm.

"What are your thoughts?"

"Not just thoughts. I just spoke to your man. The FBI guy. Special Agent Anthony Grimm."

"How?" I said stupidly.

"The time zones. They're five hours behind."

"Oh, yeah."

"Nothing new about O'Rourke. War hero. Adjusted well to civilian life. Good civil servant. There were a couple of other speeding tickets that weren't in the file. Thirty years in the IRS." "Anything controversial? Did he ever audit the wrong guy?"

"Nothing controversial. He was a mid-level IRS inspector. He wouldn't have been a prosecutor or have made any enemies."

"What was this Grimm like? Weird tone of voice, evasive, anything like that?"

"Nothing that I noticed. Happy to speak to me, it seemed like. Broke the routine. Sounded a bit bored by his lot."

Not what I was hoping for.

"There was one thing . . ." McCrabban said.

"Yes?"

"Well, when I called up the FBI's number in Virginia and asked to speak to Special Agent Anthony Grimm, I was put on hold and then the operator said that she was transferring me to the Secret Service."

"The Secret Service? Shite! What's that all about? Aren't they the ones that protect the President?"

"I asked Grimm and he laughed and he said that it wasn't as dramatic as it sounded. He'd just been seconded to the currency protection department of the US Treasury. The most boring possible assignment in the entire FBI, he said. Even more boring than preparing data sheets on dead IRS inspectors. I don't think that really means anything, but I thought you'd like to know."

"Yeah, okay, I'll write that down. As long as he sounded legit?"

"He did."

"Okay. Good. So where are we, Crabbie?"

"I think we can rule out anything from O'Rourke's past. He was a model citizen. He paid his taxes, he didn't have a record, looked after his wife."

"I had no idea he was a serial killer, he was a very quiet man, he kept to himself," I said in a Yorkshire accent.

"Stop it, Sean. He's no ripper. I really feel for the bloke. His missus dies and he takes a bloody holiday to Ireland to get over his grief and while he's here some bastard tops him. It all seems very random to me."

"Random except for the fact that A) he was poisoned and B) the murderer chopped up the body, froze it for an unknown amount of time and then dumped it in a suitcase. That is not your standard mugging gone wrong, is it, Crabbie?"

"No."

"And then there's all the distractions, as you call them. The women and the note, the deal with the widow McAlpine . . ." I said, and took a big drink of the vodka gimlet.

"Ach, mate, the note's a prank, and I never thought the McAlpine angle would get us anywhere."

"You should have told me that before I went down to Islandmagee twice," I said.

"You're the inspector and I'm the detective constable."

"All right, Crabbie, thanks. Go home now, okay?"

"Aye. Okay, bye, Sean."

"Stay frosty and drive safe."

"I will."

I hung up and rummaged in the bookshelf for my King James Bible. I made myself another pint of lime and vodka and put on Radio Albania. A five-minute rant about Ronald Reagan and the evils of American capitalism. A rant about the Soviet Union and the decadence of the Brezhnev regime. Praise only for Pol Pot, a true friend of the workers in Cambodia.

It was midnight and I was only two sips into the new vodka gimlet when somebody started banging the front door.

"Will this madness ever end?" I said, storming down the hall.

I opened the door to Bobby Cameron, who had come by with a lynch mob.

18: NOT EXACTLY SCOUT FINCH

There were a dozen of them wearing balaclavas, ski masks or scarves; they were carrying cricket bats, sticks and baseball bats—the last always an impressive get in a country that didn't play the game.

They had banged the front door rather than smashing the windows, so that gave me the feeling that they weren't here to kill me.

"This is your last chance. If you want to prevent violence, you'll have to fucking come, Duffy," Bobby Cameron said in his unmistakable burr.

"Why don't you take that thing off your face and we'll talk like civilized men," I said, pointing at the bandana over his mouth.

"Come with us, Duffy, or it'll be on your conscience," Bobby replied.

I liked that—whatever they were about to do was somehow going to be my fault.

"All right. Hold on a minute," I said.

I closed the door in their faces, ran upstairs, got the .38 from under my pillow, shoved it down the front of my jeans and pulled my Ramones T-shirt over the grip. I grabbed a leather jacket and went outside onto the porch.

"I love the kit, but I think you're all a little late for ski season, gentlemen," I said.

No one laughed.

"We have to draw a line in the fucking sand," someone said. It sounded like Mr. Cullen who once had been a shop steward at Harland and Wolff shipyard and now, like nearly everybody else, was unemployed.

"It's bad enough with the fucking fenians out-breeding us. And now this? It's a fucking disaster," someone else said.

"It's a question of jobs," Bobby said.

"What's going on, lads?" I asked.

"We want you, Duffy, because you can explain it to them, nice, like. This doesn't have to end in tears," Bobby said.

"What doesn't have to end in tears?" I asked.

"This way," Bobby said.

Cameron led the way and we followed him out onto Coronation Road. The street was deserted. Cleared. No drunks, no passersby, no witnesses. What the hell were they doing?

And I was sober now, too. And a little scared.

Two of the men were carrying vodka bottles with rags sticking out the end.

"Down here," Bobby said.

He stopped at the last house on Coronation Road, just before Victoria Road began. He turned to me.

"Now, you go in and tell them that we're reasonable men. We don't want any nonsense. Nobody has to get hurt. We'll give them half an hour to get their stuff and go. But if they don't go I won't be responsible for what happens to them," Bobby said.

I was still clueless. I had no idea who lived in this house. In fact I had thought it was vacant. Was it a child molester? What?

It was a red-brick terraced council house, identical to mine, except that I had purchased mine from the Housing Executive under Mrs. Thatcher's home ownership scheme and done it up a bit.

I opened the gate and walked down the path.

The previous renters had cemented over the garden, but the new occupant or occupants had placed half a dozen rose bushes in little pots over the raw concrete.

I knocked on the front door.

"Who is it?" a voice asked from inside.

"It's one of your neighbors," I said. "Sean Duffy from down the street."

"Just a minute."

The door opened a few seconds later. It was the African woman. She was wearing jeans and a hooded sweatshirt and she was clutching a handbag. She looked at me and looked at the mob waiting in the street.

"What is happening?" she asked, trembling, terrified.

"These men have come to intimidate you out of your house," I told her. "What have I done?" she asked. Her accent was East African, educated.

"I don't know," I said. "Why don't I ask them."

I turned to face the men milling on Coronation Road.

"She wants to know what's she done," I said.

"She just has to go! Carrick's no place for her. There's no jobs for outsiders!" someone yelled.

"We don't want any niggers in our town!" someone else shouted. Billy Took, by the sound of his high-pitched voice.

"Where do you think you are, Billy? Alabama?" I said to him.

"This is our country!" someone else said.

"They're fucking swamping us!"

"It's the thin end of a wedge."

"They're stealing our jobs!"

The rain began. I tilted my head back and let it spatter on my face for a moment or two.

I turned to face the woman.

"What's your name, love?" I asked her.

"Ambreena," she said.

"What do you do?"

"I am a student at the university."

"Which university?"

"The University of Ulster. I am studying business administration."

"Very good. Who else is in the house? Do you have any kids? A husband?"

"A boy. My husband is in Uganda."

"Do you have any relatives nearby?"

"They are all in Uganda."

She looked at the mob. "What must I do? Must I go?"

"No. Go back inside, close the door. I'll get rid of these hoodlums, and if you have any more trouble you come see me. I'm a police officer. I live at number 113."

She nodded.

Her eyes were hooded and dark and very beautiful. Old eyes that had seen much, but she herself was very young. Perhaps twenty-one.

She reached into the bag, fumbled for her purse, took three twenty-pound notes and offered them to me.

"That won't be necessary. Now go inside, close the door, and if you've any trouble, come see me. Or call me. 62670. Okay?"

"Yes."

"Do you have a phone?"

"Yes."

"Go on, then. Get inside."

She closed the door.

There was that smell in the wet street. That oh-so-familiar perfume of gasoline and tobacco and booze and fear.

Curtains twitched, lights went on, but whatever happened nobody, absolutely nobody, would hear or see anything, even if someone accidentally killed a copper. Check that. *Especially* if someone accidentally killed a copper.

Silence, save for a distant army helicopter somewhere over the black lough.

I looked at Bobby Cameron. Our eyes met above the bandana.

"Stand aside, peeler," someone said.

Raindrops pattered in the oily potholes.

Fragile lines of phosphorous flitted between clouds as the moon appeared over the terrace on Victoria Road.

Bobby smiled under the mask. "They have to leave, Duffy," he said. "We've discussed it."

"It's only one woman and her kid."

"One or a thousand. It doesn't matter. It's the start of it."

"They're taking our jobs!" someone yelled. It was Davey Dummigan from up the road, his Ards accent unmistakable.

"She's not taking your jobs, Davey. ICI moved its factory to Southeast Asia 'cause there are no unions and the labor's cheap. It's got nothing to do with her."

"You didn't hear us, Duffy. We brought you in as a courtesy. One way or another they're leaving tonight," someone else said.

I stared at the men.

They stared at me.

In the distance I could hear sirens upon sirens.

This was absurd. I reached into the front of my jeans and pulled out the .38.

Is this what you want, Bobby? Do you really want us to all leap together into the great glittering Omega? For her? For the thin end of a wedge?

"You're not the law, my lads, I'm the fucking law," I growled.

I didn't point the gun at them but I let everyone see that I had it in my hand.

Half a dozen of the men backed away, afeared of the wild-haired, maverick cop who had already topped five people on this very street.

Bobby was completely unfazed.

"I can come back with a bigger gun than that," he said, and some of the men laughed. Of that I had no doubt, there were probably AKs in his garden shed.

"I'm the law, my brave boys, and you'll have to go through me. But why would you want to? She's the only adult in the house. She's a student. She's studying business administration. She's studying business. She's come here to create jobs, not fucking steal them," I said.

A ripple went through the men.

"What did you say she was studying?" Bobby asked.

"Business administration at the University of Ulster," I said.

"Is she a fenian?" someone shouted.

"There's no fenians out there, they're all fucking heathens. They fucking put priests in the pot," someone else said, and there was more laughter.

Bobby, no dummy, seized the moment. "Well, as long as she doesn't try and cook anybody on this street, the stink's bad enough when Rhonda Moore makes lasagna," he said.

More laughter. "I've got a missionary joke, if you want to hear it," Eddie Shaw said.

"Go ahead, Eddie," I said, and I put the gun back in my trouser band.

"Very religious Free Presbyterian missionary goes to Africa, catches a disease and is flown to a hospital staffed with nuns. They put a mask over his mouth and move him to the isolation ward. 'Nurse,' he mumbles from behind the mask, 'are my testicles black?' Embarrassed, the young nurse replies, 'I don't know, I'm only here to wash your face and hands.' The Head Sister is passing and sees the man getting distraught so she marches over to inquire what the problem is. 'Nurse, please,' he mumbles, 'Are my testicles black?' The Head Sister whips back the bedclothes, pulls down his pajama trousers, moves his dick, has a right good look, shows the other two nurses, pulls up the pajamas, replaces the bedclothes and announces, 'Nothing wrong with your testicles, sir!' At this the missionary pulls off his mask and says, 'I said, are my test results back?!'"

Roars of laughter. Even Bobby Cameron. And just like that it was over. Most of the men took off their balaclavas as they walked home. Bobby grinned at me and I got the feeling that this was what he'd been hoping for the whole time. Shattered, I went back to the house, grabbed a can of Bass from the fridge and plonked myself down in front of the telly.

Bass after Bass while Alex "The Hurricane" Higgins tore up the snooker table. A lynch mob. What next?

The phone rang. I looked at the living room clock: 12:29. I had a strict rule. Never get the phone after midnight. It was never good news. Never. It rang thirteen times and then stopped and then began ringing again.

"Shit!"

I stomped down the hall. "What now, for heaven's sake?"

"Duffy, meet me at Carrick Marina, ten minutes," Chief Inspector Brennan said.

"Come on, sir, it's after twelve!" I said.

"Stop your whining and get your arse down here, pronto!"

I went outside to the Beemer, checked underneath for bombs, and drove down Coronation Road to the harbor. I parked in the harbor car park. Everything was dark except for the lights on a Polish coal boat which was leaking diesel into the water. I walked along the south pier until I came to the Marina, which consisted of a couple of dozen yachts and small fishing smacks tied against a wooden pontoon.

"Over here, Duffy!" Inspector Brennan said.

I walked along the pontoon to a messy thirty-two-foot ketch, all wood, probably pre-war. Jesus, was he living here now?

"Come here!" Brennan said.

I climbed aboard.

"Should I salute the quarter deck or something?" I said.

"Can I get you a drink?"

"Yeah."

He handed me a glass of whisky.

"Come down below."

We sat at the chart table. The place smelled bad. Clothes everywhere. A sleeping bag on one of the bunks.

"Standing offer, sir. If you're looking for somewhere to stay for a while, I have two spare bedrooms and—"

His face went red. His fist clenched. "What the fuck are you talking about?"

"If you and Mrs. Brennan are having any sort of—"

"I'll thank you not to mention my wife's name, if you don't mind, Inspector Duffy!"

I nodded

"And for your information, I am fine. Everything's normal. Sometimes I choose to sleep out here. I go fishing early. I don't know what gossip you've been listening to down at the station but it's all fucking lies."

"Yes, sir."

"A man's allowed to go fishing, isn't he?"

"Yes, sir."

"I mean, I have your bloody permission, don't I?"

"Yes, sir."

He swallowed his glass of whisky. Poured himself another.

"So, Duffy, this morning you paid a call on a man called Harry McAlpine, is that right?"

"I encountered him, yes."

"Sir Harry McAlpine?"

"Yes."

"And you went to his house without a warrant and conducted a search, is that right?"

"No. I went to see him. I was invited in by one of his servants. I waited for him. He didn't show up and I left."

"That's not the story I was told," Brennan said.

"Has there been some sort of complaint?"

"Aye. There has. To Ian Paisley MP MEP. Ian fucking Paisley."

"Sir, look, all I did—"

"Spare me the details, Duffy. I'd never heard of this cunt McAlpine before but he's obviously fucking connected. Stay away from him, all right?"

"Yes, sir."

His eyes drooped and he seemed to fall into a microsleep for a moment.

"Sir?"

"If a man pours you a fucking whisky, you fucking drink it!" he said angrily.

I drank the rotgut whisky.

"All right, Duffy, you can go."

"Yes, sir."

He sighed and rubbed his face. "It's one thing after another isn't it, Duffy?"

"That it is, sir. That it is."

19: THE CHIEF CONSTABLE

It felt like I had just closed my eyes before I heard some eejit throwing stones against my bedroom window. I checked the clock radio: 6:06 a.m. Goddamn it. If this was Cameron again I'd go out there and shoot the fat fuck.

I opened the curtains and looked down into the front garden.

It was Matty and another constable in their full dress uniforms.

Oh dear.

I went downstairs and opened the front door.

"They've been phoning you for the last hour," Matty said. Not only was he in his dress uniform but he had shaved and the ever-present cheeky grin was gone from his face.

"Am I in trouble?"

"What?"

"Who have I pissed off now? The Prime Minister? The Bishop of Rome?"

"It's not about you, boss. It's Sergeant Burke."

"What about him?"

"Accidentally shot himself last night. Dead."

"Jesus! Are you sure?"

"Quite sure."

"Fuck. How?"

"Accidental discharge of his personal sidearm," Matty said, as if he was reading it from a newspaper.

I looked at the other constable.

The other constable smelled of church and breath mints. He seemed about fourteen.

"He topped himself?" I asked Matty in an undertone.

"I wouldn't know," Matty replied.

Of course, it was well known that the RUC had the highest suicide rate of any police force in Europe, but you didn't expect someone in your parish to go off and do himself in.

"I'll get changed, you lads come in. Who wants coffee?"

I made toast and coffee and shaved and got my dress uniform out of the dry-cleaning wrapper.

We drove to the cop shop where the mood was blacker than the Dulux matt fucking black.

I found Inspector McCallister, who was always on top of things.

"What happened, Jim?" I asked him.

He was pale and his breath reeked of coffee and whisky.

"Neighbor heard the shot and called it in. I was duty officer so I went out myself. Me and Constable Tory. He was in the living room. Gunshot wound to the side of the head."

"Did he have any family?"

"He was divorced. Two grown-up kids."

"Definitely suicide?"

"Keep your fucking voice down, Duffy! We won't use that word in here. When the fucking internals come round asking questions, we'll all say that Burke was a first-class officer with no fucking problems, all right?"

I understood. Suicide invalidated any potential life insurance policy, but an "accidental discharge of a firearm," was exactly that . . .

"Just between ourselves, then?" I asked in a lower tone.

"His kids are both over the water. His parents are dead. His brother's in South Africa. There was nothing for him here," McCallister said.

"I suppose he'd been drinking?"

"He'd been drinking. I'm sure his blood alcohol level will be off the fucking chart. But that wasn't the clincher . . ."

He beckoned me to follow him into his office. He closed the door, sat me down and poured me some evil hooch in a plastic cup.

"What was the clincher?" I asked

"There were three bullets lying on the living-room coffee table."

"He'd taken them out?"

"Aye. He'd taken three out, spun the chamber, pointed the gun at his head and pulled the fucking trigger . . . He'd done that before more than once. That's why the wife had moved out."

"Christ Almighty."

"Fucking stupid, isn't it? Doing the IRA's job for them."

"Aye."

"Poor bastard. Why didn't he go to Michael Pollock?" I said.

"Who's that?"

"The divisional shrink."

McCallister gave me a queer look. Why did I know the name of the divisional shrink? And why would anyone go to a stranger to talk about their problems?

"Do you know why we're in this get up?" I said, pointing at our full dress uniforms.

"The Chief Constable's coming down to visit."

"You're messing with me."

"Nope."

"The Chief fucking Constable?"

"He thinks there's something rotten in Denmark."

"There is something rotten in Denmark."

"Aye well, we're to put on a brave face and reassure him that Carrickfergus RUC is a happy ship."

I smiled at that. No RUC station I had ever visited in Ulster had been a happy ship. In the ones along the border the pathology was a constant, palpable terror that any moment Libyan-made rockets were gonna come pouring in from a field in Eire; in the ones in Belfast you feared a riot or a mortar attack; in the quieter, less heavily defended country stations it could be anything from an ambush by an entire IRA active service unit to a car bomb parked down the street. And no peeler ever felt safe at home or in his car or at the flicks or at a restaurant or anywhere. There was never any down-time. Blowing your brains out seemed a reasonable enough way out.

And although Burke wasn't that popular a bloke, he was a familiar face and before he became a really heavy drinker had been a decent enough peeler.

I went into the main incident room. The air, like the weather, was foul. Some of the female reservists were crying.

There was nothing I could say or do. I went down to the evidence room to see if I could liberate some grass or ciggies but the duty officer was a God-botherer called Fredericks who wouldn't countenance any untoward shit.

Back up to my office by the windows. A cup of tea. A smoke.

McCrabban knocked on the door. He was in his dress greens too.

"Shame, isn't it?" he said.

"Aye, it's a crying shame."

Crabbie looked embarrassed, was going to say something, couldn't bring himself to, excused himself and left. Did he want me to put in a good word for him about the sergeantcy vacancy? Probably, but with these Presbyterians you could never tell anything.

I stared out the window for ten minutes, watching boats chug up and down the filthy lough.

Another door knock and Chief Inspector Brennan came in.

Full duds and a shave.

"Put your cock away, Duffy, the Chief Constable's on his way. I don't know what we did to deserve this, but there it is," he said.

"Well, sir, it's not really about us, it's—"

"The next promotion cycle I was going to be made superintendent. You can't have a chief inspector running a cop shop like Carrick. Superintendent they were going to make me. That's all over now. Fucking Burke and his fucking games. Fucker. Poor dumb fucker . . . Have you got a drink, Duffy?"

"I might have some vodka under the—"

"Better not, Hermon's a tough nut. Jesus! What a cock up!"

He left the office so that he could wail to someone else.

I watched the clock and around eleven the Chief Constable did indeed come down. He landed by helicopter on the Barn Field and drove to the police station in a convoy of three police Land Rovers.

Not exactly low key.

Still, Jack Hermon was a popular chief constable of the RUC. He had fought Thatcher tooth and nail for better pay and conditions, he had encouraged the recruitment of Catholic officers, he had sacked the worst of the Protestant sectarian arseholes and he had ended the use of psychological and physical torture at the Castlereagh Holding Centre (counterproductive and unreliable, the reports said). The RUC still had many many problems with bigoted, incompetent, and lazy officers but Hermon had done a decent job in only a short time and for his efforts he had recently been knighted by the Queen.

His entrance was all drama.

The bodyguard cops came into the station first, looking tough. Big guys with 'taches and submachine guns.

Then Sir Jack with his familiar peasant features, red potato face and squat frame. His uniform looked too tight for him.

Chief Inspector Brennan saluted.

They shook hands and exchanged words.

Brennan introduced his senior officers, in other words Inspector McCallister, myself and Sergeant Quinn.

Sir Jack shook our hands and told Brennan to gather everyone ("even the fucking tea ladies") in the downstairs conference room.

His speech was boilerplate stuff that didn't even attempt to deal with the "accidental discharge of a firearm" cover story. Instead it was: Morale . . . The importance of talking to people about your problems . . . Optimism . . . Things looked bad now, but in fact we were winning the fight against terrorism . . .

Maybe some of the reservists were impressed, but no one else was.

Afterwards we had tea and biscuits and a carrot cake that Carol baked herself.

We were supposed to mingle with the Chief Constable and feel free to ask him anything. I hung back near the photocopier with Matty and McCrabban, trying not to catch his eye. It didn't do any good. After a minute or two he made an obvious beeline for me. Crabbie and Matty scattered like wildebeest before a lioness.

"Get back here," I whispered.

"You're on your own, mate," Matty hissed, before making a break for the bogs.

Hermon offered his hand again. He was wearing leather gloves now, getting ready to leave.

"You're Duffy, isn't that right?" Sir Jack asked.

"Yes, sir."

"Wanted to talk to you before I go."

"Me personally, sir?"

"Aye."

"Uhm, we can go into my office if you want."

"Lead on."

I walked up to my office and closed the door.

He didn't sit or comment on the sea view.

"I've had two calls about you in two weeks. Two calls about a lowly detective inspector. You must be something pretty special, eh?"

"No, sir, I'm—"

"Do you have any idea how busy I am, Duffy?"

"I imagine that you're ver—"

"Damn right I am. And let me tell you something, sonny Jim. I am not afraid to stick my neck out for my men."

"I've never heard anything different."

"Ian Paisley? I'm not afraid of Paisley. I personally arrested that loudmouth. To a man, the politicians of this sorry, benighted, God-abandoned land are rabble-rousing scum."

"Yes, sir."

"But when I get calls complaining about the actions of one of my officers, calls directly to me, I have to take an interest, don't I?"

"Yes, sir."

"The United States Consul General in Belfast called me up and said that one of my officers was hectoring one of his officials. Do you know who that officer was?"

"Sir, I can assure you that—"

"And then I get a call from the Right Honorable Ian Paisley MP, saying that one of his oldest friends, a certain Sir Harry McAlpine, was also getting a bollocking from a bolshy young detective. Can you guess who that detective was?"

"Sir, if I can explain . . ."

Hermon got real close and I got a zoom in on his lined face, that cheap and cheerful Mallorca suntan, the tired, angry, bloodshot eyes.

"I looked at your personnel file, Duffy. You've got a medal from the Queen and you're a Catholic to boot! I suppose you think that that makes you immune. I suppose you think you're Clint Eastwood. I suppose you think you can do whatever you like?"

"Not at all, sir, if I could just—"

"Let me tell you how this place works, Duffy. It's a tribal society. Clans. Warlords. You think we're living in 1982? We're living in 1582. You can't go around ruffling the feathers of the big chieftains. Do you get me?"

"Chieftains, feathers, no ruffling, sir."

"Are you making fun of me, son?"

"No, sir!"

"Good. Because you need me. And if I'm going to back you up against them, I need to know that our masters in London are going to back me up."

"Of course, sir."

"Sir Harry McAlpine is a wheeler and dealer. He's got land here and there. And he's in favor at Stormont at the moment. He has influential friends and he has the ear of the ministry."

Aye, and he's also a big bluffing bastard mortgaged up the wazoo and to quote his sister-in-law, as poor as a church mouse, I did not say.

Hermon looked at me and held my gaze and waited until I looked away first, but I wasn't going to give the bastard the satisfaction. He may have come here in a helicopter, he may have been on the blower to Mrs. Thatcher last night, but his breath smelled of Cookstown sausages.

He nodded and finally *he* looked away. He examined my office for the first time, impressed by the view out the window and perhaps by its un-Presbyterian messiness. "So," he said, after a pause, "where do you keep the good whisky?"

20 THE UDR BASE

The media bought the tale about the "accidental shooting"—whether the life insurance company dicks would was another story but that, thank Christ, was not my concern. The funeral was on a Sunday at a small Scottish Calvinist Church up the Antrim coast. The ceremony was alien to me: singing of Psalms, prayers, nothing about the dead man. Rain and sea spray lashed the unadorned church windows and there was no heating of any kind.

A tall, Raymond Massey-like church elder said: "Whoever dwells in the shelter of the Most High will rest in the shadow of the Almighty. I will say of the Lord that He is my refuge and my fortress, my God, in whom I trust. Surely He will save you from the fowler's snare and from the deadly pestilence. You will not fear the terror of night, nor the arrow that flies by day, nor the pestilence that stalks in the darkness, nor the plague that destroys at midday. A thousand may fall at your side, ten thousand at your right hand, but it will not come near you. You will only observe with your eyes and see the punishment of the wicked."

This was definitely my kind of god but unfortunately it hadn't quite worked out that way for Sergeant Burke. At the graveside, a divisional chief super gave a eulogy mentioning Burke's years of devoted service. Of course there were no shots over the coffin or anything like that. You save that kind of thing for the Provos.

The fall-out from Burke's death was immediate. Chief Inspector Brennan was not promoted, but to keep the shifts working effectively we now needed a new sergeant. Someone with a head for detail who could help keep the place level. I knew that this was my opportunity to push for Crabbie. If they promoted him to acting sergeant now it wouldn't matter how he did on his exam as long as he wasn't a total disaster. I lobbied hard for him but I was a lone voice as everyone else wanted weasely Kenny Dalziel from clerical who could run the admin that everyone else hated.

I told Crabbie after the meeting. "They're promoting Dalziel."

He was gutted. "What have I done wrong?"

"Nothing. I'm sorry, mate. They don't know anything. I mean, of course they're going to promote a clerk like Dalziel, not someone who actually, you know, goes out and solves crimes."

The day ended.

The next began.

The week went by like that.

Rain and no leads.

On the Thursday we learned that Bill O'Rourke's body had been returned to America. His funeral was at Arlington where he got the full honor guard, folded flag treatment. We were told that his dead wife's sister had surfaced out of the woodwork to claim his house in Massachusetts and his apartment in Florida. I asked the local police to interview her and they did and a Lieutenant Dawson sent me a terse fax stating that there was nothing suspicious about her.

The days lengthened. The Royal Navy Task Force continued its southward journey. On Saturday morning a masked man armed with a shotgun robbed the Northern Bank in High Street Carrickfergus and got away with nine hundred pounds. The sum was insignificant, no one was hurt and I wasn't going to make it a priority until Brennan summoned me to his office.

"What's your progress on the O'Rourke murder?"

"It's about the same as it was when we talked last w—"

"Get on this robbery, then. Your full team. It's about time you started pulling your weight around here, Duffy!"

Brennan had aged. His hair was going from grey to white and he looked flabby. God knows where he was staying now. What was bothering him? The marriage? Being passed over? Something else? I'd never know. Crabbie had gone through troubles with his missus last year and had never said one word about it.

I investigated the robbery and of course there were no witnesses, but an informant our agent handler knew called Jackdaw told us some good information.

A guy called Gus Plant had bought everyone a round of drinks in the Borough Arms on Saturday night and boasted to everyone that he was going to get himself a new motor. Crabbie and I got a warrant and went to Gus's house in Castlemara Estate. He'd had the stolen money under his bed.

It was pathetic.

We cuffed him and his wife screamed at him all the way outside. She'd told him that that was the first place the cops would look and he hadn't listened because he never listened.

"Prison'll be good for you, mate. Anything to get away from that racket," I told him in the back of the Rover.

It wasn't *The Mystery of the Yellow Room* but it was a case solved and it kept the Chief off our backs for a couple of days.

I called Tony McIlroy and asked him about the Dougherty murder.

For a moment he was baffled.

"We yellowed that file. It's going nowhere," he said.

"You interviewed the widow?"

"Aye, I did. You didn't tell me she was a good-looking lass."

"And?"

"And what?"

"And what are your impressions? Did she have something to do with Dougherty's death?"

"Fuck, no."

"That's it? A simple no? She had no alibi."

"Or motive, or weapon, or cojones, or experience . . . Hey, I've another call, I'll call you back."

He didn't call me back.

Days.

Nights.

Rain through the kitchen window. Thin daffodils. Fragile lilacs. Gulls flopping sideways into the wind. An achromatic vacancy to the sky.

I canvassed for witnesses, tried to nail down Bill O'Rourke's last movements, but nobody knew anything. Nobody had seen him after he left the Dunmurry Country Inn.

One morning the Chief Inspector had us up to his office. "Lads, listen, I'm putting the name and number of the divisional psychiatrist up on the noticeboard. I suggest you tell the lads to avail themselves of his services. The bottle is not the answer," he said, finishing a double whisky chaser.

April marched on.

We put the O'Rourke case in a yellow binder, which meant that it was open but not actively being pursued.

This represented yet another personal defeat. Half a dozen murder investigations under my belt and not one of them had resulted in a successful prosecution.

This time we hadn't even found out who'd done it.

A man mourning his wife had come on holiday to Ireland and someone had poisoned him, chopped up the body, frozen him and dumped him like trash.

"It's sickening," I told Matty and McCrabban over a hot whisky at the Dobbins.

"It's part of the job, mate," Crabbie said philosophically. "You'll drive yourself mad if you're after a hundred per cent clearance rate."

He was right about that, but wasn't it also possible that I just wasn't a very good copper? Perhaps I lacked focus, or attention to detail, or maybe I just didn't have the right stuff to be a really good detective. Or even a half-decent detective.

On a wet, frigid, Monday morning we got a call about a break-in at the rugby club on the Woodburn Road. Trophies had been stolen. The thieves had come in through a skylight. None of us could face going up onto the rugby club roof in this weather so we drew straws. Matty and I got the short ones.

We drove up the Woodburn Road, climbed a rickety ladder, got on the roof and gathered evidence while rain came down in buckets and a caretaker kept saying "It's not safe up there, be careful, now."

We heroically dusted for prints and found nothing. A pigeon shat on Matty's back. We climbed back down, wrote a description of the missing articles and said we'd put the word out. We had a courtesy pint in the club and we were about to drive home when I noticed that the rugby club was right next to Carrickfergus UDR base.

The UDR barracks was even more heavily defended than the police station. A twenty-foot-high fence topped with coils of razor wire was in front of a thick blast-wall made of reinforced concrete.

It was an ugly structure: utilitarian, grim, Soviet. I had never been inside. You'd think that there were would be a lot of cooperation between the police and the UDR The Ulster Defence Regiment was the locally recruited regiment of the British Army and there were often joint RUC/UDR patrols, but in fact we largely operated in different worlds. We seldom shared intelligence and what they actually did apart from the odd patrol or operation on the border was a mystery. A lot of drinking, snooker and darts, I imagine. We regarded ourselves as a highly professional modern police force operating in extremis—the UDR was, at best, a panicky response to the Troubles. The Troubles was their entire *raison d'être* and if the war ever ended we would still be here but they, presumably, would have to be disbanded. Were there good UDR officers and men? Of course, but were there a lot of wasters, too? Yes. And bigots, more than likely. These days the police were getting up to twenty per cent Catholic representation, which compared favorably to the forty per cent of Northern Ireland's population who identified ourselves as Roman Catholic on the census. The UDR didn't publish its Catholic membership, but it was rumored to be less than five per cent. Of course the IRA made it their number one priority to kill Catholic UDR men, but even so, the regiment had more than a whiff of sectarianism about it. And it wasn't just the Nationalist papers in Belfast who criticized it—stories about collusion between the UDR and Protestant terror groups had appeared in the mainstream English press, too.

We were all on the same side, but if we ever wanted to get cooperation from the Catholic community we coppers had to hold ourselves somewhat aloof.

"Where are you going?" Matty asked.

"We never checked out Captain McAlpine, did we?"

"Oh Jesus, this again?" Matty said.

"Can you think of anything better to do?"

Matty thought for a second or two. "No, actually, I can't."

We drove to the fortified guard post and showed our warrant cards. A soldier with full body armor, holding an SLR, gave us a suspicious look and then waved us through.

We parked in the visitors lot and went through another checkpoint at the base's entrance.

"What's the nature of your business, gentlemen?" the guard asked us. Big Derry lad with a black beard.

"We need to speak to your commanding officer about one of your men. It's a confidential matter," I said.

He didn't like that, but what could he do? We were all supposed to be pulling for the same team.

"You're lucky, lads. The Colonel's here. I think he's down on the range. You'll have to leave your weapons, gentlemen. Only authorized personnel are allowed to carry firearms inside the base."

We left our guns and got directions to the range.

We walked down dreary concrete corridors illuminated only by buzzing strip lights. There were no windows and the sole decorations were posters on the wall warning about the dangers of booby traps, honey traps and other IRA tricks.

The honey trap posters showed an attractive blonde woman leading an unsuspecting squaddie into a terraced house with the caption "Who knows what's waiting for you on the other side of the door?"

The range was on a lower level deep beneath the ground.

We knocked on the No Entry sign and a "range master" opened the door a crack. He was a sergeant carrying a machine gun. We explained our business with the Colonel.

"I'm afraid you'll have to wait until Lieutenant Colonel Clavert is finished. You need a range pass to get in here and only Colonel Clavert or Captain Dunleavy can issue those. Captain Dunleavy's not on the base at the moment."

We waited outside on uncomfortable plastic chairs.

The sound of gunfire was muffled and distant like it is in dreams.

Finally the Colonel appeared. He was dressed in fatigues. A tall man, with jet black hair, a trim moustache and large, round glasses.

He turned out to be English, which was something of a surprise. I introduced Matty and myself and explained why we had come by:

"We're looking into the murder of Captain McAlpine and we wanted to ask a few questions about him."

"I wondered when you chaps would finally appear."

"We're the first police officers to come here asking about McAlpine's death?"

"Yes. And it's been a while, hasn't it? It was December when poor Martin copped it. Come with me to my office."

The office was another windowless bunker.

Lime-green gloss plaint covering cinder blocks. A series of framed pictures of castles. A large wooden desk, pictures of wife and kids, a Newton's cradle. The whole thing looked artificial, like a movie set.

Colonel Clavert offered us tea and cigarettes. We accepted both and a young soldier went off to make the former.

"Did you enjoy the range?" I asked conversationally.

"Oh, yes! It's wonderfully relaxing. A friend of mine in the Irish Guards up at Bessbrook sent me down a batch of AK-47s they found in a weapons cache. We had them cleaned and oiled, found some ammo. Have you ever shot one of those? Ghastly things. But fun! Sergeant O'Hanlon proved himself something of a master. Trick is short bursts. Full auto is a disaster."

I could see Matty rolling his eyes to my left.

The soldier came in with tea and biscuits. When he'd gone I got down to business.

"So, Captain McAlpine?"

Clavert nodded.

"Fourth man we've lost since I took command here. Such a shame. First-class fellow. We can't replace him. Not with the riff raff we, uh . . ." he began and dried up quickly when he realized that he was talking out of school.

He went to a filing cabinet, and took out a file. He sat back down at his desk, thumbed through the file, read it, and closed it again.

"Can I take a look?" I asked.

Clavert shook his head. "Actually, old boy, I'm afraid not. We do not have a code-sharing arrangement with the RUC and this file has been marked SECRET."

He had a young, open face, did Colonel Clavert, but now it assumed a pinched, irritated expression. He rubbed his moustache, but didn't look the least embarrassed.

"I'm investigating the man's murder," I said.

"Be that as it may, you can't see his file without authorization from the Secretary of State for Northern Ireland."

"Why? What's so bloody secret? Was he on a death squad or something? Going around shooting suspected IRA men in the middle of the fucking night?" I said, in a silly bout of frustration that I immediately regretted.

Clavert sighed. "Don't be so dramatic, Inspector, it's nothing like that . . . And if it was something like that, do you think I'd still have the file in a little cardboard folder in my office?"

"So, what is then?" I asked

He lit another cigarette and said nothing. He smiled and shook his head. Not only was the bastard disrupting the investigation, but I was losing face in front of Matty.

"This is a murder investigation," I said again.

"Yes, Inspector. But I assure you that nothing's amiss. We conducted our own inquiry into Captain McAlpine's death. His killing was a random IRA murder. Nothing more."

"What? Who conducted this inquiry of yours?"

"The military police, of course."

"The military police? I see. And did you pass on your findings to us?"

"No."

"Why not?"

"Because it was an internal investigation."

"This is why the IRA is going to win, because the left hand doesn't know what the fucking right hand is doing," I muttered.

"I don't like that kind of talk. It shows a bad attitude," the Colonel said.

I tapped the desk.

"Listen, mate, I won't need to go to the Secretary of State for Northern Ireland. I'm investigating the murder of an American citizen. Captain McAlpine's death is only an adjunct to a wider inquiry. The Consul General has been on the blower asking about this case and his boss is the United States Ambassador to the Court of St James. There's this little thing going on in the Falklands Islands at the moment, you may have heard about it, and Her Majesty's Government is doing everything it can to keep the Yanks fucking sweet, so if a call comes into your office this afternoon it won't be from the Secretary of State for Northern Ireland, it'll be from the fucking Prime Minister and she won't be pleased with you, I promise you that."

Colonel Clavert's thin, supercilious smile evaporated.

"Very well. I can let you read this, but I can't allow you to make notes, photocopy or remove it from this office."

He sighed and passed the file across the desk before continuing, "You'll understand my caution when I tell you that Captain McAlpine was our district intelligence officer. He ran our informers."

I understood. The UDR had its own network of informers and McAlpine was the man who was in charge of paying them and assessing their information. Of course the RUC had its own completely separate list of informers and it was rumored that MI5 had yet another network of its own too. A really good tout could be getting three paychecks for the same piece of information.

I read the file carefully. It was low grade stuff about arms dumps, suspected IRA men, suspected UVF men, suspected drugs smugglers. The payments were small: fifty quid, a hundred quid. There was nothing dramatic here. I passed it to Matty. I could tell that he wasn't impressed either. I read it again just to be on the safe side and then I spotted something. The penultimate entry about a week before McAlpine's murder was from an informant, codenamed Woodbine, who "had seen a suspicious character hanging round the Dunmurry DeLorean factory carpark." For this information McAlpine had paid Woodbine the princely sum of twenty pounds. I pointed out the word Dunmurry to Matty and he nodded.

"Who's Woodbine?" I asked, passing the file back.

"One moment," Colonel Clavert said.

He went to the filing cabinet and opened another file. "Woodbine, let me see, Waverly, Winston, Woodbine. Ah, yes, a chap called Douggie Preston."

"Address?" I asked.

"11 Drumhill Road, Carrickfergus."

We thanked the Colonel, stubbed out our cigarettes and were about to leave when he asked us if we were going to interview the widow McAlpine in the course of our inquiries.

"We might," I said. "Why?"

"Because she still hasn't picked up Martin's stuff and it's been here four months now."

"What stuff?"

"From his locker. His dress uniform. A pair of training shoes. There's some money. A cricket bat, of all things. I've called her several times about it."

I looked at Matty. "Aye, we can take them down to her."

We drove out of the UDR base into a heavy downpour.

"I suppose we're going to Islandmagee now?"

"Let's try Mr. Preston first."

Drumhill Road was in the ironically named Sunnylands Housing Estate—one of the worst in Carrick. Red-brick and cinderblock terraces, mostly packed with unemployed refugees from Belfast. Lots of kids running around barefoot, burnt-out cars, shopping trolleys and rubbish everywhere. This was RHC territory—the Red Hand Commando—a particularly violent and bloody offshoot of the slightly more responsible UDA.

Preston lived in an end terrace. There was a smashed row boat in the front garden, a pile of old furniture, what looked a lot like an aircraft engine and a little girl about four in a filthy frock playing by herself with a headless Barbie doll.

"So this is how the other half lives," Matty muttered.

I rang the doorbell and when that didn't work I knocked.

"Who is it?" a woman asked from inside.

"The police," I said.

"I've told you. We do not sell acid. Never have, never will!"

"We're not here about that."

"What do you want?"

"We're looking for Douggie."

She opened the door. She was mid-forties but looked seventy. Grey hair, teeth missing, running to fat. Her fingers were stained with nicotine smoke.

"Have you found him?" she asked.

"We're looking for him," Matty said.

She shook her head sadly. "Aye, aren't we all."

"How long has been missing?" I asked.

"Since November," she said.

"No word at all?"

"No."

"He lived at home?"

"Aye."

"No girlfriend, anything like that?"

"Nobody steady like. He was a shy boy, was Douggie."

Past tense. She knew he was dead.

"When was the last time that anybody saw him?"

"He was down the North Gate on November twenty-seventh, having a wee drink, said he was away home to watch the snooker. That was the last we heard tell of him."

I wrote the information down in my book.

"They've topped him, haven't they?" she said.

"I have no idea."

"Aye, they've topped him. God knows why. He was a good boy, was Douggie, a very good boy."

"Did he have a job?"

"No. He was at Shorts for a year. He was a trained fitter but he got laid off. He tried to get into the DeLorean factory in Dunmurry, but they had their pick of the crop. He went back several times looking to get in, but jobs is scarce, aren't they?"

"They are indeed," Matty said.

"Dunmurry, eh?"

"Aye, but there were ten applicants for every one job. Wee Douggie had no chance."

"He didn't know anyone up there?"

"No. More's the pity."

"Have there been any strangers hanging around? Anyone asking about him?"

"No."

We stood there on the porch while the girl behind us in the garden started to make explosion noises. Matty tried a few more lines of approach but the lady had nothing.

"Well, if we hear anything, we'll certainly be in touch," I said.

"Thank you," she said, and added, "he was a good boy."

21: FIFTEENS

Matty started bitching about another "bloody pointless trip to Islandmagee" so I ditched him at the police station and pulled in to Bentham's shop to get some more smokes. I grabbed a packet of Marlboros from the shelf. Jeff wasn't there, so running the joint was his daughter, Sonia, a sixth-former still in her school uniform. She was chewing bubblegum and reading something called *Interzone Magazine*.

"Where's your da?" I asked her.

"I dunno," she said, without looking up.

"Are you minding the shop?"

"Looks like it, don't it?"

"What's news?"

She put the magazine down and looked at me. "Philip K. Dick is dead."

"Who's that?" I asked.

She sighed dramatically. "That'll be two pound for the fags."

"Your da gives me a policeman's discount," I said, with a smile.

"Me da's a buck eejit, then, isn't he? About the only person guaranteed not to kneecap you is a peeler. That'll be two pound for the fags and if you don't like it you can fuck off."

I paid the two pounds and was about to drive down to Islandmagee when an incident report came in on the blower about two drunks fighting outside the hospital on Taylor's Avenue. It wasn't a detective's job but it was my manor so I told the controller that I'd take care of it. I was there in two minutes. I knew both men. Jimmy McConkey was a fitter at Harland and Wolff until he'd been laid off, Charlie Blair was a hydraulic engineer at ICI until it closed. "For shame. What are you lads doing, blitzed out of your minds, at this time of the day?" I asked them.

Charlie attempted to shove me and while he was off balance Jimmy pushed him to the ground.

With difficulty I got them both in the back of the Land Rover and took them home to their long-suffering wives in Victoria Estate, where the women were using a cameo appearance by the sun to hang clothes from lines and chat over the fences. The men behaved themselves when they got out. We had gone from the adolescent male world of pushing and shoving to the feminine universe of washing and talk and order. There would be no more hijinks from them today.

There was no point writing the incident up. It was nothing. It was just another sad little playlet in the great opera of misery all around us.

I got back in the Land Rover and drove to Islandmagee in a foul mood.

There was a gate across the private road. It was chained up and I couldn't break it without causing trouble for myself so I parked the Land Rover and walked to Mrs. McAlpine's cottage carrying Martin's stuff in an Adidas bag.

Cora barked at me, giving Mrs. McAlpine plenty of warning.

She opened the door gingerly.

There was blood on her hands.

"Hi," I said.

"Hello."

"Is that blood?"

"Aye."

"What are you doing?" I asked.

"This whole question question question thing is very tiresome."

"Bad cop habit."

"I'm butchering a ewe, if you must know," she said.

"Can I come in?"

"All right."

Her hair was redder today. Curlier. I wondered if she'd dyed it or was that a reaction to sunlight and being outdoors. She looked healthier too, ruddier. You would never call her Rubenesque but she'd put on weight and it suited her. Perhaps she was finally getting over Martin's death. Looking after herself a little better.

I went inside carrying the green army shoulder bag.

"Do you mind if I finish up?"

"Not at all."

We walked to the "washhouse" at the back of the farm where a sheep carcass lay spread-eagled on a wooden table. She began sawing and butchering it into various cuts of meat.

"This'll last you a while. Do you have a freezer?"

"Harry does."

"I'd help you carry it over, but I'm supposed to stay away from your brother-in-law. I got a shot across my bows from the Chief Constable no less."

She laughed at that. "My God. I suppose his Masonic contacts are the only thing left in his arsenal."

She cut long strings of sinewy meat from the bone and trimmed the fat and threw it into a box marked "lard."

Thwack went the cleaver into bone. *Thug* went the cleaver into meat and fat.

"So, uh, let me tell you why I'm here today. I was down at Carrickfergus UDR base and they asked me to take you some of Martin's things. I brought them in the bag out there."

"You shouldn't have."

"It was no trouble. Interesting place, that UDR base. Bit grim."

"I wouldn't know. I never went there."

"Like I say, pretty grim. Hard job, too, I expect," I said.

She hacksawed off the sheep's head and put it in a Tupperware box. She looked at me.

"What are you getting at, Inspector?"

"Did Martin ever talk to you about his work?"

"Sometimes."

"He was an intelligence officer. Did you know that?"

"Of course."

"Did he ever talk to you about specific cases?"

"Hardly ever. He was very discreet."

"He ever mention the name Woodbine, or talk about Dunmurry or the DeLorean factory?"

"Not that I recall."

"Are you sure?"

"If he did, it didn't make an impression."

She finished butchering the aged ewe and I helped her bag the meat. We washed up and went inside the cottage.

"I was baking today. You want a fifteen while I put the kettle on?"

"Sounds delicious."

"Wait till you taste them. My mother was the baker."

"Your mother's passed on?"

"Aye, passed on to the Costa del Sol," she said with a laugh. She brushed a loose strand of hair from her face. She caught me looking at her. She held my gaze a second longer than she should have.

"It's ages since I had a fifteen. How do you make them?"

She laughed. "Well, when I say baking, that's a bit of a fib, isn't it? The flour's only for rolling them on the board."

"What do you do?"

"They're so easy. Fifteen digestive biscuits, crushed, fifteen walnuts, finely chopped, fifteen maraschino cherries, fifteen colored marshmallows, a can of condensed milk. Flour and flaked coconut. Mix everything except the coconut. Roll into a ball. Divide the ball into two and make two log rolls."

"And then what?"

"Scatter a chopping board with flour and the coconut."

"Something about a fridge, isn't there?"

She smiled. "Roll the sausages in floury coconut and then wrap each log tightly with plastic wrap and refrigerate for two hours. Couldn't be simpler. My secret ingredient is Smarties or, for Harry's friend, M&Ms, which is the American equivalent."

"The fifteens are for Harry too?"

"You have to keep the landlord happy don't you?"

"I suppose so."

"They're for a friend of his. An American lady."

"A rich American lady? A potential bride?"

"I didn't ask."

She handed me a plate of the treats. "I must warn you," she said. "They're sweet."

I tried one and they were way too sweet for my blood. They made your head hurt. Emma came back a minute later with tea.

"Delicious," I said.

She smiled. Sipped her tea. Didn't eat.

She looked at the bag full of Martin's gear.

After a pause, she said: "You couldn't put it in the cupboard under the stairs, could you? I don't want to deal with it just at the moment."

"I forgot that you told me that you threw all Martin's stuff out. I'm sorry. I shouldn't have brought this."

"It's okay."

I put the bag in the cupboard and stood there awkwardly. "Well, I suppose I'll head on then."

"Yes."

I cleared my throat.

"Are you doing all right?" I asked.

"What do you mean?"

"Moneywise, you know?"

"Yes. I sold a dozen spring lambs and that cleared some of the debts and I'm supposed to

get the compensation money by the end of the month. Of course, that's what they've been saying since January . . ."

"Will you stay here when the money comes?"

"I can't afford to go anywhere else, can I?"

"Your parents in Spain?"

"That place? It's the living death down there. No thanks. What would I do with my time?"

"What do you do with your time here?"

"That is the question."

Silence.

I watched a drip burrow its way through the thatching onto the living-room floor.

"All right, well, I suppose this is the ... uh ..."

"Yes, Inspector Duffy, I suppose it is," she said.

I went outside.

The Land Rover back to Carrick.

Sea spray along the lough shore.

Driving rain.

Her manner hadn't been that encouraging. In fact there was a distinct coldness near the end, and yet I couldn't help but feel that there was something bubbling beneath the surface there.

Chinese takeaway for dinner. Pot from the shed out back.

I smoked the joint in the shed with the door open and the rain coming in.

I went inside, put on *Age of Plastic* by The Buggles which I snapped up for 2p at a jumble sale. I made myself a pint of vodka and lime juice. I drank and listened. It was a very bad album.

I watched the TV news: incidents all over Ulster: bomb scares and disruption to rail and bus services, an incendiary fire at the Door Store, a policeman shot in Enniskillen, a prisoner officer severely injured in a mercury tilt bomb in Strabane. I watched the Final Thought on UTV: a cheerful long-haired evangelist insisted that God was merciful and just and cared about his flock.

Midnight. It was so cold I lit the paraffin heater.

The phone rang. I got out of bed, wrapped myself in the duvet, tripped on the blanket and nearly went down the stairs head first. My face banged into the side wall. Blood was pouring out of my nose. The phone kept ringing. *Never get the phone after midnight, Duffy, you dumbass.*

I picked it up. "Yeah, what is it now?"

"You are not the detective I thought you were," a voice said.

The voice from the note. The English chick. "Why's that?" I said.

There was silence.

"I was the one who left you the note."

"Yeah, I know. You stand out. We don't get many English birds round here, do we?"

"I suppose not."

"Who sprung you from Whitehead Police Station? A couple of your mates?"

She didn't reply.

"Listen, sweetie, you're not cute and you're not funny. I don't know if you're a spook, or a reporter, or a student, or a player looking to make trouble, or what you are exactly, but pick on someone else, okay? It's enough to make me want to take my name out of the phone book."

"Perhaps you should."

"Aye, but it'd be a shame to do that, I'm the only Duffy in Carrick in there," I said.

More silence. I was weary of this. "What the fuck are you calling me up for? Why don't you just tell me what you've bloody got, if you've really got anything."

"I need someone who's good. I thought you were good. I looked you up. I read those articles about you, but you're not good."

"Not good? I almost nailed you, you dozy cunt."

"Almost doesn't count for much."

"You were shitting it, darling, admit it. You were lifted by a stop and search unit—and them boys couldn't find a fat man at a Santa Claus convention. You must have been well surprised."

"And you must have been surprised to find me gone."

"Big deal. You pull the wool over the eyes of some twenty-year-old part-time country copper. Big deal. You don't impress me."

"And my note?"

"Your note? Fuck that! We're too busy with a civil war in our laps for shite like that. We don't have time for notes or fucking games. You want to try the San Francisco Police Department and spin them lines about the Zodiac killer, or get the Ripper unit at the South Yorkshire PD."

"Maybe you're right. I shouldn't have tried to lead you. I set you a test and you failed it. I assumed that if I could find the evidence you'd be able to find it too."

"What evidence?"

"It's not my job. I was trying to help *you*, Duffy. I wanted to prod you, not give it all to you on a plate."

"Give it to me on a plate."

"No, you were right. I should have said nothing. If you'd found it, it would have made things worse for you, more than likely. I'm sorry to have troubled you, Duffy."

"Who are you?"

"You know who I am."

"I really don't."

"Then you certainly are not the detective I thought you were."

"I'm not the detective anyone thinks I am. I'm a plodding copper— no better, no worse than anyone else."

"I see that now."

"Look, love, it's late, I'm tired, do us both a favor and don't bloody call again."

"I won't."

"Good."

She hung up. The dial tone continued and then it began going *beep beep beep*. I put the phone back on its crook. And I was too fed up with it all to even call Special Branch and get them to put a tap on my line.

22: I'VE SEEN THINGS YOU PEOPLE WOULDN'T BELIEVE

Two a.m: A group of drunks coming down the street singing: "We are, we are, we are the Billy Boys! We are, we are, we are the Billy Boys. We're up to our necks in fenian blood and we're coming back for more. We are the Billy Billy Boys."

I was never going to sleep this night.

I went downstairs and grabbed an encyclopedia and read it over a bowl of cornflakes.

I had a cup of coffee, dressed in jeans, sneakers and a sweater, put on my raincoat and went for a walk around the Estate. I picked up my new Sony Radio Walkman and tuned it to the BBC World Service.

Black clouds. Rain. Sleet on the high plateau.

Bombings in West Belfast and Derry.

Rocket attacks on police stations along the border.

War news.

The other war.

In the South Atlantic.

I walked down to the lough and sat on the beach.

I watched the planes going both ways on the Trans-At.

I got cold.

At six I went into the station.

Brennan was there already, reading the newspapers in the incident room. He hadn't shaven. He looked unkempt. There was no point asking him what the fuck was going on in his life, but I wanted to talk to someone.

I knocked on his door and opened it. "Morning, sir, can I get you a coffee or something?"

"No, you can't, Duffy! But you know what you can do for me?"

"What?"

"Give my head peace and leave me alone."

"Okay, sir."

I shut the door again.

Maybe talk to McCrabban when he came in.

I went to the coffee machine, got a coffee-choc, trudged to my office, put my feet up on the desk and looked out to sea.

The sun limped up over County Down. It was a clear crisp day and Scotland was distinctly visible as a long blue line on the horizon. The guy trying to sell the goat went past without his goat. An entrepreneurial success story.

The door opened.

Brennan came in shaving with an electric razor.

"What are you doing in at this time, anyway?" he asked.

"I couldn't sleep. I was out for a walk and ended up here."

"What do you know about Epicurus?"

"Is it a crossword clue?"

"It's something I heard at a, uhhh, a meeting. I thought, I'll ask Duffy. He's a guy that knows things."

"Athenian. He taught in what was called The Garden."

"Sum him up for me in short words."

"He said that either there are no gods, or they don't care about us. Ambition is a pointless quest. In a thousand years no one will remember any of us. All we've got is love and friendship, so take pleasure where you can find it."

Chief Inspector Brennan closed his eyes and swayed a little. "You believe that?"

"I haven't thought too much about it."

"What have you thought about?"

"Uhhh—"

"That O'Rourke murder, for example. Have you been thinking about that?"

"Not lately, it's in the yellow file which means that we are at something of an impasse."

"What have you got?"

"We've established the name of the victim and how the victim died."

"And?"

"That's about it, sir, to be honest. Few red herrings along the way."

He put up his hand. "Progress, Duffy, what progress have you made since your last report?"

"No actual progress."

"That's what I thought. Is that what you boys do in here? Sit around drinking tea and concealing the truth from me? All right, so you bin it and you move on so the resources of CID can be used elsewhere."

"We solved that bank robbery."

"We need more of that stuff. Results."

He was spoiling for a fight out of sheer ennui. I was in no mood to engage. What did I care about the O'Rourke case or any other? "You're the boss. If you want, I'll move it from the yellow file to the cold case file."

"I am the boss and don't you forget it. Now bugger off home and get some kip and come back at a Christian hour."

"Yes, sir."

Home. Sofa. Kip. Cup of tea and Mars bar sandwiches and the classic *Star Trek* ep. *Arena*. You know the one. Kirk makes gunpowder to kill the guy in the rubber suit.

The doorbell went. It was Bobby Cameron with a bottle of Glenlivet. He offered it to me. "Fell off the back of a lorry," he said. "No hard feelings, eh?"

"About what?"

"About your woman up the street. Sometimes the lads get a bit boisterous. Sitting around with nothing to do, the dartboard's broke, it's too wet to fly the pigeons and before you know it, it's the fall of Saigon on Coronation Road."

"I don't know what you're talking about."

He winked, nodded and walked down the path. At the gate he turned. "You'll look after yourself now, Duffy, won't you?"

It was hard to know if this was a threat or a warning, or nothing at all.

"I'll try to," I said.

"I like you, Duffy. We'll kill you last."

"Cheers."

I decided to skip work entirely and rang a lithe reserve constable called Clare Purdy to see if she wanted to go to the pictures. She said yes and I took her to the ABC in Belfast to catch *Blade Runner.* We were the only people in the cinema. When we came out it was raining, dark, there'd been a bombing somewhere and the street was full of smoke and soldiers: it was as if the movie had come to life. It took us an hour to get through the checkpoints and the rain. I tried to get Clare to come back to Coronation Road with me but she was a Jesus freak and the flick had messed with her head and all she wanted to do was go home and lie down. I dropped her at a cottage in Knocknagullah and then it was a quiet night in with chicken lo mein, vodka and lime and a quick whizz to Helen Mirren on a repeat *Parky* talking about the nude scenes in *Caligula.*

The next day I asked Crabbie and Matty if there were any developments on any front. When they both said no I told them that the Chief wanted the O'Rourke case killed.

"*You're* willing to drop this?" McCrabban asked skeptically.

"Orders is orders," I said. "As my dear old gran used to say 'when someone shits on your chips, you have to eat the onion rings.'"

"What?" McCrabban asked.

"What do we work on then?" Matty wondered.

"Theft cases. Stolen cars. Anything," I said.

If they'd both objected I would have taken the fight back to the Chief but neither of them kicked up a fuss, so that was that. The O'Rourke murder investigation was suspended indefinitely.

I wiped the whiteboard, gathered up the materials from the incident room, put them in a box binder and placed it in the filing cabinet in my office. McCrabban was watching me out of the corner of his eye.

"If the Chief asks you, tell him it's a cold case now," I said.

"I will."

We exchanged a look and that look said that he knew that I was far too much of a stubborn arsehole to leave it there.

23: DeLOREAN

The factory was on waste ground in Dunmurry, West Belfast. A big hasty concrete and metal box that had gone up in eighteen months with the blasted city in various states of decay all around. If Coronation Road was the fall of Saigon, this part of Belfast was Hitler's last days.

Security was a couple of guys at the gate, but to get up to DeLorean's office, I had to go through a metal detector, show my warrant card and wait until it was verified by a computer.

John DeLorean was a very busy man and had his day scheduled out in tight fifteen-minute blocks. Our interview was scheduled from eleven thirty to eleven forty-five on a Monday morning. I could have pushed it but I didn't want to make waves or have him ask questions of my superiors. I wanted this encounter to be as straightforward and low key as possible.

On the inside, the Dunmurry DeLorean factory dazzled me. Perhaps it was just amazing seeing any kind of industrial activity going on in Ulster. The assembly line was clean and efficient. Raw metal sheets and engines went in one end, aluminum gull-winged DeLorean sports cars came out the other. The administrative offices overlooked the factory floor (DeLorean was big on worker/management cooperation) and I could have stood there all day watching the engines getting mounted and the transmissions going in. It really was incredible. DeLorean had brought a successful industry to Belfast in the heart of the Troubles. He had done what everybody said couldn't be done and Dunmurry was the only place in Ulster where heavy industry worked, where people actually made things.

Three thousand men were employed here and maybe twice that

in subsidiary trades. That was nine thousand men in West Belfast who wouldn't join the terrorists.

Everybody loved DeLorean: the local press, the British Government, the Northern Ireland office, the Irish government . . . Everybody, that is, except for a few privileged American auto journalists who had actually driven the DeLorean and said that it was clunky, unreliable and sloppily put together by an inexperienced workforce.

These criticisms had publicly been dismissed by John DeLorean, who trusted his own judgment, not the judgment of "know nothing journalists." He, after all, was the "man who had single-handedly saved GM" and by implication had therefore saved America.

On TV his persona was half hard-headed businessman, half televangelist. In person he was trim, handsome, soft spoken, and for our interview he was wearing a conservative, un-showy blue suit.

His hair was more grey than black. He had an interesting face: a long aquiline nose that didn't really go with his squat peasant eyebrows and cheeks. It was a tanned, handsome visage that both radiated intelligence and a kind of weary, punchy vitality.

As I entered the office he was sitting in a 'Helsinki' Java wood mahogany armchair reading a report, tutting to himself as he marked it up with a yellow highlighter.

I liked his shoes—they were hand-made Oxfords in a soft brown leather.

His socks were red which I also liked.

He smelled of cologne and cigars.

There was an engraved sign on his desk that said "Genius at Work."

"Inspector Sean Duffy of Carrickfergus RUC," a tall attractive secretary called Gloria reminded him when I came in.

He got up and shook my hand.

"Inspector Duffy. Pleased to meet you. I take it this is about the fundraising ball?" he said, with a gleaming and rather charming smile.

"No, this is about a rather different matter," I said, momentarily thrown.

"Oh?"

His big eyebrows knitted together and I knew that Gloria was going to catch it after I left.

"I'm investigating the murder of an Army captain called Martin McAlpine."

DeLorean shrugged. "Never heard of him, should I have?"

"He was an intelligence officer. He was murdered late last year, apparently by the IRA."

"What's the connection to us?" DeLorean said.

"We went through Captain McAlpine's notes and an associate of his was keeping an eye on someone who was spying on this factory. It could be unrelated to Captain McAlpine's murder but I thought I'd follow up on the lead."

"What do you want to know?"

"Would there be a reason why anyone would be interested in spying on your car plant?"

DeLorean laughed at that. "Of course! Haven't you ever heard of industrial espionage?"

"Well, yes, I—"

"They've been doing it to me my whole career!" he said. He got to his feet and pointed through the plate-glass windows to the factory floor. "You see what we're doing down there? We are radically re-engineering the model of American sports-car manufacture. In Detroit they are terrified. If I can be blunt, Inspector Duffy, I have them shitting in their pants. Ford, GM, Chrysler, Toyota. Spying? Of course they're spying. I expect no less of them. They have no original ideas. They have to steal them from me!"

"Would they kill to get information about your plant?"

DeLorean smiled and nodded. "Nothing would surprise me in this country. Nothing. You have no idea the kind of deals I've had to do with all sorts of people to get this factory up and running. Pretty unsavory characters, I can tell you." He raised his eyebrows. "Do you get my drift, Inspector?"

"Yes, I think so."

"No, nothing would surprise me, but as for actual secrets . . . Well, the blueprints of the DeLorean are well known and have been in the public domain for years. Our production design is also well known, even our factory layout is common knowledge. We don't have that many secrets as such ..."

"New models or anything like that?" I inquired.

"Oh, sure. I'm always sketching, planning, scheming, but I don't keep that stuff here."

"Where do you keep it?"

"In my house in Belfast, or my place in Michigan."

"Have you had any burglaries? Anything like that?"

"No. Certainly not in my place here. The house in Michigan's empty but I have a security firm looking after it. They would have told me."

"What about poaching of company employees, that sort of thing, I've heard that—"

"No, no, no, you're barking up the wrong tree, Inspector," DeLorean said, becoming animated. "The reason people work for me is that they want to be part of something bigger than themselves. All my people have already been offered more money elsewhere, but they want to be part of a company they can be proud of. No, my staff is loyal. I wouldn't put it past your local thugs to try and kidnap someone who works here, but they're not leaving to join fucking Ford."

"So you can't think of any reason why someone might be nosing around the plant?"

"A million reasons! Desperation! Panic! They know I'm going to wipe the floor with them. But they can't stop it! Ten years from now we're going to be the biggest car company in the world. Not just sports cars. Light trucks. Mid-sized economy sedans. You name it. Electric cars. You should see my plans for electric vehicles."

"And it's all going to be headquartered right here in Belfast?"

"You bet!"

He looked at his watch. Our time was almost up.

I gave him my card. "If anything out of the ordinary happens, I would certainly appreciate a call."

"It depends what you mean by out of the ordinary. In Belfast the 'out of the ordinary' happens every day!"

I nodded. "Well, if you think of anything, please, get in touch . . ."

"Sure thing," he said, and got to his feet. "I'll see you out."

He walked me across the office, opened the door and shook my hand again. The secretary got up from her desk to whisk me away from her boss in case I proved intractable. There was already another man waiting on the sofa. He was wearing a leather jacket, had a thin black tie, messy brown hair and he was smoking a Camel. Everything about him said "reporter."

DeLorean disengaged my hand

"Have a good day, Inspector."

"I will."

The secretary smiled at me. She was a blonde, classic high cheek-bones, blue eyeshadow, big hair, very American.

She put up a finger to prevent me from speaking and addressed the man on the sofa.

"You can go in now, Mr. Burns."

"My photographer hasn't showed up," Burns said in an East End accent. "Can we wait a few minutes?"

"If you want to talk to Mr. DeLorean you'll have to go in now, Mr. Burns, Mr. DeLorean

has another meeting at twelve fifteen."

"All right," Burns said.

The secretary pressed a button and formally announced him. "Mr. Jack Burns from the *Daily Mail.*"

Burns went into DeLorean's office.

It was unusual to hear an American woman's voice in Northern Ireland, and I tried to think if I'd ever heard one here before. I doubted it. The American news networks didn't send their female reporters to war zones.

"Is he a good boss?" I asked.

"He's a great man," she said.

"'Genius at Work,' it says on his desk."

"Oh, that? That's sort of a joke. That was a gift from Ronald Reagan when he was campaigning through Michigan."

She began to roll a sheet of paper into her electric typewriter when suddenly another secretary came running down the hall and burst into Mr. DeLorean's office.

"What!" DeLorean yelled, and then a moment later: "Goddammit!" DeLorean came out of the office, fuming.

"This, when I'm talking to a reporter!" he muttered to Gloria.

He turned to me. "I suppose you'll want me to evacuate the place? Stop production?"

"I'm sorry, I've no idea—"

A young man came breathlessly up the stairs. "Mr. DeLorean we've had a—"

"Yes, I know!" DeLorean exclaimed. The *Daily Mail* hack had come out of the office now and was writing furiously in his notebook.

DeLorean turned to the man. "You want to know what difficulties we have to deal with? This kind of goddamn difficulty! Every goddamn week!"

An alarm began sounding and the workers began putting down their tools.

"Who pulled the fire alarm?" DeLorean screamed.

"One of the shop stewards, probably," the young man said.

"Jesus Christ! All right, all right, show it to me!" DeLorean said.

"I think we should evacuate the premises," the young man said.

"Show it to me!"

The young man led DeLorean towards a fire exit. Gloria grabbed her handbag, notepad and followed and I followed her. We were met at the bottom of the fire escape by two uniformed security guards.

"Where is it?" DeLorean demanded.

"On the slip road to the south gate," one of the security guards said.

I went with DeLorean and the motley band to the south gate. And there I saw what the problem was. Someone had hijacked a Ford Transit van and dumped it there.

"There is no bomb in there—I'll show you!" DeLorean said, marching towards the van.

"Stop right there!" I ordered, and DeLorean froze in his tracks. "What's going on here?" I asked the harassed young guy.

"Suspect device. Someone called in a bomb threat," he said.

"There's no bomb in that vehicle! We get this all the time, Inspector Duffy. It's a hoax. I'll show you!" DeLorean said, and continued striding towards the transit van.

"No, you won't! You'll go back inside and evacuate the factory and call the bomb squad," I said, with a voice of absolute authority.

DeLorean glared at me with pure malice.

He pointed a finger at me, but said nothing. After a couple of seconds of this he nodded at the young man, who ran back towards the factory.

"I'll check out the van, I'll show you, Mr. DeLorean," a beefy Liverpudlian security guard said.

"Yes!" DeLorean said excitedly.

"You'll do no such thing," I insisted.

The security guard shook his head. "Every day, Inspector, it's the same story. Someone calls Downtown Radio to request Fleetwood Mac and call in a bomb threat at the DeLorean factory."

"Nevertheless, no one's going to touch that van until the bomb squad shows up," I reiterated.

"Okay, we'll wait here and I'll show you that I'm right," DeLorean insisted.

I knew he was right. Nine times out of ten it's a hoax. But that one time . . . that's the time that gets you.

The Army bomb disposal unit showed up and the robot blew open the back doors of the Transit. The robot looked inside and fired a shotgun into a wooden box, but it only contained tools. Behind us the blue-collar staff was filing out of the factory, most deciding to go home for the day. An enterprising mobile chip van showed up and DeLorean bought our little group fish suppers out of his own pocket.

The Army EOD unit still wasn't completely satisfied with the situation, so they carried out a further controlled explosion which destroyed the van completely, sending metal fragments and a fireball into the air.

There had been no secondary blast which proved that the Ford had contained no bomb or combustible materials.

DeLorean was not triumphant. He was resigned now. Fed up. He shook my hand.

"I yelled out of turn," he said. "You did the right thing. Better safe than sorry."

"It's all right," I replied.

The Army gave us the all clear but some fool had left a backpack in the executive car park in his haste to evacuate and the disposal unit roped off the car park to carry out a controlled explosion on that too. It was five o'clock now. Many of the white-collar staff were effectively trapped until the Army said that this was a negative result too.

"My car's in the visitor's car park. Anyone need a lift going Carrick way?" I asked.

Gloria put up her hand. "I do," she said.

"No problem."

We drove through the center of Belfast where rush hour and a string of incendiary devices on buses had created chaos.

"Where do you live?" I asked her.

"A town called Whitehead. An apartment overlooking the water. Wonderful view, full of charm."

"Sounds like a nice place."

"Oh, yes. Mr. DeLorean picked our accommodations out personally."

We were stuck in traffic for twenty-five minutes.

I was getting annoyed.

Worse. Losing face.

"This is ridiculous. Time for my *Starsky and Hutch* moves," I said.

I took the portable siren out of the glove compartment and put it on the roof of the Beemer. I turned it on and drove the wrong way down the one-way system at the City Hall.

"Are you allowed to do this?" Gloria asked, in what I discovered later was a South Carolina burr.

"I'm allowed to do anything, love, I'm the Johnny Law."

"You're the what?"

"Put the windows down, sweetheart!"

She wound down the window and I cracked Zep in the stereo. Good Zep. *LZIII*. We ran the one-way systems and frightened the civvies and hit the ten lanes where the M2 leaves the city. Six camouflaged sacks of shit were stopping suspicious characters where the M2 merges with the M5, but the siren got me past them and on the M5 I got the Beemer up to a ton. At Hazelbank I killed the woo woo and took us down to seventy-five.

We drove past Whiteabbey RUC.

"A rocket went through that police station," I said.

"A rocket?"

"Yeah, not an RPG. A rocket."

"What's the difference?"

"Oh, there's a difference, baby. Believe me. I was in there half an hour later."

I scoped her, and my God, she was a stunner. She looked like Miss World 1979, one of the ones Georgie Best couldn't get.

"You want to get a bite to eat? I know this fabulous Italian that just opened up in Carrick. The food's so good the place won't survive past Christmas."

"Italian food?"

"Italian food."

"I'll try anything once."

"Oooh, I like the sound of that."

She laughed and I knew I was in like Flynn.

The Tutto Bene was deserted apart from a bald gourmand who was loving everything he was given and kept sighing dramatically at each new dish. We were given the window seat overlooking the harbor. I ordered the second most expensive red. She plumped for the spag carbonara and I got the risotto.

She didn't like the grub but the desserts killed her.

I asked her if she wanted to come back chez Duffy and hear my records. She said that that sounded interesting.

Coronation Road. Nine in the p.m. Curtains drawn. I was spin-ning Nick Drake, while Gloria checked out the Nickster's sad eyes on the sleeve. *Soften them with up Nicky D. and Marvin Gaye and then unleash the inner perv with the Velvets . . .*

I made her a vodka martini and questioned her about her life and times. She was from a town called Spartanburg, South Carolina. She'd gone to Michigan State to major in business and from there it was a short hop to GM and JDL's own company.

We were getting on famously when there was a knock at the front door. I turned the TV off and looked through the living-room window. It was Ambreena.

"Shit," I said to Gloria and went into the hall.

"Anything wrong?"

"Not a bit of it, get that martini down your neck."

I opened the front door. "Hello," I said.

"I hope I'm not bothering you," she said.

She was wearing jeans and a black T-shirt. Her hair was braided. The T-shirt was tight. She looked fabulous. She was holding something covered in tin foil.

"I made you this, to thank you," she said.

"Oh, thanks."

"It is merely brandy snaps. The only thing I can make," she said.

I took the tin foil off and bit into one. It was like biting into stale bread soaked in rubbing alcohol.

"Amazing," I said, fighting the gag reflex. "Look, I'd invite you in, but I'm busy."

She smiled. It was the smile to light up the porch, to light up this whole fucking gloomy street.

"Well, thanks. Maybe another time, we could have a drink or something."

"I cannot stay long. I have to pack."

"Pack?"

"I am moving to England."

"When?"

"Tomorrow."

"Why?"

"I have been offered a place at Cambridge University. My father pulled a few strings, as fathers do."

"Cambridge?"

She leaned in and kissed me on the cheek.

"Thank you," she whispered.

"You're welcome."

She turned and walked down the path. I closed the door and went back to the living room.

Gloria was burrowing deep into my extensive, prized record collection.

"Who was that?"

"Just some chick whose life I saved."

"No, really, who was it?"

I grabbed her round the waist and carried her to the sofa. I kissed those big pouty red American lips. Damn, she tasted good.

"Just some chick whose life I saved," I insisted.

I made more martinis and played her *What's Going On* and *Pink Moon*. Everything was proceeding according to plan.

"Does he ever play in Ireland?"

"Who?"

"Nick Drake."

"He's dead, baby," I informed her. "He killed himself."

"Why?"

"I think he was depressed."

Another round of martinis and I span the Velvets.

She leaned over and kissed me. She tasted wonderful.

She seemed the kind of girl who liked to party. I got the quality hemp from the garden shed. The stars were out. It was dark. Quiet. There was a cold wind from the North Channel. I got some logs I bought from the tinker pedlars: oak and hazel and copper birch. I went back inside, rolled a spliff and put the logs on the fire. The smell from them was fennel and deer spoor and wet earth.

We lay there on the sofa.

She told me stories about America.

I took off her secretary blouse and bra and skirt and marveled at her perfect, huge, beautiful breasts and luscious hips.

I kissed her neck and between her breasts and she pulled down my jeans.

Nico sang in her tone-deaf monotone and we baked the Moroccan and smoked it neat and fucked on the leather sofa like two people who have witnessed a van getting blown apart and sped through a hostile city under police sirens.

I fucked her and it was me fucking all of America. And we kissed again and finished the Moroccan and slept.

We lay all night there on the living-room sofa until the sun came up over the Scottish coast, rising prismatically over the pink lough, over Leinster and Munster and all of red-handed Ulster, over the DeLorean factory and the McAlpine farm in Islandmagee, over the rubble of Bally-corey RUC station, over Belfast. A pale orange sun rising out of a cobalt dawn that warmed the hearts of innocent men and guilty men and men whose task it was to heal and those whose burden it was to hurt.

The sunlight came in through the back kitchen and woke me on the sofa.

The place smelled good: cannabis and martini and peat logs and *woman* and coffee.

"Is that you up?" Gloria said.

"What time is it?"

"Lie there. Don't move. I'm making coffee and toast."

She made coffee in the French press that was suitably hard-core. We had toasted soda bread and we went upstairs and showered together like people in a French film. Post-shower she was radiant. Belfast people sucked the light from their surroundings black-hole fashion— this woman was giving off about two-thousand candlepower from her smile alone.

I drove her back to the DeLorean plant in Dunmurry and walked her to her desk.

There was a box waiting on her seat with a ribbon around it.

"I love these!" she exclaimed.

She opened the lid.

A box of Irish "fifteens." With M&Ms in them instead of Smarties.

"Those look good," I said.

"They're delicious," she replied.

"Where do you get them?" I asked.

"Sir Harry brings them in. His sister-in-law makes them."

"Sir Harry McAlpine?"

"Yes."

"How do you know Sir Harry?" I asked conversationally.

"I don't! Not really. Mr. DeLorean knows him."

"How does Mr. DeLorean know Sir Harry?

"The factory is on his land. Sir Harry leased it to the DeLorean Motor Corporation at a very generous rate."

"As an incentive to get DeLorean to set up his factory in Belfast as opposed to Scotland or wherever?"

"Precisely. But over the last year Sir Harry and Mr. DeLorean have become fast friends."

"Have they indeed?" I said.

24: PEOPLE IN GLASS HOUSES

I was feeling good as I drove down the coast road to Islandmagee. I accelerated the Beemer up to seventy and then got it up to a nice 88 mph. I dug out a mix tape and put it in the player.

Plastic Bertrand took me all the way through Carrick, Eden, Islandmagee.

Sir Harry's estate.

The gate along the private road was closed and there was a man there now, sitting on a stile, wearing a Barbour jacket and holding a shotgun. Old geezer, grizzled, game-keeper type.

"This is private land," he said in a country accent.

"I'm the police," I told him.

"You'll have a warrant then," he said.

"To drive down this road I'll need a warrant?"

"This is not the King's Highway. All these farms, right down to the water, is all Sir Harry McAlpine's property," the man insisted.

"Just let me through, mate, I'm the peelers. I've been here before."

"So you say. But we have to careful. We had a murder here last year."

I got out of the Beemer, opened the gate and showed him my warrant card.

"If you want to shoot me, shoot me, but I'm going to see McAlpine."

The old geezer nodded.

It was more than his job was worth to get in the way of a determined copper.

I drove past Emma's farm.

No sign of her.

I followed the dirt trail up the hill to the big house.

The gate down that drive was also closed but there was no chain across it so I got out and opened it. I drove over the cattle grid and down the palm-lined driveway.

The Roller was parked out front.

I rang the bell. Mrs. Patton answered the door. I showed her my warrant card.

"Remember me, love?"

"What do you want?"

"I want to talk to *le grand fromage*."

"He's in the greenhouse. I'll go get him."

"The empty greenhouse? Don't trouble yourself, Mrs. Patton. I know the way."

I walked through the house and the kitchen and out into the back garden.

There had been a few changes: the garden looked tidier, neater. There were bags of soil and peat and empty terracotta pots. Sir Harry's finances must have stabilized some if he could afford a guard down there on the private road and a revamp to his back garden.

And there he was in a ratty brown shirt and brown corduroys.

I knocked on the greenhouse door.

He was pulling a jumper over his head. When the head popped through he turned round, saw me, frowned.

I opened the door and went inside.

It was warm. There was a little humidifier in the corner pumping out steam.

"What the devil are you doing here?" he asked, not even attempting to conceal his dislike, which was certainly un-Irish, but perhaps not un-Anglo-Irish.

And it wasn't that clear why he disliked me. Sure, everybody hated the peelers. We were lazy and crap at best, corrupt and sectarian at worst ... but at least I was trying to solve the murder of his brother, wasn't I?

I walked over. He was fussing with an orchid of some kind and it made me think—ah, a real horticulturist, eh?

"The last time I was in this greenhouse the place was deserted," I said.

"I'm restocking . . . and what business is of it yours, anyway?" His eyes were bulging in his face. His cheeks were red. That and the green Wellingtons and the accent. He was really an old-school character. I found myself warming to him.

"Do you ever grow rosary pea in here?"

"What pea?"

"Rosary pea."

"Never heard of it. What are you doing here? You've come to ask me about my garden?"

"I've been up to see John DeLorean."

"And?"

"The car guy. The guy who is going to save Northern Ireland from the abyss."

"I know who he is."

"Of course you do, Harry. His factory is on a piece of your land. Some old waste ground in Belfast that is now the hub of Ireland's regeneration project."

He put down the pot he was working on and took off his thick gardening gloves. He cleared his throat. "And what exactly has this got to do with anything?"

"Your brother was an intelligence officer for the UDR. He ran a series of informers for them. One of them told him something about a guy asking questions and taking photographs at the DeLorean factory. I went to see Mr. DeLorean and he told me that he's subject to industrial espionage all the time, that it's pretty much par for the course, so that's okay. But you see this tip about Dunmurry was the last entry in your brother's log book and the informer that gave your brother that tip has gone missing. And of course your brother himself was murdered. I thought perhaps that these incidents were connected somehow and I thought that maybe you might have some insight into them?"

"What are you implying?"

"I'm not implying anything. I merely thought that you might possibly have an angle on this that I, as an outsider, would not."

"I am not terribly fond of your tone, detective," Sir Harry said.

"I'm sorry about that. There was no tone, sir. No offense meant, I assure you."

That seemed to mollify him a little.

He sniffed and sized me up.

"So you're still looking into Martin's death?"

"I am."

He nodded and breathed out slowly. "I take it you think it wasn't a random IRA hit then?"

"Oh, no, I haven't got that far yet. I just want to parse this link a little. You, DeLorean, Martin's informer . . . I wanted to see where all this went."

"All right, maybe I can help. Come into the house and we'll discuss it over tea. Have you got some time?"

"All the time in the world."

"That other detective, the one who died . . . I hate to speak ill of the dead, but, well . . . I didn't have much confidence in him."

"No."

We went into a library on the ground floor.

Floor-to-ceiling shelves stuffed with old books. A formal leather sofa worn comfortable by generations of use and repair, use and repair. A few more modern chairs, an oak table, a reading lectern and a nice bay window with an easterly prospect of the coast and the Irish Sea only a few hundred yards over the fields.

Mrs. Patton brought the tea.

It was a Darjeeling. Very strong and over-steeped. Harry didn't seem to notice. He was much more relaxed now. "So you really think this could be something to do with John DeLorean?" he asked, eagerly.

"Perhaps. What exactly is the nature of the relationship between you and Mr. DeLorean?"

He shrugged. "Relationship. Ha! The man's a user. He doesn't have relationships with people. He uses people."

"How did you get to know him in the first place?"

"Two years ago I started hearing rumors that DeLorean was looking to invest in Northern Ireland. Build a big auto plant for this sports car he was designing. Lots of jobs. The whole thing would be underwritten by the Northern Ireland Office. They'd pump in fifty million. They were desperate to have any kind of investment, actual honest to God money flowing into Northern Ireland. So, as you may or may not know, I've been a having a few financial problems of my own. My father died in '69 and I'm still paying the estates taxes—that's not hyperbole, by the way, I really am still paying them off. If he'd died one year later it would have been under the Tories, but no, he had to die in 1969, when the rate was through the roof . . . Anyway, to cut a long story short, the Secretary of State, Humphrey Atkins, asked me to quote, donate, unquote, some land that I had in Dunmurry for a factory site. And I did, and that's how I know DeLorean. I'm his landlord."

That confirmed what I knew, but I didn't see how it tied into Martin's death or into anything else.

"You want to know how much he pays me for all those acres?"

"How much?"

"You'd choke on your chocky biscuits. The man's a cancer. I just hope to God the Yanks don't find out before they buy a million of his cars."

"Yes, I—"

"And I'll tell you something else. Ever been in his office? He's got a sign on his desk, 'Genius at Work.' Genius at work, my foot! You know who's behind the curtain, don't you? You know who the real Wizard of Oz is?"

"No."

"DeLorean didn't even design the car. He made a sketch, a bullshit sketch. Colin Chapman, heard of him?"

"The name rings a bell."

"Lotus! Lotus Sports Cars. Colin Chapman is the man who made Lotus. He's the real designer of the DeLorean, not John D.L., as he likes to be called."

I was familiar with the Lotus sports cars from the James Bond movies.

"Colin Chapman's the designer, the money's coming from the

British government, the land came from me, the workers are ex Harland and Wolff guys from Belfast, so what exactly does DeLorean do? He's just the front. That's all. Just the front. He's just the fucking hair and the fucking million-dollar smile."

"And if the front falters?"

He made a plane crashing sound and smacked one hand into another.

"And God help Northern Ireland if it does," he added.

"So you don't really see him very much on a social basis."

"Only when he needs something."

"Hmmm."

"So how does this tie into Martin's murder?" he asked.

"That's what I'd like to know."

We sipped our tea and we talked for a few more minutes about this and that, but nothing came of the conversation. He either knew nothing or he was a pretty decent chancer himself.

I finished my tea and stood and offered my hand.

"I'm sorry that we seemed to get off on the wrong footing," I said.

"My fault, I'm sure. Tarred all you boys with the same brush . . . If you find anything about Martin, you'll let me know, won't you?"

"Yes."

"Only . . ."

"Yes?"

His eyes moistened. "Only, he's my wee brother, you're supposed to look after your wee brother, aren't you?"

"I suppose so."

I walked down the palm-lined drive in a thoughtful mood.

I got in the Beemer.

He hadn't reacted to the rosary pea crack and he seemed genuinely interested in finding out about his brother's death.

His connection to everything might be tangential.

But that entry in his brother's book . . . it was a coincidence.

And coincidence is the sworn enemy of all detectives everywhere.

25: INTO THE WOODS

I'd driven about a hundred yards from Sir Harry's house when I saw Emma wearing army boots, a blue dress and a raincoat, walking along the sheugh and carrying a basket. Her back was to me on the road and she had an umbrella up, but she was unmistakable with that wild curly red hair.

I pulled the car beside her and wound the window down.

"Hello," I said.

She seemed a little startled.

"Oh, hi . . . What are you doing down here?"

"I was seeing your brother-in-law."

"About Martin?"

"Yes."

"Anything new?"

"I'm afraid not. Just tidying up some loose ends."

She nodded, frowned and then smiled.

"What on earth is that music?" she asked.

"It's Plastic Bertrand."

"Who's that?"

"Belgian New Wave guy."

"What's New Wave?"

"Jesus, I mean they have the wheel down here, don't they? And fire?"

She laughed.

"You're not still living in caves, hunting for woolly mammoths?"

She lifted her basket. "Mussels more like."

"You need a lift?" I asked.

"A car can't go where I'm going."

"Where's that?"

"Down to the shore."

She smiled again and something down below decks remembered last night with Gloria.

"Can I come with you?" I asked.

She hesitated for a moment. "What have you on your feet?"

"Gutties," I said, showing her my Adidas sneakers.

"They'll get soaked."

"That's okay."

I pulled the BMW over and locked it. I got my leather jacket out of the boot and zipped it up over my sweater and jeans.

"We go down the lane there and then we're back through the wood," she said.

Her hair was blowing every which way round her face. She looked elemental and slightly scary and very beautiful.

"This way," she said, and led me along a lane past a ruined farm with broken windows and a roof with half the tiles missing. The farm was pitched on a rocky red outcrop that bled down the cliff to the water. It was only about thirty feet above the surf and probably on rough days the spray would come right up. We walked through what once had been the living room and the kitchen. There were sodden newspapers and ciggies in the hearth. "One of Harry's cousins used to live here. But he upped and left for Canada," she said. "It's one of my secret places, like the old salt mine."

This one wasn't so secret. My cop's eyes took in discarded syringes, furniture broken up for firewood and an old piano which someone had taken a hammer to. The back garden led to the cliff path right down to the shore. The stone slabs were slippery and I almost went arse over tit in my gutties.

"So, you're from around here, aren't you?" I asked.

"Yeah, I'm from Mill Bay, just a few miles up the road."

"Any family still there?"

"No. Folks are in Spain, older sister's in San Francisco. She wants me to come over to America. I suppose I should. There's nothing for me now in Ireland. Nothing for any of us here, really."

"That's what everybody says."

We reached the bottom of the track. There were more abandoned cottages down here, much older dwellings. "These are from the famine?" I asked, pointing towards them.

She nodded. "Harry says that this valley used to be bunged with people. Now it's all sheep and a few of his loyal retainers."

We stepped onto the stony beach and she gathered mussels and whelks.

"Are you making a soup?" I asked, helping her.

"No, no, you just boil them up in a little chicken stock with some garlic. Delicious."

"Really?"

"Don't sound so skeptical."

In ten minutes her basket was half full. "I think that's enough," she said. "We'll take a shortcut back through the forest."

We walked along the beach past a long rusting jetty sticking out into the water.

"Harry's?" I asked pointing at it.

"Yeah, he keeps talking about renovating it, turning it into a marina, but he never will. All talk. Big plans."

We trudged back up the hill along another trail.

"Initially I got the impression that your brother-in-law wasn't too impressed with me," I said.

"Has he come around?"

"A little bit, I think."

"It's not anything personal. This part of Islandmagee has never been fond of the law. Around here it's always been about poaching and cattle raiding and rustling stolen cattle over to Scotland."

We reached the edge of the wood. The trees were enormous and warped by age into strange patterns. Big elms and ashes, beeches and huge old oaks, living statues meditating in the rain. I smiled and I found to my surprise that she was holding my hand.

"They're talking to us," she said.

"The trees?"

"You know what they're saying?"

"What?"

"Every leaf is a miracle. Every leaf on Earth is a miracle machine that keeps us all alive."

"I think they're saying, 'ooh, me aching back, from standing here all day.'"

She hit me on the shoulder. "You're all the same, aren't you?"

"Who? Cops? Men?"

There was a glint in her eye that I couldn't decipher. "Hey, do you want see something really interesting, Inspector Duffy?"

"Sure."

"This way."

We followed the woodland trail up a hill, catching the odd glimpse here and there of the motionless sea and beyond that, startlingly close, the Scottish coast.

"Down here," she said, and led me to a hazel grove where one solitary oak was standing by itself. It was clearly very old, and covered with moss and mistletoe. Prayers and petitions had been placed in plastic bags and hung from the lower branches. Little offerings and notes were leaning against the trunk. Coins, keys, lockets, photographs, at least a dozen plastic baby dolls, wooden boxes, tea cups, a silver spoon, an intricately carved woman with a belly swollen by pregnancy.

A breeze stirred the notes and photographs.

"Do you know what this is?" she asked.

"Sure I do, it's a fairy tree."

"You're not totally ignorant."

"I'm from the Glens, love, I speak the Irish. I know things."

"You're a Catholic?"

"You didn't know?"

"No."

She nodded to herself. "Yeah, I can see it now . . . come on, let's get back."

We walked back across the boggy pasture.

"Were Martin and Harry close?" I asked.

"I don't know about close. There was an age difference, but they respected each other. Martin admired Harry for taking on the debts and the burdens of the estate. Harry admired Martin for joining the Army, putting his life on the line."

"Literally, as it turned out."

"Yes," she said, with a melancholy smile. "Even when Martin got Born Again, Harry didn't give him a hard time about it, and Harry's as atheist as they come."

"Martin was a Born Again Christian?" I asked.

"Yes. About a year and a half ago there was a visiting preacher from America who came to the church, and Martin felt called."

"But not you."

"No."

"He must have tried to make you see the light?"

"That's what was so lovely about him. He knew I was more into all this . . ." she said, pointing back at the trees, and I bit my tongue before I said "bullshit."

"He never bullied me with his faith. Let me go my own way."

"Sounds like a good guy."

"He was. He really was."

We had reached the edge of the pasture and I could see the valley again. The big house, the cottages, the salt mine, my car parked along the road.

"Do you want to stay for dinner?" she asked. "I'm making the mussels. It's a shame to do all that for one."

"Sounds great."

We walked over the boggy field to the farm.

Cora started barking and Emma untied her.

"Why didn't you take her on your walk?"

"I used to, but she's incorrigible. She worries the sheep and she goes after the game. She goes for everything."

Except IRA gunmen, apparently.

A man waved to us from the road as he drove past in a Toyota pickup. She waved back.

"Who's that?" I asked.

"Connie Wilson. One of Harry's tenants from down Ballylumford way. Connie's in bad shape. He tried to coax barley out of his land this year. Got rid of his flock and tried to grow barley. He hasn't been able to pay his ground rent, Harry says."

"How many tenants does Harry have?"

"Quite a few. Twelve, thirteen. Only two or three can actually make a go of the land with the EEC subsidy; but with taxes Harry actually loses about five or six thousand pounds a year on the estate."

"He loses money on the estate?"

"That's what he says."

We went into the house and this time I noted that the door was unlocked.

"Farmers are always complaining. That's what they do best," I said.

"Well, as long as he doesn't put up my rent."

"He wouldn't do that to his sister-in-law."

"You'd be surprised what men do when they're desperate."

"No, I wouldn't."

She nodded and brushed the hair from her face.

A harsh face. Youthful—but when she was older, bitterness would make her pinched and thin-lipped and shrewish.

"Can I help make anything?" I asked.

She smiled, almost laughed again. "No, no. There'll be no man in my kitchen. Settle yourself down in the living room. I'll get you a Harp."

I sat on the rattan sofa and sipped the can of Harp. There were a few novels on the book shelf: Alexander Kent, Alastair MacLean, Patrick O'Brian. She'd got rid of Martin's clothes and his suitcase, but she'd kept some of his books.

"Mind if I use your phone?" I called into the kitchen.

"Go ahead. Although the reception down here is shocking. It sounds like you're phoning from the moon."

I called the station, asked for Crabbie.

"McCrabban speaking," Crabbie said.

Emma had the radio on in the kitchen but I lowered my voice anyway.

"Mate, listen, it's me. Do me a favor and see if there's anything brewing with Finance and Embezzlement or the Fraud Squad on Sir Harry McAlpine or John DeLorean or both of them."

"John DeLorean?"

"Aye, and Harry McAlpine."

"Well, the DeLorean factory's a great big money pit, but I've never heard of any actual fraud—"

"Check it out, will you? And don't forget McAlpine. The DeLorean factory is on his land. Some kind of deal with the Revenue Service, he says."

Crabbie hesitated. There was static on the phone line.

"Did you get that?" I asked.

"I got it. You want to me to call Special Branch and the Fraud Squad."

"Yes. What's the problem?"

"Sean, an inquiry like that will get passed up the chain. I thought you were specifically warned off involving yourself with Sir Harry McAlpine. Two or three days from now when this arrives on the Chief Constable's desk you'll be getting a bloody rocket!"

"Goes with the territory, Crabbie. We're firing blanks here anyway."

"It doesn't matter if we're firing blanks, Sean. The McAlpine case is not our case and the O'Rourke case has been yellowed," he said, his voice rising a little.

"I know, mate, look, just do it, will ya?"

He sighed. "Of course."

"Thanks, pal."

"No problem."

I hung up.

"Everything okay?" Emma shouted from the kitchen.

"Aye. Everything's fine."

I made another quick phone call to Interflora and had them deliver flowers to Gloria at the DeLorean plant. It was thirty-five quid, but it's always smart to keep the sheilas sweet.

Emma came up behind me.

"Ordering flowers?"

"Me mother's birthday."

"You are such a dutiful son."

"Aye, I am."

"The stock's on. It'll take an hour. Do you ride? I borrow Stella from Canny McDonagh down by the sheddings. She's got a young hunter called Mallarky that needs a run or two."

"I haven't been on a Dob for fifteen years."

"You don't forget."

"Are you sure?"

"Quite sure."

We put on coats and she lent me Martin's riding boots.

Canny McDonagh wasn't home, but Emma made free and easy with the farm and in the stable block she harnessed and saddled both horses. Mallarky was a big hunter but he had just gorged himself on oats and was no bother at all.

We rode over the fields till we reached a beach on the Irish Sea side of Islandmagee. She galloped Stella and I got Mallarky up to a canter. Cora barked happily alongside.

When they'd had a good run we dismounted them and walked them in the surf. It was colder now. The beach was empty. Emma threw a stick to the dog and she ran to fetch it in the water. I looked north. You could see up the glens to the Atlantic

Ocean. The wild deep blue of it chilling my retinas from here.

The sun began to set behind the cloud banks to the west.

"Look! There!" she said.

A massive gorse fire was burning on a hill in Scotland.

"Jesus, will you look at that."

"Sometimes the heather will burn for days," she said.

We watched it until the set sun. It was getting dark now.

"We better get these horses back, don't you think? I'm not that confident about riding at night."

"Yes. All right."

We rode back and Cora barked and Canny McDonagh still wasn't home, so she left him a note, telling him what she had done and that Mallarky had taken the canter well.

Mussels and country bread at the kitchen table.

She lit a paraffin lamp.

"Do you fancy something stronger?" she asked, when I finished a second Harp.

"Poteen?"

"You won't tell the excise, will you?"

"Are you joking? Cops and the excise are natural enemies."

She took an earthenware jug from under the sink.

"Everybody distils their own round here," she explained.

She poured me an honest measure and we clinked glasses.

We drank and it was evil rough stuff, around 120 proof.

We both coughed. She poured us another.

"Yikes, do you have anything to cut this with?" I asked, knocking back shot number two. "There's orange juice in the fridge."

I went to the fridge, looked out a couple of tall glasses and made us a couple of screwdrivers.

She drank hers and moved closer to me on the couch.

"You're not married, are you?" she asked, looking at me with those azure eyes and those full lips with the little dent in the middle of the lower.

The eyes. The pale cheeks. The dangerous red hair.

"Would it make a difference?"

She shook her head. "I don't think so," she said, and placed her cold hand on mine. "As you can imagine, it's been some time."

We went to the bedroom.

The big south-facing window looked out over the valley and the clear night gave up the winter constellations. Naked, she was beautiful, but gaunt and pale, like a case, like something washed up in the Lagan.

I took her, and I was gentle with her, and I held her and she slept in my arms. I listened to her heart and watched her chest heave up and down.

She was frowning in her dream.

Those closed blue eyes could not see any good in the future.

I fell asleep watching her.

She woke me in the wolf's tail—that grey Irish light that comes before the dawn.

"Huh, what is it?" I asked.

"I heard a noise!" she said. "Something's outside."

I sat up, rubbed my face.

"What?"

"Outside. I hear something. I'll get the rabbit gun."

"No, I'll go."

I pulled on my jeans and sneakers and my raincoat. I grabbed a torch and my .38.

Cora growled at me as I walked into the yard.

It was drizzling, the ground was slick.

"Hello?" I said, turning on the torch.

I walked towards the road.

I slipped on the mud but saved myself by grabbing the gate post. I saw something flash further down the track. Maybe nothing or maybe the fluorescent strip on a rain jacket or a pair of training shoes.

"Is there anyone down there?" I yelled.

I held out the .38 and shone the torch beam down the road.

Nothing. I flashed the beam up into the hills.

No movement, no sounds.

The distant lough, the even more distant sea.

I stood there, waiting for something. Anything. "There's nothing here," I said to myself. I walked a little bit further down the lane and then cut back to the farm along the hypotenuse of the nearest field. I nearly took a header into a bog hole filled with water, but saved myself before the final step. When I got back to the house Cora was barking again and Emma was standing in the doorway with a shotgun.

"Well?" she asked.

"It was nothing," I told her. We went back to bed and I kept the blinds open. The moon was giving out a yellow candle light and the sky about it was eerie and in a state of strange coruscation. Neither of us went back to sleep.

In the morning, Emma made me scrambled eggs and coffee. The coffee was like coal dust but the country fresh eggs with butter were good.

I ate breakfast and kissed her and said goodbye. I walked down to the car and I saw what the commotion had been the night before. Someone had tossed a brick through the windscreen of my BMW. A helpful note had been tied around it which read: "Fuck Off And Die Peeler Scum!"

I threw the brick into a field, carefully pushed out the windscreen, carried it to the stone wall and left it there. I brushed the broken glass off the driver's seat and headed home.

26: THROUGH A GLASS DARKLY

I stopped at Paddy Kinkaid's BMW dealership in Whitehead and parked the car in a lot full of brand new Beemers. If old Paddy wanted to keep them new he'd need to get the bloody hose out because smoke from Kilroot power station was depositing a fine grey-grained soot on all the windward surfaces, as if the golden head of the enormous chimney top was in sinister coitus with the friggin' place.

I lit a tab and went inside.

It was basically a big plywood shed painted BMW white and blue. An elderly woman was playing an electric organ in one corner of the showroom and when I saw Father O'Hare I thought perhaps the two were connected by some nexus—a wedding rehearsal or funeral preparations or the like, but in fact they were unrelated. She was Paddy's wife, playing away to herself, and Father O'Hare was in looking for a car.

"I haven't seen you in a while, Sean," Father O'Hare said cheerfully enough, although perhaps with a hint of admonishment. And if a hint was there, I didn't effing like it.

"Big mistake, Father," I said.

"What?"

"You can't be a priest and drive a BMW. It sends out a bad message."

"Sean, as I'm sure you're aware, the Popemobile, as they call it, is manufactured by BMW."

"The Holy Father survived an assassination attempt by the direct intervention of Our Lady of Fatima and can therefore pretty much do what he likes in the vehicular realm; with all due respect, Father, you're not up there yet."

He nodded and countered with "I wonder how it looks to have a policeman driving a BMW?"

"Perhaps an inspector in the Vice or the Fraud Squad might have cause for concern, but not a simple homicide detective."

The organ reached a complicated part of the Toccata and Fugue in D minor, and Father O'Hare could see from the look in my eyes that I'd already had a somewhat trying morning.

"Perhaps you're right, Sean, I was only picking up a brochure anyway. Will I see you at Mass before Lady Day?"

"Yes, Father," I assured him, and he went outside to his rickety 2CV coupe which had death trap written all over it.

Paddy was annoyed with me. He was a tubby, complacent man with a welcoming suntanned bald head, but when he heard the tail end of me chasing out Father O'Hare he was furious.

"That was a customer, Sean. A customer. You don't see me going around to your manor and solving murders, do you?"

"You're welcome to, Paddy."

Paddy went on a rant about Father O'Hare's pressing need for a new motor and pointed out that the Catholic Church used wealth to glorify God and show the common people a glimpse of the infinite. I was in no mood for the dialectic so I told him that he had a point and apologized and asked about the windscreen.

Paddy told me he couldn't possibly get a replacement in less than a week and offered me a loaner of a black BMW 320i for only fifty quid. It was a canny move on his part for he knew that I'd be hooked after a couple of days behind the wheel of that four-cylinder, fuel-injected, 125 BHP beast.

She purred right up and I notched her at 115 mph on the straight run from the old ICI factory to Eden Village.

I turned right up Victoria Road, left on Coronation Road and parked the car.

I found Bobby Cameron's wean and give him a pound note and told him he'd get another one if he kept all the wee shites away from the Beemer.

I was exhausted.

I turned on the hall light to look at myself in the mirror. A pitiful bedraggled wreck of a man.

The hall mirror.

The hall looking glass.

Alice through the Looking Glass. Alice Smith because Alice Liddell was too obvious. I see through a glass darkly.

I saw the phone sitting on the table. I recalled the conversation with our special guest mystery caller.

I walked outside to the Beemer and drove to William McFarlane's bed and breakfast in Dunmurry.

Mrs. McFarlane didn't recognize me without the riot squad to back me up

I asked if I could have a look at room #4.

She said all the rooms were the same.

I said four was my lucky number.

She said fine, go ahead.

I went upstairs to room #4.

I looked at the huge mirror above the dresser.

I looked at those strange wear marks on the carpet. Exactly where they should be if someone had moved this heavy thing out from the wall.

I moved the dresser out from the wall.

Behind the mirror someone had duct-taped an envelope.

I put on latex gloves and opened the envelope.

Inside:

Bill O'Rourke's Massachusetts driver's license, five hundred dollars in fifty-dollar bills, and a key with the number 27 stamped into the metal. Taped to the key with Scotch tape, a piece of paper that said "Ten Cent Bank Safety Deposit, Jefferson Street, Newburyport, Massachusetts."

I moved the dresser back and told Mrs. McFarlane I'd have to think about the room.

I went back to the borrowed Beemer and sat there.

The mystery caller had known about this all along.

I see through a glass darkly. She had seen through it. She'd seen through it to the other side, but was leaving it to me to do something about it.

There was only one thing to be done.

I knew the drama that would erupt if I asked for official permission to go.

The Chief. The Consulate. DeLorean. The Americans. Especially the Americans.

The case would be taken away from me.

The case would vanish into the ether.

We'd never find out who killed Bill O'Rourke. Perhaps someone would, but not us.

"No, not us," I said aloud.

I drove to Carrick RUC and found Kenny Dalziel among the pay stubs in the subbasement. I told him that before the marching season got going in a month or so now was as good a time as any for me to take my personal days all at once.

He said that he'd sound it out with the Chief.

Half an hour later the Chief called me up to his office and declared that I looked as if I needed a break. He recommended Blackpool, which was bracing and inexpensive at this time of year.

I told him that that sounded like a great idea.

I told Kenny I was taking five working days and a weekend exemption from riot duty. I told them that Crabbie was in charge of CID and he should be paid for the week as an acting sergeant. Kenny baulked at that until I said that I'd pay the extra four quid out of my own pocket.

I went back upstairs and told Crabbie about the acting sergeant thing and he was as pleased as I'd hoped. I didn't tell him about the mirror. Not yet. No point dragging him in until we saw where it all led.

I called Emma McAlpine and said that I had to go out of town for a few days but I'd really like to see her when I got back.

"That would be nice," she told me.

I ordered Emma flowers from the same place I'd got them for Gloria.

I drove to Grant's Travel Agency in Carrickfergus and had them book me a flight to Boston. Tomorrow at noon from Shannon.

I'm not a superstitious arsehole but just to be on the safe side I found out when the next Mass was going to be.

27: HIGH MASS

Coronation Road was the last street in Greater Belfast before the country began and the field behind it felt like another world. A littoral. An Interzone. A DMZ. I put a barley stalk in my mouth and listened to the commingling of music from radios and stereos and from far up the lane a piper practicing his scale. The gable graffiti said "God Save the Queen," and "No Pope Here," but on this particular April evening Coronation Road belonged to neither Queen nor Pope but to a Jewish girl from Brooklyn called Barbra Streisand. The current UK no. 1 album *Memories* was warbling from several underpowered hi-fi speakers with most of them repeating the title track, but one preferring Streisand's melancholy duet with Neil Diamond: "You Don't Bring Me Flowers." We could be over-egging the theoretical custard here, but for me these torch songs were desperate cries for help from Coronation Road's female population. Streisand's mezzo soprano expressing what they couldn't express from their marriage prisons: longings about foreign travel and roads not taken and above all about their men who were once buoyant and funny and now were aged characters brought low by unemployment and sickness and the drink.

I was hungry. I hadn't eaten as an act of contrition. Tonight I would take the sacrament of penance and in a state of grace I would go to America.

It was dusk now and the colors were from another latitude: the barley a bold yellow, the sky an epic Sicilian red. I walked past two children playing hide-and-seek behind a burnt-out car. The field had become a dumping ground for bombed vehicles, and these warped and twisted hulks of steel and aluminum possessed a strange, minatory beauty. I touched the side of a Reliant Robin that had been turned inside out by the apocalyptic power of Semtex. A kid put his finger to his lips. I nodded. I won't turn you in, son.

I reached the street and said hello to my two terrace neighbors, Mrs. Campbell and Mrs. Bridewell, while Barbra brought her rendition of "Memory" to a histrionic, emotional climax and the ladies dabbed at their cheeks. The sky, the song, the tear: the moment carved with such precision that I knew that it would scratch the iris of my mind's eye decades from now. If the Lord spared me. . .

I checked under the Beemer and drove to the chapel.

Revenge is the foolish stepbrother of justice. I understood that. I had lived with that thought for eight months. *Ever since that night on the shores of Lake Como.* What I had done then was a crime, and it was also a sin. No one cared about the crime, but tonight I was going to confess to the sin. To the act itself and to the feeling of satisfaction I got when I thought about what I'd done.

I parked the car and got out.

The chapel was ancient and barely used, covered in moss and yellow ivy. It lay now in the shadow of Kilroot power station. Only in Ulster could a charming piece of coast like this have been blighted with such a Soviet-style monstrosity. "Kilroot" is a derivation of the Irish *Cill Ruaidh* meaning "church of the redheads." The Redheads were the local Celts and supposedly Kilroot had been founded as a parish in 422 AD, which predated St Patrick's mission by a generation. At that time Ulster, and indeed Ireland, was a land of pagan, poetry-loving, warring, tribal kingdoms. Not much had changed.

Father O'Hare was only twenty-two. He was nine years my junior, but he was an old soul. In defiance of Vatican II, and for the benefit of the five other aging parishioners, he conducted the mass in Latin.

The ancient words comforted us.

When the service was over I entered the confessional.

Father O'Hare saw old Mrs. McCawley to her car and returned to the chapel.

He entered his side of the booth.

He slid across the partition.

Only the carved wooden lattice protected me now.

"Bless me, Father, for I have sinned," I told him. "It has been nearly a year since my last confession."

I confessed to the mortal sin of murder and the venial sins of pride, lust and adultery. I confessed that I did not regret what I had done and I told him that I would do it all again.

He listened and did not approve.

Technically, he should not have offered me absolution until I had explained that I was sorry for these and all the sins of my past life, but Father O'Hare was no sea lawyer and couldn't afford to be too harsh with his tiny congregation.

"*Misereatur tui omnipotens Deus, et dimissis peccatis tuis, perducat te ad vitam ternam,*" he said. "*Indulgentiam, absolutionem, et remissionem peccatorum tuorum tribuat tibi omnipotens et misericors Dominus. Amen. Dominus noster Jesus Christus te absolvat: et ego auctoritate ipsus te absolvo ab omni vinculo excommunicationis, (suspensionis), et inter-dicti, in quantum possum, et tu indiges. Deinde ego te absolvo a peccatis tuis, in nomine Patris, et Filii, et Spiritus Sancti.*"

Outside the confessional it was a different world and we exchanged unembarrassed pleasantries.

"It was the lovely day today, wasn't it?"

"Aye, it was indeed, Father, although I heard it was going to be cold tomorrow."

"Oh, and my roses just coming through!" he said, and shook his head.

"I won't see it. I'll be in America."

"America? A holiday?"

"Something like that."

I drove home and, absolved and at peace, I called McCrabban.

I told him about the mirror and the note and what I was planning to do. He was silent for a long time.

"Don't do this, Sean. The whole thing smells. Pass it up the chain of command," he said, finally.

"Why did you become a detective, Crabbie? Truth and justice, right? If we pass this up the Yanks will take it, the Brits will take it. We'll never get the truth. Never."

"This is a game being played on another level, Sean. A game you play carefully. Pass it up and our job is done."

"You know what will happen, Crabbie. It'll vanish. The higher ups and the Americans will make it vanish and we'll never find out what happened to Mr. O'Rourke."

"You don't know that for certain, Sean."

"You said it yourself, mate, this whole thing stinks."

"At least tell the Chief."

"The Chief's a company man, I won't be out of his office before he'll be on the phone to the FBI."

Crabbie hung on the receiver for a long time, *thinking*. I knew he was conflicted. He wanted to talk me out of it, but he wanted to know, too.

"So, what's your plan?"

"Find out what Mr. O'Rourke has hidden away in that safety deposit box and retrieve the evidence. Fait accompli, mate. No interference from Special Branch, goons, FBI or anyone else."

"And then what?"

"Depending on what I find, we'll take it from there."

"Let me go with you," he said suddenly.

I considered it for a second or two. It would be great to have him with me, but it would selfish to drag him into the black pit of banjax if it all went wrong.

"No, Crabbie, if this shit fucks up, it'll be my head on the block and mine alone."

"What could go wrong?"

"I don't know."

"That's why I should go with you. You need me, Sean."

"I do need you, Crabbie, but I don't need you catching any flak from this. I'll retrieve the evidence from the box and see what it is and then we'll talk."

"I'm your mate, Sean, I should be there to help."

I was touched. "I know, Crabbie. And that's why I want to keep you out of it. You've got a family to look after."

Another long period of silence before a hurt and worried and confused McCrabban said: "Okay."

"Thanks for understanding."

"You sure you know what you're doing?"

"No."

"Take care, Sean."

"I will."

I hung up the phone.

Coronation Road was quiet. I poured myself a pint of vodka and lime. I flipped on the UTV news: a shooting in Crossmaglen, a suspicious van in Cookstown, an incendiary attack in Lurgan—nothing that serious. I went upstairs, packed and set the alarm for six.

28: AMERICA

Of course I'd been before. New York in '78 when I'd stayed with my old girlfriend Gresha for two weeks in the West Village. Happy days. It was the New York of The Ramones and *Serpico* and CBGB and *Dog Day Afternoon*. Gresha's then boyfriend was a fuckwit who had not been cool about me staying in the first place and hated me after I'd gone to the fridge and eaten his "Reggie Bar." "I got that at the Yankees' home opener, man. I'm not into material possessions, man, but that is going to be a collector's item one day, man." When Gresha banged me for old time's sake I didn't feel a bit bad about it.

This trip was to Boston. Bus to Dublin. Dublin to Shannon. Shannon to Logan. I flew Aer Lingus and sat in the smoking section and watched Ingmar Bergman's *Fanny and Alexander*. It was so long that it hadn't actually ended when we touched down.

The whole Irish-American thing did not manifest itself at Logan Airport or at the Avis where I got myself a huge brown '71 Robert Bechtle style Buick. I stayed the night at a Holiday Inn in Revere, and on hearing my accent the desk clerk asked if I was from Australia. At ten o'clock that evening I was idly flipping through the TV channels when there was a knock at the door. It was a prostitute who was also from our own fair island and who'd been sent here by the manager so that we could "cheer each other up." She was a chubby girl from Mayo with black hair that she had misguidedly dyed platinum. She said that she had come to America in 1979 after she'd seen the Pope conduct an open-air Mass at Phoenix Park. I poured her a glass of Maker's Mark from the mini bar and asked her her name. She told me it was Candy which seemed unlikely. She asked if I wanted to have sex with her and I told her that I was very tired having just arrived today. She told me that a quick hand job would ensure that I would get a good night's sleep and would only cost ten dollars. She had big peasant hands that looked as if they could wring the neck of a chicken without any bother at all and I said thanks but no thanks and gave her five dollars for her trouble.

She thanked me for the drink. I had read *The Catcher in the Rye* and was prepared for the desk clerk or manager to come barging in five minutes later demanding full compensation for his girl's time, but no one came and no one bothered me and I slept until seven the next morning.

I shaved and dressed in black jeans, a white shirt and a black sports jacket.

I bought a map and drove the Buick north on Route 1A towards Newburyport. Before reaching town, I took a mini diversion to find the O'Rourke homestead. I was surprised to discover that in the weeks since Mr. O'Rourke's body had been sent home, his house had been completely cleared out, filled with rented furniture, and was now on the market. There was a lock box on the front door and the number of a realtor who would let you see inside.

I called the realtor from a payphone at the gas station and asked if I could see it this morning. How did ten suit me? I wondered if she had an earlier appointment, and she said no. I said that ten would be no problem.

I drove to a place called the Village Pancake House just over the town line in Ipswich. I got the pecan pancakes and they were excellent.

The realtor was a large bubbly woman called Buffy. She had blonde, curly hair and a perma-tan, and she was wearing a light blue leisure suit that made her look like a member of a cult.

She showed me inside the O'Rourke residence.

My hunch about the rented furniture proved correct.

All the late Mr. O'Rourke's effects had been cleared out "and the house fumigated," Buffy assured me.

"What happened to Mr. O'Rourke?" I asked.

"I heard that he wasn't well and that he went home to Ireland to die."

I told Buffy that I was a keen gardener and she showed me a completely empty greenhouse in the back yard—as empty as Sir Harry McAlpine's had been.

I thanked Buffy and drove next to the VFW post. I wanted to talk to O'Rourke's mates and I'd brought that roll of five hundred dollars I'd found behind the mirror, which I wanted to leave as a donation to his fellow veterans. I parked outside the small, white clapboard building and tried the door, but it was locked.

I got a coffee roll and a coffee from Dunkin' Donuts on Route 1 and waited for any of O'Rourke's VFW buddies to show up, but no one did. It was obviously way too early. I ate the coffee roll; it was great and made up for the coffee itself which tasted like it had been percolated through a tube previously used for stealing petrol from parked cars.

I drove back to O'Rourke's house and rang the doorbell of the neighbors on either side. The Browns were not at home, but his other neighbor, Donna Ferris, a home maker in her forties, told me that Bill was an amazing guy. A very proud man. A great neighbor who could fix just about anything.

"You wouldn't believe what he went through when Jennifer died. She was in so much pain. He tried to take it all on himself. They should have given that guy a medal."

I told her that they had given him several medals, and this was news to her.

I asked her about his work for the government and she said that he never discussed it. She said that she was devastated to hear about his death. That he was the most honorable man she knew.

"Most people these days don't even know what the word 'honorable' means," she said.

At lunchtime I drove into Newburyport and found the Ten Cent Savings Bank. The main branch on State Street was not the one that contained the safety deposit boxes. I had to go to the adjunct branch on Jefferson Street; but I knew that already.

I had a toasted cheese sandwich at Fowles Diner and found a review of *Fanny and Alexander* in an old Boston Globe someone had left lying around. The reviewer liked the film, but didn't say what happened at the end.

I walked down to the little harbor and strolled along a pier that had rows of lobster boats and fishing smacks. An attractive lady with a screaming infant asked me the way to the McDonald's. I told her I was a stranger here myself and she hazarded a guess that I was from Down Under. "Belfast," I said, and she smiled and wished me a pleasant trip.

I found an Irish pub called Molly Malone's. It was an embarrassing explosion of kitsch and sentimental Oirishness. Comedic leprechauns jostled for space with photographs of the dead hunger strikers and framed newspaper headlines celebrating infamous bombings. There was a collection tin for the IRA on the bar and posters that said things like "Death to the RUC," and "Death to the Brits." No Mick with any self-respect would ever drink in a place like this, which was why it was packed to the rafters.

I went next door to a dive bar and got a bottle of Sam Adams for a buck fifty. I knew that I was only delaying the inevitable, so I gulped my brew and went back outside.

Jefferson Street.

The Ten Cent Saving Bank's adjunct branch was a brown concrete single-story structure

that had all the aesthetic charm of a nuclear fall-out shelter. But perhaps that was the point. Your stuff will be safe here even in the event of the apocalypse . . .

I took out my key and walked boldly inside.

You had to go past a clerk who was sitting behind bullet-proof glass.

He was a thin, bald man with a comb-over and a caterpillar moustache that conveyed a great well of sadness. He was reading *The Parsifal Mosaic* by Robert Ludlum.

The boxes, presumably, were in a room to his right behind a locked metal door.

"Key number," the man said.

"Twenty-seven," I said.

"Let me see it, please," the man said.

I took out the key and passed it under the partition. He examined the key and looked at something in a book and passed the key back.

"Do you have any identification, Mr. O'Rourke?"

I slid O'Rourke's license through the partition. I had a story ready that Mr. O'Rourke had passed on and I was his son-in-law closing up his estate, either that or a policeman investigating his estate. I hadn't completely decided on the narrative, but neither proved necessary. The guard nodded and passed the license back and even though O'Rourke and myself looked nothing alike, he pushed a buzzer which opened the inner door.

I went through into the next room which was a kind of ante-chamber. An armed security guard was sitting on a stool and staring into space. He was a big white guy, about thirty, who looked like he could handle himself. There was a TV monitor above his head.

"Good morning," he said, cheerfully enough.

"Good morning," I replied.

The boxes were behind an armored door. "Through here?" I asked.

"Yeah. Take as long as you like," he said. "But we close at four."

"Thank you," I said.

"I'll buzz you through and lock you in, but I'll keep an eye on you on the TV monitor. When you want out, knock the door one time. I'll hear."

"Okay."

He unlocked the armored door and I went inside the room and waited until he closed the door again. There were a hundred safety deposit boxes in two rows. In the center of the room there was an oak table.

I went to box 27, put the key in and turned it.

I pulled out a long metal box and set it on the table.

I opened the box.

Inside was a brown envelope.

I opened the envelope.

Photographs. A dozen 8x10s. Black and white, taken with a tele-photo lens.

They were all of the same subject.

A group of four middle-aged men having some kind of meeting at a restaurant. There were photographs of the men going inside the restaurant, photographs of the men sitting by the window and shots of them coming out again.

One of the men, unmistakably, was John DeLorean.

I stared at the photographs for five minutes to confirm that I was right, but there was no possibility of a mistake. Who the other men were I had no clue at all, and I wasn't sure where the photographs had been taken. The only car I could see was a Volkswagen Beetle, and you can get those all over the western world.

I put the photographs back in the envelope and put it under my arm.

I closed the empty safety deposit box and locked it.

I knocked on the door.

The guard opened the door and buzzed me into the street.

The sunlight startled me.

What to do now?

Only one thing to do now. Find out who these men were. Who was DeLorean meeting and why had O'Rourke taken photographs of the meeting? And why were the photographs in a safety deposit box? And who the fuck *was* O'Rourke?

Jesus, what the hell was going on?

Should I take this to the local peelers or the FBI? Maybe. But, I'd have to think about it. Have a think, find a phone box, maybe call Crabbie, get it all sussed.

I walked to my car which was parked in the lot behind State Street.

I decided that I would drive to the VFW Post, give them the five hundred dollars and perhaps try to talk to some of O'Rourke's buddies. What if he wasn't a retired IRS agent? What if post-retirement he'd taken on a new career? A PI or something? Maybe someone would know.

I got in the Buick and drove out of Newburyport along the 1A. I'd gotten about a mile out of town when I saw flashing lights behind me.

It was an unmarked police car.

Had I been speeding?

Who knew what the limit was around here.

I pulled the Buick to the side of the road.

Thick woods on either side of the car. An odd patch of snow in the deeper parts of the forest. I wound the window down. There was a smell of salt water and marsh gas.

A man wearing sunglasses and a suit and tie got out of the unmarked prowler behind me. He had a gun drawn. Didn't traffic cops always have to wear uniforms?

"Get out of the vehicle and put your hands on the hood."

I sighed, got of the car and put my hands on the roof of the Buick.

"Spread them!" the man yelled.

I spread my hands far apart.

I heard him come up behind me.

"Was I speeding, Officer?" I asked.

"Give me your right wrist and do it real slow," he said.

I put my right hand behind my back. He slapped the cuff on. He asked for my left hand and cuffed that, too.

"How can I get my driver's license out now?" I said.

"We won't be needing that, Duffy," he said.

I just had the time to experience a little rush of panic before he hit me in the neck and I crumpled to the ground.

I wasn't unconscious, but I was dazed.

Two men were dragging me into the trees. There was a third man keeping an eye on the road.

When I was well off the road one of the men kicked me in the head. Another kicked me in the gut. The wind was knocked out of me and I winced in agony. Somehow, I scrambled to my feet, but I was hit twice in the ribs in quick succession by a really big guy with a long reach who was a fighter and fast and strong.

My heart was pounding and there were white spots in front of my eyes.

I threw up in my mouth and I felt myself being tossed down a small embankment.

A momentary respite and then more kicks.

Blood in my eyes.

Scrapes all down my back.

Pain everywhere.

Red out . . .

Black out . . .

Faces.

"Shut the fuck up, he's coming to!"

Tape over my eyes, and then they were holding my mouth open, pouring in bourbon.

I choked, spat, and they poured in more.

It was a goddamn classic.

I almost laughed.

Someone held my head in his greasy paws and they made sure I got the bottle down.

I was scared now. Drunk and scared. They could kill me and make it look like an accident.

"Motherfuckers! What is this all about? I'm a cop."

A punch in my kidneys.

"You're not a fucking cop. You're a fucking Brit, you're a fucking black and tan bastard." "Stop talking to him," another man said.

They slapped my face. Gut punched me. Sucker punched me.

Hands squeezing my throat.

More booze.

I was well gone now.

Beyond the pain. Across the border. Into the dark.

I watched as the world erased itself.

I was being carried.

I was in the car.

"This is a good one, lads. This is an old-school fix up," I said.

The engine kicked into life. The car was moving. Fast.

Death stamped her iron hooves. She was coming. With Finn's spear and Ossian's bow. At the speed of understanding.

The car hit.

Exquisite silence.

Fire.

I was on the car's ceiling. I was upside down.

I wanted to lie there.

I couldn't breathe. The seat was burning. The seatbelt had trapped me in.

"Help!" I said weakly.

"Help!"

"Help!"

Smoke.

Vomit.

No breath.

Smoke.

An ellipsis.

Breaking glass.

An arm around my neck.

Air.

Sweet, beautiful air.

"Christ, son. Are you all right?"

I breathed.

"My God, you're lucky I was passing!" the voice said.

"Lucky," I said.

29: DRIVING UNDER THE INFLUENCE

I wasn't here. I was at the Langham Hotel on Regent Street watching a man clutching his chest, falling, his right hand flapping like a dove in a magician's act. I was eleven years old with my aunt Beryl. The man was yelling without sound and we sat there under the palms, taking in the wonder of it as if we were at the starblown circle of the Giant's Ring. Everything frozen save for the man's right hand which was scrabbling for a finger hold on the air which he thought would save him and pull him vertical once again.

It did not . . .

No.

My mistake.

Not his finger in the air.

Mine.

My finger connected to a pulse monitor. A drip in my arm. Nurses and morphine.

Two days of this and everyone, how shall I put it, a little bit aloof.

A doctor told me I had two minor first-degree burns and three cracked ribs. It could have been worse.

A British consular official came on the third day. He was called Nigel Higgs. He was a tall good-looking spud with a slight stammer. He seemed to be just out of his teens, although presumably he was much older, having gotten a plum like America.

"Nothing broken at least. You're jolly lucky to be alive," he said.

"What happened?" I asked.

I knew full well what had happened but I wanted to hear the official story.

"Well, I'm afraid you had a little too much to drink, old boy. You pranged your car. Total right-off . . . You could well have been killed. You certainly would have been burned alive had not a passing motorist pulled you out."

"What motorist?"

"He was an EMT."

"What's that?"

"A fireman."

He talked for a while and I listened.

"The Yanks are being awfully nice about the whole thing . . .The local police say that they'll only charge you with a misdemeanor DUI."

The upshot was that if I left the country immediately, everything could be swept under the rug. No one needed to spell it out for me. I got it, even if this fucking Nigel didn't. However, if I kicked up a stink I'd be charged with dangerous driving, drunken driving and so on. They'd make sure they threw the book at me. They'd probably plant narcotics in the car. I'd be looking at jail . . .

Oh, yeah. That's how it would play.

If I forgot the photographs and everything I'd seen and quietly left the country with my tail between my legs then all this would go away. I don't know what the average bloke would do, but let me stress the fact that I am no fucking hero.

"Tell them I'll take their offer but I want talk to a goon first. I want to talk to an FBI man. Off the record. That's my condition."

"FBI? What are you talking about? You were drunk driving. You're being prosecuted by the Massachusetts State Police."

"You heard me, Nigel. That's my condition. I want to talk to the FBI, off the record. They'll speak to me. They'll know what this is about. They already know this whole thing is a crock of shite. Someone tried to get rid of me and someone royally fucked it up."

He left in a state of confusion.

He didn't come back. Special Agent Ian Howell did.

He was tall, tanned, pock-marked. Handsome. North of forty. Serious. He looked like he could happily listen to you yakity-yak or he could coolly inject an overdose of morphine into your drip—whatever the situation demanded. He was wearing a brown wool suit with very wide lapels. He had a tape recorder running in one of his jacket pockets, that I wasn't supposed to see.

He introduced himself.

I was sitting up now. I was a lot more comfortable. I was keeping down the solid food. I was ready for him.

"So, I hear you're preparing to make a serious allegation against a local police department?" he said.

"I'm not making any allegation," I said.

"You're not filing a complaint?"

"No."

"You're not alleging theft or the violation of your person?"

"No."

He took off his absurd aviator sunglasses. His eyes were light green. Squinty.

"What is it that you want, Duffy?"

"I only want one thing. But I'll tell you what I don't want first. I don't want to know who was in the photographs with DeLorean. I don't want to know what operation you or other agencies are planning with or without the cooperation of John DeLorean. I don't want to know why you followed me to the Ten Cents Bank Safety Deposit or why you did what you did with me and the car. I just want to know one thing. Tell me that, and I'll leave this green and not so fucking pleasant land and I won't come back."

"And what is that one thing, Mr. Duffy?"

"I want to know who killed Bill O'Rourke."

"What if we don't know who killed Mr. O'Rourke?"

"Then I want to know what you do know about him and his mission in Ireland."

Howell grimaced.

He thought about it and stood.

"Wait here," he said.

"Where am I going to go?"

He went out to make his phone call.

He came back two hours later with a document for me to sign on a roll of fax paper. It was a confession to the charge of DUI and dangerous driving.

"This stays sealed as long as you keep your mouth shut," Howell said.

I didn't like the look of it, but I signed.

"Good," he said, with a smile that didn't suit his face.

"Now your part of the bargain," I said.

Howell sat on a chair and pulled it close to the bed.

"O'Rourke was a Treasury Agent recruited from the IRS. He kept his IRS cover but he was Treasury his whole career. He looked into currency fraud and fraudulent currency transactions. Occasionally he went into the field. He was good," Howell said.

"What was he doing in Ireland?"

"Well, he was compulsorily retired from the IRS at sixty. Officially retired, so to speak."

"But unofficially?"

"He still worked for the Treasury Department."

"So what was he doing in Ireland? Was he investigating DeLorean?"

Howell grimaced. "Yes."

"As part of something bigger?"

"Yes."

"What?"

"That, I am not permitted to tell you."

"A Treasury thing?"

"It was only after Agent O'Rourke's death that we realized that two agencies of the United States government were working on the same problem."

"Jesus! The FBI and the fucking Treasury were both investigating DeLorean and you didn't tell one another?"

"I am not at liberty to discuss that at this time."

"Okay. Tell me this: when did O'Rourke file his last report? Where was he? What was the situation on the ground?"

"O'Rourke wasn't required to file daily reports. He didn't generally present his findings until he knew what he was talking about. Treasury didn't expect a report until he had concluded his field work."

"But he came back to America after his initial visit."

"To attend a colleague's retirement party."

"And leave off those photographs?"

"Apparently."

"You didn't know about the photographs until you started tailing me?"

"No."

"Why did you start tailing me?"

"Immigration alerted us to your arrival in the country. We thought you might try and do some digging over here."

I leaned back into the sturdy hospital pillow. Through the double-glazed window of Mass General I could see rowers and little sailing boats gliding past on the Charles River.

"Who killed O'Rourke?"

Howell shook his head. "We don't know," he said.

"You *really* don't know?"

"We don't know. We were hoping that the RUC would find out for us."

"Maybe we would have if you had cooperated with us from the start."

"You must understand, Inspector Duffy, we have bigger fish to fry here. Special Agent O'Rourke would have understood that."

"What *do* you know about his death?"

"No more than you do, Inspector Duffy. Your investigation has been the primary information vector for us."

"You knew that he was investigating John DeLorean, which I didn't discover until the last few days."

"Inter-agency suspicion and communication problems have been a feature of this investigation from the beginning. You, for example, were not supposed to have been injured, never mind nearly killed. Our apologies for that."

"So why was I nearly fucking killed?"

"Our surrogates got carried away."

"I see."

"They have been disciplined."

"I would hope so. You have no idea at all about who killed Bill O'Rourke?"

"No."

"Why should I believe you?" I asked.

"I can't think of a reason after the way you've been treated, Inspector Duffy, but nevertheless it's the truth."

I nodded.

There was a period of silence.

"It has come to our attention that your investigation into Special Agent O'Rourke's death has more or less been suspended?" Howell asked.

"Yes, it has. We can't close the case because we never found his killer, but the investigation has reached a natural dead end," I said.

Howell's eyes narrowed. "It is in the interests of the United States Government that the investigation into Special Agent O'Rourke's death remain suspended at least until our own investigation into John DeLorean has concluded."

"I'm sure you don't want to tell me how to do my job, Agent Howell, but I will say that in the absence of any new evidence I don't really see how I can proceed with the O'Rourke case at the moment."

Howell nodded, picked up the faxed confession and put it in a briefcase.

"Do you have any more questions?" he asked.

"A million."

He looked at his watch. "Well, Inspector Duffy, I'm afraid that those are the only answers you are going to get, today." He tapped the briefcase. "I trust that I can count on your discretion?"

"Of course."

"You'll keep your nose clean, I'm sure," he said.

"Once I get the bloody scabs out of it, I'll keep it clean."

He walked to the door, opened it, but didn't leave.

He looked at me and then, in a lower tone of voice, he said: "There is one thing, Duffy."

"Yes?"

"Bill O'Rourke had a condo in Florida."

"I know."

"He grew plants on the balcony. We had them analyzed. You know what those plants were?"

"Rosary pea?" I gasped.

He nodded and closed the door behind him.

30: BACK TO BELFAST

They took me out of Mass General on a gurney and across Boston to Logan in a black windowed private ambulance. I felt like Howard fucking Hughes. They flew me first class to New York LGA on the Delta Shuttle.

An FBI driver met me with a wheelchair.

JFK. The first-class lounge. The Concorde from JFK to Heathrow.

Christ, they wanted rid of me *fast*. Whatever they were cooking up was hot, hot, hot. And speaking of food. Canapés and champagne; Russian caviar with traditional accompaniments (blini, chopped egg white and yolk, chopped spring, white, and red onions); free-range chicken breast with black truffle, foie gras, savoy cabbage; lobster and saffron crushed potato cakes with spinach and bloody Mary relish; cheese service with Stilton, chevre and pecorino with balsamic vinegar, biscuits, walnuts, dried apricots and berries; a hand-made box of chocolates; port wine and tea; a sweet of mango and almond gratin.

We left New York at 5:00 p.m. The jet stream was strong and we crossed the Atlantic in three hours dead.

I spent the time thinking about Bill O'Rourke. He must have refined and milled the Abrin himself. Perhaps all this time he was carrying his depression around with him.

Suicide?

If I had to spend any time in William McFarlane's bed and breakfast in Dunmurry,

West Belfast, it might push me over the edge too. Suicide and then McFarlane fakes an American Express bill, sends the body to a mate who runs a cold storage who finally cuts him up and dumps him?

Maybe.

It would certainly be fun bringing McFarlane in for questioning.

Heathrow. And then the British Airways Shuttle to Belfast. So fast it made your head spin. I was in my bed in Coronation Road by ten thirty p.m. Eastern Standard Time—a not unreasonable three thirty in the morning GMT.

Vodka and aspirin.

A death sleep.

I woke groggily and looked at myself in the mirror. I was no oil painting. Bruises, cuts. My ribs were aching. I needed some painkillers.

Still in my dressing gown I went outside, looked under the Beemer and drove down to the newsagents. "SAS Recapture South Georgia!" or variations thereof, the yelled headlines on all the papers.

It was the cheeky girl again. Sonia. Her nose was pierced. Her hair was dyed orange.

"Philip K. Dick, *Blade Runner*," I said.

She looked at me with contempt.

"You mean *Do Androids Dream of Electric Sheep?*"

"Do I?"

"Aye, you do."

"Have you got any aspirin?"

She looked up from her magazine. "The fuck happened to you?" she said.

"The FBI got me drunk and crashed my car with me in it so I wouldn't spill the sensitive information that I knew about John DeLorean's dirty dealings."

"That's the best one I've heard today. Aspirin won't do you any good. Hold on a minute."

She went into a back room and came back with a plastic bag filled with white pills.

"What are those?" I asked.

"Two every four hours. Be careful with them. It's a low dose diamorphine. They've been cut with chalk, but they'll do for you. Street value a hundred quid. I'll let you have the packet for fifty."

"Do they work?"

"If you're not satisfied I'll give you your money back, fair enough?"

"Fair enough."

"And I'll take a Mars bar and an *Irish News* and the *Daily Mail*."

I drove home, popped two of the 'low dose diamorphines' with my coffee and the Mars bar. They worked immediately. The pain reduced itself by several degrees of magnitude and my head felt better.

I took the phone off the hall table and carried it on its lead into the living room.

I made myself a cup of tea.

I stared at the phone with a growing sense of annoyance.

Presumably the mystery caller knew what had happened to me. She knew what had been taped behind the mirror in room #4 of McFarlane's bed and breakfast and presumably she'd been too cowardly to go to that safe deposit box herself. Yes, I gave her credit for doing a better job of searching the bed and breakfast than my team, but I gave her no credit at all for sending me off to America to get nine kinds of shite kicked out of me. What was she? MI5, Special Branch, Serious Fraud Squad, Army Intel, MI6? Did it matter? The whole thing was baroque. This whole situation was ridiculous.

Fuck her.

The tea went cold. I stuck on *Bitches Brew* by Miles Davis, the album where he'd had to train like a prize fighter to bend those notes and solder the rock riffs to the jazz.

I took two more pills.

There was a knock at the front door.

It was Bobby Cameron. He was holding a massive cardboard box. Anything could have been in there. A bomb, the head of an informer...

"Yeah?"

"You've got a freezer, don't you?"

"I do."

"Mine's already full. I brought you some meat," he said.

I looked inside. It was a box of steaks. I took it from him, but it was so heavy I had to place it on the floor.

"What happened your face?" he asked.

"Car accident," I said.

He nodded. "Aye, I've had car accidents like that when the missus catches me with some bird down the pub."

"No, it really was a—"

"I was only joking—I saw that you had a BMW loaner. Assumed your own was in the garage. Nice wee runner?"

"Yeah."

He pointed at the steaks. "From the EEC," he explained again. "Prime Angus. Good stuff. Look inside."

I opened the box. There were maybe fifty steaks in here.

"Why give them to me?" I asked.

"Well, you have a freezer, don't you?"

"Aye."

"And it's a sort of a wee thank you, anyway," he explained.

"What for?"

"For getting rid of the black bint without any trouble. I don't know what you said to her, but she's gone."

"I didn't say anything to her. She's off to Cambridge University."

He winked at me. "Sure," he said. "Anyway, the point is, she's back in Bongo Bongo Land, no blood spilled, everybody wins. That's the kind of police work I like."

He walked down the path and I stood there with the box of steaks at my feet.

I felt nothing but hate for him, for this street, for this town, for this whole country, if you could call it that.

I closed the front door and kicked the box.

I called up the station and asked for McCrabban.

"Acting Sergeant McCrabban," he said.

"Crabbie, it's me. Can you meet me at my house in twenty minutes?"

"You're back in one piece?"

"Not exactly."

He arrived in his Land Rover Defender, smoking a pipe and looking worried.

"You want some steaks?" I asked, showing him the box.

"Are they stolen?"

"Aye. They're from the UDA," I said.

He shook his head. "No, thanks."

We went into the living room. I made tea and put on Alessandro Scarlatti to calm my nerves. I told him everything. I told him about the photos, and the cops and the car accident. I told him O'Rourke was Treasury. I told him that the FBI and Treasury were planning some kind of hit on DeLorean and O'Rourke was part of the intel gathering team.

Crabbie's dour, unsurprised, unflappable expression did not change.

"You want to hear my theory?" I asked.

"Go on," he said.

"The DeLorean Motor Company is a fucking disaster. DeLorean has been keeping fraudulent books to hide this fact. US Treasury Agents are all over it. One of them is an old, experienced field hand called O'Rourke who they send to Ireland to scout for local info. He comes to Ireland, he takes photographs of DeLorean's meeting with Provos or paramilitaries or whoever. He goes back to America and puts them in a safe place. He comes back here. He starts to feel lonely. It's raining all the time. He has no kids, no wife, he wonders what the fuck he's doing with his life. He's in Ireland. The Old Country. Where there's riots every day and eighteen percent unemployment and things are fucked beyond all imagining. And his job now is to destroy the DeLorean Motor Company? The only firm that's providing manufacturing jobs in this pathetic country. He misses his wife. He spent two years helping her fight the fight. He watched her die, perhaps he even helped her die in the end . . ."

"What do you mean?" Crabbie asked.

"He was a chemical engineer. He knew about pharmacology. He grew rosary pea plants on the balcony of their condo in Florida."

"He made the Abrin himself?"

"It would take some skill. But O'Rourke had skills."

"So then what?"

"He's sitting in that bed and breakfast in Dunmurry. His wife's dead, his friends are getting old and dying. It's raining and miserable and he just doesn't see the bloody point. He swallows one of the Abrin pills he's brought with him for just such an emergency."

"No suicide note? No explanation?"

"Maybe he did leave a note and McFarlane destroyed it. Maybe O'Rourke had a hunch about that thieving bastard, which is why he taped his stuff behind the mirror. Who knows? The point is McFarlane finds him dead and goes through his gear and figures out that he's a fucking federal agent and panics and calls in a couple of lads who work in the meat business and they take the body away and throw it in a freezer until McFarlane can figure out what to do with it. In the meantime a greedy and stupid McFarlane forges O'Rourke's signature on an extortionate American Express bill."

"And the body?"

"Time marches on. Either the heat's coming down or McFarlane just can't see any good coming of keeping Mr. O'Rourke in a freezer forever so he has his mates chop up the body and dump the poor lad in a skip. They do this to avoid us and keep their boss Richard Mr. Connected Coulter out of the loop."

Crabbie finished his tea and leaned back in the armchair.

"It's possible," he said. "How would you go about proving something like that? McFarlane's an old lag. You could beat him with a rubber hose and he wouldn't talk."

"Maybe he will talk. What are we accusing him of? Disposing of a body? Concealment of evidence? What's that? A year? Six months? If he pled guilty he could be out in ten weeks."

"Maybe he doesn't want to go to prison at all. Maybe he feels that if he's inside for any length of time, he'll be looking shaky."

"Perhaps."

Crabbie looked at the bag of pills sitting on the coffee table.

He sipped his tea and leaned back in the chair.

"Your face is a mess, Sean."

"Aye, they give me a good hiding and no mistake."

"I told you not to go."

"You did."

"This case had plenty of warning signs all over it."

"It did."

"We'll both have to learn how to read those signs better, won't we?"

"You're sounding like the Chief Inspector, mate."

"I've got a couple of kids, now. Gotta think of my future."

I said nothing.

The nothing went on a for a while.

Even after two years with him I couldn't tell what the hell he was thinking. Opprobrium? Annoyance? What?

Finally he sighed. "This is too deep for the likes of us. Too deep."

"I know, Crabbie," I said.

He got to his feet. "You need to rest up, Sean. I don't think we should bring McFarlane in formally. Not yet. I'll take a wee run up to the B&B and see if they'll tell me anything. I'll go softly softly."

I stood too and offered him my hand.

"I'm sorry about all this, Crabbie. Like you say we'll have to learn to read the arcana better."

"And listen to me next time," he said shaking my hand.

I waved to him as he drove off.

I had a can of Harp and popped two more of the white pills.

They were helping.

I called up Emma.

"Hey, it's me," I said.

"You're back? Did you bring me a present from the Land of the Free?"

"I forgot."

"I was only kidding. I don't want a present."

"I've got a huge box of steaks here that nobody wants."

"Steaks?"

"Yeah."

"I'll take them."

"Have you got a freezer? It's a big box."

"I don't, but Harry's got one."

"Okay then. I'll see you in about half an hour . . . Don't be freaked, but I, uh, I had a bit of a car accident, I'm slightly beat up."

"Oh my God, are you okay?"

"I'm fine. Shouldn't have mentioned it."

"Should you be driving?"

"Yes! I'm fine. Look, I'll see you in a wee bit, okay?"

"Okay."

I hung up and wondered if I really should be driving all the way down to Islandmagee.

Well, we'd soon find out.

I dressed myself without much difficulty and went out to the Beemer.

I was wearing jeans and a tight black sweater. They'd shaved my head in the hospital to put the stitches in. The ensemble made me look like I was a paramilitary thug. To complete the thing I went upstairs, got my .38 and shoved it in my belt.

"You look like an eejit," I said to my face in the mirror.

I kept the BMW at a reasonable pace down to Islandmagee.

The private road to Sir Harry's land had a different goon guarding it now. A kid with big ears, red cheeks and a red hunting hat that he was wearing backwards.

"Is that thing loaded?" I asked, looking at his twelve-gauge shotgun.

"Aye, it is, so you better piss off, mate! This is private land," he said.

"I'm a peeler, son, open the bloody gate!"

He got off his arse and opened the gate.

I drove down the lane to Emma's house.

It began to rain.

I parked the car. Took the box of steaks out of the boot. I'd stuffed the freezer compartment of my fridge full but there were still thirty or forty of the bastards left.

I carried the box to the front door while chickens pecked about my feet and Cora barked at me all the way. I leaned them on top of the oil drum for the central heating.

Emma opened the door. "Hi," she said, and then, "Oh my word."

"I'm not a pretty sight, am I?"

"Not in the least."

"Where do you want these?"

She looked in the box. "That's a lot of meat. I'll cook two for us tonight and we'll leave the rest up in Harry's freezer."

She was making an assumption that I was staying for dinner and she suddenly felt embarrassed about that. Her cheeks colored and she looked all the more beautiful for it. "That is unless you have plans, or work, or—"

"I'd love to say for dinner. And there's no work this week. I'm still officially on leave."

"Have a seat, leave those things on the kitchen table."

I carried the steaks inside to the kitchen and then joined her in the living room.

"Get you a drink?" she asked.

"A stiff glass of anything except that moonshine of yours."

"Johnnie Walker Black?"

"That'll do nicely."

She poured me a glass.

"Thanks," I said and sipped it.

"Sit yourself down there, Sean. I'll go marinate those steaks in garlic and red wine."

"Sounds good."

I drank the Johnnie Walker and watched the sun head towards Magheramorne and the west side of Larne Lough. She came back with a glass of Johnnie Walker for herself. She snuggled next to me on the sofa.

She was wearing a soft wool sweater and faded blue jeans and her hair was tied back.

I liked her being close to me.

It was a nice moment.

"So, what happened to you? Was it driving on the wrong side of the road?" she asked.

I span her a few lies and she went for them. And then, feeling guilty about that, I told her about some stuff from my previous New York trip. She laughed at the story of the Reggie Jackson bar, but she hadn't heard of The Ramones or the New York Dolls or even Blondie and I vowed that I would rectify that.

"How do you like your steak?" she asked, getting up.

"Call me squeamish, but I'm no fan of rare," I said.

"Medium okay?" she asked.

"Sure . . . How long will it take?"

"Twenty-five minutes."

I got up.

"You've no freezer at all?" I asked.

"None."

"Well, I don't want them to spoil. I'll leave the rest of the box up at Harry's. The only thing that worries me is Mrs. Patton giving me the evil eye."

"Oh, don't be silly, she's harmless. Well, she's outlived two husbands, but that's neither here nor there, and you won't even have to go to the house. He's got a curing shed for hanging his pheasants and there's a big freezer in that. Just bung them in."

"Where is it?"

"You just go through the gate, turn left and follow the wall about a hundred yards and you'll see it."

"Is it out the back with the greenhouse and everything?"

She tapped my forehead. "What's the matter with your brain? No, you don't need to go through the house. Immediately you enter Harry's estate turn left, go long the wall and . . . you know what, sit there, I'll do it. I'll be back in ten minutes."

"I'll go," I said. "I've been taking some pills. I need the air."

"I'll phone him and tell him you're coming."

"No need, no need, I'll be fine. Have you got a torch?"

Of course I wasn't fine. You try carrying a box of steaks uphill in the rain at night over muddy ground with a dog barking at you.

I reached the gates to Red Hall.

My brain was fugged. Did she mean go down the driveway to the house and then go left, or go immediately left here?

"I think she meant here," I said.

I walked towards a clump of trees and I saw an old timber curing shed, where they would hang the pheasants for five or six days.

That must be the place, I thought.

It was easily a hundred years old and in the shade of a couple of willow trees that would keep the shot pheasants at a nice 55 degrees year round.

The door wasn't locked.

I opened it and went inside. I fumbled for a light switch and found one.

There were a dozen hooks hanging from the ceiling. There were no birds but there was a massive meat freezer against the far wall.

I hefted the box of steaks over to it and rested it on top.

The meat freezer had a chain and padlock on it, but the padlock was unlocked.

I lifted the lid. The freezer was completely empty.

I tipped the box of steaks inside and closed the lid.

I threw the empty cardboard box in a corner and walked back across the curing shed. I put my hand on the light switch.

I hesitated with my finger on the switch.

Hesitated.

While synaptical connections formed a pattern.

I walked back to the freezer and opened it.

I shone the torch inside. There was something on the freezer bottom.

It was a patch of human skin.

I reached into my raincoat pocket and found a pair of latex gloves. I put the gloves on, leaned into the freezer and tugged at the skin. It came loose. I flipped it over and there on the back was a faded blue ink 't.' It had come from a tattoo which said "No Sacrifice Too Great."

This was the freezer O'Rourke had spent time in after he had been murdered.

This was where Harry had kept O'Rourke's body before he'd decided to get rid of it once and for all. He had probably done it himself—the getting rid of—I mean.

He had driven down to Emma's and asked if she had any old suitcases knocking around and she'd said of course. And he checked it to make sure that it didn't contain anything that could be traced back to him or Emma and wiped it of prints and he'd chopped up the body and disposed of the head and arms in a bog and the big torso he'd dumped miles and miles away with no hope of it ever coming back to him.

Except that he hadn't quite checked the suitcase as well as he should have.

And Emma when questioned by us had lied, and after we'd left had called him in a panic. And he knew we were on to him but he told her to play it cool. *The cops? Don't worry about the cops. The cops have nothing.* And she did play it cool. And he played it cool. And the cops had nothing.

The question was why?

The question was what was going on?

I'd have to think about it.

I had to get away from here and process this evidence and think about that.

I folded the latex glove around the piece of skin and put it in my pocket. I closed the freezer door and turned.

"Anything interesting in there?" Harry asked. He was carrying a Remington pump action.

"Nope. Just leaving off some steaks."

"So it *was* open then. Usually we keep it padlocked in case kids would go in there while playing hide-and-seek," he said in a monotone.

His face a mask. A sickly yellow mask. The Remington had one in the breach, it was pointed down at the ground, at my feet, but it would be nothing, nothing at all to raise it and pull the trigger.

Hell, you'd have a great place to put the body. "Yeah, I've seen those public information ads on telly. That wee kid is playing hide-and-seek. He gets locked in the freezer. He yells but no one can hear. Sensible to keep it locked."

"But it was open."

"Yes."

"Careless on my part."

"No harm done at all, mate. I was just leaving off some steaks. Heading back to the house now. Emma's got dinner on the burner."

He looked at me.

He didn't know. He couldn't be sure if I'd found anything or not. Was there anything in there? Had they been thorough? If he let me go was he signing his own death warrant?

"What's that in your pocket?" he said looking at a finger of latex.

"Nothing, piece of plastic, so I don't get freezer burn handling the steaks."

"Can I see?"

"You want to see a piece of plastic?"

"Yes."

"I have to go, Harry. I'm late for dinner."

He raised the shotgun and I grabbed the .38 from my belt.

Shotgun and .38.

Cop and robber.

Blue eyes/green eyes.

All those dichotomies flitting by at once. Wonderfully.

I smiled at him.

"It's a piece of skin, Harry. It's the missing piece of Bill O'Rourke's tattoo. A 't' from the motto 'No Sacrifice Too Great.' You didn't even know it was there, did you?"

He shook his head.

"Why did you kill him, Harry?"

"I didn't kill him."

"Was he digging into your relationship with DeLorean? And for that matter, mate, what is your relationship with DeLorean?"

"I didn't kill him."

"Who did?"

"Give me that piece of skin. Give it to me."

I laughed. "I don't think so."

"I'll fucking blow your legs off before you get near the trigger of that pop gun," he said.

"No, it won't play like that. Look at my .38. It's fully cocked. The slightest motion or noise will set it off and it's pointing right at your heart, me old mucker. You're not surviving that. Aye, you're right, that shotgun will take my fucking head off. But for you . . . It'll be a bad death. Your heart will be ripped out of your chest. Blood will pour into your chest cavity from your arteries. Your lungs will fill. You'll drown in your own blood. Like your brother Martin. Can you imagine? There'll be no white light for you, me old China plate. No friendly waving from the far shore. You'll be fighting it to the last, desperately trying to breathe."

Now he looked even more yellow.

"What happened to O'Rourke, Harry? Tell me," I said softly.

He smiled.

"All right," he said.

31: IN EXTREMIS

Harry cleared his throat. "The whole thing started with one of Martin's touts who spotted O'Rourke lurking around the DeLorean factory, taking photographs, asking questions. He stood out. He was an American."

"And your brother came to you?"

"Yeah, Martin told me about it all. Martin knew that John DeLorean and me were pulling off a big score. He knew this guy was bad fucking news."

"What did you do with the information?"

"I decided that we should bring O'Rourke in to answer a few questions."

"How did you do that?"

"Got a few lads in balaclavas, stole a white Transit, grabbed him off the bloody street in front of some bed and breakfast in Dunmurry."

"So you don't know Willy McFarlane?"

"Who?"

Sweat was running down my forearm onto the .38. It was hard standing in this position with me ribs aching and the painkillers wearing off. Harry, by contrast, looked pretty fucking relaxed with the Remington.

"You brought O'Rourke here?"

"Nah. Took him down the salt mine."

"And then what happened?"

"Nobody was going to kill him. That was never the plan."

"What was the plan?"

"We just wanted to know who he was working for, what he knew, that kind of thing. We chained him to the generator in the mine and put the fear of fucking God into him. Martin did. He was used to interrogating touts and informers."

"Did you torture him?"

"No. It was all talk. Torture? Martin wouldn't have it. He said we didn't need to torture him anyway. He said O'Rourke would tell us everything he knew, given enough time."

He moved his shotgun a little and I straightened my arm to aim the .38 at his face.

"And then what happened?"

"Nothing. We lifted the informer who told us about O'Rourke, and gave him some money to disappear. He went over to England. So that took care of that, but O'Rourke was our main problem. Who was he? What did he want? Did he know about me and DeLorean and the deal? We needed answers."

"So what did you do?"

"Martin said he could handle it all. I trusted him. I mean, O'Rourke was down the fucking mine. Have you been down there with the lights off? It's like a pit of hell. Martin knew that that would work him and he told O'Rourke that if he didn't tell us everything he'd fucking suffer the torments of the damned . . ."

"And what did O'Rourke say to that?"

"He said he would never talk. He said that we could do what we liked but he would never tell us anything. Eventually Martin grew to believe him. He started telling me that probably we should let him go."

"But you didn't agree to that, did you?"

"Did I fuck? So we kept on him day in and day out. And then one morning we go down to talk to him and his legs are still chained up to the generator, but somehow he's got a hand free and he's dead. At first we thought he'd had a heart attack but then we saw that he must have done it himself. He must have thought we were never going to let him go and he fucking topped himself. He must have had a hidden pill somewhere. Dumb fuck."

"Suicide?"

"Suicide."

"That's good, Harry. That's good for you. What can I do you for? Kidnapping? Sure, that's only five years. You'll be out in three. That's nothing."

I started moving towards the door.

"Stay where you are!" he growled.

"No, I'm going, Harry. I'm going to walk out of here and back down the hill to my car and you're going to let me go. There's no point escalating this. All I have is a piece of forensic evidence that says O'Rourke was stored in this freezer at some point. I can't prove you kidnapped him. I can't prove anything. So there's no sense killing me with that there shotgun, not when a half decent lawyer will get this case thrown out of court. Okay?"

I started inching closer to the door and I gave him a wide berth as I went past. He kept his gun on me, I kept mine on him.

"It'll ruin me," he said.

"No, not if you're acquitted. You'll be fine."

"I won't be acquitted. You'll fit me up. And I didn't do it! I didn't kill him."

I was at the door.

"I believe you, Harry. And I'm leaving now. You'll not do anything stupid, will you?"

"You're not going anywhere, peeler!"

He should have fired the Remington from his hip—sure, there would have been a nasty kick but I'd have been wasted.

He didn't, though. He was too well trained in the use of firearms. His father must have imprinted that lesson in him at an early age and in the second it took him to raise the shotgun to his shoulder I dived out into the rain.

There was a blast behind me and fire spat out of the barn door into the darkness.

I ran to the wall and hid behind an old combine.

I was plotting my next move when I suddenly heard a klaxon blaring up at the house. It sounded like one of those air-raid sirens from the war. It was no fucking air raid, it was Harry calling in his tenants. I'd have to get bloody moving.

I ran from behind the combine straight into a spotlight. There was a shotgun blast from somewhere near the house.

White hot shot flew over my head.

I ran behind a hay rick.

Men were yelling now. A posse of Harry's friends and tenants. Old fucking retainers who would do anything he wanted, no questions asked, even if it was killing a copper. Maybe *especially* if it was killing a copper.

"He's down there!" someone said.

"I seen him!" someone else shouted, and fired.

I hit the dirt, slewing into the mud.

"I nailed him!" a voice yelled.

No, you didn't, but you bloody will soon.

I climbed over the stone perimeter wall that surrounded the estate.

"There he is!"

"He's going over the wall!"

"After him! Billy, get your dogs! And Jack, cut the landlines at the junction box! He'll not get away and he'll get no help."

I tore up into hills, heading out into the bog where the dogs would hopefully lose my scent. I ran through a stream, tripped on something, took a nasty spill and lay there panting for a minute before I got up again.

I doubled back towards the lane and Emma's cottage. My ribs were screaming and I was covered in filth. Cora barked at me as I shambled across the farmyard.

I ran into the house.

"My God! What's happened?" she said, her hand to her mouth.

"Where's the phone?"

"What?"

"Where's the fucking phone?"

"In the bedroom."

I limped into the bedroom and dialed 999.

"Which service do you require?" the operator asked.

"Police! Quickly, Islandmagee out at—"

The line went dead.

I tried again and again but there was no dial tone.

"What happened?" Emma asked.

"Harry tried to kill me. He killed O'Rourke and threw him in his freezer. I've got the proof."

Her face fell and she shook her head.

"No, Sean. He didn't kill Bill O'Rourke," she said in a monotone.

"He told you? You believe that?"

"It's true."

I took her by the shoulders and squeezed. "Tell it and tell it fast!"

"O'Rourke was spying on DeLorean. Causing all sorts of problems. Harry is landing something for DeLorean at his private slipway on the lough. The one you saw. Drugs, I think. It's a big deal. They had to know if it had been compromised. Harry had Martin and a couple of his lads grab O'Rourke off the street. They were wearing balaclavas. They were only going to interrogate him and then let him go. They took him to the salt mine to question him. They must have gotten rough with him or he panicked or something. They weren't going to kill him. They left him alone down there and one morning when they came to wake him he was dead. Martin thought he'd had a heart attack. Nobody knew what to do."

She looked me square in the face. She'd confirmed Harry's story and there was no nonsense about tears or throwing herself on the mercy of the court.

"It was no heart attack, Emma. He was smart. He knew this could happen in Northern Ireland so he made his own fucking suicide pill. Planted the plants, refined it himself. He didn't want to be tortured to give the game away."

She nodded. "We didn't know about that."

We, she said *we*.

"Martin told you about O'Rourke's death, didn't he? And you told him to go to the police, and Harry—"

She laughed bitterly. "Me? Me tell him to go to the police?"

And then the tears did start welling in her eyes. "The police? Nobody in this part of Islandmagee would ever go to the peelers."

"So what did happen?"

She shook her head. "They put the body in the freezer. They would have cut him up and got rid of him and it all would have been fine, but for Martin. Fucking Martin."

"What about Martin?"

"Martin was a fool. He had found Jesus. Jesus didn't mind him helping his big brother do a dodgy deal with John DeLorean but Jesus apparently told him that now a man had died, he had crossed a line and he had to tell his commanding officer about this entire fucking escapade."

"Martin wanted to turn you all in?"

"Yes."

"So you shot him?" I asked, astounded.

She shook her head. "I didn't shoot him."

"Who did?"

"I called Harry and told him about Martin's plans. He said he would take care of it," she said simply, and sat on the sofa. "Martin was going up to check on the yearlings but Harry came down over the fields. I heard them talking. Harry gave him every chance, but Martin wouldn't take it. Jesus wanted him to tell the truth to his commanding officer and that's what he was going to do."

"And then?"

"And then I heard the shot. And Harry came in and told me it was done. We cooked up the story about the IRA and I called the police."

"What about O'Rourke's body?"

"That? We didn't even think about that. Harry just left it there, padlocked in the freezer. Nobody would look there, nobody could get in there."

"But he couldn't leave it there forever, could he?"

"No. A couple of weeks ago he tells me that we have to get rid of it. The place was going to be hot what with DeLorean's shipment coming in."

"So he came to you to ask for one of Martin's old suitcases."

She nodded and fumbled for a cigarette.

"And that's everything?"

"It is."

"All right. We don't have much time. I went out over the fields—laid a good trail, so that's where they'll be looking for me, but if they've any brains at all they'll be coming down here soon enough. This is what we're going to do. We'll kill the house lights and sneak out to the yard. You'll come with me in the BMW. I'll run it without lights until we're well away from here. I'll take you to Carrick police station. It'll be okay. You'll turn Queen's evidence. All you've done is conceal information from the police. I'll see to it that you won't do a day in jail."

She shook her head. "I won't be doing that," she said simply.

"It'll be okay. I'm not bullshitting you. You won't do a day in jail. If you're nervous, we'll get you a new identity in England or Australia, wherever you want."

She thought about it for a moment and shook her head. "No. I'm not going with you, Sean."

"For God's sake, woman! We don't have fucking time for this!"

"You go."

"We don't have time for this! Come on!"

"No!"

"I won't ask you again, we really have to—"

Headlights from several vehicles suddenly lit up the yard in front of the house.

"Come out, Duffy! You've got no chance!" Harry yelled from behind the stone wall.

"Shit! They got down here fast!"

"Come out, Duffy! Don't make this hard on yourself!" Harry yelled from outside.

I looked to where the BMW was parked. Maybe twenty feet from the door to the driver's side. And they were a hundred feet away armed only with shotguns. If we turned off the lights and we legged it, maybe we could make it.

"We can still make it to the car," I said to her.

"*You* can make it to the car. I'm not going with you."

Her arms were folded across her chest. Her eyes were half closed.

In the kitchen I could smell the steaks burning.

"What are you talking about, Emma? I explained it to you. You won't have to go to jail."

"I'm not testifying against Harry."

I gripped Emma by the shoulders and shook her.

"He killed your husband."

"Martin grew up around here. He knew the score. You don't go to the police. You don't talk."

"Are you mad? He shot your husband in cold blood."

She nodded. "I know . . . I know. You go, Sean!"

The tears were streaming down her cheeks.

"You're doing this for Harry? The man's a sociopath."

"You don't understand."

"The Larne copper. Harry took him out the same way he took out Martin, didn't he?"

She nodded.

"But it wasn't quite the same way. He shot him dead and then he shot into the garage wall three times. Why do you think he did that?"

"I don't know."

"I know. It was insurance. He wanted to make it look like a woman had done it. Like she'd missed with the first three and she got him with the others. He was setting you up, Emma. No doubt if everything went to shit he would have leaked other evidence implicating you in your husband's murder. I'll bet you he's got your prints on key pieces of evidence."

"He wouldn't do that."

"Why not?"

"Because he knows I wouldn't talk. I'm from here. We take care of our own problems."

"Like Martin?"

"Like Martin."

"He'll kill you too, Emma. Come with me! Come on, now, while we have the chance!"

She shook her head. "You go, Sean. You go!"

I couldn't argue with her all night.

"Fuck it, then. Are you sure about this?"

"Yes."

"Will you be okay?" I asked.

"They won't harm me."

"I'll be back with the law, you realize that?" I said.

"Yes."

"Okay."

I turned off the living-room light, got the car keys, opened the front door and ran. I got five feet.

Half a dozen separate shotgun blasts.

A white-hot pellet caught me on the shoulder and knocked me down. I landed flat on my back.

The car was impossible.

It might as well have been a million miles away.

More shotgun blasts and rifle cracks. I dived back into the house and closed the door.

Emma ran over to me. "You're hit," she said.

I took off my raincoat. It was only a glancing wound in my shoulder. But my cracked ribs were on fire.

"Help me up," I said.

She put a hand under my shoulder and lugged me to my feet.

There were maybe half a dozen men out there now. They had shotguns *and* rifles. I had a .38 revolver with six rounds.

"What will you do now? Give yourself up?" she asked.

"Give myself up? They'll kill me. You know they'll kill me, don't you?"

Her face was blank, distant, but then she nodded.

"There's got to be a way out the back," I said.

"Yes," she said.

She was talking as if she was in a trance.

Her features were frozen.

A rifle bullet smashed the living-room window and thudded into the back wall. The lights were off except for a side lamp next to the TV. I crawled across the living-room floor and knocked it off its stand.

I fumbled in my raincoat pocket for my pills. I swallowed two of them dry.

"The back door?" I asked again.

"Through the kitchen. If you open the door, you'll see the chicken run and there's a hedge. If you get over the hedge and keep going across the fields you'll make it down to the lough shore."

"And from there?"

"I don't know."

We'd cross that bridge when we came to it. Maybe I could get out into the water and float my carcass across Larne Lough to the Magheramorne side.

"All right. I'm going," I said.

I couldn't see her face now, but she whispered "Good luck."

I crawled through the living-room doorway but as soon as I opened the back door shotgun pellets thudded into the door and into the gap above my head.

Fuck.

The house was surrounded.

I crawled back into the living room.

"They're there ahead of me. Is there any kind of cellar or cellar door or priest's hole, or anything like that?" I asked her.

"No. Nothing like that. A front door and a back door. That's it."

"There's no way out!" Harry shouted.

I slithered to the broken window and looked out. Half a dozen shadowy forms arranged behind the stone wall. Maybe two more out back.

"I called the cops, Harry! The fucking cavalry is on its way! You boys better run if you don't want to go down with your boss!" I yelled.

"We heard your conversation to 999 and we yanked the cable! Do you think we're daft, Duffy?"

"Fuck!" I whispered. "Fuck, fuck, fuck."

"Come out and it'll be quick, Duffy. No nonsense. No torture. We've got marksmen. You won't even know it."

I was beat already and the whole night was ahead of us. Night and into the morning and however long Harry wanted to keep at it on his private land.

The cars were still shining their headlamps at the farmyard and it was hard to see what was going on, but I did notice one careless fucker stand up to take a shot at the house. I lifted the .38 two-handed, carefully sighted it and squeezed the trigger. A crack, a slight recall, the man went down.

"That'll gentle his condition some, eh, Harry!" I yelled. "And that goes for all of you fuckers! Who wants it next? Just remember that when Harry tells you to charge the house!"

"Peeler scum!" somebody shouted by way of retort.

"You're doing this for Harry? You're going to risk your life so he can make some cash in a drug deal? And what do you get out of it! Nothing! Think about that, too, before you charge!"

"We'll be all right, you can't watch both doors at once, can you, Duffy?" Harry yelled.

It was a good point.

Emma's arm was on mine.

She was looking at me.

"He can't, Harry! But together we can. I'll cover the back with Martin's shotgun and he can cover the front! The first man I see in my backyard is a dead man!" Emma yelled.

I couldn't make out all of her face in the dark but I could see that smile and the fact that she was holding a double-barrel shotgun.

"You don't have to do this, I'll send you out under a white flag," I whispered.

"I'm staying here!" she said and kissed me on the cheek.

Why the flip? Guilt? Resignation? Death wish? They were all good.

A volley of gun shots smashed the windows and sent sparks flying across the floor.

We hit the deck.

"You better cover the back door. Don't expose yourself. Keep low," I whispered.

She nodded and crawled towards the kitchen.

I waited for whatever was going to happen next.

No movement that I could shoot at.

The rain was getting heavy and the sky was moonless, starless, black.

Nothing happened for a minute. Two. Then I saw two arcs of fire and a Molotov cocktail landed on the thatched roof and another tumbled through the broken living-room window into the house, exploding in a sheet of crimson flame across the hardwood floor.

I pulled a curtain off the wall and threw it over the conflagration. The curtain caught fire and I had to smother it with my body. It singed my face, fizzled for a moment and then went out.

I knew now that it was all over. Of course, they would simply burn us out.

Why would they charge the house when they could stand behind the wall and lob Molotovs at us?

"Are you okay, Emma?" I yelled into the kitchen.

"I'm okay, are you?" she shouted back.

"I'm fine."

I crawled into the kitchen. "What are we going to do?" she whispered.

I peered into the backyard. I could see bobbing lights beyond the fence. They were getting ready to fire another round of Molotovs.

"They're going to torch the place," I said.

"Oh, God! I'd rather be shot," she said desperately.

"Do you want me to parley with them? You still have a chance."

She shook her head. "No. No, it's too late now. I've made my choice. I should never have . . . I've made my choice."

I kissed her tear-stained cheek.

The men launched their Molotovs and I broke the kitchen window and shot at one of them as he threw. I missed him and both petrol bombs landed on the thatched roof.

Yeah, that was the way to do it.

Smoke rapidly began filling the kitchen.

"Follow me into the living room," I said, and she slithered after me, but it was just as bad there too.

Thick black straw smoke from the thatch.

We began to cough.

I dry-retched.

"What are you thinking about now, Duffy?" Harry yelled.

I was thinking of a Butch Cassidy style run into oblivion.

"I was thinking how good it's going to feel when I kill you, you cunt!" I yelled back.

And then I heard it.

Was it a hallucination?

No.

No, that was no trick of a desperate mind.

That was a fucking siren. Sirens.

"Sirens!" I said.

I turned to Emma. "I hear sirens."

"Sirens!" I yelled out the broken window. "The peelers are coming for you, lads! If I were youse I'd bloody leg it!"

I turned to Emma. "Are you hurt?"

She nodded. "I'm all right."

The sirens were tearing up the Mill Bay Road. Two police Land Rovers at least. Of course they had traced the 999 call. They didn't need to hear the address. They needed only to triangulate the call line backwards through all the tumblers and switchboards, and Harry had helped them with local geography by giving them a nice big fire to steer towards.

I edged open the front door so we could breathe. We kept low to the ground and no one shot at us.

"Come back, you dogs!" Harry was yelling at his men who were sensibly making a run for it back to their houses.

"I really won't have to go to jail, Sean? I couldn't stand to go to prison," Emma said in a low, ashamed voice.

"No. I give you my word."

The sirens were now less than a mile away.

"It's over, Harry! You've been abandoned! It's finished!" I yelled into the darkness.

"Not quite, Duffy! Not quite!" he yelled back.

I heard an engine rev and a hand brake slip. I looked up and out into the farmyard. Harry's Bentley was speeding towards us. There was a burning rag sticking out of the petrol tank. He had put a weight on the accelerator pedal.

He was walking behind it with the shotgun.

"Jesus! Quickly! Get into the back kitchen! He's—" I yelled at Emma.

And

then

everything

was

light.

32: IN THE WORLD OF LIGHT

Silence. The silence of mice in graves. The silence of non-being. Nothingness singing to itself.

Time passing.

Ash.

Death's hand. Warmer than I was expecting. Welcoming.

Rain on my face. Starlight. Pain naming me into consciousness.

A sleepwalker getting to his feet.

Me.

Comparatively unscathed.

Two arms. Two legs.

A ringing in my ears.

Lucky.

Lucky Sean Duffy, that's what you should call me.

The house?

There is no house.

The house is leveled.

"Emma! Emma!"

I see her.

It must have been from a heavy stone in the wall.

It would have been instantaneous.

I kiss her shattered face. Her blood on my lips.

I walk away from the debris.

The Land Rovers are coming to me across the valley.

The sirens so close now.

A melody.

Glissando-like runs from two pianos, the first playing that Chopinesque descending ten-on-one ostinato while the second playing the more conservative six-on-one.

And there's Harry, spread-eagled in the yard. An arm missing. Severed by one of the Bentley's side panels.

I bend down next to him.

"What were you thinking, McAlpine?" I say.

He gives a little laugh. "I wasn't thinking. I forgot about the oil tank for the central heating."

"Emma's dead," I said.

"Why didn't you send her out, Duffy, you fuck?"

"She wouldn't go."

"You should have forced her."

"Tell me all of it, Harry. You killed your brother and called in an old IRA code word."

"You know that."

"You shot three times into Dougherty's garage door after you killed him. You were setting her up, weren't you, in case we didn't buy the IRA story?"

He laughs. "God, you peelers! You overthink everything. I missed. I bloody missed, that's all. I'd never fired a handgun before."

"Oh."

"Have you a cigarette, Duffy?"

I kneel down next to him.

"All this, Harry, all this for what?" I ask him.

He winks at me, grins.

"Millions mate, millions and millions," he says.

I could save him, I know that. A tourniquet. The rubber seal from the Bentley's door. He'd have a fighting chance.

I get to my feet and walk towards the flashing lights.

33: CASHIERED

I was debriefed at the hospital by Special Branch. I told my tale and they told me that John DeLorean was the subject of an international investigation between various government agencies and that I had to keep my mouth shut. I knew that and I would have kept my mouth shut anyway without Special Branch goons forcing me to sign the Official Secrets Act.

Sinister men with public-school accents and sharp suits met with me and we concocted a story that Sir Harry and his sister-in-law Emma had been killed in an explosion and fire from a faulty oil heater. I had valiantly tried to save them from the inferno but had not succeeded.

We knew no one in Islandmagee would talk to the press, so the official version would stand unchallenged.

The local papers accepted this narrative without complaint and I was even a bit of a hero for a couple of days. Fanciful details of my attempt to save Emma from the flames were printed and mention was made of my Queen's Police Medal. The news briefly dominated page one of the *Belfast Telegraph* and then got sandwiched between various victories and disasters in the Falkland Islands.

I still was okay when they began reporting that Sir Harry was involved in some dodgy deals and knew the famous John DeLorean and that he had been in some kind of dispute with his sister-in-law.

But then the Yanks stuck their oar in.

Apparently they must have felt that I had reneged on our deal. I had promised to stay away from DeLorean and the O'Rourke case, but as soon as I'd got off the shuttle to Belfast I had gone digging . . .

They released their report about my drunk-driving incident in Massachusetts. The local press began to suggest that I was a maverick, a rogue cop at the center of some kind of scandal between a baronet and his sister-in-law. The theories got wilder: Sir Harry and Emma were lovers who had killed themselves in a spectacular murder/suicide; Sir Harry, Emma and I were the three points of a love triangle.

The preliminary coroner's report accepted accidental death as the most likely explanation for the events at Red Hall cottage, but some of the press still liked the love triangle twist that sucked in a "hero cop."

As the story refused to die I began to think that maybe I could be in trouble. I had been ordered to keep away from Sir Harry McAlpine. I'd been told to yellow a case which I had subsequently investigated on my own time. I had concealed information from my superiors. And the fact that the only evidence—the piece of tattooed skin—linking Sir Harry with the death of Bill O'Rourke had been destroyed in the explosion did not help matters.

I had a harsh *in camera* internal review conducted by two chief superintendents.

Had I been given order X? Had I disobeyed said order . . . That kind of thing.

I knew my failures better than them: Sir Harry had escaped justice, Emma was dead. DeLorean—whatever the hell he was doing—was going to keep doing it as long the Northern Ireland Office let him and as long as he kept those precious precious jobs in Northern Ireland.

The press finally got bored of the story and the whole thing died for a while after my *in camera* review; I resumed duties, assuming, foolishly, that it would all blow over.

All seemed normal down at Carrick RUC until one day, out of the blue, in June, I was summoned to a formal disciplinary hearing. This was the real deal: dress uniform, charges, and I was told that I would have to get myself legal representation.

The hearing convened in a civil service building in the center of Belfast. The board was made up of old men. Their faces grey, their noses blue. They had joined the police during or perhaps just after the war, and the RUC back then was a different animal: a Protestant force for a Protestant people. The timing of the hearing made me more than a little nervous, for they had picked a moment when the story could be buried. The Argentinians were on the verge of surrendering in The Falklands. Scotland, England and Northern Ireland all had teams in the World Cup. Nobody would waste that much ink about a former hero now disgraced. They could fuck me up or let me off without anyone giving a damn.

The case against me was read out by a sleekit-looking chief inspector from the internal affairs unit. The meat of the O'Rourke case was barely mentioned at all. The only evidence the tribunal seemed interested in was what particular orders I had disobeyed and whether I had correctly followed RUC procedures. It was pure chicken shit.

And it dawned on me that this punishment was coming not from Belfast or London but from Washington, DC.

I had pissed off the Americans, and the Americans wanted to see me punished.

The old men on the board listened to the case against me, heard my defense, read their notes and retired to consider what should be done with me.

I waited.

The room was stuffy, but no one thought to open a window. The panel clearly were not going to be away for very long—and sure enough, they came back in after a pro forma fifteen minutes.

Chief Superintendent Pullman called my name. My RUC counsel gave me a nudge, which meant that I should stand. I stood to attention. My thumbs pointing down along the seam of my trousers. My heels together. My gaze steady. My dress uniform spic and span.

Chief Superintendent Pullman shuffled his papers, cleared his throat and read the verdict: "Detective Inspector Duffy, after long and careful deliberation, this tribunal has found that you have committed four separate breaches of the RUC code of conduct. . ."

The stenographer began recording my various infractions. She knew it was chicken shit, too. I mean, until very recently they were still beating suspects with rubber hoses down the Castlereagh Holding Centre—they couldn't talk to me about breaches of their fucking code of conduct.

"You have disobeyed direct orders on several occasions. You have embarrassed the force on foreign soil . . ." Pullman continued.

Embarrassed the RUC? Our name is mud in America. Read the *Boston Herald* some time, mate.

Pullman continued talking. His lips moved, the other men nodded, I looked at them with contempt. Old men. Stupid men.

". . . In conclusion, Inspector Duffy, it is with great regret that we must inform you of the unanimous judgment of this disciplinary panel."

I swallowed and looked at a crack on the back wall.

"Effective immediately, you will be reduced to the rank of sergeant."

Shit.

"Back-dated to January first, 1982, your accumulated leave, personal days and other benefits will be similarly reduced to the benefits accruing to a sergeant."

Shit.

Okay so it was bad. I'd lost a rank. But if they let me stay in Carrickfergus I'd still get to lead a team of detectives. Maybe if I kept my nose clean for a year they'd quietly bump me up again to inspector. And if they posted me to a big station in Belfast, a DS could get himself involved in some of the more interesting cases . . .

Pullman took off his glasses and stared at me.

"Do you understand and accept the verdict of this tribunal?"

I was expected to respond in full for the benefit of the stenographer.

"Yes, sir, I am being demoted to the rank of detective sergeant with full loss of seniority and remission, sir!"

Pullman looked up at me with surprise.

"No, Duffy, you've misunderstood—you are being demoted to a sergeant in ordinary. You are being removed from the CID lists."

My knees buckled.

An ordinary sergeant? I wasn't going to be a detective?

A regular copper? A regular copper was little people. A regular copper was nothing.

I sat down again.

My lawyer looked at me to see if I was all right. He passed me the glass of water when he saw that I was not.

"Do you understand the verdict, *Sergeant* Duffy?" Pullman said.

"Drink this," my lawyer whispered.

I got back up and returned Pullman's gaze right into his ugly mug.

"No, I don't bloody understand it! This is bollocks! Have you any idea what it's like out there? Have you any idea what it's like to be out there on the line every day of your fucking life?"

Pullman shook his head at the stenographer who immediately stopped typing.

"Duffy, we appreciate your service and we take these measures with great regret. But you have embarrassed the name of the—"

"Fuck your regret and fuck all of you! And make sure you write that down, love," I said.

I clicked my heels together, saluted and stormed out of the room.

They had a car for me but I went home by myself on the train.

It was full of school kids and I had to stand, enraged, the whole way. I got off at Downshire Halt and made for the off license. I bought a bottle of Jack Daniel's and a six-pack of Bass.

I walked up Victoria Road.

"Oh, you look very nice, all dressed up," Mrs. Bridewell said, pushing a pram.

"Thanks," I replied curtly.

I went into 113 Coronation Road, searched through my records and put on "Hellhound on My Trail" by Robert Johnson.

I ripped the uniform off my body and threw the police medal against the wall.

It bounced and nearly landed on the turntable.

I popped the first can of Bass.

"A sergeant in ordinary! I'll fucking resign first. That'll show you, you fucks," I said.

The phone was ringing.

The first of many phone calls: McCrabban, Matty, Sergeant Quinn, Tony, Inspector McCallister, even Chief Inspector Brennan, who was slap in the middle of messy divorce proceedings.

They had all heard. They talked to me like there was a death in the family.

I called my parents.

My dad said I *should* resign. All the bright people were leaving Northern Ireland for England and America. I had so much potential. I was wasted in the sectarian, poisoned atmosphere of the RUC . . .

I drank and listened to the blues and at nine put on the BBC.

Port Stanley had fallen to the British forces.

The Argentinians were formalizing a surrender.

The BBC correspondent was ecstatic: "There is jubilation here in the streets of Port Stanley as the Falkland Islands flag once again rises above the Governor's—"

I turned off the box and sat in the silence with the Jack Daniel's.

Just before midnight the phone rang again and I picked it up.

"It could have been worse, Duffy," a female voice said.

It was her. Little Miss Anonymous. She who had caused me so much trouble.

"Could it have been worse?" I said.

"Oh, very much worse. The Americans are terribly cross with you."

"The Americans say jump and you ask how high."

"Quite."

"Why did you do it? Why did you pick on me?"

"I was trying to help you, Duffy."

"You set me up. Why didn't *you* go to America, love? Why didn't you look in that safe deposit box?"

"That wasn't my scene. Not my scene, at all, Duffy."

"No, but you sent me, didn't you? Turned me round and pointed me in the right direction. Did you know what was going to happen when I went to that bank?"

"Of course not. We wouldn't have done that to a friend."

"Who do you work for? MI5? I already have friends in fucking MI5."

"Look . . . Duffy, or can I call you Sean?"

"Don't call me anything! Don't call me again! I'm hanging up on you."

"Wait! Wait a minute. As you well know, Sean, life is cheap in Northern Ireland, so why is it, do you think, that you have been allowed to live after all the trouble that you've caused for us and our allies across the sea?"

"Why don't you fucking tell me?"

"I have no idea. I can only imagine that to the powers that be, you are, as yet, of some value. Some of us play the long game, Sean."

"This isn't a game," I said, and hung up the phone and pulled the jack out of the wall.

I went to the kitchen and wrote out a hasty letter of resignation.

I stuck it in an envelope and addressed it. I found a stamp and walked to the post-box at the end of Coronation Road. I stood there for a minute, thinking.

"Best to sleep on it," I finally decided, put the envelope in my jacket pocket and returned home.

EPILOGUE: A FOOT PATROL THROUGH THE ABYSS

Images from the asymmetric wars of the future: curling pigtails of smoke from hijacked cars, Army helicopters hovering above a city like mosquitoes over a water hole, heavily armed soldiers and policemen walking in single file on both sides of a residential street . . .

Night is falling.

The sky is the color of porter.

The soldiers are carrying semi-automatic SLR rifles and wearing full body armor. We, the embedded cops, are wearing flak jackets and carrying Sterling submachine guns.

We are watching windows and rooftops. We are spaced well apart so that a bomb or a rocket-propelled grenade cannot kill all of us.

Every hundred meters the point man alternates. Every dozen paces or so the man at the rear does a one eighty and walks backwards for a step or two.

Even we seasoned veterans are pumping adrenalin. The street is full of civilians and any one of them could be a watcher for an IRA button man, ready to detonate a booby trap under a car or dug into a road culvert. There could be unseen assassins waiting behind windows and doors with sniper rifles or anti-tank rockets.

Is this what the squaddies signed on for? These British soldiers who were brought up on *Zulu* and *The Longest Day*.

This is the way it's going to be from now on.

Wars in cities.

Wars with civilians all around.

Make one mistake and you're dead.

Make another kind of mistake and you're on the TV news.

We walk through the maze of red-bricked terraced houses off the

Falls Road. This part of West Belfast that has been ruined by endemic conflict and economic catastrophe and suicide martyr cult.

Bomb sites. Waste ground. Helicopters throwing up dust from pulverized brick and stone.

Recall the noise boots make on cobbles. Recall the eyes watching you. Recall the fear.

Recall the sights: the scene of a notorious ambush, the graffiti proclaiming death to enemies of the IRA, a bonfire in the middle of a street.

At a road junction a cat has been shoved into a birdcage. A young private hesitates and turns to look at his commanding officer. He wants to save the cat but everyone shakes their head at him. It could so easily be a booby trap. Such things and worse have been done in the past.

People jeer as we walk by.

Others make throat-cutting gestures.

I thought that my days of foot patrols were behind me. Already the sweat is pouring down my thighs. A kid playing kerby with a soccer ball catches my eye.

"Bang, bang, you're dead," he mouths at me.

I fake a bullet in my gut and he grins.

Hearts and minds.

One heart and one mind.

The patrols turns on Divis Drive.

It's getting dark now. The sun has set behind the Knockagh. It's cold. Later they say it might snow. We're now at *Reilig Bhaile an Mhuilinn*, as the Republicans call it. Mill Town Cemetery, to you and me.

This is where the IRA buries its dead.

"Let's take a look through the graveyard, lads," the commanding officer says. He's a Scot from Edinburgh. A boy really. Fresh out of Sandhurst. Must be twenty or twenty-one. A young officer of the Black Watch. My life completely in the hands of a green lieutenant walking through a city he doesn't know, on his first or possibly second combat patrol.

We cross the Falls Road in single file.

The traffic waits for us.

We walk through the cemetery gates. An experienced staff sergeant whispers something to the lieutenant. The lieutenant grins and nods, agreeing to the sergeant's suggestion.

I look at the other two policemen on patrol with me. They shrug. They have no idea what the squaddies are up to either.

The patrol makes straight for the Republican Plot. The graves of all the IRA men and women who have died for Ireland.

We reach the final resting place of Bobby Sands. The martyr in chief. The IRA commander in the Long Kesh prison who starved himself to death over sixty-six days.

The sergeant takes something from a pocket underneath his Kevlar jacket and leaves it on the marble headstone.

It is a packet of digestive biscuits.

The soldiers laugh.

The other policemen and myself do not.

Later . . .

A drive to Carrickfergus through sleet and rain. I go inside and cook sausages. I pour myself a glass of Islay whisky. I eat and drink and doze in front of the TV.

Suddenly the power flickers and goes out. I wait, but the lights don't come back on. The IRA has undoubtedly blown up the high tension lines or a substation.

I sit in the dark drinking the peaty, smoky, pungent, almost painfully good whisky. I get bored and put batteries in the shortwave. I tune in Radio Albania, my old favorite. Dramatic piano music blares from my stereo speakers. The music ends abruptly and an announcer with an American accent continues the news bulletin in mid-sentence: ". . . production levels. Comrade Inver Hoxha met with a delegation of workers' Soviets and praised them for their three-fold increase in steel output."

Later . . .

I stoke the fire and lie under a duvet, listening to the sounds of the outside: babies gurning, kids yelling, peelers racing along the top road, Army choppers clipping menacingly over the black water . . .

"I hate your drunken face!" a woman shouts over the back to backs.

"I hate yours more!" a man responds.

I put the sofa cushion over my head. And then finally there is quiet...

The TV buzzes into life at seven in the morning with the news that John DeLorean has been arrested for cocaine smuggling. DeLorean apparently thought he could sell a vast quantity of cocaine in Ireland as a way to save his ailing car company, but the whole thing was an FBI sting operation.

"The bloody F bloody B bloody I."

I sit closer to the TV.

The DeLorean factory in Belfast has suspended operations. Three thousand workers are being laid off immediately with the effect that the unemployment rate in Belfast is going up to twenty per cent.

Men are filing out of the factory gates looking utterly bereft.

One commentator says that this marks the end of Northern Ireland as a manufacturing center.

"Maybe the end of the province itself!" another reporter agrees.

A guy from the union comes on the tube and promises riots and demonstrations. Later that morning we get a message that leave is being canceled. But in the end there are no riots because the unions are weak and the workers are weak and the real power in this land belongs to the men with guns.

The small crowd outside the Dunmurry plant chants "We want jobs! We want jobs!" over and over for the cameras; but eventually even they are sent scurrying inside by the bitter rain from a big storm-front which has stalled in its inexorable eastward progress and which is destined to remain over Belfast for a long, long time.

ABOUT . . . ADRIAN McKINTY

I was born and grew up in Carrickfergus, Northern Ireland. After studying philosophy at Oxford University, I emigrated to New York City, where I lived in Harlem for seven years, working in bars, bookstores, building sites, and finally the basement stacks of the Columbia University Medical School Library in Washington Heights.

In 2000 I moved to Denver, Colorado, where I taught high-school English and started writing fiction in earnest. My first full-length novel, *Dead I Well May Be*, was shortlisted for the 2004 Ian Fleming Steel Dagger Award and was picked by *Booklist* as one of the ten best crime novels of the year. The sequel to that book, *The Dead Yard*, was selected by *Publishers Weekly* as one of the twelve best novels of 2006 and won the Audie Award for best mystery or thriller. These two novels, along with *The Bloomsday Dead*, form my trilogy of novels starring hitman Michael Forsythe, the DEAD trilogy.

In mid-2008 I moved to St. Kilda, Melbourne, Australia, with my wife and kids. My book *Fifty Grand* won the 2010 Spinetingler Award and my last novel, *Falling Glass*, was longlisted for Theakston's Crime Novel of the Year.

Visit Adrian's blog at http://adrianmckinty.blogspot.com/